Exposure!

Julia Boggio

ALSO BY JULIA BOGGIO

The Photographers Trilogy
Shooters
Chasing the Light

A Photographers Trilogy Novel
Camera Shy

Exposure!

A Novel

Julia Boggio

HOME BY MIDNIGHT PUBLISHING

To request permissions, contact the publisher at hbmpublishingUK@gmail.com.

Paperback: 978-1-7392151-7-0

First edition.

Cover design: Bailey McGinn

A CIP record for this book is available from the British Library.

For my beautiful neurodivergent family,
James, G & H

1

STELLA

THE ROOM SIMMERED WITH TALENT: THOSE WHO HAD IT, THOSE WHO wanted it, and those who would always suck no matter how hard they tried.

After ten years as a professional photographer, Stella finally knew where she fell on that scale. As she entered the hotel lobby full of eager convention delegates, she pretended not to notice the heads turning towards her and the whispers of 'OMG, that's Stella Knight!'

An excited thrill shivered up her spine, chased immediately by her ever-present insecurity. How long until they all realised that she was a fraud? That other photographers were better or knew more than she did? Despite her many awards and glowing client testimonials, her imposter syndrome remained strong.

To her right, Liliwen rolled her bright pink suitcase over the maroon and gold carpet. 'Holy Tom Jones, this place is glorious,' she said in her strong Welsh lilt. Perching her over-sized sunglasses atop her voluminous white pixie haircut, she ogled a well-endowed marble statue of a Greek god, her elfin features dripping with appreciation. 'Did you see that man out front in a leopard-print unitard with the red mohawk? Reminded me of my Camden Market days and a short fling I had with a contortionist. I wonder what ever happened to Barry...'

Side-eyeing her diminutive travel partner and temporary personal assistant, Stella asked, 'When did you live in Camden?'

'There's a lot you don't know about me, lovely.' Liliwen winked, her blue eyes twinkling with their usual youthful mischief. At 65, she was one of the most entertaining women Stella knew—and glamorous, too, with her petite frame, chic cropped trousers, and boxy floral top.

However, not for the first time, Stella questioned her judgment in bringing Liliwen on this trip. Stella had a lot of work to do and didn't possess the brain space to keep Liliwen out of trouble. But her friend needed something to occupy her after becoming a widow twelve months ago, and Stella needed a PA. So when Liliwen suggested she could step into the role, Stella had agreed. She only hoped she didn't come to regret it.

Stella scanned the lobby. It was the first time the conference was being held at this venue, and Stella was unfamiliar with the layout. Up ahead, at the top of a short staircase was a lounge bar called the Wild Card. In the dim lighting, groups of photographers were already gathering for the first of many drinking sessions. After all, the International Photography Expo—aka IPE—was like spring break for photographers.

On the opposite side of the lobby next to the lifts, an open, plant-filled atrium no doubt led to shopping, gambling, and food. Behind the check-in desks stretched an aquarium teeming with colourful fish. Stella would need a map to navigate this place.

Little hands seized her arm, making her jump. Liliwen pointed and said, 'Is that Connor here to greet you?'

Stella's head whipped around and her heart rate revved at the mention of her estranged husband. She followed Liliwen's finger towards a tall, dark-haired man with broad shoulders and a muscular build talking to an attractive blonde woman. A jealous spark flared to life in her chest, but then the man turned, and it wasn't Connor. Not nearly handsome enough.

Her stomach dropped. 'It's not him,' Stella said, her voice unsteady.

'I'm sorry, lovely. I didn't mean to stir things up.'

'It's okay. He probably won't arrive until the end of the week.' When she'd spoken to Connor about this trip, they'd agreed that he would be there by Friday for the awards ceremony. Then on Saturday, they'd drive to the boutique hotel she'd booked in Joshua Tree, where they would decide the future of their marriage.

Would he want to try again? More importantly, was *she* ready to try again? Or was this the end of the road for them?

She frowned and pushed a lock of long red hair behind her ear.

'Stella Knight!' called a deep voice, snapping her out of her thoughts. She looked up to find Blake Romero grinning as he approached, arms wide open in welcome, his white teeth bright against his California tan. In the flesh, Blake Romero was even better looking than his online persona on MuseTV, the creative education platform he'd launched last year.

Only a few years older than Connor, he was a fine specimen of Italian manhood. He wore his sun-streaked blond hair loosely gelled, ensuring his high cheekbones and light brown eyes were on full display. A golden cross on a thin chain peeked through the neck of his casually unbuttoned shirt. Her Venetian mother, raised Catholic, would love that.

Stella hadn't expected to see Blake so soon. She smoothed a hand over her flight-tousled hair and quickly reversed the corners of her lips into a smile, keen to make a good impression.

'*Benvenuti a Las Vegas,*' he greeted her, placing his hands on her shoulders and planting a kiss on each cheek.

'*Ah, parli Italiano?*' asked Stella.

'I wish I did,' Blake said. 'My nonno and nonna were from Rome, but my father never spoke to me in the mother tongue.'

'*Peccato,*' she said with the appropriate sad face.

'I'm so glad you've managed to crowbar me into your schedule this week.' His eyes flicked up and down, and she had the distinct feeling he was weighing her up. Now she was both tired *and* nervous.

'Of course! No problem, anything for you,' she replied, struggling to appear unfazed while inside she was 100,000 girls at a Harry Styles concert. One month ago, he'd messaged her, requesting a meeting at the convention along with an offer to upgrade her flights and room.

He obviously wanted something.

Part of her feared what it was; part of her craved it. Blake Romero had the power to skyrocket her career. MuseTV was the biggest seminar streaming service in the business, and the photographers he handpicked to be presenters were the new industry rockstars. But all of MuseTV's classes were initially streamed live. What if she said something stupid or messed up a photo shoot with thousands of people watching?

Liliwen coughed politely.

Indicating her travelling companion, Stella said, 'Blake, this is Liliwen Thomas.'

'You didn't say you were bringing your sister.' Blake reached out and took Liliwen's hand, kissing her on the knuckles like she was this Season's Incomparable from *Bridgerton*.

Liliwen giggled. 'Oh stop!' she admonished, her wide smile belying her words. If she'd had a fan, Liliwen would have flicked it open and fluttered it.

Blake chuckled and turned back to Stella, 'Is the other member of your party here yet?'

'His flight from Mexico City gets in late tomorrow morning,' she said.

She had warned Tristan that she wasn't in Vegas to play, but her old friend insisted that he wanted to see her and that they could meet up whenever she was free. Listening to her heart instead of her head, she said yes. It had been a year since he moved away and she missed him terribly.

Besides, she needed her friends close to bolster her before the Big Conversation with Connor.

'Is that the queue to check in?' Stella asked, surveying the long line of people in reception with travel pillows looped around their necks, piles of luggage, and bleary expressions.

'I've already done it. A suite with three rooms, as requested,' Blake said, taking the handles of her and Liliwen's suitcases.

'I think I love you,' joked Stella. Time was precious, and she could put the hour she saved not having to queue to better use. Just because she was at the convention didn't mean her business stopped operating.

Blake waved over a hotel porter. Stella could tell he was the kind of man who expected to be obeyed—like a president or a tech billionaire. He pointed towards the bags and the porter rushed towards them. As the porter loaded the bags onto his trolley, Blake pulled a wad of ten-dollar bills from his pocket and peeled off a few, handing them over as he announced the room number.

'Oh, I can pay for the tip...' said Stella, before remembering she had no cash. She would ask Liliwen to procure some tomorrow.

'Please, it's my pleasure,' said Blake, shoving the wad back into his pocket. 'Now, do you want me to show you to your room...or do you want to get a drink, or can I even tempt you with dinner...?'

Eager as she was to discover his intentions, all the tiredness she'd been holding at bay rushed through her body at the mention of her room. Her eyelids grew heavy at the mental image of crawling between crisp, cold hotel sheets... as soon as she'd fired off a few emails.

'Let's go up now,' Stella said at the same time as Liliwen said, 'Definitely a drink,' while threading her arm through Blake's.

They all laughed.

'Tell you what,' said Blake. 'Let's get you both settled. Then,

Liliwen, if you're still thirsty, I know a great bar not far from here with the best champagne cocktails in town.'

'You're quickly becoming my favourite person,' Liliwen flirted back. Again, Stella wondered if bringing Liliwen to Vegas had been a good idea. She immediately felt guilty at the thought.

Before Stella could tell them that she would head up to the room by herself, a young woman with thick make-up and large hoop earrings accosted them. 'Oh my gawd,' she said in a nasal, New York accent. 'Stella Knight, right?'

Stella opened her mouth to reply, but the woman continued, 'I check your blog, like, *every day* to see if you've posted any new tutorials! And I've booked on, like, *all* of your masterclasses this week. I'm, like, your *biggest* fan. Hey, can I get a selfie with you?'

'Of course,' said Stella, despite her exhaustion. She couldn't disappoint a fan. She willed her face to look bright and happy, like she hadn't just spent eleven hours on a plane.

The young woman pressed herself to Stella's side and threw a thin arm behind her back. Stella could smell her strong, floral perfume and sickly sweet gum, which made her mildly nauseous. Her eyes cut briefly to Blake who was watching the exchange with keen interest.

Like he was possibly auditioning Stella as the next star presenter for MuseTV.

'Say *IPPY-KIY-YAY!*' commanded the woman, IPE pronounced *Hippy* without the H. IPPY-KIY-YAY was the battle cry of the seasoned attendee.

Stella said the words and struck her 'selfie-pose': head tilted to the side, chin up, big grin, wide eyes. She held the position until tears gathered and her cheek muscles twitched. Finally, the woman proclaimed, 'Got it!' then thanked Stella and skipped off. Stella was sure she'd see her name tagged in that picture when she checked her socials.

'Shall we?' said Blake, ushering them towards the elevators.

As they reached the line at the lift bank, Stella overheard another person whisper loudly, 'It's Stella Knight!'

How had Connor dealt with this level of attention? Stella remembered the BAPP conference in London where she first met him. He'd been swamped by photographers itching to be near him. Hell, she'd been one of them. She'd harangued him into giving her a spot on his sold-out residential course in a French chateau.

How different would her life have been if she hadn't done that? If she'd never gone to France, where the first tendrils of their relationship developed?

Her chest tightened with sadness.

She loved Connor. And if she hadn't met him, then she wouldn't have her daughter, Grace, and that was the one thing that made everything worthwhile. Stella only wished that Grace didn't have two crap parents who couldn't seem to communicate with each other. The idea of breaking up their family tore Stella apart, but sometimes love just wasn't enough.

As they waited for the lift, Stella pulled out her phone to check if her parents had sent any more pictures or videos of Grace. They had taken her to London Zoo that day and already shared thirty-plus images over WhatsApp. But of course, there were no new notifications. They'd all be asleep now.

Her phone vibrated in her hand.

Her breath caught. It was from Connor.

I'm here. When can I see you?

2

CONNOR

FROM THE BAR IN THE LOBBY, CONNOR WATCHED HIS WIFE QUEUING for the lifts with that twat, Blake Romero. He saw her read the text message he'd sent, and ignore it in favour of Blake.

What the fuck was she doing with *him*? Connor fought the impulse to rush over there and find out. He forced himself to stay put, imagining what would happen if he accosted them, how Stella would react. Verdict: not well. He inhaled a thin breath through his nose, counted to ten, and blew it out through his lips. Curbing his impulsive behaviour was one of the things he was working on, and accosting that wanker would be a step in the wrong direction.

The thought brought back a memory: Romero laid out on the floor with a bloody, busted lip courtesy of Connor. That was almost twenty-five years ago. He scowled.

His phone vibrated in his pocket, and he quickly plucked it out, hoping to find a reply from Stella. But it was from Krish.

Sorry. Held up. See you in 5.

Closing his eyes, Connor took a series of deep breaths and calmed his racing thoughts, the way his therapist had taught him.

Since five o'clock that afternoon, he'd been sitting in the noisy hotel bar, hidden in the low, tungsten mood lighting, waiting for Stella to arrive. He wanted to welcome her. Surprise her. Be the man she wanted him to be: attentive and available for her. For four hours, he remained in that seat, imagining all possible outcomes of their reunion. In some versions, she was happy to see him; in some, she wasn't and they'd argued.

When she'd finally walked into the lobby with Liliwen ten minutes ago, Stella looked tired but beautiful, her fiery hair a memory of warmth between them. He didn't recognise the body-skimming yellow jersey dress she was wearing. Something new, then. He squinted at her hand as though squinting would turn his eyes into binoculars. Was she still wearing his ring? He couldn't tell.

He'd been waiting ages for this moment, but uncharacteristically paralysed by indecision, Connor froze in his chair. With women, he usually knew exactly what to do, but with his wife, fear of screwing up overwhelmed him. Would greeting her as soon as she arrived be a good idea? Or would that put her off? She'd be exhausted, and he didn't want her to feel like he was ambushing her. But if he did go to her, should he kiss her? Shake hands? Flash a peace sign?

Then Blake Romero had shown up, and she'd given that bellend the smile that Connor craved.

It made him want to hit something.

A slap on his shoulder startled him. 'If it isn't the legendary Connor Knight! What're you doing here?'

Even before he looked up, Connor knew who it was: Damian McGillicuddy, a photographer who'd been in the business longer than Connor. In fact, Damian had mentored him in the early days of his career.

Damian perched on the leather arm of a nearby chair. He appeared the same as ever: glasses, jovial expression, black t-shirt, bald head, and a skinny, grey ponytail hanging down his back.

Momentarily distracted from the Romero issue, Connor leaned

back and crossed his legs, resting his ankle on his knee. 'I was in between jobs so I thought I'd honour you all with my presence.'

'Fuck off,' chuckled Damian, pretending to bonk Connor on the head with the bottom of his beer bottle.

Actually, Connor was there because Stella had insisted that they should catch up after IPE, 'far away from our daily lives'. His very own Last Chance Saloon. Make or break. Winner takes it all.

But if he lost...

Connor shut down that line of thought. Failure was not an option. He would fight tooth and nail to save his relationship with his wife.

He recalibrated his gaze on Romero and Stella, still waiting at the lifts. She looked quizzically over her shoulder as though sensing his eyes on her.

Damian swigged from his bottle and asked, 'So...really. Why are you here? Teaching a masterclass? Didn't see your name on the schedule. Or...Ha!' he barked, as though a thought had just occurred to him. 'Or are you expecting an award? Biggest ego in photography?'

Out of the corner of his eye, Connor saw Stella roll her head left and right, obviously tired from her flight. He'd give anything to be the one to rub the ache from her shoulders. He hadn't touched her in six months.

'Hello? Earth to Connor?' Damian waved his hand in front of Connor's face. 'Still daydreaming, I see.'

Dragging his attention away from Stella, Connor dredged his recent memory for what Damian had asked and answered, 'Just here for the atmosphere and to catch up with losers like you.'

At the lifts, Romero said something and Stella laughed.

As though reacting to the same joke, Damian hooted. 'Too big for us now, huh? You hanging out with Annie Leibovitz yet?'

Connor snorted. 'Yeah, I had lunch with her last month.' He said it like he was being sarcastic, but it was true.

'Damian!' called someone from the bar, another photographer

Connor recognised from days past. 'Come on. We're heading to the restaurant.'

'Shit. Well, I guess I'll see you around,' Damian said as he launched himself to his feet and ambled after his friends.

Connor remembered a time when he would have been invited along as one of the gang. A dull ache of longing pinched his heart, surprising him.

Maybe it had been a mistake to come to the conference early. He didn't have a reason to be there. It had been five years since he last attended IPE—since he transitioned from weddings to high-end fashion and commercial photography. His career had outgrown events like this. After all, Annie didn't go to photography conventions. So why was he here?

He sighed, knowing the reason full well: he wanted to be near Stella.

Back at the elevators, Romero relieved Stella of her heavy laptop bag. Connor squeezed his hand into a fist and rested it against his lips, grey eyes narrowed. How well did Stella know Blake? As the doors opened, Romero placed his palm on the small of Stella's back and guided her into the lift. The gesture seemed intimate.

What the fuck? Connor sat forward, his pulse racing and nostrils flaring. Was something going on between her and Romero? The thought took hold and wouldn't let go of him.

His phone buzzed. A reply from Stella.

> Hi, didn't realise you were already here. I have a full schedule, but could squeeze in a quick dinner tomorrow night? Just heading to bed now. S

Heading to bed...? Heading to bed *with* Blake Romero?
Over my dead body.

This time, he didn't stop to consider consequences. He pushed himself up from his chair, but a hand clamped onto his shoulder and pushed him back down again.

'Hold on there, Boss,' said Krish, dropping two beer bottles onto the table. 'Where do you think you're going?'

Connor growled, 'Did you see that maggot touch my wife?'

'I saw.' Krish lowered himself into an adjacent chair and made himself comfortable. His natural laid-back energy was the opposite of Connor's.

'So... what? I'm supposed to let whatever's going on—'

'You really think Stella would do that?' Krish sipped from his bottle.

With an aggravated sigh, Connor grabbed his beer. 'I'm not sure. When she asked for the separation, we never discussed... you know... whether we were on a *break*—' he widened his eyes and lowered his voice '—or a break.'

'Have you...?'

'No, of course not.'

'I don't think Stella would either. She loves you. I'm sure of it.'

Connor's head dropped into his hand. 'I wish I was.'

Krish clapped him on the leg. 'You need to talk to her. You have issues to work out, but you can do it. Because who are you?' he said with the attitude of Ted Lasso giving a pep talk.

'I'm Connor fucking Knight,' he mumbled.

Deep down, Connor knew Krish was right. The Stella he loved wouldn't start something with anyone else while there were unresolved issues between them. Besides, Connor hoped that Stella would be able to see through Romero and guard herself against his manipulation. Blake could be very convincing. Even Connor had fallen for it once upon a time.

For his own sanity, Connor needed to trust Stella, even if she didn't seem to trust him, thanks to how he'd handled the whole Valentina Vavilek incident all those years ago. With all his heart, he wished he could go back in time to change his actions. That had been the point when their problems had really started.

Taking another sip, he tried to relax and asked, 'When did you become so wise?' Krish used to be his student and assistant for many years before leaving Connor's business to start up on his own. Now Krish ran the preeminent Asian wedding production company in the UK. Photography, videography, event design—his company did it all.

And along the way, Krish had also become Connor's best friend.

Krish laughed and pushed a hand through his shoulder-length black hair. 'I guess fatherhood has changed me.'

'Cheers to that.' They clinked their beer bottles. 'How's Francesca getting on with Soraya?'

Six months ago, Krish and his wife, Francesca, who couldn't have children, had adopted a one-year-old girl with Krish's colouring and Francesca's green eyes. Adoption services couldn't have found a more perfect match.

Krish chuckled. 'She's attacking motherhood with gusto. You know Francesca...'

'You mean the woman who told me I was an arsehole the first time she met me?'

'She's very astute.'

'Haha.'

'Anyway, she's home alone with Soraya and she's not used to it, so I'm heading back early.'

Connor raised his eyebrows. 'You're not staying for the whole conference?'

Krish shook his head. 'Sorry. Once my masterclasses and sponsorship meetings are over, I'm outta here. This is crazy but... it physically hurts to be away from them.'

A frown pulled at Connor's mouth. He knew exactly what Krish meant. Nowadays whenever he took Grace to the park or the cinema or to play mini-golf, there was a Stella-shaped absence, an echo of missed memories he wished they were making together. An image of Grace's smiling face crossed his mind—a smile so much like her mother's. Grace was the perfect combination of her parents, with her mum's red hair and her dad's grey eyes. A lump formed in Connor's throat.

He coughed it away. 'Fatherhood does that to you,' he said, hiding his sadness in a swallow of beer. He just had to salvage his marriage and hold his family together.

Compulsively, he looked down to check his phone, catching another glimpse of Stella's text message: no X after her initial. Just S. It was difficult not to read into that.

Selfishly, he wished Krish was sticking around. In light of the things Connor was learning about himself in therapy, he understood why he was so drawn to Krish's unflappable presence. He helped Connor stay calm and curtail his impulsive tendencies. Connor suspected that he might need more of that if things with Stella didn't turn out as he hoped. The city of Las Vegas wasn't famous for inspiring self-control, especially for people like him.

The siren sound of his ringtone cut through their moment of bonhomie. He groaned, 'Ugh. Speaking of fathers.' Armstrong Knight's name flashed on the screen. 'Do you mind if I...?'

'No, go ahead.'

Connor's father rarely called, so it must be important. When they'd last spoken, it was to tell him that Armstrong had taken another diplomatic posting in Australia, despite the fact that he was knocking on seventy's door. Flicking his thumb across the screen, Connor answered, 'Armstrong?' It had never been 'dad' or 'pops' or any other fatherly term of endearment for them. 'Everything okay?'

'Where are you?' Armstrong said, not wasting time on pleasantries.

'Las Vegas,' Connor said, not wasting time on them either.

'I know that.'

Connor's face twisted with confusion. 'How do you know I'm in Las Vegas?'

'It says so on your Instagram.'

His assistant in the UK had been posting on Connor's behalf and must have mentioned it. 'You know how to use Instagram?'

Armstrong scoffed, 'I'm not an idiot, Connor. So where are you?'

Connor looked at Krish and rolled his eyes. 'At my hotel. Why?'

'Where in the hotel?'

'At the bar in the lobby.' This was the most surreal conversation of his life. 'Why?'

'Because I'm here!'

Connor shot to his feet. 'What?'

Through the line, he heard a commotion, like somebody wrestling the phone away. Another, deeper voice that sounded a lot like Connor's workaholic brother, Michael, said, 'What dad's trying to say is we need a drink as a matter of urgency. Where the fuck are you?'

3

CONNOR

'SURPRISE,' SAID MICHAEL, FLASHING HIS INFECTIOUS SMILE AS HE AND Armstrong approached a stunned Connor.

No words. Connor had no words.

He blinked a few times to see if his father's tall, slim, grey-headed body and his equally tall, blond brother might disappear.

Nope. Still there.

Jumping into the silence, Krish stood and reached out to shake Armstrong's hand. 'Mr Knight. Nice to see you again.'

'Krish, right?' said Armstrong as their hands pumped up and down. 'The Oxford-trained lawyer turned photographer, if I remember correctly.' He always *remembered correctly*—a skill honed from almost forty years as a senior diplomat.

However, Connor rankled at the way his father said *photographer*. Since the day Connor told him that he wanted to take pictures for a living, it was clear what Armstrong thought of it as a career. He'd encouraged Connor to go into law or science or civil service, like him. Connor couldn't think of anything he'd rather do less.

Snapping out of his shock, Connor stood, a slow smile lifting the corner of his mouth. 'What the fuck ...?' He addressed his brother, hugging him close with a fraternal slap on the back before stepping away to run his eyes over Michael's lean, muscular frame. Feigning concern, he squeezed Michael's upper arm. 'No time for the gym these days?'

In turn, Michael squinted at Connor as if inspecting a bug and said, 'Going grey at the temples, I see.'

'Bugger off,' Connor smiled and hugged him again.

They hadn't seen each other for over three years, both busy with work. When Connor moved out at age 18, Michael had been 10. They'd managed to stay in touch, talking on the phone and visiting each other when they could. But in general, the Knights were not a close family. As a child, Connor had watched bootlegged VHS recordings of *The Brady Bunch* and *Family Ties* and *Growing Pains* and wondered what it would be like to be one of those families.

Pulling away, Connor asked, 'What the hell are you doing here?'

'Ask dad. He's the one that called this round table.' Michael lived in New York, where he worked as a human rights lawyer. The three of them hadn't been in the same room since Connor and Stella's wedding seven years ago.

Connor's smile slipped. *Shit. Something must be wrong.*

He looked Armstrong up and down in his expensive blue suit as though x-raying him like Superman. From the outside, his father appeared fine, more than fine, even. He was in good shape with an uncanny resemblance to *Color of Money*-era Paul Newman, but with grey eyes instead of blue. Stella called him the Silver Fox for a reason. 'Are you ill?' Connor said, his brow furrowed. 'Are you dying? Is that what this is about?'

Armstrong made a pfft sound. 'I ran a half-marathon last week. Why do I need an excuse to see my boys and that beautiful daughter-in-law of mine? Speaking of which, where is Stella?'

'Uhhh...' Connor and Krish's eyes locked a second before Connor's shifted away and he rubbed the skin at the back of his neck. *Bollocks.* He hadn't divulged to his dad and brother that he and

Stella had separated. The only people he'd confided in were his therapist and Krish. Telling anyone else would have made it too real.

Krish clapped his hands together. 'Anyway, I have some prep to do for my talk tomorrow, so I'm going to head upstairs. Armstrong, Michael, great to see you again.'

'Are you sure? I was about to order a round,' said Armstrong, switching to host mode—another hangover from a lifetime spent as a diplomat. Armstrong would probably welcome the hangman to his own execution. Offer him an aperitif and ask how business was going. Connor had observed long ago that his father's first instinct was to ensure people felt comfortable and interesting... unless they were related to him, of course.

Krish graciously declined. 'See you back in London,' he said to Connor, with an added 'Good luck' under his breath.

While Armstrong went to the bar, Michael pulled over another armchair. He collapsed into it like he was in his own living room and enthusiastically drummed his hands on Connor's leg.

'It's really great to see you, Con. How have you been?'

Sometimes Connor forgot that his brother was a respected lawyer because he was also an excitable puppy. 'Busy, as always.'

'I hear you.' A momentary shadow passed over his face, but he recovered so quickly that Connor dismissed it as a trick of light. With his clean jawline, blond widow's peak, and earnest blue eyes, Michael had one of those open, genial faces that made others like him immediately. He bore more than a passing resemblance to their late mother. 'Hey, I saw that Chris Seals is performing in Vegas this week. Didn't you shoot him for Omega?'

'Yeah. Nice guy.' Seals was an iconic rockstar whose career spanned decades. He had a reputation for being a rebel, crossing genres and surprising fans with unexpected albums—like his latest, an Irish sea shanty/hip-hop mix. The tabloids liked to paint him as an arrogant tosser, but during the shoot, Connor and Chris had spent ten minutes crowing over pictures of each other's kids on their phones.

'You going to see him?'

'God, no. I don't like big arena shows.' He found they over-stimulated his senses. He preferred small, intimate performances—unless he was the one on the stage. Then the bigger, the better. He felt a nostalgic twinge for the days he used to speak in the biggest rooms at this convention.

Michael's brow pinched with disbelief. 'Really? I still remember that time you snuck out to see the Backstreet Boys in Paris when you were 15 and my nanny called the police to file a missing person's report.'

Connor tipped his head back and chortled at the memory. The Backstreet Boys had toured Europe before they made it big in America. 'If you ever tell anyone, I will deny it.'

'Are you kidding me?' Michael said. 'You were their number one fan. Remember how you used to walk around the house practicing all their harmonies? And the curtain hair! Oh my god, that hair!' Laughter bubbled out of him.

'Bugger off.' Connor grinned, picturing the Kevin Richardson-inspired look with the long, dark fringe framing his forehead. Connor hoped the photos of him with that haircut remained lost. Stella would never let him live it down.

At the thought of her, his smile faded.

Fuck, if a picture of him with a bad haircut would make her love him again, he'd frame it for her himself.

His gaze fell on his father, who was still at the bar, flirting with a woman a fraction of his age. Unsurprised, Connor leaned towards Michael. Close up he noted the dark circles under his brother's eyes. He'd broach that subject later.

Pointing his thumb towards their dad, he asked, 'Any idea what's wrong with Armstrong?'

'Not a clue,' Michael said. 'He called and commanded me to meet him in Vegas. Said you were here. I needed a break and I had a window in my schedule, so I came.'

'Shit. Do you think it's serious?'

'No... I think he'd be less... *chipper* if he were dying.'

'Here we go,' said their father, cutting the conversation short and putting three tumblers on the table. 'Whiskeys all around.'

Michael made a face. They all knew he hated whiskey.

'Come on! Whiskey is a man's drink!' declared Armstrong as he settled into his chair, crossing his legs. 'It'll put hair on your chest.'

Connor ruffled at Armstrong's comment. Was he taking a pot shot at his gay son?

Michael laughed it off. 'Actually, dad, I pay good money to have the hair waxed *off* my chest.'

Bristling, Connor jumped in. 'I'll get you a drink, Michael. G and T?'

Ever the peacekeeper, Michael said, 'Don't worry, it's fine.' He picked up the whiskey and smelled it, struggling to hide his distaste.

Connor hailed a passing waitress and ordered a gin and tonic. He was tired of whatever game their father was playing. 'Armstrong, why don't you stop being an arsehole and tell us why we're all here.'

Armstrong narrowed his eyes at Connor. 'Nice to see you, too, son.'

Under his breath, Michael muttered, 'Weddings and funerals...'

'Actually,' said Armstrong, sitting forward, 'I bring glad tidings.'

The brothers exchanged a dubious look.

Grinning like he had a sackful of toys he couldn't wait to hand out, Armstrong announced, 'I've finally retired and I'm moving home! To London! To be near my granddaughter.'

Connor choked on his whiskey. The last thing he wanted while his marriage was in crisis was his philandering father around all the time. He was about to say something when Michael cut in: 'Dad, did you ever think I might want you to move to New York? Just because I don't have a husband and kids doesn't mean I don't want to spend time with you.'

Armstrong obviously wasn't expecting this. 'Um, I... sorry, son, I didn't think—'

Michael started laughing. 'Just kidding! I've never been happier to be single and childless in my life. I love you, but you'd be a nightmare. He's all yours,' he said to Connor. Picking up the whiskey he supposedly hated, he swallowed a celebratory swig.

'Great.' This was not what Connor needed right now.

When Connor had started therapy a few weeks after Stella instigated their separation, it didn't take long for his therapist to hit upon the subject of Connor's father.

They'd talked about him. A lot.

They discussed how, after the death of his mother, Connor was raised by a string of nannies who changed every three years when Armstrong received a new assignment; therefore, both Connor and Michael lacked a stable female role model and struggled to form attachments.

They discussed how Armstrong always put work before his sons and how he had a string of women coming in and out of his bedroom—behaviour that Connor had modelled in his own life for a while until he realised how empty it made him feel.

They discussed how, no matter what Connor achieved—the awards, the high-profile assignments, the reputation—none of it seemed to impress his father. Ironic that he'd come to see Connor at a photography convention.

In therapy, Connor realised that he had idolised his father for a long time. He believed Armstrong's way was the only way to live.

Then Stella had come along and showed him what real family was, and he'd re-examined his upbringing with a new lens.

'I don't know what to say,' Connor said, his brow furrowing as he sipped his whiskey.

Armstrong cocked his head. 'How about congratulations?'

'Why now?'

They were interrupted by a waitress delivering Michael's drink.

As soon as she left, Armstrong said, 'Because I'm seventy years old on my next birthday, and for some insane reason I thought it might be fun to spend time with my granddaughter before I die.'

Connor studied his father. Something about this wasn't adding up. Armstrong had forgotten three out of Grace's six birthdays and never remembered Connor's. With his famously good memory, that had to be a choice. And Connor was supposed to believe that family was suddenly his father's priority?

Armstrong's excitement waned in the face of his son's lack of enthusiasm. He grumbled, 'Where's Stella? She'll be happy for me.'

Connor disagreed. Stella would have the same reaction as him. She'd simply hide it better.

Fidgeting with his glass, Connor exhaled and said, 'Stella and I separated six months ago.'

It was their turn to be shocked.

Michael spoke first. 'I'm sorry to hear that.' He squeezed Connor's leg.

'What does separated mean? Divorced?' Armstrong said.

'No, not divorced.' Connor sighed. How could he explain this to his father? The best analogy had occurred to him while he was watching Peppa Pig with Grace. Connor loved Peppa Pig. It was written for kids but also had plenty of tongue-in-cheek content for adults. He remembered the moment of his epiphany clearly: in the episode where Mummy Pig's computer wasn't working, Daddy Pig told her to turn it off and on again, magically fixing it.

In a burst of insight, it struck Connor that Stella was doing exactly that to their marriage: turning it off and on again.

He just hoped that it magically fixed them, too.

'We're taking stock. It'll be fine.' Connor wished he felt as confident as he pretended to be.

'Well,' Armstrong patted Connor on the knee, 'I've been there. Marriage is hard. I'm not sure us Knight boys are cut out for it. We're lone wolves.'

The anger hit Connor right in the gut. How had his mother ever put up with his dad? Maybe Armstrong wasn't cut out for marriage, but Connor was. He had to believe that. 'Why would you say that?'

Michael laughed uncomfortably. 'Anybody fancy a steak? There's supposed to be a great steakhouse in this very hotel...?'

Armstrong flapped his hand in the air as though wafting the tension away. 'Listen, I don't want to fight with you. We're in Las Vegas. Let's just... have fun. I want to spend as much time with my sons as I can.'

Connor would believe it when he saw it.

4

STELLA

'MUMMY! LOOK! I MADE A PICTURE OF YOU, ME, AND DADDY!' SAID Grace over video call the next morning. Her red hair was neatly brushed, her grey eyes shining with pride as she showed off a stick-figure drawing of their family, plus a mysterious dog.

Sitting at the dining table in her suite, Stella fought back tears. Her airways thickened with grief, as if someone had crumpled the picture and shoved it down her throat. *I'm a terrible mother*, she thought, a regular refrain since the separation. *I ruined our family.*

But she couldn't let Grace see her distress. Instead, Stella swallowed hard, slapped on a smile and said, 'It's beautiful, Gracie.' She squinted at the brown scribble with ears. 'Who's the doggy?'

'It's my puppy!' she said, as though Stella should know that.

'I'm sorry, what?' *Shit, have my parents bought her a dog while I was away?* Stella wouldn't put it past them. Both Angela and Bill had trouble saying no to their granddaughter. If Grace asked for something, their response was usually *how many?* Which was why they had enough Squishmallows in their house to pad a gymnasium.

A dog would be another problem Stella didn't need. Her parents knew she was afraid of dogs ever since she was bitten as a child, but Connor and Grace had been bugging her for one for a while now.

She half expected Connor to adopt one during the separation, but of course, he wouldn't be able to care for a dog with his hectic work schedule.

Grace walked off screen, leaving Stella staring at her unusually tidy living room. A moment later, Grace returned with a large stuffed Cocker Spaniel. *Phew.*

'Say hello to Princess Poopy Paws!'

Stella barked with laughter.

'What's wrong?' asked Grace.

'Nothing. Um, hello, Princess Poopy Paws.' *Note to self, don't let children name pets.* Stella made the necessary small talk with the stuffed toy, learned that her favourite colour was green, and that she preferred pancakes with Nutella rather than bananas.

Abruptly, Grace announced, 'Bye, mummy!' and flounced away. Elsewhere in the house, she heard Grace inform someone—probably grandpa—that they needed to take the dog out for a walk before bedtime.

Stella called out, 'Hello? Anybody there?'

'*Ciao, cara,*' said Angela, Stella's mother, as she slid into view, wiping her hands on a dishtowel. Her faded auburn hair was tied back, and she wore a fancy top patterned with large blue flowers.

'*Ciao, mamma. Tutto bene?*' she asked.

'Grace misses you.'

And there it was. The first—and probably not the last—sword of maternal guilt aimed by her mother straight at Stella's heart. 'I miss her, too.'

Angela narrowed her eyes. 'Have you seen Connor yet?' she asked, moving swiftly to sensitive subject number two.

'Not yet,' Stella said. 'I'll see him tonight.'

'I don't understand why you forced him into this separation in the first place.' *Here we go,* thought Stella. She had enough doubts without her mother piling on her own. 'You know, this is what happens when you go to bed angry. Anyway, I've spoken with Father Jacob at St James down the road, and he is happy to make time to speak with you and Connor about your... marital disorder.'

The force with which Stella had to resist rolling her eyes gave her a headache. In all the years they'd lived in Maida Vale, Stella had never been into St James. She didn't plan on starting now. 'Mamma, we don't need to speak with a priest.'

'I'm just saying... *non si può avere le botte piena e la moglie ubriaca.*' In other words: *You can't have a full barrel of wine and a drunk wife.* Angela pressed on, 'Marriage isn't easy. It's about sacrifice. You can't always have it all.'

'Thanks for the advice.' Stella had endured a lifetime of lectures about what marriage was and wasn't from her mother. Marriage was beautiful. Marriage was ugly. Marriage was a joy. Marriage was a struggle. Marriage was a many-layered flower. Marriage was a hard nut to crack.

Angela shrugged, stuck out her bottom lip, and bucked her chin —a typical Italian expression. 'By the way, I have a bone to pick with you.'

'Another one?' Stella groaned.

'Eh! This is serious!' Angela chopped her hand repeatedly at the screen. 'Your daughter's Italian is atrocious. What have you been teaching her?'

'She speaks perfectly well for a six-year-old.'

Now, Angela was slapping the back of one hand into the palm of the other. Stella was getting the full library of Latin gestures. 'She needs to go to Italian school every Saturday, like you did. I've made some research—'

The alarm on Stella's phone sounded. Time to get ready for her meeting with Blake. 'Sorry, mamma. I have to go,' she said, glad to have an excuse to end the call.

'Don't hang up, Stellina, I'm serious—'

'*Ciaoooo!*' Stella said as she hit the red button. The screen went dead. She loved her mother, but sometimes she drove Stella up a wall. Some people paid for childcare with money. Stella paid for it by suffering hours of commentary on her personal life and parenting skills. Nothing she ever did was good enough... Except marrying Connor and having Grace. In her mother's eyes, those were Stella's shining achievements.

She pushed her laptop away, crossed her arms on the table, and dropped her head on top of them. Didn't her mother know? Stella had more than enough self-recrimination all on her own.

AN HOUR LATER, Stella was navigating the rabbit warren of a hotel to find the room where she was meeting Blake. She'd already lost her way a number of times, which only served to increase her nerves. She wasn't even there yet, and her palms were sweating. Having taken a wrong turn at one point, she had to stop in the food arcade to ask for directions. It was a ramen restaurant/bubble tea/karaoke bar where some drunk punter who'd probably been up all night was murdering 'Oops! I Did It Again'—the Millennial anthem for bad decision making.

Stella memorised the instructions that the girl behind the counter gave her and set off again.

Pop music blared in every thoroughfare, making it hard to think. Nowhere in this place was quiet except her room. On the casino floor, which lay between the guest rooms and the conference centre, guests were already manning the slot machines, losing their fortunes one quarter at a time. The jolly bleeps and bloops of the machines made it sound significantly more fun than it was. Around her, the air smelled fruity and floral, but underneath, Stella could detect the historic odour of stale cigarette smoke and desperation.

She yawned and slapped a hand over her mouth. Jet lag had awoken her at 4AM. Wide awake and alone in her bed, that was the moment she missed Connor the most, wishing he could hold her and reassure her everything would be okay, that she hadn't destroyed their family. While she stared at the ceiling, her thoughts had descended into a dangerous place—a regular occurrence in the last six months. Had separating from Connor been a mistake? Could she have done things differently? Was she part of the problem?

Perhaps she should have made time to see a therapist. It wasn't the first time the idea had occurred to her, but she'd been so busy living day by day, shooting clients, running her blog, and spending time with Grace, that there hadn't been space in her schedule. And then six months had passed and she was in Las Vegas. She expected Connor to change his habits in that time, but had she wasted the opportunity to work on herself?

To silence the barrage of her thoughts, she'd rolled out of bed and grabbed her laptop. Working always helped quieten her mind. She'd edited some images for a client before jumping on the call with Grace.

Stella wished her schedule today had some time for a nap built into it—especially because she had plans to see Connor later for... what? A date? Her stomach fizzed at the thought. She wasn't ready to have any big discussions yet. She had a busy week to survive first. Would it be possible for them to simply enjoy each other's company for an hour? Or would it devolve into arguing?

Whenever they fought, she'd end up raising her voice, getting more and more passionate. In turn, Connor would go calm, making her look comparatively unreasonable. Well, opposites attract, right?

As usual, conflicting emotions rolled through her when she thought about him. Excitement tinged by caution. Exasperation mingled with hope.

As if conjuring him, she passed an advertisement for a famous jewellery company featuring a photograph that Connor had taken. Pride in his achievements warred with her feelings about the personal cost.

Seven days, she thought. That's how long Connor had been away in Florida for that particular shoot, missing Grace's ballet show.

She shook her head to clear her mind. She couldn't dwell on that now.

This meeting was important. If Connor hadn't changed and they divorced, then she would need a steady, passive income to allow her to spend less time shooting for clients and more time raising Grace. The royalties and following from an opportunity to record a class or two for MuseTV would give her that financial cushion. Her friend, Lada Lovechild, the newborn photographer who took Grace's baby photos, taught a popular class for MuseTV and now received a cushy £10,000 cheque every month.

After locating the right lift, Stella finally found the meeting room: the Athena Suite. Goddess of wisdom. She could use some of that now.

Stella inhaled deeply. She opened her eyes wide, willing herself awake, then pinched her cheeks and stretched her mouth into a friendly smile. Smoothing her hands over the front of her green jumpsuit, she wondered if she'd made the right clothing choice. She'd wanted something not too formal, not too casual. Approachable. Professional. And most importantly, photogenic. Green was her colour.

Tits and teeth, she intoned the mantra she and Tristan used to say pre-performance, when they'd been dance partners on the competitive ballroom circuit. She raised her fist and knocked.

'I APPRECIATE you making the time to see me.' Blake placed a fresh cup of coffee in front of Stella and sat in the chair next to hers. With only the two of them, the boardroom seemed extra enormous with its long table and the wall of windows that overlooked a busy avenue. Harsh, desert sunlight streamed in through the tinted glass, making rectangular parallelograms on the carpet.

Stella dared not drink the coffee. Her hands were already trembling, and she'd just end up spilling it all over herself. Blake, on the other hand, seemed calm as ever—a man who clearly took pride in his appearance with his jaw cleanly shaven and his ecru suit pressed and crisp. He even smelled successful. Spicy. Expensive.

It did nothing for her nerves.

She willed herself to appear relaxed, too, even as one of her wayward fingers picked at a loose red thread on her chair. Noticing that she had already unravelled two inches, she moved her hand to her lap. 'Of course,' she said. 'I'm interested in hearing your proposal.'

'Fabulous. And I'm excited to tell you what I have planned for you.' Her pulse sped up at his words. 'Have you watched any of the content on MuseTV?'

'Yes, of course. It's brilliant. I've been especially impressed with how quickly you've established market dominance.' In preparation, she'd read everything she could in the business press about Blake and his online venture.

'Well, having the right tech and the right investors with the right connections helped,' he said. Blake started to open his laptop and paused. He pursed his lips, his brow furrowing. 'Before we begin, I wanted to say that I heard about your impending divorce from Connor...'

Shock made her smile slip. How did he know about their marriage issues? The only people she'd told were her parents, her best friend Claudia (and her husband Magnus), Liliwen, and Tristan, of course. Stella had been careful not to spread the news. She hated the idea of people gossiping about them. Had Liliwen said something last night?

Or maybe Connor had been less circumspect.

She reinstated her smile. 'We're only separated. We're not divorced.' The unspoken *yet* hung in the air.

He nodded in a way that made her feel like he knew which way it was heading. 'I'm sorry. Separated. Of course. I didn't mean to—'

'It's fine.'

Blake glanced away before returning his gaze to hers. 'I've been through a tricky marriage myself, so... I understand what you're going through.'

'Thank you,' she said, hoping that would be the end of the discussion and they could move onto the reason she was sitting in this boardroom. At least she now felt less nervous and more... annoyed.

'Right.' He flipped open his laptop. Picking up a remote, he hit a button and blackout blinds descended over the windows. On his computer, he typed something, and a large screen at the end of the table flared to life. A presentation appeared. The first slide was covered in numbers: website hits, social media followers, reach, all under the heading 'Stella Knight Feasibility Study'.

She gulped as silently as possible.

Blake launched into his pitch. 'Obviously I don't have direct access to your website analytics, but from our research, we estimate that you get about twenty-five thousand hits per month.'

'Closer to forty thousand,' she said, sitting up straighter in her chair. She knew her numbers were solid.

He grinned. 'Even better. And looking at the engagement not only on your blog posts, but on social media, I'd say that you hold the attention of a wide spectrum of photographers, both male and female, all over the world, all interested in your unique brand of glamour photography.'

Not to big herself up, she added, 'I try to respond to all the comments and emails I get. There's a lot of them.'

'It's the personal touch. It's admirable that you care about nurturing your fans. The Taylor Swift of photography.'

'I wouldn't go *that* far,' she said, glowing at the comparison.

'We conducted market research with a group of twenty-five of your top fans. Did you know they have a nickname for themselves?'

Stella's face contorted in surprise. 'What? No. You're kidding me,' she laughed. 'What is it?'

'The Starlings.'

'Wow.' Stella pursed her lips. Her name meant 'star' in Italian, so that made sense. But also, *how crazy was that?* Didn't these people know she was making it up as she went along?

'Wow, indeed. And here's the interesting thing.' He leaned forward and folded his hands on the table. 'I think they're right. I think you've got star quality, and I'd like to help you reach that potential.'

Stella could only nod, too excited to speak. *Here it comes, the offer of fronting a class on MuseTV...!*

'I think you have a unique way of teaching. People love the unpretentious way you explain technique in your vlogs. You don't make anyone feel like they need a better camera, or that they have to buy expensive lighting equipment and hand-painted backgrounds to create better pictures. You show them how to do it themselves, down and dirty, no frills. But the results... I mean, you're the queen of posing and styling.'

'Thank you.' Stella was starting to blush now, a bit overwhelmed by all the praise. She had Connor to thank for everything she knew about posing, lighting, well...everything.

Blake paused. The only sound was muffled pop music from the hallway outside. Stella wished he would make his offer. Put her out of her misery.

She leaned towards him, just an inch.

He mirrored her. 'What I want...'

Stella leaned forward another inch. 'Yes?' For one odd second, she thought he might try to kiss her, he was so focused on her face.

But then he tapped the forward arrow on his computer. On the big screen, another slide appeared. 'What I want is to build a whole new membership platform around *you*.' The screen showed a website mockup: KnightSchool dot com. Blake scrolled through the next slides, revealing a new logo and design. 'You can post regular content—lessons on posing, on business, on DIY background making...whatever you want. You'll have a budget for live creative shoots so you can get the best models, best wardrobe, props, etcetera. You'll have a full-time camera person on staff to capture and edit all the material. And of course, we'll pay for the studio space.'

Her jaw had dropped somewhere around 'whole new membership platform'. Was this for real? Her heart was pounding, and she had to pinch herself under the table to make sure this wasn't some jet-lag-induced fever dream.

'Blake, I don't know what to say—'

'Say yes! The investment is already lined up. And we've done our research. We've looked at a number of different candidates to roll this out with—Jen Kingman, Amy Lin, Royale Lefevre...' Three female photographers Stella knew by reputation, but not in person.

'We're searching for a female lead specifically, and your name kept floating to the top every time. You're unique. Your numbers are so far in front of everyone else's; there's no one that comes close. We all think you'll be a great success. And with your looks and that accent, the American market will be eating out of your hands.'

He forwarded to another slide with financial projections. Her eyes almost jumped out of her head at all the zeroes.

'Is that—?'

'Millions, Stella. This would make us both millionaires.'

Holy Tom Jones, as Liliwen would say.

This was far beyond what she had expected. At home, she had been gearing up to offer paid photography content online. For professional photographers, it was a lucrative way to make money to supplement—and often exceed—what they made from their photography itself. But between everything going on with Connor, raising Grace, the demands of her clients, and creating fresh content for her blog, working on the online classes had fallen further and further down her list.

What Blake was offering could change her life.

If only it didn't fill her with dread. It felt like a lot to carry on her shoulders. All that investment... what if she messed up?

Her father's voice bubbled to the forefront of her thoughts: *Winners don't turn down opportunities like this*, he would say. Even at age 38, her parents still occupied a broadcasting station in her brain.

She could do this. Other photographers would kill for this opportunity, and here it was, offered to her on a silver plate.

Brimming with excitement, she said, 'Okay! I'm in! I mean, we need to discuss the details, but in essence, it's a yes.'

Blake slapped the table and smiled. 'Excellent news. This is going to be an amazing collaboration. I see so much potential. Not only online, but picture this: your own *conference*. The sky's the limit.'

Stella couldn't believe this was happening. All the years of hard work and slowly building her brand were paying off. She'd deal with the Imposter Syndrome later.

Blake's smile faded. 'There's just one thing.'

In response, her joy faltered. *Here it comes.* The catch. There always had to be one. 'Okay. Tell me?' She hoped it wasn't something she'd have to reject, like wanting her to shoot a certain number of nude female models every month to keep male subscribers happy or give up all her current sponsorship deals.

He crossed his arms on the table and strummed his fingers on the polished surface before going completely still. Long seconds ticked by. Stella was on the point of passing out from holding her breath when he said, 'The problem is...the production company is in the US. You'd have to move to Los Angeles.'

5

CONNOR

'ONE, TWO, THREE!' MICHAEL COUNTED BEFORE HEFTING THE WEIGHT into the air. Standing behind his head, Connor monitored his brother as he lay on the bench, pressing 100 pounds.

The hotel gym was only half full but impressively equipped. An attractive woman speed-walking on a treadmill in pink camouflage workout gear caught Connor's eye and cocked her head at him, smiling flirtatiously. Connor focused on his brother.

Next to them, two men in their late twenties were pumping dumbbells, watching themselves in the floor-to-ceiling mirror as they chatted.

'You decide on a new camera yet, bro?' asked the man in a red Chicago Bulls singlet.

Overhearing, Connor chuckled to himself. Photographers were always obsessed with buying new kit.

Bulls' friend answered, 'Think I'm going for the Fuji. Forty mega pixels, thirteen stops dynamic range...'

Connor shook his head. When would photographers learn that the most important equipment was the person behind the camera?

'Solid choice.' Bulls nodded. 'I think that's the camera Ali Kazan uses. Isn't he a Fuji Ambassador now?'

'Aw, man. His photos are sick,' said the friend. 'You going to his masterclass?'

'Fuck yeah. All three of them.'

Ali Kazan, Connor thought. The new wedding photography rockstar. *Professional Photo* magazine recently ran a ten-page feature on his work. The headline read, 'The Future of Weddings'.

Connor clicked his tongue. Kazan's photography was decent, if a little over-processed.

'Um... Connor? Connor!' called Michael, the weight slowly descending towards his neck.

'Sorry,' said Connor as he lifted the bar and deposited it back on the safety hooks.

'No problem.' Michael sat up on the bench and wiped his sweaty face with a small white towel. 'Who needs an intact windpipe anyway? Your turn.'

Connor added another ten pounds to each end of the bar.

'Show off,' said Michael.

Taking Michael's place on the bench, Connor gripped the cold metal in his hands, counted down, and hoisted the weight. His chest, shoulder and arm muscles leapt to attention, burning as he took 120 pounds into his hands and pressed slowly up and down.

Working out kept him sane by helping him burn off his extra energy. It gave him not only physical fitness, but mental, too. While exercising, he could give his brain a break from the constant deluge of thoughts and ideas.

It was his natural medication.

'Done,' he grunted as he pushed the weight towards the safety hooks. Michael helped secure the bar before Connor let go.

'Impressive... for an old man,' said Michael as he wiped down the bench.

'I'd like to see you do it,' Connor said, zapping Michael playfully with his workout towel.

They'd been in the hotel gym for an hour, and Connor was starting to dream about big stacks of American pancakes, melted butter, warm maple syrup and blueberries that popped in his mouth. He'd allow himself one indulgence on this trip, and today was the day. Unhealthy, but delicious. 'Shower then brunch?' he suggested.

Michael cocked an eyebrow. 'I have a better idea, if you're up for a little friendly competition.'

CONNOR SPUN his racket on the lacquered beech floor. Annoyingly, it fell towards Michael.

'My serve.'

Cursing under his breath, Connor took his spot on the opposite side of the squash court. As always, Michael crashed into the game with a vicious serve, the little blue ball hitting high on one wall, then the other, speeding towards Connor lightning fast. Thankfully, he had the reflexes of a fighter pilot despite his 45 years. He returned the ball with equal power.

Michael smashed the blue missile with a forehand, sending it to the left corner and forcing Connor to use his backhand—his weaker swing—to return. Michael kept hitting the ball on that side. As their swings moved closer and closer to the left wall, Connor eventually made a mistake.

'Out,' said Michael, unable to hide his grin.

'Fuck it,' said Connor, slashing his racket through the air.

His little brother was fast. And condescendingly smug. Michael was the nicest person outside of a squash court, but as soon as he had that little ball in his hand, he turned into a monster. If Connor wanted any chance of winning this, he'd need to attack on a psychological level, too.

As Michael prepared to serve again, Connor said, 'So, how's work?'

His brother's nostrils flared. 'You know me,' Michael bounced the ball several times on the floor. 'Saving the world one homosexual at a time.' He slammed his racket into the ball.

'Lost any—judgments lately?' Connor grunted out in two parts as he returned a couple of tricky shots, his words echoing around the court along with the squeak of their trainers.

'Yes,' said Michael through gritted teeth.

'Boyfriends?'

'No time.'

Connor scored the point. 'One all,' he said calmly.

Michael hissed.

They switched sides. As Connor readied his serve, Michael said, 'So what happened to your marriage?'

Oh, that's dirty, thought Connor, trying not to let it rile him. 'We just needed to switch it off and on again.' He thwacked the ball hard.

'What did you do—' Michael backhanded the ball— 'to piss Stella off?'

Thwack! 'Is this an inquisition?' Connor's shoulders tensed..

'Just interested.' *Thwack!*

The ball came out of nowhere, bashing into Connor's right butt cheek.

'Fuck!'

'Sorry.' Michael grinned.

Connor peeked under the elastic of his workout shorts and rubbed his backside. 'That's going to leave a bruise.'

'Two-one,' Michael said, as though Connor needed help keeping score.

On the next volley, Michael wrestled another point, hitting a beautiful shot into the corner that was dead before Connor could slide his racket under it. To be fair to himself, Connor hadn't played squash in a while. He was out of practice. That was his excuse, anyway.

By the end of the game, Michael was in the lead, and Connor needed a water break.

Breathing hard, they exited the court and plopped down next to each other on the tiered seating outside. The hallway was empty.

'Nice game,' said Michael.

'Don't patronise me,' said Connor, squirting water on his face and wiping it off with a towel.

Michael's knees jiggled up and down as he swigged from his bottle. Some part of him was always in motion with nervous energy. 'I really do want to know, by the way.'

'Know what?' Connor extended his leg and grabbed the tip of his trainer to stretch out his calf.

'What happened between you and Stella.'

Releasing his foot, Connor leaned forward to rest his forearms on his knees. He sighed and the floodgates opened. 'We were both so busy, and I think Stella felt ignored. I was travelling a lot, shooting all over the world for my clients. My advertising career took off quicker than either of us expected. For a while I was juggling that with finishing off my wedding bookings, and I didn't have Krish to help anymore.' He shrugged. 'I thought I'd pass the wedding business on to Stella, but turns out she didn't want it. She had her own plans. So she turned the basement of our house into a studio, and *that* took off—'

'Doesn't she have a blog or something?'

'Yup—*Stella's Boudoir*. She started it to connect with other photographers and share behind-the-scenes videos from her shoots, and it just... went mad. People were asking her to show how she made her props, sewed her costumes, painted her backdrops, diffused her light. I was really proud of what she created...'

'But?'

Rubbing at the bridge of his nose, Connor said, 'I feel like such a luddite saying this, but... I wonder if it's humanly possible for two ambitious people to raise a family together and have enough time left for each other. Because we completely failed. Or at least, I have.'

'Sorry to hear that, Con.' Michael slapped him on the back. 'Didn't you have a nanny or someone to help out?'

Connor was silent for a moment. 'After *our* experience with nannies, I wasn't keen on having that for Grace.' His memory flicked to the nanny he'd had in Barbados, who used to hit him with a wooden spoon whenever he misbehaved, which was often. She'd much preferred baby Michael, whom she wore in a sling across her buxom chest as she was berating Connor.

Michael threw a towel across the back of his neck. 'Yeah, but... Grace has two loving parents, while we had... dad.' Connor watched Michael's gaze turn wistful, introspective, as it did whenever the spectre of their mother appeared. Connor wondered if his brother would ever stop feeling guilty for her passing during his birth.

Blowing out a mouthful of air, Connor said, 'I know. I realise now that I should've gone with it. Stella told me she was finding it hard dealing with nursery drop-offs and pick-ups *and* running her business... and fuck, I didn't listen.' He paused, closing his eyes as he relived his own idiocy. 'Anyway, I've been going to therapy.'

Michael sat up in shock. 'You? You've been in therapy? *You?*'

'Yes, very funny.'

Even as a young boy, Michael had seen therapists. He suffered from panic attacks and anxiety, which was how Connor knew what to do all those years ago when he found Stella having a panic attack at the BAPP convention. Completely the opposite, Connor had always thought he could handle any problems by himself, no help needed. He was independent to the core, just like his father raised him.

'So how's it going?' Michael asked before sipping from his water bottle.

Connor rolled the squash ball under his shoe and pushed down on it hard. 'Well enough. We talk a lot about Armstrong.'

'Ha, no shit,' said Michael without a hint of surprise.

'And...there's something else,' Connor said.

It was in his second session. Levi, his psychologist, presented as a quiet, zen old man with square glasses and too many bonsai trees. But in reality, he was a smiling Exocet missile hiding behind a grey beard. The session started as usual. Half an hour into a painful line of questioning about Connor's womanising days, Levi suddenly asked, 'Have you ever been diagnosed for your ADHD?'

Connor had no idea what Levi was talking about. Wasn't ADHD that childhood disorder where they fed kids speed to make them behave in school? Connor didn't know adults could have it.

But sure enough, Levi led him through a questionnaire and gathered some anecdotal evidence through conversation, and —

'I have ADHD,' Connor said.

He hadn't spoken about it with anyone else. He hadn't even mentioned it to Krish. Part of him had wanted to tell Stella first, but he hadn't expected to have a face-to-face with his brother, one of the few people who knew him best in this world.

'Really.' Again, Michael didn't seem surprised.

'What? You knew?' Connor wasn't sure how he felt about that. Was it that obvious? Did *everyone* know?

As though reading his mind, Michael said, 'Don't worry. They did a workshop about it at the office, and I immediately thought of you. What did the teachers used to say on your reports?' He put on a high voice, '*Connor is an intelligent child, but he is often disruptive in class and becomes easily frustrated with other students. Attempts at discipline are met with what we can only describe as weaponised charm.*'

'How do you know what my school reports said?'

'Dad kept them. They made for a fascinating read when I was bored. Like, remember that time you brought a frog to school and left it on your teacher's desk in a shoe box but then forgot, and it escaped and ended up in her coffee?'

Connor raised his shoulders. 'I thought it would be a cool class mascot.'

'Or the time you took butter from the school cafeteria and greased the hallway floors to see how far you could slide in your loafers?'

'Children should be inquisitive...'

'Or when—'

41

'Okay, I get the gist.' Connor sat back and ran his hand through his dark hair. 'I was a nightmare.'

'Your science teacher said you were *spirited.*'

'*Anyway,* the point is—it turns out that it's had some negative effects on my marriage.'

When he'd started unpacking it with Levi, Connor was amazed by how much of his behaviour and judgment had been influenced by his ADHD.

'Specifically?' Michael probed.

'You know how Stella, me, and Grace travelled for six months just before she turned one?'

Michael nodded.

'Well, when we returned to London, Stella complained that I was obsessed with work and kept forgetting about her and Grace. While we were on the road, that's where I had the idea of moving from weddings to advertising—'

'—which you succeeded at doing because you are goal-motivated.'

'Exactly. While we were traveling, it was stimulating—every day, something different. Before we left, we had a new baby to keep us occupied. And before that, it was Stella's pregnancy, and before that, the wedding...' Connor leaned his head on his hand. 'Obviously, I love Stella and Grace, but she's right. I completely lost focus on them. I didn't even realise I was doing it, and when Stella pointed it out—'

'—you dug in your heels and refused to see her point.'

'I thought she was nagging. Trying to clip my wings.' There were also his time-blindness issues. And what he called his 'ideas roller-coaster' episodes, when he stared into space for long periods of time while his brain leap-frogged from creative idea to creative idea—usually resulting in him being late for dinner.

'You've always been like this,' said Michael, and for a moment, Connor wondered if his brother had his own memories of Connor's ADHD affecting him.

He shook his head sadly. 'I used to think, "Well, that's just me", but as it turns out, it's more than that.'

Michael lifted an eyebrow. 'Sorry to sound like your shrink, but... how did that make you feel?'

'Well... *free*—in a way.' Getting the diagnosis had been like a light-switch flicking on in his brain. When he looked back at his life through the lens of the disorder, he understood certain things he'd done weren't him being a prick or over-reacting. Now as he read more and more about it, he found himself nodding along, feeling seen.

He realised that ADHD had been his friend—giving him the need to get on stage, the drive to achieve goals with focus, the ability to read a room. But it had also been his enemy, and not only in his marriage. 'Remember in Paris, when we lived next to that photographer—'

'Vaguely. The one that looked like Santa Claus?'

'That's the one. Maybe you don't remember, but that's when I became hyper-focused on photography, to impress him. Once, I showed him a portfolio of images I was working on—thought I was the next Henri Cartier-Bresson—and he told me they were childish, immature, and lacked style. I didn't just sulk. I was destroyed. Felt like a complete failure.'

Without waiting for Michael to respond, he continued, 'I've always thought it was an extreme reaction. And turns out it was Rejection Sensitivity.' In his research, he found out it was common in people with ADHD.

'Nobody likes rejection.'

'No shit, but for people with ADHD, it's worse. Just...trust me.' When Stella and Krish both left his business around the same time, Connor now realised that he'd resented it. He'd felt rejected and angry, but never expressed it. Only in discussion with Levi did he realise how much it had hurt.

Michael put the tip of his racket on the ground and spun it. 'Have you told Stella about this?'

'Not yet.' Connor ran his palms over his face. 'We've booked a week together at the end of the conference to… talk things over.'

'Are you on meds? I know people who say they really help.'

Connor flubbed his lips. 'I tried them. But I didn't like how they made me feel. A big part of who I am is the performer. The man who loves a stage. The pills made that part of me… less. And I didn't like it.'

'So… how are you dealing with it?' Michael spun his racket again.

'I've been functioning and… *mostly*… doing well my whole life. Simply being more aware of my symptoms helps.' Still, he was nervous about telling Stella. He worried that she'd think he was making excuses, but Levi said awareness was half the battle. If she took him back, they'd hopefully find ways to communicate and work through it, together.

In the meantime, he was still discovering what being neurodivergent meant for him: trying to slow down his reactions and use the mental tools Levi had given him.

Michael clapped him on the back. 'Come on. I'm not done whipping your arse in squash.'

In answer, Connor's stomach growled loudly. The pancakes beckoned. 'Actually, can we take a rain check? Old men like me need regular meals.'

'Saved by the bell,' Michael laughed. 'I'll text dad and let him know the plan.'

They threw their towels in the laundry bin, left the hotel fitness centre, and entered the lift. The doors closed. Connor smiled quietly to himself. Sharing his ADHD diagnosis with his brother had been the right call. He'd been keeping it in for months now, and Michael's understanding gave Connor hope that Stella would understand, too.

His thoughts turned to the dinner planned with her that evening. A nervous shiver ran through him, like the delicious anticipation of a first date. He'd made reservations at a fancy sushi restaurant, her favourite, and requested a table with some privacy.

She had complained that he didn't pay enough attention to her, so now he was laser-focused on exactly that. If he had to woo her all over again, then goddammit, that's what he would do. But first, he needed a thorough stretch and a long shower. He stunk.

The lift stopped on the first floor. The doors slid open.

And Stella walked in.

6

STELLA

STELLA FROZE ON THE SPOT WHILE HER HEARTBEAT WENT INTO Ferrari mode. This wasn't how she expected to see Connor for the first time in Vegas, his muscles straining against his grey workout shirt and his dark hair damp with perspiration. She couldn't help but compare him with the other dads she saw on the school run, their pectorals rounded and soft. Connor's were like cut marble.

She swallowed hard.

Their eyes locked: green to grey. If he was surprised to see her, he hid it well behind his inscrutable gaze. Still, he'd been smiling when the lift doors opened.

And now he wasn't. Sadness expanded in her chest like a dry sponge meeting water.

'Surprise!' said the other man in the lift.

It took her a second to realise it was her brother-in-law. 'Michael? What are you doing here?' she said, a wide grin unzipping across her face. A person couldn't help but smile at Michael. She stepped towards him for a hug before realising he was just as sweaty as his brother.

'Family holiday,' he said, offering her a fist bump instead. 'Dad's here, too.'

Good, she thought. When Damian McGillicuddy had contacted her on behalf of IPE to say they wanted to give Connor a Lifetime Achievement award on the final night, she'd messaged Armstrong, suggesting he might like to be there for his son. She knew Connor felt his dad never approved of his career, but if Armstrong showed up, he could see for himself what his son had accomplished.

All she'd received back was a quick 'Thanks for letting me know.' Nothing more. She assumed he wouldn't be attending, but he'd come after all and even brought Michael—a pleasant surprise!

Now, though, she had to pretend she knew nothing about it, so she laughed and said innocently, 'The Silver Fox in Vegas? Watch out, ladies! What's the occasion?'

Connor cleared his throat. 'Which floor?'

'Oh...um. Thirty please,' she said.

The doors closed and the lift slid into motion.

She was glad Michael was here. It took the pressure off her to make conversation with Connor, especially when all she could think about was the proposal Blake had just made.

Move to LA. Be a star.

Michael's lips were moving, and she realised he'd asked her a question. 'Sorry, what did you say?'

'I said how are you? I hear you're a big star now, with your blog...'

'A star?' She blushed. His words flitted too close to the thoughts circulating in her head. 'No, I wouldn't say that.'

Connor said, 'Are we still on for dinner tonight? Seven o'clock okay?'

Her stomach flipped. 'That's fine...' Then she had an idea, one that would save her from being one-on-one with Connor and give her more time to organise her thoughts. She was afraid that, if she were alone with him, she'd blurt out everything about Blake and LA. It would only add to their problems, especially because she had a vague memory that Connor didn't like Blake Romero. Some old petty photographer rivalry.

No, better to wait until the end of the week, when they'd have time to discuss it properly. 'Hey! Why don't you and Armstrong join us for dinner? I can ask Liliwen to make a reservation somewhere.'

'Um...' Michael's eyes shot to Connor, as though seeking permission.

'Come on, it'll be fun,' she said. 'I haven't seen you all in so long. It'll be nice to catch up.'

Connor sighed and bucked his chin in assent even though his disappointment was palpable. She couldn't look directly at him, afraid he'd see right through her ploy to avoid alone time with him. Still, it was for the best. This week was her time to focus on her career; next week was for her and Connor.

'Okay, then. Yes,' said Michael as the lift dinged. 'That's my floor.'

The doors opened. Michael exited, throwing a 'See you later!' over his shoulder.

The doors closed. Connor and Stella were alone. *Shit.* Stella swept her eyes up from his feet to his chest. That glorious chest. She remembered the many occasions when she'd kissed it, licked it, stroked it. Before the separation, his body was hers to touch. She bit her lip.

Trying to appear nonchalant, she moved to the wall opposite him and pressed her back against it, pinning her hands behind her bottom to keep them trapped.

'So...' began Stella. 'You okay? I mean, with your dad here...?'

'It's fine. Apparently, he's retiring.' He sighed and shook his head.

That was a surprise. The man lived for the civil service. 'Really? Why?'

'I'm not sure. He's being very cagey about his reasons.'

The lift dinged again. Connor's floor, thankfully. The door swooshed open, but neither of them moved.

Her awareness of him increased. The very cells in her skin were like magnets seeking connection. She crossed her arms to reinforce her personal shield.

Six months separated them. He might as well have been standing behind a glass cage. Hers, but not hers.

Would they ever be able to break through this barrier? The offer from Blake had only added more bricks. They already had enough problems to deal with.

The doors began to close, and her hand snapped out to catch them. He stayed still.

Connor stepped forward. 'Stella, I—'

'I'm teaching a masterclass in an hour.' She gulped, hoping he didn't notice her trembling. 'So...I have to prepare.'

A beat passed before he said, 'Got it. I suppose I'll... see you at dinner.'

'Bye,' she said, and he stepped out. The doors closed.

She finally breathed.

This tension sucked. When had they lost the ability to talk to each other? She'd asked herself this question so many times. Thinking back, it had probably started with the Valentina Vavilek situation, when Connor had lied to her about working with his over-sexed, over-affectionate client again, despite promising Stella that he wouldn't. He'd been so focused on getting what he wanted from Valentina professionally that he forgot to consider what it might cost him personally.

He'd apologised a million times. And he'd never done anything like it again (that she knew of).

Regardless of his apologies, she found it hard to trust him one hundred percent after that. She had no idea what he did while he was travelling for work, which was constant. She liked to think he was faithful to her, but then she'd remember what he was like before he met her...

The constant conveyor belt of women. The lack of commitment. Acting like his father.

And then she'd worry whether she could possibly ever be enough for a man like that.

Could a leopard really change its spots?

It didn't matter how much she hated that saying. It passed through her thoughts at least twenty times a day.

WHEN STELLA ENTERED HER SUITE, Liliwen was sitting at the dining room table, laptop out with Rat Pack songs playing from the TV stereo. Stella had been a little disappointed by the ordinariness of their accommodation: brown patterned rug, brown beds, corporate grey sofas. Being Las Vegas, she'd expected a gilt edge or two and a tinge of tackiness, but it was a surprisingly normal hotel room, boring and functionally furnished, only bigger.

Liliwen glanced over the pink-rims of her reading glasses. 'Hello, lovely. How was your meeting with that beautiful blond hunk of man?'

'It went well,' said Stella, avoiding specifics.

With a high whistle, Liliwen said, 'Let me tell you, if I were a few years younger, I'd be all over him, good and proper.'

Stella rolled her eyes. 'I'm married.'

Liliwen shrugged. 'You're separated.'

'Speaking of which, did you say anything to him last night about Connor and me while you were having drinks?'

'No, of course not, lovely. We mostly talked about why he loves LA so much. Apparently you can go skiing in the morning and hop over to the beach in the afternoon, which sounds exhausting if you ask me, but he seemed to think it was a selling point. Oh, and he said the fruit and veg is lush.'

Stella pursed her lips. She wondered if he'd told Liliwen those things on purpose, to turn her into an unwitting LA cheerleader. Stella still couldn't get her head around his offer. It was too good to turn down, but it was hard to consider when things were still so unsettled between her and Connor. If they stayed together, would Connor put her career first for once and move with her? And if they didn't stay together...

One brick at a time.

'Blake seemed to know about our separation. It caught me by surprise.' Stella had already sent her best friend, Claudia, a message to check if she'd told anybody. The response had come back straight away: *Fuck no.* Claudia never missed an opportunity to swear.

Remembering their exchange in the lift, Stella said, 'Could you please make a dinner reservation somewhere for tonight? Six people at seven o'clock. Sorry—assuming you want to come to dinner with me, my estranged husband, his gay brother, and their lecherous father?'

'Sounds divine. I wouldn't miss it for the world,' said Liliwen, scribbling a note on a Post-It. 'Any particular type of food?'

'Surprise me.' She couldn't spare the brain cells to think about that.

'Leave it with me.'

Stella had less than an hour before her first masterclass, a two-hour session teaching different ways to photograph a model using only one light. She should leave soon to set up, but first, she wanted to post a blog entry she'd meant to finish up last night.

Sitting at the table, she'd just opened her laptop when Liliwen said, 'I've replied to most of the messages from your website with those templates you wrote, but there are a few I'm not sure how to handle.'

'Okay,' Stella said, multi-tasking as she found the Word file she needed. 'Go on.'

'One woman wants to know if you used any artificial light in that shoot you did with that stunning Nigerian model on the beach. And where the bikini was from.'

'No, all natural. And I have no idea. Model's own.' She scanned the document to make sure it was the latest version. 'Next.'

'I'm afraid you've had three dick pics. One of the dicks wants to know if you're visiting Miami any time soon. And do you like waffles.'

'Sorry. What? As in pictures of penises?'

'Yes. None of them particularly tempting, I must say. Even to a sex-starved old lady like me.'

'You're not old. And delete. Delete. Delete.' What was wrong with people? As she gained more followers, she also gained a greater appreciation for how many perverts there were in the world. Though most of the comments on her social media posts were from people genuinely engaged in the content, there were more than a few from strange, often illiterate men apparently in the military, making either inappropriate or nonsensical comments about her looks. And she didn't even want to think about her DMs...

That would be a good use of AI. Somebody needed to create a bot that would scrub lewd comments from her messages. Stella shook her head and refocused on her computer.

A clicking noise at the door caught her attention. The handle turned, and Tristan's head popped through. 'Ding dong! Did anybody ring for a toy boy?'

'Eeeee!' Stella shrieked, slamming her laptop closed and giving up on work. 'You're here!' She ran over to her oldest friend and former dance partner and threw her arms around his 6'5" frame, hugging him hard.

Tristan returned the hug, lifting her off the ground. As he set her feet back on the floor, she moved to disengage, but he continued to hold her, rocking her from side to side. He must really miss her. The sunglasses he had latched into the V of his shirt pressed into her chest so hard she worried about crushing them.

Finally, he pulled back, put his hands on either side of her face, and kissed her forehead with a noisy *smack*.

She grinned and soaked in the sight of him. He'd changed since moving to Mexico. He was tanner, for one thing. His dark brown hair, partially covered by a baseball cap, was longer and wavier, and he sported a short beard. In all the years she'd known him, he'd always shaved. Always.

But the biggest change were his amber eyes. They looked tired. And there were more lines around the edges than she remembered.

He was still gorgeous though. She hated how men seemed to grow more handsome as they aged. It was not fair.

Stella leaned over to pick up the duffle bag he'd dropped on the floor when he came in. 'How was your flight?'

'Traumatising,' he said, following her into the suite, taking off his hat, and tossing it onto the table. 'I was sitting between some grandmother who must have eaten her bodyweight in *frijoles* before getting on the plane and a gentleman who probably should have had two seats.'

'Weren't you in business class?' Stella asked with surprise. The Tristan she knew wouldn't be caught dead in steerage.

'Not this time.' He didn't elaborate.

'Okay... well, you remember my friend Liliwen?'

'Of course!' He waved.

'I voted for you on *Strictly*,' said Liliwen with a wink, as though it were her vote that swung the win his way.

With a surge of emotion, Stella threw her arms around him again, pressing her face into his olive green jacket. 'We have so much to catch up on.'

'Totally, Stels. But first, I need a coffee.'

A knock sounded on the door, startling them all. 'Not expecting anyone,' Stella mumbled as she crossed to the door. Opening it, she came face to face with a humongous bouquet of beautiful orange poppies.

'Stella Knight?' said the delivery man.

'Yes?'

'These are for you.' He handed them over, and then stood there, as if waiting for something.

'Ugh, sorry, I don't have any cash,' she said. She'd forgotten to ask Liliwen to get some.

'It's okay. You can Venmo it to me,' he said.

'Cheeky sod,' said Tristan, pushing the door closed. 'Are you starting an opium factory?' He took the heavy bouquet from her and set it on the table.

'Who are they from?' said Liliwen.

Stella pursed her lips as she searched for a card. Did Connor send these?

Among the stems, she located a mini pink envelope. The note inside said, 'The Golden Poppy is the state flower of California. Looking forward to working with you. Blake.'

'Well, what does it say?' said Liliwen, pushing her glasses up the bridge of her nose and holding her hand out for the note.

'Uh, nothing. They're from Blake.' She slipped the note into her pocket, silently freaking out. She didn't want anyone else to know about the LA offer until she'd had time to think about it. Speaking of time, her schedule was packed. She checked her watch. 'Bugger. I have to go. My class starts in twenty minutes.'

Tristan stretched his hands in the air and yawned. 'No problem. We can catch up after.'

'*After*, I'm on a stand in the trade show, doing posing and lighting demos until five-thirty. But we have dinner reservations. Seven o'clock. Sound good?'

'*Perfecto.*'

'Ooh, your Spanish is practically fluent,' she joked. 'Liliwen, could you text Connor the details of the restaurant?'

'Aye-aye, captain,' she saluted.

With no time to change, Stella grabbed her camera bag. Her lighting sponsor should have delivered her strobes and stands straight to the classroom, so at least she didn't have to carry those around. After saying her goodbyes, she ran out the door and caught the lift. Her emotions ping-ponged between excitement at seeing her friend, nerves over the class, conflict over Blake's offer, missing Grace, and despair at her marital situation. Her brain was a slot machine, cycling through topics at pace before landing on one, only for her to pull the handle again.

That's why it was only as she reached her classroom that she remembered something important: Tristan used to date Connor's brother, Michael. And it did *not* end well.

7

STELLA

L<small>ILIWEN</small>, T<small>RISTAN</small>, <small>AND</small> S<small>TELLA</small> <small>APPROACHED THE HOST'S DESK AT THE</small> restaurant, manned by a bored teen with an oversized red sombrero and a face of angry pimples. 'Reservation for Knight,' Stella said, wishing that she *had* been more specific with Liliwen about the kind of restaurant to book.

'Isn't this place fun?' said Liliwen, scrunching her button nose. 'The reviews said the food is very authentic.'

Tristan wore the standard costume of celebrities in disguise: baseball cap and sunglasses. Taking the sunglasses off and hanging them on his shirt, he eyed the decor like it was a crime against humanity: colourful murals of partying skeletons playing roulette and blackjack covered the walls. The ceiling was swathed in fake, dust-covered foliage that had probably appeared lush and green ten decades ago, but now made Stella wonder how much dust ended up peppering the food. And was that a *real* spider dangling from a gossamer thread?

Tristan clicked his tongue. 'This place is a travesty, darling. I've never met a *real* Mexican wearing a sombrero. And I've lived there for over a year.'

Stella groaned. This definitely would not have been her first choice.

The oily smell of fried food hung in the air. Stella would probably have a salad. Even though she did love to eat Mexican, she had too much to do this week to chance any sort of funny tummy.

'The rest of your party is already here.' The teen greeter tried to ring toss a sombrero onto each of their heads. Stella politely declined. Tristan grimaced and batted it away like it was a live octopus.

'You two are missing out! Where's your sense of adventure?' said Liliwen as she caught hers and fastened the elastic under her chin. Of course, she looked adorable. The electric fuchsia hat complimented her candy pink dress.

Tristan slipped his baseball cap off and ran his hands through his hair. 'How do I look?' he said to Stella.

'Handsome as ever,' she replied.

When Stella had informed Tristan that Michael would be joining them at dinner, he'd said tersely, 'It's fine. We're both adults,' before disappearing into the bathroom, shaving his beard, and gelling his hair back from his face. He'd also changed into a loose, khaki linen shirt and trousers that emphasised his tan. Now, he bore more resemblance to the top model he used to be.

Stella was not looking forward to this. Thankfully, she had an excuse to leave after an hour. Her album sponsor was throwing a party in some fancy bar, and considering how much money they paid her to be an ambassador, she needed to show her face. She was already wondering how long she'd have to stay there before she could slip back to her room and pass out—that is, after sending some images to a big client who'd emailed demanding them that afternoon.

As the teen host led the way, a mariachi band surrounded a group of diners across the room and sang the restaurant's happy birthday song. Struck by the sudden image of what Armstrong's reaction must have been when he'd arrived, Stella smiled. He was more of a fine wine and dine sort of guy.

They turned a corner and found the Knights arrayed around a round yellow table. Stella's eyes shot straight to Connor, devastatingly handsome as always in a white shirt, blue suit jacket, and jeans. She thanked the Time Gods that she'd been able to shower and redo her make-up before coming out. And she knew the short black dress she wore showed off her legs.

Of the three Knights, only Michael wore a silly green sombrero. He flashed her his big grin before his gaze shifted to the man standing behind her.

His smiled disappeared.

'Michael,' said Tristan.

'Tristan?' said Michael. 'What are you doing here?' He defiantly readjusted the elastic strap around his neck.

'I really love Mexican food,' Tristan deadpanned.

Oblivious to the drama playing out next to him, Armstrong stood and exclaimed, 'There's my lovely daughter-in-law!' before sweeping around the table and taking her into his arms. As always, he smelled of expensive cologne, reminding her of Blake. One of the things she'd always loved about Connor was that he never doused himself in scent. He had a natural, woodsy smell that was all him.

'Hi, Armstrong, good to see you,' she said, kissing him on each cheek. They'd always gotten on well.

'Listen,' he said close to her ear, 'I don't know what my idiot son did, but I know you two will work it out.' He patted her on the arm and stepped back.

A blush crept up her cheeks and she avoided looking at Connor.

'And who do we have here?' Armstrong said, his eyes locking on Liliwen, who giggled with delight.

'This is Liliwen Thomas. You met her at our wedding.'

'Charmed,' she said as Armstrong kissed her on the knuckles. Seriously, why were all the men doing that? Did she have honey on them?

'Ah, yes! I remember.' He squinted his eyes. 'I spoke with your husband for a while. Gareth... is it?'

Liliwen frowned. 'Yes, that was him, poor love. Sadly, he passed last year.'

'Oh, I'm sorry to hear that.' His brow furrowed. 'What was it?'

'Pancreatic cancer.'

They both nodded their heads for a moment before Armstrong said, 'Well, come and sit next to me, Liliwen. I'm certainly the most interesting of this lot.'

Tristan had already claimed the chair on the opposite side of the table, as far as he could get from Michael, which left Stella with the seat between Tristan and Connor. She exhaled, tucked a lock of hair behind her ear, and went to her chair.

Connor pulled it out for her. 'You look beautiful,' he said so only she could hear. A shiver ran through her, straight to her toes and back to her middle.

'Thanks. Um... you too.' *You, too? Come on, Stella.* Why was she feeling nervous? She'd been married to the man for seven years. She'd folded his underwear, for heaven's sake.

Their young waitress approached the table, wearing a colourful striped sarape and a fluorescent green sombrero. As soon as she clapped eyes on the four handsome specimens of alpha manhood sitting before her, the poor girl turned bright pink, obviously regretting the garish restaurant uniform. 'Um... hola! I'm Sally and I'll be satisfying all your needs today,' she said, flushing even deeper as she realised the subtext. 'I mean, in your mouth. Your food needs. Um, can I get you something to drink?'

Stella would need a margarita to get through this. Liliwen and Armstrong decided to share a pitcher of sangria. Connor and Michael ordered beers, and Tristan said, 'Just water for me, no ice. Gracias, darling.' Stella glanced at him. Tristan ordering water? The man had never met a cocktail he didn't like.

Mexico had changed him.

Armstrong and Liliwen nattered away to each other, but the rest of the table seemed to have lost their tongues. Michael studied the specials board like he was going to be tested on it later. Connor was disfiguring a napkin. Tristan had leaned his chair back onto its hind legs and was casually rocking like a bandito in a saloon. Stella had to say something, or this was going to be a miserable hour.

'So, Tristan, tell us about Mexico City.' Stella looked at Michael and explained, 'He's been living there for the past year.'

'What's to tell?' Tristan said. 'The weather is hot. The food is hot. And the men are hot. *Olé.*'

Michael snorted and picked up his menu.

'Something wrong?' enquired Tristan, grounding his chair and leaning onto the table with interest, eyes narrowed at Michael.

'No.' He put down his menu. 'I just thought you might have something more interesting to say about the city of Frida Kahlo and Diego Rivera, a city known for its amazing food, lively neighbourhoods, and diverse culture.'

Now would be a really good time for those drinks, Stella thought.

'Why do I need to say it when you've obviously memorised Lonely Planet?' said Tristan, his lips curled with distaste. 'We can't all be as intelligent as you, mister Oxbridge.'

Okaaaaaay. Stella had greatly underestimated the acrimony between these two. She'd never seen Michael say an unkind word to anybody, and Tristan could be bitchy, but this was another level. They did not bring out the best in each other.

'Armstrong!' barked Stella, interrupting his tête-à-tête with Liliwen. 'What's new in your life?'

'Didn't Connor tell you? I've retired!'

'Oh, that's fabulous!' said Liliwen, clapping her hands.

'Congratulations!' Stella said, genuinely happy for him. 'What will you do next?' He'd probably buy a beach house in the Maldives or somewhere equally hot and full of women where he could continue his elderly bachelor lifestyle.

He held out his hands like he was about to do a magic trick. 'I'm moving to London to spend time with my granddaughter.'

Wait? What?! Stella's mouth froze in a rictus grin, eyes wide. Where the *fuck* were those drinks?

'Yeah. Isn't that great,' said Connor flatly.

'That's great,' she repeated robotically. Inside, a volcano erupted, Stella's brain overflowing with panic. The timing could not be worse. Here she was, considering a move to Los Angeles, when her father-in-law was planning to relocate next door to babysit in London.

Fuck, fuck, fuck.

Blood rushed through her as her heartbeat picked up speed.

In that moment, she experienced clarity: she wholeheartedly desired what Blake was offering, even if it scared her. If she didn't take this opportunity, she'd regret it for the rest of her life. At age 38, now was the time to do something like this. Grace would be able to adapt.

Connor, however... well, she'd cross that bridge later.

The waitress appeared with the drinks. Stella grabbed hers off the tray, threw the plastic skeleton stirrer on the table, and downed her margarita in one. 'Another,' she said, replacing the empty glass on the tray and licking the salt off her lips.

Everybody stared.

'What?' she said with more force than she meant.

'All okay?' said Connor, touching her bare leg with concern.

She startled. Her skin tingled where his fingertips had brushed her knee. Why couldn't any of this be simple?

Her breath turned shallow, the first stirrings of a panic attack. She hadn't had one of those in a long, long time. Since before she married Connor, at least. Wanting to nip it in the bud, she shut her eyes and tried to remember the method that Ula, her ex-cleaner, had taught her: first pause, then breathe through it, observe her symptoms, and proceed—Sod that. What she needed was to leave.

Her eyes popped open. 'You know what?' she said, wiping her mouth with a napkin and throwing it on the table. 'I'm so sorry. But I don't think I'm going to have time to eat, after all. My next appointment is across town, and it's going to take longer than I thought to get there.' She stood, pulling her dress down as she straightened up.

Connor pushed his chair back and jumped to his feet, worry clear on his face. 'I'll come with you.'

'No! Please. You stay. Enjoy dinner.' She grabbed her bag.

'Are you going...' Connor paused for a beat. His hand gripped the back of his chair, his knuckles turning white. 'Are you going to meet that wanker Blake Romero?'

'What?' How did Connor know about Blake? She knew they had some sort of history but calling him a wanker was a bit rude. She took a step back. Anger edged out any residual panic. 'Have you been following me?'

'No! Of course not.'

'Then how do you know about me and Blake?'

Connor flinched. 'What do you mean *you and Blake?*' He paused a moment, breathed in and out like he was wrestling with his own panic, and stated calmly, 'I happened to see you in the lobby with him yesterday, that's all.'

Her shoulders relaxed. 'Oh. Well, no. It's something else tonight.'

'Good. Because I'm warning you. He's an opportunist and a liar. I don't want you having anything to do with him.'

She recoiled from the heat in his words. 'Good thing I make my own decisions.'

His forehead furrowed, his gaze sharpened, and she watched his pupils turn hard as anthracite. They stared each other down, the air between them crackling with thunder. They may as well have been the only two people in the restaurant.

'*Feliz cumpleaños a ti!*' The mariachi band singing happy birthday nearby shattered their stalemate. Stella looped her purse across her body and sighed. 'Listen, we'll talk soon. I'll text you,' she said to placate him.

Turning on her heel, she exited the restaurant as fast as she could.

8

CONNOR

WHAT THE FUCK WAS THAT ABOUT? THOUGHT CONNOR. IT WAS LIKE SHE couldn't wait to get away from them.

From him.

It took everything he had not to run after her. That would create a scene, which she would hate. But why wouldn't she talk to him? Why was she *avoiding* him? And what did she mean when she'd said 'me and Blake'?

An uneasy, hollow feeling settled in his stomach. One part fear, one part despondency, all parts nausea.

Had she already made a decision about their marriage? Devastation rolled through him at the thought of never waking up next to her again, of never sharing another grin over Grace's precocious antics, of never getting the chance to expand their family and give Grace a sibling—a hope that still smouldered in his heart.

What would he do without her? Return to his pre-Stella ways? The idea held zero attraction.

He swigged his beer and slammed the bottle down on the table.

'Hey,' said Tristan. 'You all right?' He shifted into the chair that Stella had recently vacated.

For a second Connor had forgotten where he was. 'Yes. No. I just... wish I knew what she was thinking.'

'Chin up, love,' said Liliwen from across the table in that ridiculous hat. 'I promise there's nothing romantic going on between her and that Blake Romero. You're still in the fight.'

'She's right, son,' said Armstrong. 'Don't give up. I raised you to be a winner.'

Oh, that was rich. His father's false parental platitude made Connor's shoulders tense. 'Armstrong,' he said through gritted teeth, 'you didn't raise me *at all*.'

Armstrong opened his mouth to rebut, but Michael clapped his hands and rubbed them together. 'Shall we order? I fancy the chimichanga special.' He called the waitress over.

THE END of the meal couldn't come soon enough. Connor would have left, but Liliwen seemed to be having fun, and she deserved it. She and Armstrong spent the whole dinner harmlessly flirting on the other side of the table.

Meanwhile, Tristan and Michael weren't particularly talkative, and Connor was in no mood to provide the conversational lubricant, so the three of them passed most of the meal on their phones. Connor scrolled through photos of Grace—the only thing that could calm him down. He missed her so much.

When the bill came, Michael grabbed it and said, 'It's on me.'

'I'll pay for myself,' said Tristan, who slipped some bills out of his wallet and threw them on the table.

Michael rolled his eyes and handed his card to the waitress.

She took one look at it and laughed. 'Haha. Michael Knight. That's funny.'

'Why is that funny?' asked Michael, with seemingly genuine curiosity. Connor knew what was coming.

'Well,' she stammered, 'be-because of that old TV show. You

know. *Knight Rider*? The David Hasselhoff character was Michael Knight.'

'Really? Never heard of it,' he said, his face completely serious. After a beat, his lips curved up. 'Just kidding. That's the problem when you have parents who never watched television in the eighties.' He winked. She laughed. People always laughed at that joke.

Tristan scoffed, 'Still wheeling out that tired old line, I see.'

'Excuse our friend here. He's a bit feral,' said Michael, handing the card terminal back to the waitress.

'You're Tristan Hughes, r-right?' she said. 'The model?'

'No.' He crossed his arms.

She blinked at him, probably expecting him to laugh like Michael had when he tricked her. But Tristan remained straight-faced.

'Okay, then.' She turned and walked away.

'That was mean,' said Michael.

'The last thing I want is the paparazzi on my trail because I took a selfie with a fan. You might not care about who I am and where I've been, but there are plenty of people who do,' Tristan said. He stood up, jammed his baseball cap onto his head, and put on his sunglasses despite the fact that it was dark outside. 'This has been an absolute delight. Liliwen, are you ready to leave?'

She and Armstrong exchanged a the-night-is-young look. 'Don't worry about me, lovely. I'll make my way back later.'

'Fine. Just don't do anything I wouldn't do,' Tristan said cautiously.

'And what exactly is that?' said Michael under his breath, just loud enough for Tristan to hear.

'Have a nice life,' Tristan snarled as he left.

Exhaling loudly, Michael ran his hands over his face. 'Shall we head back?' he said to Connor.

'Hell, yes.' Connor could think of nothing he wanted more than to leave the scene of this horrendous dinner.

To Liliwen, he said, 'Are you sure you're okay?'

Armstrong put his arm around the back of her chair. 'Don't worry. I'll take very good care of her.'

'That's what I'm afraid of,' mumbled Connor.

'Thank you for your concern, lovely,' said Liliwen with a wink. 'But I'm a big girl.'

For a moment, Connor stopped to consider whether it was actually his father he should be worried about. Then he dismissed the idea and followed Michael out of the restaurant.

They walked in silence for a few minutes, the music that spilled from different venues deejaying their progress. Guns N' Roses segued into Pink which morphed into Frank Sinatra. Lights danced on the marquees of hotels and bars, bright explosions of colour that made Connor's eyes ache. When had he become so old?

He was grateful that he had his little brother with him. He needed somebody to talk to, a temporary Krish replacement.

'Well, that was fun,' said Michael, shoving his hands into his jeans pockets. He was still wearing the sombrero.

The words burst out of Connor: 'What if she's done with our marriage?'

Michael shook his head. 'I saw the way she looked at you when you weren't paying attention. She still loves you.'

Connor ran a hand through his hair. 'I wish she'd talk to me about whatever's going on with Blake Romero. I don't trust him after—'

'Is that your old business partner who—'

'Yep. That's the one.'

'You need to warn her.' Michael poked Connor with his elbow. 'I mean, without making it sound like you're laying down the law.'

Connor grimaced. 'I... shit, that's what it came off as, isn't it?'

'Kind of. Yeah.'

'Shit.' He'd been no better than Stella when she'd forbidden him to work with Valentina Vavilek. They both knew how well that had gone down.

They continued past the flashy entrance of their hotel. Neither were in a rush to immerse themselves in the filtered, over-oxygenated hotel air. Much better to stay outside, in the unfiltered, traffic-polluted air instead.

A group of tipsy bachelorettes swaggered past, tightly packaged in matching red dresses. Once upon a time, when Connor was young and stupid and overflowing with hormones, he would have been right in there. His therapist pointed out that Connor's particular flavour of ADHD made him more sensory seeking than neurotypical men, which partially explained his constant merry-go-round of women pre-Stella.

But now he only wanted sensory engagement with one woman.

A blonde bachelorette tripped and stumbled into him. He caught her by the arm as she fell.

'Careful!' he said in his dad voice, setting her back on her feet.

Her mascara-rimmed eyes fixed on him. 'Wow. You're hot. Are you, like, famous?'

'Yes,' said Michael, jumping in. 'He's in that Netflix show. The one about the alien sex gods?'

Connor threw his brother an unamused look. 'Don't listen to him. He's pulling your leg.'

She grabbed her heart. 'Oh, and you're BRITISH!'

'Have a good night,' Connor said. He stalked briskly away, his brother chuckling behind him like he'd done something sooo clever.

Behind them, the woman yelled, 'Will you sign my butt with a Sharpie?'

Ages ago, he might have, but those days were long gone.

'Sorry,' said Michael, still laughing. 'It was too perfect to resist.'

They turned into Fremont Street, which was even brighter than the road they'd just been walking. The curved ceiling was an LED screen with pictures of clouds and sky rolling across it. It would be too easy to lose track of whether it was day or night in this place. 'Larger Than Life' by the Backstreet Boys was blaring from the speakers, and Connor's head automatically bounced to the beat, his bottom lip caught between his teeth. He could feel Michael smirking at him. Sure enough, when he cut his eyes towards his brother, Michael was sniggering like a child.

'Shut up,' said Connor.

Michael winked. 'Your secret's safe with me.'

At the end of the song, Connor turned to Michael and asked, 'So what about *you*?'

Michael screwed up his face like he had no idea what Connor was talking about. 'What about me, what?'

'What was that between you and Tristan?'

'Oh. That.' Michael sighed. 'Well, remember how we used to date?'

'How could I forget.' Connor had been shocked when Stella showed him a picture in *Hello!* of Tristan and Michael at some famous-people party shortly after they met at Connor and Stella's wedding.

Michael laughed dryly. 'I think he still hates me for breaking up with him.'

Connor didn't know much about it. Maybe Stella had told him, but he'd forgotten. 'What happened? Did you do it via text or something?'

'No. Face-to-face. You know me and doing the right thing.' He said it like it was a negative trait. 'I told him that our lifestyles didn't align.'

'That's fair enough. International model slash reality TV celebrity and international human rights lawyer. It would never work,' Connor joked, thinking of the Clooneys.

'Right?! That's what I thought!' said Michael, completely missing the joke. 'I mean, he was hanging out with all these gorgeous men all the time. Jet setting around the world. If I were him, I wouldn't want to settle down with me.'

'What are you talking about? You're a catch.' Connor couldn't believe that his handsome little brother who had graduated with a first from Oxford and whose dissertation was printed in the *Human Rights Law Review* felt insecure about dating anyone.

With a low groan, Michael confessed, 'Yeah. What a catch. I told him he was too shallow for me. You know, to make sure the message really got through.'

'Ouch.'

'The thing is...' Michael's sagged. 'The thing is, I really did care about him. A lot. We only dated for six months, but we had fun. And oh my god, the sex. It was on another level.'

'Then why did you end it, you idiot?'

'Because I couldn't afford the distraction!' A police siren blared above the noise of the crowd, somewhere in the distance. 'You know how seriously I take my work. It has to come first, right?'

It felt like Michael was begging Connor to agree with him rather than stating a fact. 'Of course. You help a lot of people.' He had always been proud of his little brother. Michael specialised in assisting LGTBQIA+ individuals and communities around the world to take on their governments for fairer laws and better treatment. He was one of the most driven people Connor knew, which was why he'd been so surprised to see Michael in Vegas.

'But you know,' Connor stopped and faced his brother. 'You deserve to be happy, too. You're not a machine.' *Huh, perhaps I should take some of my own advice,* he thought.

Michael shrugged. 'I know. But the work never stops. Next week, I'm flying to the Middle East to advocate for a 17-year-old boy accused of propositioning another boy for sex. He didn't even *do* anything.'

'The world is a shit show,' agreed Connor.

A caricature artist stepped forward and tried to funnel them into his stall. 'Seventy-five bucks for the two of you! Best caricatures in Vegas!'

'No, thanks,' said Connor as they skirted around him. 'Shall we turn around?' In unison, they swivelled and headed back towards the hotel. The constant, moving lights were overwhelming. His eyes darted everywhere, like a kitten with a laser dot—another symptom of ADHD that he discovered during his research.

He glanced over at Michael. 'Shame you two hate each other now.'

'I don't hate him.'

A beat passed before Connor said, 'Stella's worried about him. Something happened a year ago—'

Michael stopped short, and a man walking behind them almost barged into his back. 'Watch it, asshole!' shouted the man as he moved past them.

Ignoring him, Michael grabbed Connor's jacket. 'What happened a year ago?'

'You don't know? It was in the papers. Tristan was supposed to replace one of the judges on *Strictly*. It was all go-go-go for his career, and suddenly he pulled the plug and took off for Mexico.'

They continued walking. 'What? Really? But that's mad. He's always wanted that.'

Connor shrugged. 'He wouldn't talk about it. Not even with Stella.'

'So… what is he doing in Mexico City?'

'The most un-Tristan thing ever. Volunteering! At a charity that helps gay teens. I don't know much more than that.'

'Wow.' Michael held his hands near his temples and made an explosion gesture.

'I know.' Connor wasn't usually a gossip, but something told him Michael needed this information. Some sort of older brother Bat Signal.

For the rest of the way, they strolled without speaking, each lost in their own thoughts.

It had been helpful to focus on somebody else's problems for a few minutes—a reminder that everyone was dealing with their own crap.

But as they approached the hotel, Connor's feelings of rejection moved to the forefront of his mind again. Did Stella love him anymore? Could he save his marriage? Could he convince Stella to cut ties with Blake Romero?

A good night's sleep would help clear his head. Hopefully, he would wake up with some clarity.

Little did he know what the next day would bring.

9

STELLA

THE ALARM RANG, SLICING INTO STELLA'S DREAM. SHE'D BEEN ON A beach with Connor and Grace, watching them make a sandcastle together while the waves lapped gently on the sand. It was so tangible she could feel the sun on her skin. Pure bliss.

And now she was awake.

The tsunami of reality washed away the dream.

Connor. Armstrong. London. Los Angeles. Blake.

Her head protested as she lifted it cautiously off the pillow. The margarita she downed at the restaurant last night had been the first of three she'd consumed throughout the evening. Not a lot by most people's standards, but these days, three seemed to be enough to give her that uncomfortable low-level throb in her brain. After this trip, she'd detox for at least a month, maybe more.

Her first masterclass of the day started in ninety minutes. Just enough time to drink some coffee and send the images to the client since she hadn't gotten a chance to sort them last night. After the masterclass, she had a podcast interview, then a quick lunch followed by a Q&A on the Canon stand, demos on some other stands, and portfolio reviews for newbie photographers in the

Mentor Zone. That night, she'd been invited to a penthouse party for all the conference speakers—and she wanted to go, but also she wanted to sleep. If she could cut one thing out of her schedule, that was it.

She needed to be well-rested for lunch with Blake tomorrow, her chance to ask all the questions that were swirling in her head about his offer.

But first, coffee.

Pulling on the white hotel robe, she opened the door of her room and was confronted with Tristan's butt sticking up in the air. He was doing yoga in the middle of the open-plan living room.

'Good morning,' she said, keeping her voice low so she didn't wake Liliwen, whose door was still shut.

'*Buenos días*,' said Tristan as he manoeuvred into a picture-perfect side plank. He wore comfortable neon yellow shorts and a matching tank top that hugged his muscular torso. The colour contrasted nicely with his tan.

'Bit early for you, isn't it?' In the past, she'd never known him to be awake before ten, but here it was, only eight o'clock. And when did he start practicing yoga?

'I'll have you know I've already been to the gym, darling.'

'Who are you and what have you done with my best friend, Tristan?'

He chuckled, pushing himself into a Down Dog. 'I lead a yoga class every morning at Sin Pecados for the residents.' Sin Pecados, or Without Sin, was the name of the charity where Tristan volunteered in Mexico City.

'I should really get back to doing yoga,' Stella mused. Lately, her exercise routine consisted of short classes on her Peloton bike whenever she could fit them in. She never had time to run anymore, something she used to love.

She started towards the kitchenette and stopped short. A huge basket brimming with oranges was on the dining table next to the poppies. 'Where did that come from?'

'It was outside our door this morning. Who's this Blake fellow, again?'

'Um...nobody. Just somebody I might be doing some business with.' She wasn't ready to talk about the offer yet. As the Italians said: *acqua in bocca!*, which meant *water in your mouth*. That is, if you want to keep a secret, don't tell anybody.

'Mm-hmm,' he said, signalling that he didn't believe her. He left it at that.

The open envelope and note were discarded on the table, where Tristan must have thrown them. She read: *Orange you looking forward to working together? Seriously, the oranges in California are magnificent. Blake.*

Rolling her eyes at the terrible joke, she kept hold of the note and took it straight to the kitchenette bin, where she deposited the evidence. The gifts were nice, but Blake really didn't need to send them. They wouldn't have any bearing on her decision. Besides, what was she supposed to do with three dozen oranges?

'Coffee?' she asked, shifting her attention to the Nespresso pods on display.

Tristan flowed into Warrior Two. 'No thanks. Is there anything herbal?'

'I'll check.' As she rifled through the tea box, she studied her oldest friend. Being his ex-dance partner, she knew his body almost as well as she knew her own. He had always been toned for his modelling, but looking at him anew, there was a softness to his form now. Not overweight by any stretch of the imagination—she could still see his muscles rippling. But he obviously wasn't following the extreme lifestyle of a top model any longer: no more counting macros and eating the right amount of protein every day. No more sharp features. It suited him.

She found a yellow paper square in the tea box. 'Chamomile okay?'

'Perfect. It has anti-inflammatory properties, which is what I need after that god-awful dinner.'

'Yeah...apologies for that.' She felt bad for ditching Tristan and Liliwen, but the pressure in her head after Armstrong's announcement made it impossible to think clearly. 'How was the rest of the evening?'

'Oh, a barrel of laughs, Stels. Thanks for that. Michael explored his Villain Era for the whole night, Connor brooded after you in the way only a truly gorgeous man can, and Liliwen told the waitress it was Connor's father's birthday so they'd sing that horrid song to him.'

Unfortunately, Stella could picture it all too clearly as she heated a mug of water in the microwave. How did Americans live without electric kettles? If she moved to LA, she'd bring one with her. 'I've never seen Michael like that before. You two really rub each other up the wrong way.'

'Once upon a time we very much rubbed each other up the *right* way, darling, but those days are long gone.' Tristan's full lips bent into a frown as he finished his practice. Standing at his full height, he stretched his arms above his head.

'Shame,' she said, dropping a capsule into the Nespresso machine. 'In a weird way, I always thought you two balanced each other out.' The microwave dinged. She retrieved the mug and steeped the tea bag.

Padding into the kitchenette, Tristan picked up his mug and leaned his bottom against the counter. 'On the theme of troubled super couples, what about you? What's going on with Connor?'

'Ugh. I don't even know where to begin.'

Stella watched the dark coffee dripping into her cup, replaying the *exact* moment she thought it had begun. Aged one, Grace had fallen down the stairs because Connor hadn't put up the gate despite Stella asking him to do it several times. Thankfully, Grace was fine. However, the larger issue was that Stella hadn't been able to get hold of Connor because he'd turned off his phone. He was having a meeting that included Valentina Vavilek, a client who had tried on multiple occasions to have sex with him and whom he'd promised never to work with again. In the end, Stella had to call Krish to find Connor and bring him to the hospital.

Trusting him was difficult after that.

'Lately it just feels like he's a square and I'm a circle and our life is a triangle. Nothing fits,' she said, doing her best to explain their new dynamic.

Tristan jiggled his tea bag up and down. 'Ah, and you don't know the shape of things to come.'

Stella clicked her tongue at his bad attempt at humour. When the first capsule finished filtering, she replaced it with a second shot. This was a double espresso kind of day. 'Connor switched to high-end commercial work, as you know, and he was travelling *constantly*. Like, three out of four weeks per month sometimes. And then my career took off, and I was receiving lucrative invitations to speak in other countries, but I'd have to turn them all down because Connor was away. I couldn't keep asking my parents to watch Grace, you know? I felt like a single parent, only with him using our house as a rest stop on the weekends so we could have sex and I could do his laundry.'

Tristan chucked his tea bag in the sink and crossed back towards the sofa. 'How long have you been married now? Is it—'

'Seven years. Don't say it!'

'Okay, I won't, but Marilyn Monroe sends her regards.'

Stella groaned as she followed him, coffee in hand. She refused to believe this was merely a Seven-Year Itch.

They sat on opposite sides of the sofa, facing each other like mirror images, both tucking their feet under their bodies. 'I tried to talk to him about it so many times. But it's like he never really hears me. I even suggested marriage counselling, and I found this woman —highly recommended by a friend—but she insisted that we both had to have an exploratory phone chat with her beforehand to make sure we were equally invested.'

'And...?'

'And Connor never made the time to call her. Which showed me just how important saving our marriage was to him.' Exasperated, she dug her free hand into her hairline.

'Hmmm. What does Claudia say?'

'She was the one who suggested the separation. Said it would give me time to figure out what I wanted and scare the, quote, "fucking shit" out of him—you know, show Connor what he stood to lose. Like the Ghost of Christmas... whichever ghost it was.' A stab of doubt pierced her heart, as it always did when she thought back to that conversation. Claudia had painted such a clear, logical case for the separation. Had Stella done the right thing? Or had she just made things worse? She pushed the thought away. Too late now...

'And did it? Work, I mean?'

She shrugged. 'A little, I guess.' Almost immediately, Connor had moved out and started rearranging his schedule to make sure he saw Grace every weekend and most Wednesday nights, sometimes more. From that point of view, the separation had been a success. Grace and Connor were closer than ever.

However, also immediately, that wall had formed between Connor and Stella, further damaging their ability to communicate with each other.

'What's she up to these days, anyway?' Tristan asked, cutting into her musings.

She shook her head, having lost the thread of conversation. 'Who? Grace?'

'Claudia!'

'Oh—her art has taken off. She makes acrylic moulds of women's boobs and torsos and suspends sentimental items in the plastic for her clients, like fridge magnets or a pair of Louboutins or a vibrator. Whatever. People pay her tens of thousands of pounds.'

'Unexpected. I like it.' Tristan sipped his chamomile. 'Now back to your imploding marriage.'

Stella sighed. 'I don't know if this whole separation thing worked. But even if it did… something else has come up.'

'Whaa-aat?' he said, making it into a two-syllable word.

Stella downed her double espresso in one. Maybe it was time to confide in Tristan, *acqua in bocca* be damned. The secret was burning a hole in her. 'I've had an opportunity. A big one. And I really, really want to take it. It could completely change my life.'

Tristan scrunched his nose. 'I'm hearing a huge *but* here.'

Sucking on her teeth, Stella said, '*But…* we'd have to move to Los Angeles.'

She watched as understanding lit up his eyes. 'Ah, that's why you freaked when Connor's dad said he was relocating to London.'

'I didn't "freak".'

He pulled his chin back and widened his eyes in disbelief. 'Okay then. Whatever you say. So, what about Connor? Is he up for the move?'

Stella cringed. 'I haven't told him yet. It only happened yesterday. And… there's one more thing.'

Tristan propped his head on his hand, like she was about to read him a bedtime story. 'Go on.'

She groaned. 'Connor hates the person who's offered me this opportunity. Like, *loathes* him.' She hadn't realised just how much until dinner last night.

'My god,' said Tristain. 'This is more exciting than a telenovela.'

'Even if we managed to fix our marriage, I don't think he'd be keen on moving to LA, especially at the behest of Blake Romero.'

'Ooh, Blake *Romero*. What a great name. Sounds like a villain in *Amor en Sombras*.'

'What's that?'

'Darling, it happens to be the best telenovela *in the world*. There's this couple, right? Marisol and Alejandro. She's a poor up-and-coming artist, and he's the rich son of a wine baron. Super hot. They fall in love when he walks into a gallery where she's exhibiting, but his ex-girlfriend, Isabella, is jealous and tries to keep them apart. She hacks into his phone and sends fake messages, spreads rumours that Marisol is having an affair with an art critic. Total bitch. I love her. And then she hires a man to seduce Marisol, but then Marisol finds out he's her long-lost brother...' He sipped his tea while Stella wondered if there was a point to this story. 'Anyway, most of their issues stem from extreme lack of communication and—well... sometimes accidental incest—but you know what would solve almost all of their problems?'

Stella narrowed her eyes. She suspected a trap. 'What?'

'TALKING TO EACH OTHER.'

Stella sighed. 'We *are* talking. At the end of the conference, we have five days blocked out at a hotel a few hours' drive from here.'

'Well, maybe you need to talk sooner than that. Being near you two is like being caught in an electrical storm.'

'I can't! I'm here to work.' She checked her watch. 'Shit, speaking of which, I need to go. I have a class in forty minutes.' And she hadn't sent those images yet either. She screamed inside. She'd have to do it later.

The whir of the front door unlocking caught them both by surprise. Was it the cleaner? This early?

Liliwen wobbled in wearing the same pink dress from last night, sunglasses and sombrero still on. In one hand, she carried her high heels looped over a finger. In the other, she was hugging an over-sized unicorn plush.

'Liliwen!' cried Stella, putting her mug down and leaping off the sofa. 'I thought you were in bed. Are you okay?'

'Oh!' the pixie woman exclaimed, dropping the unicorn and putting a hand to her head. 'Could you turn the music off, lovely? It's a bit loud.'

Tristan raised an eyebrow at Stella when their eyes met. 'There is no music,' she said, taking Liliwen by the arm and leading her to the sofa. The petite woman frisbeed her sombrero across the room with a 'weeeee!' and collapsed, a dopey smile on her face. Stella rushed to the kitchen to fill a glass of water for her.

'Looks like you had a good time last night, darling,' said Tristan.

Liliwen snatched the sunglasses off and smiled. 'I had a *marvellous* time. This town is full of surprises. And so is Armstrong!'

Handing Liliwen the water, Stella kneeled in front of her. 'Have you been out with him all night?' Her eyes searched for any signs of wear and tear.

'Oh, yes! And we went to a *strip club*. I had a lap dance from a lovely girl from Wyoming named Chantilly. How utterly thrilling!' Liliwen downed half the glass. 'And then we made out on a huuuuuuge ferris wheel that overlooks all of Las Vegas! I felt like a teenager again.'

Stella was going to kill Armstrong. Her friend was drunk, and he'd taken advantage. An ache began to throb between Stella's ears. Spying a bright red mark on Liliwen's ankle, Stella said, 'What happened here?'

'Oh! I almost forgot about that. We had matching tattoos done. They only cost ten dollars each!' She pointed her toe to show off the artwork.

Stella squinted at it. 'Is that—'

'Ms Pac-Man! Armstrong had the same but without the bow on top. Isn't it cute?'

It was *something*. Seriously, the next time Stella saw her father-in-law, she was going to poke him hard in the... tattoo. How dare he get her friend drunk and then hit on her?! Where was Connor during all this? He knew better than anybody what his father was like.

'And then—' Liliwen finished the rest of the water. 'This is the best part...'

A sense of dread unfurled in Stella.

'—and then we *got married!*'

Tristan burst out laughing. 'Oh, this is priceless.'

'You WHAT?!' shouted Stella.

'The ceremony was lush. Just the two of us and Prince! Well, not

Prince, but a man dressed as Prince. The wig wasn't very good, mind.'

Stella collapsed onto her bottom and clutched at her head. What was happening here? Had the world gone *mad*?

Liliwen held out her hand to show off a slim gold band. 'Let me introduce you to the new Mrs Armstrong Knight!'

10

CONNOR

'I'M SORRY. *WHAT?*' SHOUTED CONNOR, SURE THAT HE'D MISHEARD. After all, his dad's mouth was full of scrambled eggs.

Armstrong swallowed and sipped his orange juice before replying, 'Liliwen and I married last night. Or maybe this morning. I can't recall the exact time. Excuse me, miss?' He hailed the waitress. 'More coffee please?'

As she refilled his mug, Armstrong winked at her. Connor and Michael exchanged a horrified look.

'When I told you to take care of her, this is not what I meant,' said Connor through gritted teeth. He couldn't believe his father had—

No, scratch that, he *could* believe it. He was just extremely disappointed. Poor Liliwen. He never should have left his father with her. Of course, he'd taken advantage. Same old Armstrong.

Michael stirred a spoonful of sugar into his cappuccino. 'Don't worry, Connor. We can get it annulled.'

'But I don't want it annulled,' said Armstrong as he sliced into a hash brown.

'You bloody well will!' Connor exclaimed, and a woman at the next table glanced over. Lowering his voice, he said, 'Armstrong, of course you want to.'

'No, I don't. Besides we can't get an annulment. We've already consummated it.'

Connor dropped his fork. 'I'm going to be sick.' At least he knew what he'd be talking about with his therapist next time.

'Dad, you can't just go around *marrying* people,' said Michael.

Armstrong slathered butter on his toast. 'We're consenting adults. We both decided to do it. And besides, I quite like her.'

'Quite like her? Wow, you should write Valentine's Day cards,' Connor scoffed as he sat back, throwing his napkin on the table. He'd lost his appetite.

'Listen, this might be hard for you boys to understand, but I've been lonely. I'm ready to settle down again—and Liliwen? She's the most fun I've had in a long time.' His lips curled into a wolfish grin.

Uncomfortable with the lustful gleam in his father's eyes, Connor said, 'For fuck's sake. Liliwen is like family to me.'

'Well, now she is actual family to you.'

Connor dropped his head into his hands. Stella. He needed to talk to Stella about this. She'd be furious, and she'd blame him for leaving them together. The last thing he needed was to give her another reason to be angry with him. He had to get ahead of this. He pulled out his phone and sent her a quick text.

> Have you spoken with Liliwen this morning? Can we talk?

He positioned his phone next to him on the table, so he could see when she replied.

'It's my life, boys. And I'll do with it what I like,' said Armstrong, taking a forceful bite of his toast.

'Did you stop to think for one second,' said Connor, 'how this might affect my relationship with Stella? She's already mad at me. This is going to compound matters.'

This seemed to give Armstrong pause. With a sigh, he said, 'I'm sorry, son. No, I didn't think about that. Liliwen just makes me feel so... well, so *alive*. I haven't felt that for a long time.'

Connor's face twisted into a sneer. 'That is the biggest load of—'

'Wait,' cut in Michael. 'Hold on a second, Connor. Dad? What's really going on with you? Why did you decide to retire now? You really need to tell us if you're dying.'

'I'm not dying. Not yet, at least.' Armstrong exhaled and glanced away. He crossed his arms on the table, tapping his right hand, like he was deciding whether to tell them something. Looking back at Connor and Michael, he said, 'I had a frightening experience. I was in a meeting with Frank Gilroy... do you remember him, Connor? He was in Paris the same time as us. Used to come over for dinner sometimes.'

Connor vaguely recalled a heavy-set man with a tendency to tell off-colour jokes and smoke cigars. 'Sort of,' he said.

'Well, we were in a meeting, talking about... something unimportant, some new sports initiative we were planning... when he grabbed his chest and died on his desk. Simply fell over and was gone. Like that.' He snapped his fingers.

'Oh, dad, that must have been hard,' said Michael, reaching out to squeeze his father's hand.

'Thank you, son. It was horrible. Frank's wife divorced him about ten years ago. Tired of the diplomat life. And his two girls weren't talking to him because of the way he handled the settlement. Hiding funds, etcetera etcetera. Anyway, he died. And I flew back to Manchester for the funeral. And you know what?' He hit the table with his hand. 'Almost nobody turned up. Just me and his brother and a few people from the foreign office. It felt empty. Hollow. This man had given his whole life to diplomatic service, and he ended up in a muddy grave.' His gaze went distant. 'He was only 59. He had plans to retire next year. He wanted to live somewhere that he could fly-fish all day. I know—sounds like hell. But that was his dream. And he never had the chance to do it.'

As Armstrong talked, Connor's thoughts turned to his own life.

Time was too precious to waste, and he felt like he and Stella were doing exactly that. He checked his phone to see if she had replied. Nothing.

'So I decided to leave the service and do what Frank couldn't do.'

'Take up fly-fishing?' asked Michael, lifting his eyebrow.

Armstrong scoffed. 'No, of course not. I'd rather dig my own liver out with a spoon. But I've been part of the diplomatic corps for so long, never growing roots, always moving, always saying goodbye to friends. I thought it would be a good time to make a change. Settle down. Spend more time with you boys and my beautiful granddaughter before I get too old to do so.'

'So you married Liliwen. That makes sense,' said Connor, unimpressed by his father's little speech. 'Where are you going to live? *Cowbridge?*' For some reason, he couldn't picture Armstrong settling in the quaint Welsh market town.

Armstrong threw his hands up in the air. 'Connor, we could all die tomorrow. Last night, I met a woman who is funny, sexy, cheeky, smart, and who was actually alive when Bob Boothby had affairs with both the prime minister's wife *and* Ronnie Kray—'

'Wait. Ronnie Kray, the famous East End gangster who killed loads of people, was *gay?*' said Michael.

'Didn't you know that?' said Armstrong.

'Well, this is a surprising day,' muttered Michael before finishing his coffee.

Connor couldn't believe that his father had done this, especially given how quickly Armstrong's infatuations tended to fizzle out. Liliwen had been part of their extended family since he married Stella, and whenever they visited Cardiff, they used to have dinner with her and Gareth—a nice guy with an excellent sense of humour who doted on Liliwen.

They'd been at Gareth's funeral only twelve months ago. Liliwen was obviously in a vulnerable place. And his father must've sensed that, like a blood hound.

Connor's phone buzzed. He picked it up and scanned Stella's message, his heart plummeting as he read:

> Have you heard that Liliwen is now my mother-in-law? What are we going to do about it? S

11

CONNOR

IF CONNOR HAD TO RANK THE MOST ENJOYABLE DAYS OF HIS LIFE SINCE birth, day two of this year's IPE would be low on the tally. Somewhere around the 15,893 mark—above the day that Stella asked for a separation, but below the day he and the Japanese ambassador's daughter sledged on cardboard down the stairs and he broke his arm.

Life was not going his way right now.

First off, no matter what he said, his father could not be swayed to do the right thing and divorce Liliwen. Connor knew they were both consenting adults, but he also knew his father's history and didn't want Liliwen to get hurt.

After breakfast, Armstrong had blithely returned to his room for a nap because he 'and his new wife' had plans for dinner and a show later.

Second, Connor couldn't find Stella anywhere. He wanted to talk to her about the situation and ensure she knew he was on it. But by the time he'd left Armstrong and Michael, her only masterclass of the day had finished. He assumed she'd be speaking on various stands in the trade show, so he headed there. He trawled the showroom floor searching for her, but she was always gone whenever he arrived. The closest he came to finding Stella was when he bumped into a life-sized cut-out of her on a lighting supplier's stand, advertising a new flash head. He had a strong urge to fold it up and take it with him.

He checked her Instagram to find out where she might pop up next, but she hadn't updated her feed with today's appearances. Not knowing her schedule meant it was hard to pin her down—this place was too big: the convention hall alone was two times the size of a football pitch—plus the thick crowds made it impossible to navigate the booths speedily. He growled with deep frustration. In the distance, he caught a glimpse of red hair, and at the same moment, the portly woman in front of him suddenly stopped. He barrelled into her.

'So sorry,' Connor said, helping her pick up some brochures she'd dropped while the redhead slipped out of sight.

'No problem, sugar. You can knock into me any day,' the woman said with an impudent grin. He made sure she was all right, then scanned the crowd, but the redhead had gone. Annoyed, he stepped out of the flow of human traffic to regroup behind a booth. He cracked his neck left and right and rolled his shoulders.

'Come on, man. You're Connor Fucking Knight. Remember?' he muttered to himself.

All he wanted was to find Stella so they could figure out what to do about Armstrong and Liliwen together. Teammates working towards one goal. After all, she'd written, 'What are WE going to do about it?'

It had been a long time since they were on the same side of an issue.

Readjusting the strap of his satchel, he soldiered on.

In front of the Fuji stage, he got trapped in a crowd watching Ali Kazan photograph a pair of models. Intrigued, Connor stopped to observe 'the future of weddings' at work.

'The hands are the most expressive part of the body,' said Kazan, as he posed the models. Of course, Connor had heard that very same line before—because he had said it himself.

He watched for a while, a wistful smile on his lips. Connor had to admit that Kazan demonstrated a comfortable rapport with the couple and the audience, cracking jokes and teaching good content. The next generation of photographers was in safe hands.

Behind him, somebody whispered, 'Isn't that Connor Knight?' But nobody approached him. Years ago, he couldn't take two steps without being surrounded by photographers eager to pick his brain. Now, people seemed to shy away from him, like he was too big a fish for this pond. He frowned.

After he left home a quarter of a century ago, the IPE crowd had become his found family. But life moved on. This year, he recognised barely half the names giving masterclasses. He was out of touch.

Connor furrowed his brow. He realised that he truly missed being a part of this. The ache was compounded by the thought that he might lose his real family, too, if he couldn't sort things out with Stella.

Failure is not an option, he repeated to himself.

He continued on and reached the competition print gallery, where all the finalists for the year's awards were on display: rows and rows of images in white mounts. He searched for Stella's entries. He knew she would have put something in. His heart sped up a notch when he counted ten of Stella's prints in different portraiture categories, all scoring above 85 and one with a perfect 100. That meant she had a good chance of winning Photographer of the Year at the ceremony on the final night. *That's my girl*, he thought, pride welling up for his wife.

While admiring the images, he recognised a name under a beautifully composed wedding photograph of a bride and groom in silhouette: Gunner Hurst—a former student of Connor's. In fact, both Gunner and Connor had connected with their future wives on the same French residential course. Gunner and Karen married shortly before Connor and Stella.

Connor's thoughts strayed back to France, replaying the first time he'd acknowledged his attraction to Stella. It was karaoke night. She'd wandered outside and found him sitting alone, drinking wine on the porch with a fire burning in the chiminea. She sat next to him, and they'd talked, getting to know one another past the mentor-and-student level. They discovered their common love of Dolly Parton. He'd opened up about his mother and warmed to Stella's quiet strength, which he'd witnessed first-hand during her panic attack at the BAPP conference.

Their connection that night had been electric, intangible. He'd wanted to kiss her so badly that it scared him. For once, instead of acting on the impulse, he chose self-control. What was it he'd said to her?

'Don't fall in love with me. I'm bad news.' After dropping that ludicrous line, he'd run away, back to his room to sort out the raging hard-on she'd given him.

He laughed at himself. What a twat he'd been. He should have just kissed her.

BY THE CLOSE of the working day, he still hadn't found Stella. His text messages to her went unread and unanswered. She must be avoiding him for some reason.

Connor ran his hands over his face in frustration. He needed a drink.

Ten minutes later, he was sitting at the counter of the Wild Card bar with a cold bottle of beer in one hand and his phone in the other. He'd been neglecting his emails since he arrived. His agent needed his availability next month for a big fashion job. It required travelling to South Africa, which sounded fun, but in reality, would take him away from Stella and Grace for two weeks. For the past six months, he'd been killing himself to make sure he was always around to see Grace on weekends and Wednesdays, sometimes even flying home mid-job and then back again. On the plus side, he had a fuck-tonne of air miles.

If he wanted to fix his marriage, he'd have to start by being in the same country as his wife more often. He replied to his agent saying he wasn't available and that she should only book London-based shoots for the foreseeable future.

'Well, well, well. If it isn't the amazing Connor Knight,' purred a seductive voice with the hint of a southern twang.

He swivelled to find himself face-to-face with a blast from his past, although the woman in front of him was far removed from the fresh-faced girl he remembered, the one with mousy brown hair who favoured jean shorts and tank tops. She'd reinvented herself as a platinum blonde, her hair swept into a smooth bun. Her perfectly applied eyeliner flicked up at the corners, giving her wide eyes a feline, predatory air. Her dress sense had altered, too: less Daisy Duke and more Jessica Rabbit. She wore a tight, red, off-the-shoulder dress that pushed her tits up. Though, honestly, he never remembered them being that big.

'Betsy Wiener,' he said with a half-smile.

She leaned in and gave him an air kiss near each cheek. Her perfume surrounded him in a floral, cotton-candy haze. 'It's Royale now. Royale Lefevre.'

'You changed your name?'

'I always hated it, as you know. But I believe in this life we can choose who we want to be. So I thought, why not change it to something with more—' she waved her manicured hand in the air— *'je ne sais qois?'*

Connor couldn't help but imagine John Travolta talking about how, in Paris, they call the Quarter Pounder a *Royale with Cheese*. He cleared his throat to hide his amusement. 'You changed your hair, too.'

'Somebody told me that gentlemen prefer blondes.' Her eyes

raked down to his chest and back up to his face. 'Speaking of gentle-men, buy me a drink?'

Inside, he sighed. He was in the mood to be alone, but his father had taught him to be chivalrous, at least. 'Of course. What are you having?'

'Never too early for a Cosmopolitan.'

He attracted the bartender's attention and placed the order.

She slid her silk-covered bottom onto the stool next to Connor and crossed her legs. 'So, what's been keeping you busy for the last twenty-five years? Still hitting the gym, I see?' She reached out to squeeze his bicep and laughed. 'Remember when you used to go down to Muscle Beach to work out with that old bodybuilder... what was his name?'

'Chad.' An image of a man with light hair and a handlebar mous-tache filled his head. Connor hadn't thought about Chad in a long time.

She hummed, as though picturing Connor's 20-year-old body. 'Those were the days...'

Connor shifted uncomfortably. He preferred not to dwell on the period of his life when his younger self lived in LA with Blake and Betsy—Royale. Whatever she called herself now.

Those memories were not pleasant ones. He'd been cocky, inex-perienced and naive, in a hurry to make a name for himself in wedding photography. Desperate to be the one on everyone's lips. If only he'd been more patient...

Post-diagnosis, he recognised this lack of patience and his hyper-focus on a goal as symptoms of his ADHD. His older self wished he could go back in time and tell his younger self that it would all happen in good time. Not to rush it. Not to trust the wrong people.

Person.

On the other side of the bar, a group of photographers yelled 'IPPY-KIY-YAY!' as they collectively downed shots.

'Ah, to be young again,' said Royale.

To be fair, if he met her now, he'd place her in her mid-thirties.

Betsy had always been beautiful. 'So where are you living these days?' he asked, changing the subject and bringing it back to the present.

'Still Los Angeles.' Her Cosmopolitan arrived, and she fished out the curled lemon rind with her long, red fingernails, giving it a sharp squeeze over her drink.

'What happened to moving to New York?' he asked. She used to say that LA was too two-faced for her and she'd had enough of that growing up in Houston. New Yorkers would always tell a person what they thought.

Royale shrugged. 'I changed my mind. In LA there are plenty of horny housewives who think they could be the next Dita Von Teese. They keep me busy.'

'Glad it's working out for you,' he said and sipped his beer. He meant it. He wanted nothing but the best for Betsy. Royale.

'Have you seen Blake yet?' she asked.

He coughed into his drink. The memory of Blake greeting Stella on the first day of the conference slithered into his mind's eye. 'Why would I want to see Blake?'

'You two used to be best friends. I thought you'd forgiven him by now.'

'Unlikely,' Connor sneered.

She sipped her drink and looked at him over the rim of her glass. 'Besides, he's working with your wife, isn't he? Or is it ex-wife?'

He slammed his beer bottle down harder than intended. Royale licked her red lips and raised her defined eyebrows. 'She's still my wife,' he said. 'Where did you hear that?'

'You may not be in touch with Blake, but I still am. I'm filming a class for MuseTV.'

Connor had heard about MuseTV. Blake's latest attempt at making millions, taking advantage of other people's talent while he raked in the profits. In a flash of insight, he realised what Blake wanted from Stella. With her skills, she must be on his hit list. 'Then I suppose Blake is as full of lies as he's always been. We're not getting a divorce.' He turned towards the bar and swiped up his beer bottle. Had Stella told Blake that they were getting a divorce?

Royale finished her drink. 'I stand corrected. So does that mean you're moving back to LA?'

'What? God, no. I hate the place.' Living in LA had been some of the darkest days of his life. Ranking even lower than today. 'Why would I do that?'

'Oh! Ohhh.' She tapped her fingernail against her rouge lips. 'I think I've put my foot in it.'

His heart thumped faster. 'Betsy. Tell me what's going on.' A sense of doom swept over him.

'I'm sorry.' She uncrossed her legs and slid off the stool. 'I think you really need to talk to your current wife.'

He gave her a don't-fuck-with-me look.

Royale sighed, her eyes darting left and right before sidling up to him and standing so close that her breath tickled the shell of his ear. 'He's offering her a huge opportunity. One that I would *kill* for.'

'A class on MuseTV?' he surmised.

'No. *Bigger.*'

She paused and Connor had to resist yelling at her to *hurry up*. But if there was one thing he knew about Betsy, it was that she wouldn't be rushed. Finally, she said, 'He's creating a whole new online learning platform around her brand.'

'What does LA have to do with it?' He held his breath. Why did it seem like the lights had dimmed?

A little too gleefully, Royale revealed, 'Why, because she's moving there.'

What. The. Fuck?!

Connor didn't bother to say goodbye before seizing his bag and rushing towards the lifts.

STELLA

THE SLAM OF HER FRONT DOOR REVERBERATED THROUGHOUT THE suite.

Stella was livid.

She threw her purse and laptop bag onto the dining table. Thankfully, nobody else was there to see her stalking the room like a caged tiger. She kicked at some petals that had fallen from the giant bouquet of Golden Poppies and considered smashing an orange against the wall.

It had been a long day. One class, a podcast interview, and countless hours doing demos on supplier stands, moving from booth to booth with barely a break in between.

The last stop had been reviewing photography portfolios for new, hopeful photographers in the Mentors' Corner. The previous years she'd participated, Stella had enjoyed the process of sharing her knowledge, helping the next generation of award-winners to attain 'glass' (aka trophies).

This time, she'd been paired with a young man whose portfolio needed significant work. 'I don't understand why my prints keep scoring so low,' he said. 'Can you help me?'

But when she pointed out that his highlights were too hot, he replied, 'It's a creative choice.'

When she suggested his model's hands needed shaping and that he should take a second to pose them before taking the picture, he insisted, 'I can't do that. It would break the spontaneity of the capture.'

And when she critiqued his composition, he objected, 'But my family and friends have always told me I'm a really great photographer. You just don't like my style.' By the end of their session, he'd become so stroppy that he accused her of not knowing anything about photography.

But that wasn't even why she was angry.

After the critique, she'd gathered her things and left. Eager to get to her room, she pretended to talk on her phone as she rushed to the lifts so that nobody would stop her for a chat—

When she spied her husband flirting with some blonde bombshell in a tight red dress at the lobby bar. The sight enraged Stella despite the fact that she'd been ignoring his texts all day.

She grabbed one of the bland grey pillows off the sofa and catapulted it at the wall.

'Argh!' she yelled, anger and hurt rolling through her as she sent two more pillows flying. She should've been clearer with Connor when they discussed their separation, but to be honest, she didn't think it had needed to be explicitly stated:

No fooling around.

Shouldn't it have been obvious? Plenty of men were interested in her. A single dad at the school gates had been flirting with her for a while and had even asked her over for 'coffee' at his house.

But she'd said no, of course. Connor had ruined her for all other 'coffee'.

Stella picked up one of the pillows and screamed into it.

A banging at the door cut into her Rage Journey.

She froze. Probably somebody checking she wasn't currently murdering anyone.

Inhaling deeply, she smoothed her hands over her hair and marched towards the door, wrestling her inner demons down. It was probably another present from Blake.

The banging came again.

'Just a minute,' she called, schooling her face into a calm mask.

She pulled open the door.

Connor stood in the hallway, hands on his hips and a stormy expression on his face. He stepped past her into the suite.

'Why don't you come in?' she said and slammed the door.

He swivelled towards her. 'I just heard a rumour that we're moving to LA,' he roared.

Stella's eyes widened with surprise. How did he know about that? Were there no bloody secrets in this industry?

Right now though, she had her own reason to be furious with him: one particular blonde reason in a tight red dress. 'Have you been cheating on me?' she yelled back.

He reared back as though she'd slapped him. 'No, of course not. Why would you even think that?' Recovering himself, he crossed his arms and tucked his hands under his biceps, as though demanding a rational explanation for her accusation.

'I saw you in the bar with that... that *Amazon*.' Her Italian hands described angry shapes in the air.

'Betsy? We were just talking.' The opposite of her, he stayed statue still. She hated when he did that—like he was demonstrating that he was the calm one, the reasonable one, while she was the one losing her shit.

Naturally, Stella's volume increased. 'Ha! She was *talking* very close to you.'

He shrugged dismissively. 'We knew each other in a past life.'

'I'll bet you did.' A small part of her was listening to her outburst and cringing. She knew her jealousy, especially when it came to how other women reacted to Connor, was not one of her best qualities. But right now, it seemed to be in control. Maybe he was right.

Maybe she was being unreasonable. But it felt so good to let the demon loose.

Connor threw his hands in the air, his facade of calm finally crumbling. 'Stella! You're being ridiculous.'

'*I'm* being ridiculous?!' She stepped towards him.

'Yes!' he yelled. 'Because whether you believe me or not, I love *you*!'

'Well, whether you believe *me* or not, I love you, too!' she bellowed.

For a moment, they glared at each other, chests heaving with sharp pants.

The next, Connor closed the distance between them, and their lips crashed together. His hands slid into her loose hair, and her fingers grasped at his hips, pulling him towards her. He broke contact for a second to divest himself of his satchel before reuniting his mouth with hers.

It felt... amazing. And familiar. Heat rushed through Stella as his hands found the buttons on the front of her blouse and deftly undid them. She craved his touch on her naked skin. As soon as the last button was free, she shrugged off her shirt, followed by her bra, and Connor ran his fingertips down her ribs. She groaned. Goosebumps popped up all over her body.

Lacking his patience for buttons, she grabbed his white shirt in both hands and tried to rip it open. Nothing happened.

'Dammit,' she said. It always worked in the movies.

She felt him smile against her lips as he seized the fabric in his own hands and cleaved his shirt in two.

'That's so hot,' she breathed. She pushed the scraps of fabric off his shoulders to join hers on the floor.

'If you think that's hot, wait til you see what I'm going to do to you next,' he said.

Leaping into his arms, she wrapped her jeans-clad legs around his waist, their mouths still attached, tasting each other like starving animals.

He strode towards Liliwen's room. 'Wrong one,' she said breathlessly. Correcting course, he aimed for Tristan's. 'Nope,' she said. 'The other one.'

With a guttural noise, he swung her towards the last bedroom, his strong arms cupping her arse to keep her in place. She could feel his excitement, hard against her inner thigh.

A tiny voice inside her head warned that they hadn't actually discussed any of their problems yet, but in that moment, Stella didn't care. She just wanted to experience the joy of making love to Connor again. It had always been their favourite method of communication.

In her room, he dropped her onto the bed, and she bounced on the super king mattress. Kneeling at the edge of the bed, he undid her jeans and tugged them down, along with her underwear.

His hungry grey eyes roamed over her naked body. 'You're so beautiful. I've missed you.'

'I've missed you, too.'

Watching her, he removed the rest of his clothing. She couldn't look away. He was still the most beautiful man she'd ever seen. Then her eyes fell on a purpling bruise on his right butt cheek. 'Whoa, what happened there?' She sat up and ran her fingers lightly over the mottled skin.

Connor shrugged. 'Michael hit me with a squash ball.'

'Bad Michael,' she said and kissed the spot.

'I'll live.' He nudged her back onto the bed.

Stella shuddered in anticipation of what came next. He smiled the sexy half-smile that she loved so much as he crawled over her with lust in his eyes. Bracing himself like he was doing a push-up, muscles straining, he kissed her on the lips, then moved down her neck to her breasts, taking each nipple between his teeth and biting it gently before moving further down her stomach. Shifting her body towards him so that her bottom lined up with the edge of the bed, he kneeled in front of her and propped her feet on his shoulders so her knees fell wide open.

She bit her lip. Time stood still while she waited for first contact.

French slang for an orgasm was *la petite mort*—'the little death'—because of that momentary transcendence to another plane. As though she were about to die, Stella's life with Connor flashed through her head: the thumb war the first time they met, the chateau, unbuttoning her dress, their first time making love in Italy, kissing in the rain, their wedding, laughing on their travels... all of their history filled her.

And then his mouth descended, and her mind went blissfully blank.

13

STELLA

Afterwards, Stella fell asleep immediately, even though it was only 7:00PM. Between jet lag and her schedule, she'd been so busy since arriving at the conference that her body needed oblivion. She always slept better with Connor beside her, the world's sexiest comfort blanket.

When she woke up around midnight, a strong, warm pair of arms tightened around her body.

She hadn't felt this safe and hopeful in a long time.

'Hey, sleepyhead,' Connor said, nuzzling behind her ear. She lay spooned against him, both of them naked under the duvet.

Stretching, she turned so that their noses almost touched. 'That was, um...'

'Yes, it was,' he said, moving his hand to her waist. The hard nub of his familiar calluses scratched against her skin, and his thumb rubbed over her hip bone. Her body automatically responded, even as her brain inserted itself. They had things to discuss.

'We should probably talk,' she said.

His thumb paused before resuming its task. 'Okay, you're right. But before we dive into it, I have something I want to say.'

She nodded. 'Okay?'

Connor fixed his eyes on hers. 'I love you, Stella Knight. With everything that I am. If I ever made you feel like you aren't the centre of my world, I'm sorry... because you are. You and Grace. I've never loved another woman like I love you.'

A tear slid down her cheek, and her heart pumped faster. He had no idea how much those words meant to her. All she'd ever wanted was for him to be present in their marriage, present for *her*. 'I love you, too, Connor Knight,' she whispered.

In her head, the wall between them began to crumble. They were talking. They were touching. This was everything.

'If we're going to make this work,' she said, 'we need to vow to be one hundred percent honest with each other. Always.'

'I swear it.' He dropped a kiss on the tip of her nose. Disentangling their bodies, he pushed himself up to sit against the headboard, ready to talk. Stella laid her head on his chest, her legs hugging his under the sheets.

She'd thought many times about what she wanted to achieve from the separation, about what would make it worth the pain. She pictured the stack of relationship-focused self-help books next to her bed, and the framework she'd planned of topics for their five-day self-imposed marriage retreat. But right now, just after midnight, with his skin pressed against hers, she had trouble remembering it in any detail. The mountain of what they needed to cover towered in her mind. Where should they start?

At the very least, she needed him to commit to seeing a marriage counsellor. But she also wanted some acknowledgement from him that he understood why she'd asked for the separation in the first place. He needed to prioritise her and Grace above his latest assignment for *Vanity Fair*. But there was also:

Los Angeles.

The offer.

Changes going forward.

What he'd been up to for the past six months.

The memory of him speaking intimately with the blonde woman

stampeded over her list, so she decided to start there. 'Me first. Who was that woman in the bar?' She tipped her head back so she could look him in the eyes.

'Betsy?' He shrugged. 'Nobody. Like I said, she's someone I used to know a long time ago.'

She laid her head back onto his chest. 'I was just worried because... well... we never made it clear whether we were seeing other people during the separation.'

His body stiffened next to her. 'I didn't. Did *you?*' he asked.

'No, of course not!' For a moment, her temper was piqued and she said sharply, 'When would I have had the time, Connor?' Being a mum and running a business by herself was not conducive to dating, even if she'd wanted to do it.

Then she remembered his shocked face when she'd accused him of cheating earlier and remorse cooled her ire. 'I'm sorry I jumped to the wrong conclusion.'

He relaxed. 'I would never cheat on you,' he said and kissed the top of her head. 'Okay, my turn. What's going on with Blake Romero? And why does he want us to move to LA?'

The big question. 'What he's offering me, it could make us millionaires.'

'We have enough money.'

That was true. They owned a house in Maida Vale and Connor's studio in Old Street. Plus Connor was very well paid for his fashion and advertising work. Stella also brought in good money and didn't have many overheads because her studio was in their home. Added to that, they had a shrewd financial advisor who helped them invest wisely.

Stella grimaced. 'Sorry. I don't know why I said that. To be honest, it's not about the money.' She gathered her thoughts while plucking at a rogue grey hair on his chest. 'For most of my career, I've been Connor Knight's wife. People assumed that you were the talent and I was the... I don't know... the sidekick.'

'Well, they're idiots. You're extremely talented.'

She loved how he never made her feel like an amateur. That's why he was such an amazing teacher, and she'd been lucky to learn from him. Shame he wasn't taking on students anymore. The world was missing out.

Even so, her insecurities were hard to smother. 'Thank you. But *they* didn't know that.'

'Who's they?'

She swatted him on the chest. 'Don't be obtuse.'

'Fine. So... let me guess: Blake has offered to run a business on your behalf. All you have to do is take pretty pictures, and he'll make you a star. Is that about right?'

Stella shifted, uncomfortable with how close his summary came to the mark. 'Well, yes, I suppose so.'

Connor snorted and muttered, 'That fucker is up to the same bloody tricks.'

'What do you mean?' A queasy sensation settled in her stomach.

'Blake has a habit of latching onto talented people and trying to make money off them. You can't trust him.'

In all the years they'd known each other, Connor had never talked much about Blake Romero. Only a snarky comment here and there alerted her that they had history. If she were going to walk away from what Blake was offering her, she needed a good reason.

'Tell me the full story.' Stella sat up and leaned against the headboard. Connor slipped his arm behind her, pulling her close so she nestled into his side.

'All right.' He tapped the back of his head against the wall as he gathered his thoughts. 'Twenty-five years ago—god, I feel old just saying that... Anyway, twenty-five years ago, I met Blake at this very conference. You know how I left Armstrong and Michael when I was 18? Well, I moved to London for a while—shot a handful of weddings, but I wasn't making great money. I had zero business sense at the time. Then I heard about IPE and decided—if I really wanted to be the best, I had to learn from the best. So I borrowed the funds from Armstrong and hopped on a flight.

'Blake and I met on the first day. Both of us were newbies, even though I was a few years younger than him. And this place was... you know how it is. Intense. Overwhelming. Invigorating. Inspiring.' He stopped to swig water out of the bottle on the bedside table. 'Blake quickly realised that I had talent. Lots of it. More than him.'

'Humble much?' Stella joked.

He tickled her under the armpit. She laughed and snuggled closer to him, inhaling his natural scent, closing her eyes. She enjoyed being close to him again. His attention was like a drug: heady and intoxicating.

Connor continued. 'At the end of the conference, Blake approached me with a proposition. He wanted us to work together. He would be a sort of business manager, and I'd be the talent. He'd grown up in his family's art gallery, and he understood the luxury market. He said he could help get me the kind of weddings that would skyrocket my career—for a small percentage. I didn't know anything about running a business yet, and I thought it sounded like an easy win. So I said yes. And I moved to LA.'

Stella turned her head and looked at him. 'You lived in LA? I never knew that.'

'I don't talk about it much.'

'Oh.' Stella winced inside. She didn't like to think there were things in Connor's past that he didn't want to share with her. Before this, she thought she knew everything about him.

Oblivious to her thoughts, he continued, 'Blake convinced me that if we could make my name in the right circles, then we could be charging a hundred grand per wedding. At the time, that seemed crazy to me. He told me I wasn't thinking big enough. But we couldn't do anything unless I had a great portfolio. So I set about shooting that while he made connections in the luxury wedding market.

'Now, I used to work out at an outdoor gym on Venice Beach. Full of body builders. I was there because I found the people fascinating. They let me use the weights for free in exchange for taking photos—a side project. I wonder if I still have them anywhere?' He stared off into space for a second.

She pinched him gently to return his attention to the story at hand. He was always going off on tangents. Shaking his head, he said, 'Sorry. Anyway, I met this bodybuilder named Jack. Attractive guy. And he was getting married. I knew his fiancée because she used to hang around while he was lifting. She was an actress. Beautiful. Long, thick black hair down to her arse. They didn't have a lot of money for their wedding, but they were holding it in a picturesque spot—and I knew that they'd be great for my portfolio. So I made a deal with them. Only a few hundred dollars to cover expenses, but I was excited about shooting it. I put them in touch with Blake to handle the details.'

His thumb absentmindedly stroked her hip again. With a big sigh, he said, 'A week before the wedding, Blake sniffed out a big opportunity. He still worked occasionally at his parents' gallery because we weren't making anything yet. He was chatting with a client who was the best friend of a celebrity wedding planner, and he heard about a couple from Beverley Hills. The bride was the daughter of some famous producer, and the groom was a sports talent agent. Their photographer had to pull out due to health reasons, which meant their planner was scrambling for somebody amazing to step in. The usual photographers were already booked, so Blake went after it. And he won it.' He paused. 'I never questioned how.'

Stella's stomach fell. She hadn't heard anything yet that would change her mind about Blake's offer, but she could feel it hurtling towards her. She dropped her head onto Connor's shoulder, and he kissed her hair.

'When he told me about it, I pointed out that Jack's wedding was the same day. Blake convinced me that this was too good an opportunity to miss. It was the break we needed. He promised me that he'd sort something out for Jack and Laura. He'd shoot it himself if he had to. He was a decent photographer, so I agreed. I had a lot of pre-planning to do for the wedding, and I needed to visit the venue, meet the couple.'

Connor shifted on the bed as though uncomfortable with the next part of the story. Stella turned towards him and placed her hand on his chest, rubbing her thumb back and forth reassuringly.

'I never should have gone along with it. I was too trusting. But I can't change the past.' He inhaled and blew it out slowly, preparing himself for the grand finale. 'I shot the wedding and it went well. Really well. The couple were thrilled when I presented the images and their album design. The wedding planner put me on his books. The money hit our accounts, and Blake took his percentage. But then a few weeks later, I ran into Jack at the gym.'

Stella held her breath.

'One minute I was doing bicep curls, the next I was up against a wall with Jack's forearm cutting off my oxygen supply. Turns out that Blake sent some talentless hack to photograph the wedding. The guy didn't know what the hell he was doing, and the images were Shit with a capital S. Laura cried when she saw them. Harsh lighting. Bad composition. Underexposed.'

'Oh my god! What did you do?'

'The only thing I could do. After Jack let me breathe again, I apologised and explained that I had no idea and offered to do a post-wedding shoot with them for free. And then I went home and confronted Blake.' Stella could feel Connor's body tensing next to her. She cuddled in closer.

'At first, he tried to play dumb. But then it eventually came out when I had *him* against the wall with my forearm cutting off *his* oxygen. He'd hired an actor to shoot Jack and Laura's wedding. No photography experience.'

'That's terrible!' said Stella, appalled. Having shot weddings for many years, she was filled with sympathy for the bride and groom.

'It gets worse. Because then I found out that when the wedding planner put out the call for replacement photographers, he was only considering vendors who had shot at that venue before. So Blake *stole images* from another photographer's display album at the venue, mixed it with my actual portfolio, and presented it all as my work.'

Stella felt ill. That was the worst sin that a photographer could commit. She had trouble marrying the image that Connor was painting of an amoral trickster with the authoritative, confident businessman she'd met. 'He did that? Really?'

'And to make it worse, the wedding planner realised it after the wedding. He felt like we'd taken advantage of him, so he struck me off his list and said I'd never work in Los Angeles again.'

A chill slithered down Stella's back. If there was one thing she knew about Connor, it was that his reputation was sacrosanct to him. 'What did you do?'

'I punched Blake, did the shoot for Jack and Laura, packed my bags, and returned to London on the next flight. Never spoke with Blake again.'

Disappointment settled on Stella like a fine layer of dust, all the dreams of her shiny future disintegrating before her eyes. She couldn't work with Blake if he'd done all of this to Connor. A small voice inside of her piped up and asked: *What if he's changed?* But a louder voice shouted: *Il lupo perde il pelo, ma non il vizio—The wolf loses the fur, but not the vice.*

What a shady arsehole! If everything Connor said was true, then she couldn't uproot their entire life in London and drag her family to LA—even if it seemed like the opportunity of a lifetime. Despite Blake's recent indisputable success with MuseTV, she couldn't risk it. Not if there was any possibility it could turn out to be a con.

At that thought, her eyes widened. What if this whole thing was some sort of revenge ploy to get back at Connor?

She wanted to cry. She'd been excited about what Blake was offering. It had all seemed so above board and well planned out. There were numbers! Projections! Now she realised that all those things he'd said had probably been a conman's lies.

And she was still in the shadow of her super-talented husband.

14

CONNOR

THE NEXT MORNING, CONNOR KNIGHT WOKE UP SMILING.

He watched Stella's chest rise and fall as she breathed, deep in sleep beside him. Her lips were slightly parted, her eyelashes brushing the tops of her freckled cheeks. He felt privileged to be the man who had the pleasure of seeing her like this. Relaxed and unguarded.

He fought the urge to wake her up. The temptation to make her face transform again with need for him was strong.

But she looked so peaceful.

Last night, he'd finally told her about his past with Blake, something he should have done a long time ago. Why had he held it back? Embarrassment? Injured pride? Either way, his ego was definitely involved. But now he was glad he'd shared it with her and that she'd realised Blake couldn't be trusted. Besides, she didn't need Romero to be a star. Connor knew she could do it all on her own, if that was what she wanted.

He'd hoped to tell her about his ADHD as well, but she'd been so downhearted after his revelations. All he'd wanted was to make her happy again, so he made love to her slowly and assiduously, lavishing attention on every part of her body. They'd fallen asleep afterwards. Perhaps the right time for another revelation would come today.

She murmured something that sounded like 'Wolverine' in her sleep, and he had to purse his lips to stop himself from laughing at how cute she was. In his head, the first notes of 'As Long as You Love Me' started up. His big toe tapped out the beat underneath the covers.

His thoughts meandered back to a conversation they'd had a year or so ago. Stella had asked Connor how often he thought about the Roman Empire after seeing a meme on social media that implied men thought about it every day. Why? Something about how it glorified masculinity. Hand on heart, Connor answered that he never gave much brain space to it. Maybe six times a year at most.

However, it would surprise her—and most people who knew him—to learn how often he thought about the Backstreet Boys. They were the soundtrack of his teenage years. While the other kids in his Paris-based high school were listening to Nirvana or Hootie and the Blowfish, he was dreaming of being the sixth member of BSB. His brother was probably the only person who knew about Connor's secret love, having lived through it. Connor understood that it was not normal or cool for a 45-year-old man to love the music of a 90s boy band—which was why he didn't talk about it.

What did he love about them? Was it their seamlessly blending voices? Their range of music? Their synchronised dance moves? Their way with the ladies? He admired all these things, but it went deeper than that. Compared with the other boy bands of the era, BSB seemed to have a genuine connection. A true friendship. This had always appealed to Connor. That's why they were still together today.

He had spoken about this with his therapist, who surmised in his quiet voice, 'Your obsession—'

'Obsession is a strong word,' interrupted Connor.

'All right, shall we say your *deep regard* for the Backstreet Boys was your way of seeking stability during your chaotic teenage years?

Your family moved a lot, so you stopped making new friends. Why bother? You'd only have to leave them in three years. Instead, you fixated on the Backstreet Boys as surrogates. They travelled with you.'

Connor pondered Levi's words. 'Are you suggesting... that the Backstreet Boys were my imaginary friends?'

'Exactly!' said Levi.

'That's insane,' Connor had disagreed. He just really loved their music, okay?

His big toe continued tapping out the beat under the duvet.

Stella stirred and he stopped moving. Although he hadn't slept this well in their six months of separation, he couldn't sleep any more. Jet lag, probably. His throat was dry from the air conditioning, and he could really use a drink. He looked at the bottle on his bedside table. Empty.

Sneaking from the bed so he didn't disturb her, he pulled on his boxer shorts and slinked out of the room. He closed the door quietly and turned around—

Only to be confronted with Tristan's arse.

'Morning,' said Tristan as he peddled his feet in Down Dog.

'Uh, yeah. Morning,' said Connor. He skirted around Tristan and headed for the kitchen, stopping for a second to eye the large bouquet of poppies and the tower of oranges on the dining room table.

'Good night?' asked Tristan, transitioning into a plank.

'Great night.'

Under his breath, Tristan said something like, 'Bloody sounded like it.'

Connor ignored him, distracted by the two open bedroom doors. In all the excitement of reconciling with Stella, he'd forgotten about his father and Liliwen.

Pointing towards her door with his thumb, Connor asked, 'Is she...?'

'I believe she spent the night making sweet, sweet love in your dad's hotel room.'

Connor gagged. 'Was that necessary?'

Tristan chuckled. 'One hundred percent, darling.'

Poor Liliwen. Connor didn't want to think about what the two of them were doing, especially since he'd spent his younger years with a ringside seat to Armstrong's Broken Hearts' Club. He remembered one incident, when a woman whom Armstrong had dumped after only a few weeks showed up at their door and yelled obscenities through the mail slot all night long, keeping everyone awake. Good times... not.

'Do you think Liliwen is okay?' said Connor before downing a glass of water.

'They're having fun. Life is short. What's wrong with that?' Tristan held his plank like he could stay there all day.

'Well, Michael is on standby for when she realises my dad is an emotional infant and she wants a divorce.' Connor opened and closed drawers, searching for the room service menu. Neither he nor Stella had eaten any dinner, and they'd screwed away a lot of calories. A lopsided grin broke across his lips at the memory.

From the living room, he heard Tristan snort. 'The Great Michael Knight is abasing himself with family law?'

Bitterness dripped from Tristan's voice. After what Michael had said about their breakup, Connor wasn't surprised. Michael's parting words to Tristan had been brutal. Still, Michael was his brother, and Connor would defend him until his dying day.

'Fuck off,' he said. 'He's one of the good guys.'

'Unless you're dating him,' Tristan scoffed.

Finding the menu, Connor laid it out on the counter. 'He doesn't need any crap from you. He has enough shit going on in his life.'

Tristan stood in one fluid motion. 'Why? What's wrong with Michael?'

Connor raised an eyebrow, surprised by the sudden intensity in Tristan's voice.

Just then, there was a knock on the suite door. Tristan and Connor's eyes met in a standoff over who would answer it.

'I can't do it.' Connor pointed towards his boxer shorts.

But Tristan had dropped back to his mat and twisted his body into some sort of awkward pose. 'I can't break my flow.'

The knock came again.

'Fine,' said Connor with an exasperated sigh, crossing to the door. He peeked through the peephole to see a hotel employee holding something in his arms. Connor swung the door open. 'Can I help you?'

'Delivery for Stella Knight,' said the man, not even blinking at Connor's state of undress. He wondered how many outrageous things the man had seen working in a Vegas hotel. A guest in underwear probably ranked low.

The delivery man handed over a heavy wicker basket containing six wine bottles.

'Thanks,' said Connor, kicking the door closed with his foot. He carried the basket to the table and placed it next to the oranges. Curious, he pulled one of the wines out and studied the label. A Californian Pinot Noir, Mondavi Rothschild. Expensive. Delicious. Whoever sent this had excellent taste. Probably one of Stella's suppliers.

He put the bottle back and searched for an envelope.

The bedroom door banged against the wall, and Stella rushed out wearing a white bathrobe, her wet hair secured in a turban. 'Morning,' she said, darting past Tristan and zipping around the breakfast bar into the kitchen. She beelined straight for the coffee machine, missing the wine basket on the table.

Connor said, 'Time for breakfast? I was going to order room service.' Walking up to her, he caged Stella with his arms from behind and nuzzled her neck while she sorted through the Nespresso pods.

She groaned. 'No time. Photo walk at 9:00.' She selected the black capsule and fed it into the slot, positioning a mug underneath to catch the espresso. She swivelled in his arms, pecked him on the lips, and pushed past him to the fridge.

A crease formed between his eyebrows, disappointment surging through him. He'd hoped they could chat. He wanted to tell her about his ADHD.

Stella plucked a yogurt from the fridge and opened a few drawers until she found a spoon. Peeling off the lid, she shovelled yogurt into her mouth.

'Are you free for lunch?' Connor asked, pressing his bottom against the counter and crossing his arms.

'Can't—I... I already have plans.' Her gaze flicked to the dining table covered in gifts, her eyes widening in surprise when she saw the new addition. 'When did that arrive?'

'Just now.'

'Did you read the note?'

'No...?' Suspicion needled through him. Returning to the table, Connor fished out the envelope between two fingers like a cigarette. Ignoring his urge to tear it open and read it, he carried the note to Stella and held it out. 'From an admirer?'

She laughed nervously. 'Not quite...'

He raised an eyebrow.

'It's from Blake,' she sighed, taking the envelope from between Connor's fingers. Reluctantly she slid her nail under the seal, freed the note, and scanned it before showing it to him.

Some elegant reds for an elegant redhead. California wines are among the best in the world. Looking forward to lunch. Blake

Connor's blood ran hot. Now it made sense. Californian wines, California oranges, California poppies. How *dare* Blake send gifts to his wife, trying to flatter her into taking part in his schemes. 'Blake is your lunch date?'

She tossed the card in the bin and picked up her yogurt pot. 'We planned it yesterday, so I could follow up with any questions I had. Don't worry, I can handle it.'

His first urge was to insist on coming along, or even to take the meeting for her. But if things were going to get better between them, they needed to start working on their marriage *now*. And a big part of that was trust.

'Okay,' he said, even though it killed him to think of Blake alone with Stella.

'Okay?' She froze with the yogurt spoon in her mouth, eyebrows raised in surprise.

'Yeah. *Okay*. I don't trust him. But I *do* trust *you*.' He raised the corner of his lip into his signature half-smile.

Stella threw the spoon in the sink, tossed the yogurt pot into the bin on top of the card, and stepped into his arms. 'Thank you. That means a lot.'

Score one for Connor. He hugged her to him. He would have encouraged her back to the bedroom if she didn't have to leave for her class. The coffee machine hissed as though to remind them that she had to go.

She nibbled him lightly on his neck, stepped away, and grabbed the coffee. 'I'm free for dinner tonight. But Tristan is coming, too. I haven't seen him much since he arrived.'

'Fabulous. I love being a gooseberry,' Tristan called out as he rolled up his mat. Connor had forgotten he was there.

'You know you do!' Stella retraced her steps to the bedroom and shut the door.

Tristan tossed his mat into his room and said, 'If you're still ordering breakfast, I'll have two poached eggs with steamed spinach and oatmeal. Three bananas.'

Putting aside his worries about Blake, Connor rubbed his hands together in a servile way. 'Of course. Would you like orange juice with that?'

'No, I don't drink—' Tristan stopped as realisation dawned. 'You're not ordering breakfast anymore, are you?'

'Nope.' Connor placed a capsule in the coffee machine for himself. Maybe he'd call Michael to see if he wanted to get breakfast.

'Tease.' Tristan grabbed a protein bar from the countertop, ripped open the wrapper, and slammed his bedroom door behind him.

Seconds later, the main door cracked open and Liliwen strolled through, humming Frank Sinatra. 'Holy naked Knights!' she said when she saw Connor, loosely shielding her eyes with her hand. 'Two in one day! I should hit the casinos with all this luck.'

'Oh! Hey, Liliwen,' said Connor, hiding behind the counter— although he was less embarrassed about his boxer shorts than about her having sex with his father.

Her laugh tinkled through the room. 'Don't mind me. I've just popped in for a quick wash and a change. Armstrong booked us a helicopter ride around the Grand Canyon today.' She scrunched up her nose. 'Why didn't you tell me he was such a romantic?'

Romantic? Huh.

So much for spending time with his boys. Same old Armstrong. Dropping his kids as soon as there was a new skirt to chase.

Before he could say anything, the bedroom door crashed open, and Stella marched into the room, dragging her camera bag behind her with her laptop clenched under her other arm. 'Ah, Liliwen! Just the person. Did you organise the lights I need for my class later?' She sat on the sofa and wrenched her laptop open. Her freshly braided hair left a wet spot on the shoulder of her light blue dress.

'The three o'clock?' Liliwen pulled out her phone and poked at it.

Checking her calendar, Stella tapped the screen. 'You mean the *four* o'clock?'

Liliwen squinted at her phone. 'Yes, of course. Silly me. I'll confirm them now before I head out.' She dropped it back into her handbag.

Stella's head snapped up. 'Where are you going?'

'On a helicopter with Armstrong. Sorry, lovely. Is that okay? Did you need me for anything today?'

'Oh. No... no, that's fine.'

Stella's nostrils flared, and she started stroking the cleft in her chin, sure signs of stress. Going into problem solving mode, Connor crossed the room and kneeled in front of her. 'Tell me how I can help.'

Her eyes widened. 'Really? You don't have your own stuff to do?'

He shrugged. 'I'm all yours.'

'Okay... well, I need some images retouched?'

'Send them over.'

'You're a saviour.' She located the folder of raw images on her computer and transferred the files to Connor. He was the one who taught her to retouch, so he knew her style.

'Anything else?' he asked.

She exhaled a long breath, her mouth shaped like an O. 'No. Just... that would be a big help.'

He remembered how full-on these conventions could be. He moved his hands to her legs and massaged her thighs. 'Call me after lunch.' He raised his eyebrows, not wanting to mention Blake in front of Liliwen.

'Will do.' She checked her watch. 'I'm late.'

Pushing himself to standing and wondering when his knees had started to ache so much, he walked her to the door, holding it open for her. Before she left, he caught her by the waist and pulled her to him, kissing her thoroughly. 'I love you,' he said. He was already dreaming about getting back into bed with her after dinner.

'I love you, too. Thanks for the help!' she called over her shoulder as she raced for the lift.

The suite door closed behind her.

'Thought today might be chocolates. Ah, well,' said Liliwen, poking through the wine basket and reading the labels, 'I'm so pleased you two have made things up.'

'You and me both,' Connor said. Liliwen lost interest in the wine and turned towards her door. Before she could disappear completely, he called out, 'By the way, sorry about my father. Michael will help sort a divorce, assuming that's what you want.'

'Oh, don't bother yourself, lovely. I have everything in hand.' She smiled wickedly. 'To be honest, after forty years of marriage, I'm quite enjoying having a new willy to play with.' She winked and sauntered into her room.

For the second time, Connor wondered if he should be more worried about his father than Liliwen.

15

TRISTAN

DOROTHY. DOROTHY. SOPHIA. DOROTHY.

Tristan picked up another quarter and slid it into the coin slot. He pulled the metal arm.

Blanche. Dorothy. Rose. Rose.

Another quarter.

Rose. Sophia. Blanche... Rose.

So close. He needed one of each character's face to come up on the four spindles to win. He clicked his tongue and retrieved another quarter.

'Thank You for Being a Friend' blared out from the machine on repeat. This particular slot machine had called to him through the morass of noise on the casino floor, a beacon in the dark. If there was one thing that could always cheer him up, it was *The Golden Girls*.

Another coin rolled down the chute.

He remembered when his deep and abiding love of *The Golden Girls* started—when Stella and he were competing in the British Open Youth Dance championships, two years before they won. Stella's attention had been snagged by one of the other dancers,

Robbie somebody, and she set about losing her virginity to him (big mistake). The boy was entirely forgettable in Tristan's opinion. Her taste in men had always been abysmal—until Connor. Tristan actually quite liked him.

In contrast, Tristan had excellent taste. There was no better playground for a burgeoning gay man than a dance championship. It was like a candy shop.

A flirtation had erupted between him and the reigning champion from Glasgow: a slim blond Adonis with a massive cock and, to this day, the dirtiest mouth Tristan had ever had the pleasure of kissing. Callum MacDonald. He was a couple of years older than Tristan and more experienced. Tristan learned a lot of moves from him... and he wasn't talking about dancing.

One night after they hooked up, Callum had pulled out his laptop and inserted a DVD of *The Golden Girls*.

It was the episode where Blanche's brother, Clayton, tells her that he's gay. At first Blanche doesn't accept it, but by the end of the episode, she's on board. Watching that as a young gay man from Wales who hadn't yet come out to his parents... it made him feel like he could do it. And so he did. His hippy parents were unsurprised.

After that, Tristan was hooked.

Here were four older women, unashamedly having great sex, living full lives even though society said they shouldn't. They were practically gay men themselves.

And the laughs! If there was one thing he could appreciate, it was a witty one-liner: Sophia and her insults delivered with a sweet smile. Rose and her ridiculous, often scary, and sometimes poignant life lessons from St Olaf. Blanche and her Big Daddy southern charm, covering a spine of steel. And nobody, but *nobody* quipped like Dorothy. She wore her humour like armour, and Tristan learned to do the same.

Homophobic comment? Brush it away with a sardonic retort.

He understood that through the lens of the new millennium,

there were problems with the 80s sitcom. Times had most certainly changed. But he was smart enough to avoid those episodes and only watch the ones that brought him joy.

A few weeks ago, Tristan had Googled Callum, curious to see what he had done with himself. He was running a stage school for kids in a small town in Scotland—Tristan's idea of hell. He noted that Callum still loved a spray tan.

Living under the relentless Mexican sun, Tristan had the real thing. It was only March, and temperatures had already reached over 100 degrees. He'd never worn so much sunscreen in his life.

Somebody plonked down in the chair at the next slot machine over, and Tristan automatically pulled his baseball cap down until the visor obscured part of his vision. At the same time, he pushed his sunglasses up. In Mexico, he enjoyed anonymity for the most part, but in the States, people remembered the famous supermodel Tristan Hughes...

...And his mysterious disappearance from the spotlight.

The tabloids went mad with outlandish theories: alien abduction, secret spy life, heart broken by Greek billionaire.

He played another quarter. Out of the corner of his eye, he saw his neighbour's trainer-clad feet as he swivelled left and right, left and right on his stool. His machine was *Game of Thrones*-themed. It was a strange juxtaposition to *The Golden Girls*.

Another minute passed.

'Hey,' said a deep voice he recognised.

Tristan startled and looked up to find Michael sitting next to him, wearing beige shorts and a collared, light blue t-shirt—the sort of outfit that could be found in department stores in the 'Lawyer Leisurewear' section, although the shirt was tight enough to show off his firm pecs.

'Hey,' Tristan said. He didn't have the energy for a fight. His inner Dorothy was taking a nap. He put another coin in the slot and pulled.

'You're up early,' said Michael.

It was 10AM. Tristan had already spent an hour in the gym, done half an hour of yoga, eaten breakfast, and showered. Searching for entertainment, he'd wandered down to the casino.

'You'll be glad to know your brother and Stella seem to have made up, loudly,' Tristan said, changing the subject.

'Ah. Well... happy for them,' said Michael. 'Whether they realise it or not, they need each other.'

Their eyes met and held for a second longer than necessary. Tristan was glad he had his sunglasses on. A thin barrier against Michael Knight.

Tristan licked his lips and inserted another quarter. The spindles twirled and stopped one by one, each revealing a smiling Golden Girl: *Dorothy. Sophia. Blanche...!*

Sophia.

He sighed and sat back. Not his lucky day.

'Thank you for being a friend' repeated again.

Michael strummed his fingers on Jon Snow's face. *Always full of nervous energy*, Tristan remembered from when they dated, a six-month period of his life he tried not to think about too often. Tristan also tried not to think about those clever, clever fingers touching him, stroking him, loving him...

Or so he'd thought, until Michael suddenly broke things off. Six months was the longest Tristan had ever dated one person. What was it that Michael had called him again? Ah, yes. *Shallow and artificial.* Tristan huffed. Annoyingly, he'd probably been right.

The strumming fingers stopped, and Michael stood up, reaching his hands over his head in a cat stretch. Out of the corner of his eye, Tristan watched a sliver of Michael's stomach appear as his shirt and shorts parted ways for a moment. He remembered licking that skin once upon a time on his way below, below, below.

Cracking his knuckles, Michael said, 'I can't stand the smell of this place. It's very—'

'Artificial?' Tristan supplied. 'Shallow?' He couldn't help himself.

Michael chuckled in recognition of the words. A warm sound. They used to always laugh together.

Neither spoke for one full chorus of *The Golden Girls* theme song. Then Michael leaned towards Tristan, so close he could smell the sea-fresh scent of his soap. What Michael said next was completely unexpected: 'So... do you wanna get out of here?'

16

STELLA

ONE FISH, TWO FISH, RED FISH, BLUE FISH...

The refrain from one of Grace's favourite Dr Seuss stories circled through Stella's head as she observed the colourful, cylindrical fish tank dominating the middle of the restaurant. She wondered what Grace was doing right at that moment and felt a pang of longing in her chest.

Her eyes followed the shapes inside the tank. Some were swimming like they had someplace to be; some were doing the aquatic equivalent of a leisurely stroll; and some were just floating. These were the zen fish. The kind of fish that, if they could talk, would say thought-provoking maxims like: *When we realise that we are the ocean, we are no longer afraid of the waves.*

She wished she were a zen fish.

Instead, Stella was a half-Italian, half-Welsh fish. And the voice floating through her head said: *Non sa chi pesci pigliare—She didn't know which fish to catch.* Which was another way of saying Stella felt conflicted.

In her heart, she wanted Connor to be wrong about Blake. What he was offering was such an opportunity. A chance to reach a wider

123

audience, to do the work she wanted to do. On top of that, her pesky instinct insisted that Blake's offer felt genuine.

But in her head, her husband's words reverberated: *Blake has a habit of latching onto talented people and trying to make money off them. You can't trust him.*

She'd spent the whole morning chewing on the problem as she led a class of fifteen photographers around the hotel on a photo walk. The automatic part of her brain took over: choosing the shooting locations, posing the model, taking the shots, explaining her creative choices. Meanwhile in the back of her head, she tried to decipher a way to have everything she wanted: the husband, the happy child, the career, the success.

The conclusion she'd come to for the millionth time was that she couldn't take the chance. To relocate her family to another country with a risk this big hanging over her... it was preposterous. Crazy. Especially with Armstrong moving to the UK to be near Grace. The timing was all off.

She knew which fish she had to grab.

'Right this way, ma'am,' said the lithe hostess in a black sheath dress. 'The other member of your party is already seated.'

She led Stella through the maze of perfectly laid tables, their white tablecloths reflecting the neon blue light from the tank. Around the back, Blake was sitting in a booth with space for six people. She noted the bottle of champagne chilling in a bucket next to him.

He stood and kissed her on both cheeks. 'Stella, so glad you could make it.'

'Blake.' She scooted onto the bench opposite him. She found it hard to look at him now. Connor's story had given her double vision when it came to Blake: today's shrewd, enticing dealmaker overlaid with Connor's manipulative, ambitious opportunist. Which one was the real Blake Romero?

'How's your week going so far?' He pushed a bowl of edamame towards her.

Well, my PA married my father-in-law. I slept with my estranged husband. And I found out that you're a big, lying cheat. 'Great,' she said. 'Busy. Thank you for the gifts, by the way. You didn't need to.' Originally, she'd viewed them as benign flattery, but in light of Connor's words, she wondered if they were actually Trojan horses.

'Please, it's my pleasure. Champagne?'

She should say no, tell him they didn't have anything to celebrate. But then again, she could use the reinforcement for the conversation she needed to have with him. Her nerves were off the charts; in fact, she was amazed that she wasn't convulsing from the adrenalin rushing through her. Her heart certainly received the memo—it was pounding so loud that the fish probably thought there was a jackhammer in the room.

If she weren't so much of a coward, she would have launched straight into the speech she'd prepared in her head. But she *was* a coward as well as a terrible people pleaser. 'Why not? One will be fine.'

He lifted the bottle, droplets of water free-falling onto the tablecloth, and filled their glasses. 'I hope you don't mind. I know we only have an hour, so I've already ordered for us. You're a sashimi person, right? Not sushi?'

Stella tilted her head in surprise. 'How did you know?'

'Instagram.'

'Oh, yes, of course.' She'd done one of those 'get to know me' posts and had mentioned it in the copy. Blake had conducted his research thoroughly. He probably knew which deodorant she used as she'd written that in a post, too.

The thought suddenly made her uncomfortable. A harmless reel about her raw fish preference had given away something about herself that he was now using to impress/manipulate her. She'd take the post down later.

'*Salute,*' he said, holding his flute aloft.

'*Salute,*' she returned, sipping sparingly from her glass, wishing this lunch was already over.

A waiter showed up balancing a large tray of sashimi on crushed ice, the fish glistening with freshness, as if they'd just been plucked from the tank. *Oh my god.* Had they just been plucked from the tank? Stella felt the urge to hide the platter from tiny eyes. The fish were watching.

She wasn't sure how much she could eat anyway; her stomach wobbled like jelly. She hated confrontation—especially because Blake had been nothing but friendly and welcoming so far. Would that change when he realised she was saying no?

The waiter placed the platter in the middle of the table. As he took them on a tour of the different varieties of sashimi, Stella's inner voice counselled her to tell Blake the news and get it over with. Rip off the plaster.

'After you,' Blake said when the waiter left. She wished he wouldn't be so polite. She wanted to see a glimpse of the shark that Connor knew.

Picking up her chopsticks, she settled them as well as she could between her trembling fingers, the lacquered surface cool against the curve of her thumb.

It took her a few goes to select some salmon and whitefish. The pieces kept slipping from her shaking chopsticks. If Blake noticed her nerves, he didn't let on. She needed to get a hold of herself. Her jaw had fused closed with tension. She forced her mouth open and took another sip of champagne to loosen up.

As Blake filled his plate, he said, 'I invited a friend of mine to join us a little later. Royale Lefevre? Do you know her?'

'I know *of* her.' She knew that Royale specialised in pin-up style glamour photography. Cheeky, colourful, sexy work with an edge. But Stella had never met her. There were countless small friendship groups within the industry, and theirs never crossed.

'I think you two will get along well, and you might like to know somebody who already lives in LA,' he said. Stella appreciated his thoughtfulness, even if it butted against the snakelike profile of him she was clinging to. He continued, 'She's recording a class for MuseTV next month.'

'Oh. Great.' At the mention of MuseTV, she swallowed hard. The luxury of taking her time disappeared. She had to have this talk with him soon—before Royale arrived. Or else it would be too late, too awkward.

She could sense Blake watching her stirring wasabi into her soy sauce, dark spots staining the tablecloth when she accidentally tipped it to the side. 'Whoops.'

He wasn't an idiot. He'd know something was wrong.

'So,' he started. 'Have you considered my offer?'

Her time was up. Stella put down her chopsticks and smoothed her hands over the napkin on her lap a couple of times. 'I have,' she said, looking down at her plate. 'Blake.' She pursed her lips and dragged her eyes up to his. Who was looking back? She tried to see the opportunist, but Blake looked so genuine.

'Why am I getting a bad feeling about this?' He dropped his chopsticks, leaned back in the cushioned booth, and crossed his arms.

She groaned with frustration in her head. 'It's not that I don't want to do it. I do. But the timing is off for me.'

'It's okay. I'll wait until you're ready to get started,' he said, blowing that excuse away.

'Blake, it could be years…'

'Mm hmm,' he said, his hand migrating to his face to rub at his jaw. 'That's not really the reason, is it?'

She caught her breath. He knew. He must have expected this would be a problem. With a long exhale, she admitted, 'No. Well, not all of it.'

'You've spoken to Connor, then.'

'Yup.' She popped the P.

'And he told you about—?'

'How you stole images from another photographer, lied to Connor about covering the other wedding, sent a charlatan in his place, and ruined Connor's reputation with a major wedding planner?'

'I mean, when you say it like that, it makes it sound bad,' he joked with a self-deprecating smile.

Stella shook her head. 'Are you surprised that I'm questioning whether I can trust you on this?'

Blake folded his hands together on the table, his thumb digging into the joint of its twin while he studied the fish tank. The blue light glinted off the cross around his neck.

As her mother always said: *Chi dorme con il cane, si sveglia con le pulci. She who sleeps with the dog, awakes with fleas*, meaning he'd inevitably turn on her, too. She had to remember that.

Looking her dead in the eye, he asked, 'Stella, haven't you ever made a mistake before?'

Ha, if he only knew. The spectre of her old boss hazed through her thoughts. Despite going to therapy years ago, the guilt from her affair with that sleaze bag still gnawed at her, even though she realised now that he'd targeted her, like he had so many girls before and probably after. The disappointment in herself still burned, still made her question her judgment. 'Of course, I have.'

'Are you the same person who made those mistakes?'

'No...' Over a decade had passed.

'And, because of those mistakes, did you vow to become a better person?'

'Well... yes.' She learned a slew of life lessons from the experience, like never to trust men in power who claimed to have her best interests at heart.

Nodding, Blake said, 'So did I. I fucked up.' He threw his hands in the air. 'I was young. Stupid. Too ambitious. And not a day goes by that I don't regret what I did. *Mea culpa*. I was wrong. Not only did I let myself down, I lost my best friend. But... that was also twenty-five years ago. I've learned my lesson. Believe me, I've learned it.'

Twenty-five years *was* a long time. Twenty-five years ago, she was thirteen. She and Tristan were just starting their journey of competing on the ballroom dance circuit. If she went back and asked her thirteen-year-old self what she'd be doing in twenty-five years, she probably would have said something about owning a dance studio with Tristan. But here she was, thirty-eight, already on her second career, married with a child, and she hadn't danced in ages. Her last barre class had left her sore for a week. Twenty-five years was indeed another lifetime. But still...

'Blake, you have to realise... it's *a lot* for me to ask Connor—who still hates you by the way—to pick up and move to LA. Surely you knew that.'

He rolled his eyes to the side. 'I know. It's all about timing. I thought I was getting you at the right moment...'

She understood exactly what he meant. He thought he was getting her in the midst of a divorce from the one man who stood in his way. 'You can see how I might perceive that as being opportunistic.'

Holding his hands wide, he said, 'I'm still a chancer. That's what makes me a good entrepreneur. I take calculated risks. I've simply learned not to lie or screw people over while I'm doing it.'

He sounded so authentic, so sincere. Her instinct reared up again to ask the question: *Are you sure his offer isn't legitimate?*

Worrying her napkin between her fingers, she said, 'I just don't think it's going to work out, Blake.' He was saying all the right things. She might even have been tempted to say yes... if Connor wasn't trusting her to say no.

'With all due respect, you're making a mistake, Stella. There are thousands of photographers who would bite my hand off for this opportunity. But we don't want any of them. We want *you*. I still believe you're the only one who can help me realise the vision I have for this project.'

'Blake...' She closed her eyes to avoid his beseeching gaze.

'Can't a person change?' On each hand, he touched his thumbs to his forefingers like a clam closing, a gesture she recognised as distinctly, familiarly Italian.

She blew out some air. 'Of course they can, but—'

'Well then can't I change?' He touched his hands to his chest. His eyes shone with genuine sadness. Or was it fake? Was he trying to manipulate her? Suddenly she couldn't tell what was real and what was an act.

'You're forgetting it's not just about me. Connor—'

'I'll speak to him.'

She widened her eyes. 'Yeah okay. Do you have a death wish?'

'He's still angry, I guess.'

'Um. *Yeah.*'

Tapping his fingers on the table, he said, 'I'm happy to sit with you both, take you through the proposal, the numbers—'

'Blake. The answer is no.' As soon as she said it, a painful ache settled in her stomach. *You're making a mistake*, said her inner counsellor, echoing Blake's words. She packed them away in a box and shut the lid.

Movement caught her eye. The hostess had reappeared with someone behind her.

Noticing they were about to be interrupted, Blake said sottovoce, 'I'm not giving up on this yet.'

Frowning, Stella wiped her napkin over her mouth and readied herself for small talk—the last thing she wanted right now. What she *did* want was to leave. Call Connor. Get his reassurance that this was the right decision.

Blake hoisted himself out of the booth and stood, the smile on his face belying the conversation they'd just been having. Another act. 'Royale. You found us.'

'Hello, Blake,' purred an alto voice with a sexy hint of Southern roots. Stella turned in her seat to welcome Royale to the table—

And stopped dead.

This was unmistakably the tall, curvy Amazon that Connor had been speaking with in the bar last night. The front matched the back: tight dress (green this time) and blonde hair up in a chignon. She had full, red lips and perfect make-up, the flicks at the corners of her eyes applied with the kind of precision that made other women feel inadequate.

And hadn't Connor said her name was Betsy?

Blake indicated Stella. 'Royale, this is—'

'Stella Knight. Of course.' She held out her hand. Fingernails shiny red. Perfect. Not chipped and nibbled like Stella's.

'Um, hi.' Stella shook it, feeling suddenly like the person who had misread the dress code on the invitation. Her light blue dress appeared mumsy in comparison, her plaited hair plain. 'I love your work.'

'Oh, it's mutual,' Royale said. She shimmied into the booth, and Blake sat next to her. 'You've really come out of nowhere these past few years.'

'Well, not *nowhere*,' said Stella, unsure what Royale was implying. Another photographer who didn't realise Stella had been a photographer for a decade. 'I'm in London.'

Royale scrunched up her nose. 'I *love* London. It's so full of history. You can literally *taste* the industrial revolution in the air.'

To Stella, that did not sound like a good thing.

Clocking the champagne glasses, Royale asked, 'Are we celebrating?'

Blake signalled to the waiter for another flute. 'No... not yet.' His eyes swished to Stella with a cheeky wink before flying back to Royale. She had to admire his perseverance.

Royale laid a hand on his arm, and Stella wondered if there was something going on between the two of them. There was a familiarity in the way they interacted: the closeness of their bodies, shoulders touching. Good friends, definitely. Lovers, maybe.

The sharp chirp of a mobile phone rang out, and Blake reached into his suit. Glancing at the screen, he said, 'Damn, I've got to take this. Do you mind? Be right back.' He slid out of the booth, answered the call with a 'Hey, Robert! I'm glad you called,' and jogged out of earshot.

Royale followed him with her mascaraed eyes. 'Always doing

business,' she said, shaking her head fondly. She leaned her elbows on the table, balancing her chin on top of her entwined hands. 'So.'

'How long have you and Blake known each other?' Stella asked to make conversation.

Ignoring the question, Royale said, 'I'm so glad I'm finally getting to meet you. I can't believe we've never met before—especially because we have so much in common.' She helped herself to Blake's champagne, leaving a bright red lipstick mark on his glass.

Stella laughed. 'Oh! We do?' From her point of view, she had absolutely nothing in common with this glamorous creature who seemed like she'd stepped out of a 1940s film. She couldn't put her finger on it, but she had a feeling that she and Royale would not be great friends, contrary to Blake's prediction. In her experience, men often said things like 'I think you'll really like so-and-so' when the only basis for this was that both women hailed from Planet Earth. Connor did it to her all the time. He was usually wrong.

Royale made an amused sound. 'Of course we do! We both shoot women—exquisitely, I might add. We're both utterly gorgeous—'

A blush crept up Stella's cheeks. She'd never been adept at accepting compliments, but her mother taught her to reply with gratitude. 'Oh, thank—'

'And we both married the same man.'

Stella spit out her champagne all over the expensive plate of sashimi. 'Oh, god! I'm sorry!' She put down her glass and picked up a napkin, dabbing at the wet fish. She laughed as she said, 'I thought you said we both married the same man!'

What an absurd idea! When they'd been on the course at the French chateau ten years ago, Connor was so staunchly marriage-phobic that they had a fight about it in front of the entire class. Once, Connor even confessed that before her, he'd never had a relationship that lasted longer than three months. For a while, Stella was worried he'd turn out exactly like his dad.

No one was more surprised than her when he proposed in Madrid after they'd been dating for a year and a half. It was so romantic. He got down on one knee and said, 'You're the only woman I've ever wanted to marry.' She remembered that line specifically.

An unexpected flicker of hurt flashed in Royale's eyes, gone quickly, but not before Stella noticed it. Recovering, Royale said, 'Didn't he ever mention me? The naughty boy.' She laughed low in her throat, a 40s femme fatale, with extra helpings of the fatale bit.

'I'm sorry. I'm confused. Didn't *who* ever mention it?' Stella said through a forced smile, making one last attempt to deny what Royale was so obviously insinuating.

Royale sipped Blake's bubbles, her gaze hard on Stella. 'Why... Connor Knight, of course.'

17

TRISTAN

AFTER A QUIET JOURNEY WHERE BOTH OF THEM STARED OUT THEIR respective windows, the taxi dropped off a surprisingly nervous Tristan and an annoyingly calm Michael at the Red Rock Canyon gates. The dry, rocky landscape stretched out in front of them as far as the eye could see—much like Tristan's sex life for the past year.

Before leaving the hotel, Tristan had changed into breathable khaki shorts, a bright orange t-shirt that would be easy to spot if they got lost in the desert (and also showed off his olive skin), and his well-loved Diablos Rojos baseball cap to protect him from the sun.

Michael, on the other hand, had topped off his lawyer leisurewear with a brown Fedora. Tristan really wanted to tell him that he looked silly. Who did he think he was? Indiana Jones?

He held his tongue. It wasn't easy.

When they found the path to the Visitors' Centre, Tristan broke the *detente* by graciously (and also sarcastically) saying, 'After you, Dr Jones.' Michael gave him an unamused look before setting off. Tristan fell in behind him. Better to remain behind thine enemy to keep a close eye on him. Definitely *not* because Tristan wanted to observe with impunity the way Michael's sinewy leg muscles bulged and retracted as he walked.

In the Visitors' Centre, they picked up a map, bought extra water to stash in their backpacks, and headed out into the wide open terrain of the Mojave Desert. Compared with Mexico, it was practically arctic at a steady seventy-five degrees.

Tristan questioned why he had agreed to this jaunt with the bane of his existence. Ennui? Curiosity? Masochism? Unfortunately, it was either this or spend all day with *The Golden Girls* slot machine. For a city that apparently had so much going on, Tristan found Las Vegas desperately dull and boring—especially without company. Being stuck in that hotel in the dry air was a far cry from the healthy, invigorating life he led in Mexico City. Sunshine. Exercise. Working with the kids at Sin Pecados. Learning *español*.

But the heat, he could do without. When Stella told him she was heading to Vegas for a week in March, he'd decided to tag along, partially to catch a break from the soaring Mexican temperatures. He'd wanted to bathe his naked body in air conditioning, but he'd also wanted to catch up with Stella. Finally ready to talk, he had so much to tell her.

Michael's presence had been an unexpected surprise. Not a good one.

'Shall we do the Calico Tanks trail?' asked the devil himself, studying the map. 'The trailhead is 5k or so away, but the trail itself is only a few kilometres round trip.'

'Whatever,' snapped Tristan like an obstinate teen. Anger was better than any other emotion right now. Anger was safe. He understood anger.

Vexingly, Michael smiled at Tristan like he could see through his facade, packed away the map, and they set off. Tristan followed after, carefully choosing his steps on the stony path. As they climbed over a pile of rocks, Tristan came face-to-arse with Michael's toned buttocks.

Nope. Not going there, he thought, tearing his gaze away. He tucked his thumbs defiantly under the straps of his backpack.

To distract himself from thoughts of Michael's tight arse, Tristan forced his mind back to Mexico.

Aside from the heat, he loved living there. The people, the architecture, the joyful attitude towards life, the fresh street food—especially tamales. Mmm. His mouth watered just thinking about the *masa* filled with chicken and cheese, wrapped in a banana leaf.

The Tamale Man was like Batman: you never knew when he was going to turn up. Sometimes Mondays. Sometimes Thursdays. Some weeks, never. As dusk fell and the edge of the intense Mexican heat softened, Tristan would listen for the Tamale Man's calling card: a nasal recording of a male voice singing *'Ya lle-gar-on sus ric-os-ta-ma-les Oaxa-queños!'* Like Pavlov's dog, Tristan would jog down the apartment building's stairs and chase the bicycle cart until he stopped. He could practically feel the juices dripping down his chin now. He wished he had some tamales in his backpack full of snacks; Michael would love them.

No! he reminded himself. *Michael is the arsehole who dumped you, remember?*

Yeah. No tamales for Michael.

A pot of anger boiled in his belly, as it often did when he thought about what could have been. How his life might be different if they'd stayed together.

Then again, if that version of reality had happened, Tristan would never have stumbled away from his barren existence and found some meaning in Mexico.

A pair of hikers passed them, going the other way. Michael picked up the pace, like he had a meeting scheduled at the end of the trail. Tristan would have preferred slowing it down. Not because he couldn't keep up—with Michael just scratching six foot and Tristan hitting 6'5", their strides were long and well-matched. No, it was because one thing that Mexico had taught him was the value in taking things slow. Enjoying the journey. But there was no way

Tristan would say anything. He wouldn't give Michael the satisfaction of thinking Tristan couldn't hack the pace.

The trail tracked up and down, over large sandy rocks, pebbles rolling under their feet. Overhead, clouds dotted the blue sky, and a whisper of breeze brushed their skin. The only sound was their heavy breathing, a rolling rock, or the occasional ragged cry of a bird. Tristan kept his eyes open for rattlesnakes and other creepy crawlies. The last thing he needed was a tango with the native wildlife.

They covered the distance to the trailhead in under an hour.

'Water break?' called out Michael, the first words either of them had said since setting off.

They unslung their packs and dug out their water bottles. While he had his pack open, Tristan removed his t-shirt. The fabric was unpleasantly clingy against his skin. It wasn't at all because he wanted to show off his own toned physique. He slid the shirt over his head, scrunched it up, and shoved it into the backpack.

'Wow,' said Michael, choking on his water. 'When did you get *that?*'

Ah, Tristan had 'forgotten' about the massive phoenix tattooed across his back. 'I started it eight months ago,' he said. The whole thing had taken twelve visits to the tattoo artist and hours of work. And a lot of pain. In his old life as a model, he never would have considered marking himself with something so big.

But then he'd had a dream when he arrived in central America. It involved a phoenix, flying over Mexico City like that kid in *The Snowman*, and running around in some ancient Aztec city. It had been a real trip.

Tristan wasn't usually the sort to believe in the symbolism of dreams, but when he woke up, he understood the message: he should forgive himself. Renew himself.

And get a big, sexy tattoo of a fucking phoenix.

'I like it,' said Michael, that annoying, ever present smile on his face.

'I'm so pleased. Your approval is important to me,' deadpanned Tristan, eyes flat. But inside, he smiled.

They packed up their bags and set off on the Calico Tanks trail.

This trek was harder, but more beautiful than the earlier one. The rocks shifted from grey limestone to red sandstone, their mounds plopped onto the landscape like layered confections. The climbing was more rigorous, too. Tristan spent a lot of time looking at Michael's arse. Hard times.

Tristan had no idea how Michael was navigating. There were no markers that he could see and sometimes they had to double-back and take a different fork. At one point, Michael pulled out his map, straddling a large rock as he consulted it, the sun silhouetting his body and making him look like some sort of sexy grown-up Boy Scout. Tristan shook his head and shifted his gaze to a scraggy bush nearby.

Eventually, they came to a watering hole full of tiny brown tadpole-like creatures.

'This is technically the end of the trail,' said Michael, holding the map as he wiped his brow. His blond hair curled at the tips with sweat. 'But I think there's an amazing viewpoint a little further on. Shall we?'

Tristan shrugged, feeling petulant. 'Fine,' he said flatly, even though he really wanted to go. He caught Michael rolling his eyes. Tristan didn't know why he couldn't simply be nice to his ex. He knew Michael was a generous, kind, funny man who made the world a better place simply by being in it.

Then he remembered: *It's because Michael broke your fucking heart.* Bastard.

After climbing up another steep track, they emerged into an open space on top of the rocks. Tristan could see Las Vegas in the far distance. Other hikers were scattered over the smooth ledges, eating lunch and admiring the view.

'Shall we climb up there?' asked Michael, pointing towards a formation that was slightly away from the crowd. 'I wouldn't mind a sit down and some food.'

As if on cue, Tristan's stomach growled loudly, and he saw Michael's eyes dip down. His gaze lingered a moment too long before he turned swiftly in the direction of their lunch spot.

Tristan couldn't resist the miniature, smug smile that tickled his mouth. So Michael wasn't *completely* immune to him. Served him right. He hoped Michael's dreams were plagued by memories of his washboard abs and everything below them.

Together, they scrambled up the lumpy beige rocks and ascended onto their private ledge, leaving the other hikers below. At the top, chests heaving with exertion, they surveyed the scene. Tristan took off his baseball cap and fanned himself with it.

'Wow,' said Michael.

Wow was right. They could see for miles, the arid, brown hills in the distance disappearing into a warm haze. Tristan shivered as an echo of his dream with the phoenix resonated through him—a strange sense of déjà vu, even though he was sure he'd never been here before.

Michael collapsed cross-legged onto the heated rock and Tristan considered sitting further along the ledge, away from him. But then Michael pulled out a packet of Chips Ahoy! and said, 'Cookie?'

'Thanks.' Tristan folded his legs and sat next to his nemesis.

They chewed in silence for a minute, appreciating the view. Tristan missed silence. He loved many things about Mexico City, but it was a noisy place. The Tamale Man was only one of many vendors that sang out their presence. Restaurants, bars, and taxis constantly played music. Mariachi bands roamed in search of couples to serenade. Even the bin men rang a loud bell every morning to let people know to bring out their rubbish—more effective than any alarm clock.

Out of the corner of his eye, Tristan noticed that Michael was completely still for once. No body parts tapping. Almost peaceful.

A bird cawed as it flew past them.

Inside Tristan's belly, a funny feeling bubbled up. He tried to ignore it, but it tasted annoyingly like curiosity. He wanted to know what Michael had been up to lately. Why did Connor say he'd been stressed? But there was a fine line between curiosity and caring, and Tristan definitely didn't want to care. He helped himself to another cookie.

'This is the perfect temperature,' Michael said, lifting his face to the sky.

Tristan huffed. 'You'd burn to a crisp in Mexico City.'

'So,' said Michael, wiping a crumb from the corner of his lips. 'Why Mexico City?'

'Because.' Tristan leaned back on his hands and glanced away, towards the shimmering puddle of buildings that was Las Vegas. He didn't really want to delve into his reasons for ditching his life, so he changed the topic. 'You're in New York now?'

'Been there for a couple of years.' Michael reached into his bag and pulled out a sandwich.

Tristan did the same. Tuna salad on white bread. He wouldn't normally eat white bread, but there hadn't been much choice in the shop. 'Enjoying it?' Tristan asked.

Michael stretched his feet in front of him and jiggled his toes like he couldn't help it. Back in motion again. '*Enjoy* is a strong word.'

'Explain.' Curiosity was winning.

With a sigh, Michael bit into his sandwich, chewed, and swallowed before answering. 'Do you ever feel like your life doesn't matter?'

Whoa, this had turned deep, fast. And yes, Tristan knew exactly what that felt like. 'Surely that doesn't apply to you? With your job?'

'You'd be surprised. Sometimes I feel, when I win a case, that I'm just putting plasters on issues. A temporary fix until the next wave of lunatics comes into power and undoes all the good. Did you see in the news... they're trying to overturn a ban on female genital mutilation in The Gambia?'

Tristan flinched. What a disgusting, barbaric practice. 'That's why I don't read the news.'

Michael's toes stopped jiggling. 'You don't read the news? *Ever*? How do you find out what's going on in the world?'

'I don't.'

'Do you care?'

This sounded more like the villainous Michael he had created in his head. Judgmental. Thinking Tristan was too superficial to live. 'Of course I care,' said Tristan. 'I'm not a machine. But for my own mental health, I can't. It's too bloody depressing, darling.' He took a fierce bite of his sandwich.

'Hmmm,' said Michael.

'What does that mean?'

'Nothing.' Michael paused. 'Or I guess it means that we, as an oppressed minority, need to be constantly vigilant. We can never take for granted that the rights we have are permanent. I couldn't live without knowing what was going on.'

Tristan pushed his lips out into a disbelieving moue. He wasn't buying what Michael was selling. He'd noticed the dark circles under Michael's eyes. 'Fair enough. It's your job. But does it make you *happy*?'

'What? Reading the news?'

Tristan tossed out his arm, indicating the entire planet in a sweep of his hand. 'Knowing everything that's going on in this mad, fucked up world, all the time.'

Michael was quiet as he chewed on that—and his sandwich. 'Hmph.'

'See? Maybe your problem is *too much* news.'

Tristan remembered a conversation they'd had a few months into their relationship. They were in bed on a lazy Sunday morning, rays of sun slicing through the window, dust motes dancing in the strong, hot light. They were talking about their childhoods, and the discussion had turned to the day Michael realised how his mother had died.

As he told it, Michael had been seven, and it was his birthday. Except it wasn't. Every year they celebrated his half-birthday, and he didn't understand why. At this point, they were living in Istanbul, if Tristan recalled correctly. Michael decided to ask his nanny, 'Why don't we celebrate my birthday on the real day, like the other kids?'

Cementing her nomination for Nanny of the Year, she replied, 'Because your mother died bringing you into this world! Your real birthday? Nobody wants to celebrate that.'

Michael had always known that his mother wasn't around. But he'd never known it was because of him.

From that day, he'd started having panic attacks.

He explained to Tristan that, growing up with this knowledge, he developed a belief that he had to live a life that mattered to make up for the one he'd taken. He wanted to make her proud.

Tristan remembered Michael telling him this story very clearly. He remembered holding him afterwards, wishing that he could take the pain away. It was also when Tristan began to suspect that his own feelings for Michael went deeper than a great fuck.

He shoved the memory aside. It was a long time ago.

Michael nudged him with his elbow, playful. He smiled and Tristan's traitorous heart beat faster. 'So... too much news. Is that the official diagnosis, doctor?'

A shiver ran down Tristan's spine. He knew Michael had meant it as an olive branch, but the words struck a little too close to home. The corner of Tristan's mouth turned down.

Stretching, he laid back on the rock, cushioning his head on his hands. Realising this wasn't comfortable, he shoved his backpack under his head. Michael followed suit next to him. The sun warmed their skin as it came out from behind a cloud. A breeze feathered across Tristan's bare chest, making his nipples harden like pebbles.

If Tristan were honest with himself, he'd admit that he was enjoying this time with Michael. They always had interesting conversations and laughed often. As a celebrity, Tristan found it difficult to be himself with people, but with Michael, that had never been a problem. He missed this. No one he'd dated since had come close to what he'd felt for Michael Knight. The years had done nothing to dull the disappointment and regret at what could have been.

Shame walloped him out of nowhere, hitting him square in the chest and making his breath catch. Things had changed since they dated seven years ago. Tristan had changed. He squeezed his eyes shut, glad that they were hidden by his dark sunglasses.

Next to him, Michael shifted. A knee brushed against Tristan's leg and disappeared. An accident, he was sure, but the spot where their skin had touched burned from the contact. His much-neglected dick stirred with interest. *Down, boy.*

It had been over a year since he'd touched another man sexually.

The knee returned, gently resting on the rock, the hairs just tickling Tristan's leg.

Inside, he groaned in pain. He didn't want to have this conversation with Michael. Not many people knew his secret. Not even Stella. Only Pablo, his friend at Sin Pecados, knew, because they were in the same boat. Tristan had always been afraid to tell anybody else, nervous it would leak to the press. If this story ever came out, he wanted it to be because *he* made it known.

But maybe it was time to tell *someone*. A person who was generous and kind who made the world a better place simply by being in it.

Despite their history as lovers, he knew he could trust Michael. Not with his heart, of course, but with this. Gay man's code of ethics or something.

The pressure of Michael's knee against his leg shifted slightly. And Tristan knew he needed to say something.

Taking a deep breath, the words rushed out of him before he could change his mind: 'Michael, I have HIV.'

18

STELLA

IN THE TRADE SHOW, STELLA STARED BLANKLY AT THE CROWD OF photographers surrounding her, waiting for her to impart some knowledge, but all she could think was: *I've never loved another woman like I love you.*

She replayed the words Connor said last night—right before he promised never to lie to her.

And then he'd lied straight to her face.

Her skin felt too small for her body. She wanted to burst. Extreme emotions centrifuged through her on rotation: rage, hurt, sadness, anxiety, confusion, and then back to rage again. Mostly rage.

Last night after they'd made love the first time, she asked him point blank about the woman in the bar, and he'd brushed it off like she was nobody. If there had ever been a time to tell Stella about Royale, that was it. She couldn't have crafted a more perfect moment if she'd hung up streamers and a banner that said: *Tell me about your ex-wife now!*

On the other side of the spectrum, Royale had been more than happy to talk about it. 'We were married for a whole, blissful year,' she'd said, her eyes brimming with fond memory.

Twelve months? That wasn't 'nothing'.

'We lived together in LA… near Venice Beach,' Royale had added.

Venice Beach was where Connor said he worked out. He'd mentioned *that* part. But it obviously slipped his mind that he'd had a *wife*, too.

Connor left out half the story—a story Royale seemed keen to tell. Before she could reveal any more, though, Stella had made her excuses and left as Blake was returning from his call.

Somebody in the audience coughed, and Stella snapped out of her deliberations. She was on the trade room floor in the middle of giving a live lighting demonstration. She tried to recall what she'd been saying. Like that nightmare where you're naked in front of an audience and you haven't learned your lines, Stella blinked at the crowd surrounding the stage, cheeks blazing.

The model gawped at her, waiting for instructions. Finally, a helpful voice called out, 'You were talking about feathering the light!'

'Right! Yes, sorry about that. I suddenly thought I'd left the iron on.' The crowd laughed politely at her lame joke, even as mortification made her want to disappear. 'So, if you angle the soft box away from the subject like this…'

How dare Connor hide this from her.

How dare he make her think that they were going to be a family again.

She blinked away the tears.

Somehow, she struggled through the rest of the demo. She still had a masterclass and a panel discussion on women in photography to chair.

After she finished, the usual gang of people vied for her attention, asking questions about her camera settings and requesting selfies with her. She smiled like she'd attended the Brit School of Acting.

When she finally managed to escape, she headed straight for the toilets: the closest place where she could be alone. Thankfully, there were plenty of stalls, and she managed to lock herself into one without having to queue. A shiny metallic cubicle of solitude.

She huddled on the toilet and cried.

Around her, she could hear flushing, the rush of water, and the roar of the hand dryer. She tried to hide her sobs, burying her face in toilet paper. The scratchy texture rapidly turned moist with tears and snot against her skin.

Her heart was breaking. The pain of it scissored through her chest.

How could he do this to her?

What she needed was Grace. Nothing would soothe her pain like her daughter's sweet voice. She rummaged through her handbag for her phone, desperate to rewatch the videos that her parents had sent through that morning, wishing there wasn't an eight-hour time difference between Las Vegas and London. She imagined Grace at home, tucked up in bed under the unicorn-themed duvet, her red hair fanned out on the pillow. Stella wished she were there. She needed a *cwtch* (pronounced *kutch*). It was the Welsh word for *cuddle*, but it was so much more than that. It was warmth and comfort and contentment and safety.

She found her phone, and the first thing she saw was a message from Connor:

How was the meeting? Call me. Love you. Cx

She snorted.

Love you, but not enough to be honest with you.

She felt like she didn't know him at all. What else had he kept from her? She recalled the previous occasion she'd caught him in a lie. Valentina Vavilek. He had gone to great lengths to hide his meeting with the model, knowing that Stella had told him point blank not to work with that woman anymore. He would have gotten away with it, too, if Grace hadn't taken a tumble that landed her in hospital. The incident happened five years ago. She thought they'd moved past lying, but here they were again. Had there been more instances that she never discovered?

Last night, she had allowed hope that he had changed to cloud her judgment. Today, she knew with certainty that he had not changed at all.

Their marriage was over.

Tears welled again. How could he do this to her? To their family?

With shaking hands, she shoved her headphones into her ears, keen to block out the noise around her, even though most of it was inside her own head.

Then she opened WhatsApp and played all the films of Grace one by one.

FORTY MINUTES LATER, Stella was still hiding in the toilets.

She had packed her phone away some time ago. Now, she sat in a semi-stupor with her temple pressed to the cold metal of the cubicle wall, staring into space and regulating her breathing. She would need to motivate herself to leave her refuge soon; her next master-class started in twenty-five minutes, and her face must look like a Jackson Pollock painting.

Stella was at a crossroads. She had a choice to make.

The divorce wasn't the choice. In her mind, that was a done deal. She couldn't stay with a man she didn't trust. She'd been there, done that. She wasn't a young girl in her twenties anymore. She was 38. She had responsibilities, not only to her daughter, but also to herself.

She deserved better.

She deserved what Blake was offering her.

But could she really move to LA on her own with Grace? Stella had no friends there. Except Royale—*ha!* She snorted bitterly. There were numerous issues that scared her about America: the guns, the healthcare system, the political upheaval. But there was also oppor-tunity. Los Angeles was a vibrant city with great weather, close to breathtaking national parks and the beach. She imagined Grace becoming a surfer girl. Her parents could come out to visit for months at a time, if they wanted. She'd rent a place with ample guest rooms. Connor was always travelling with work anyway. What did it matter if he played dad in London or LA?

And it didn't have to be permanent. Maybe just five years. Her exit strategy could involve moving back to the UK eventually.

She needed to talk to somebody about this, to help her sort out her head. And she needed to do it sooner rather than later. She checked her watch. Three o'clock. That meant it was eleven in the UK. Claudia would probably be up. Stella fished her phone out of her bag again and fired off a quick text:

> You awake?

She stared at the screen, willing three dots to appear. Eventually, they did, followed by:

> Trying to read in bed, but Magnus is snoring like a ducking chainsaw. What's up?

> Argh! Fucking autocorrect.

Stella cracked a tiny smile, surprised Claudia's phone didn't have every swear word hard-coded. She could picture the exact scene of married life from Claudia's text: she, in stylish silk pyjamas, glasses perched on her nose, book on her lap. Magnus probably wearing something paisley, passed out next to her, an eye mask covering half his face. It still surprised Stella that, out of the two of them, it had been Claudia—the wild child— who achieved true marital bliss. Stella typed out her next question:

> Should I move to LA?

> Fuck no. You'd miss me too much. Why?

> I've had a huge offer. Bigger than MuseTV. But I have to move here for it.

> Okay, that's exciting. What does Connor say?

At the mention of Connor, Stella's heart squeezed with pain. Tears leaked down her face again. She soaked them up with toilet paper.

> Stels? You still there?

> Sorry. Things not going well. Also he's against it.

> Fuck him. In LA you can have Nicholas Galitzine as your toy boy.

> So I should do it?

> Stels. I love you, but you need to woman up. Do what's right for you. Even if I'll miss the ducking shit out of you. Bright side: gives me an excuse to get away from this mad house and visit :o)

She was right. Stella tended to people please, to put everyone else's needs and desires before her own, from Connor to Grace to her clients to the photographers who emailed her with constant questions. But she couldn't ignore that this move would affect people she loved.

> What about Grace? My parents?

> They'll adapt. You only get one life. OMG I can see Grace as a surfer babe!

Stella buried a laugh in her hand, amused that Claudia had the same thought as her.

> Okay, I have to go. Thanks for the chat. X

> Take care, babes. Give Nicholas my love and tell him I'm available for threesomes. X

A toilet flushed. The water tap flowed. The hand dryer whooshed. Stella inhaled and exhaled deeply while she re-read the conversation, then quietly dropped her phone into her bag, ran her fingers over her braided hair, and left the cubicle. At the faux-marble bank of sinks, she washed her hands, shaking them to remove the excess water. A thirty-something brunette woman that Stella vaguely recognised appeared at the basin next to her, and their eyes met in the mirror.

'Loved your photowalk yesterday,' the woman said and smiled.

'Thank you,' said Stella.

The woman hesitated before adding, 'I hope you don't mind me saying this, but... the things I've learned from you have really helped me in my business.'

'Oh, thank you. I'm so glad.' Stella pasted a smile on her face, finding it hard to engage in conversation when her body was struggling to hold her heart together.

'You see, my husband and I divorced two years ago.' She pointed to herself. 'Single mom!'

Stella dug her fingers into her palm, the words hitting a nerve. She didn't want to cry in front of this stranger. 'I'm sorry to hear that.'

The woman flapped her hand. 'No, it's fine. He was a jackass. But suddenly, I had to earn enough money to support my son and me. I never went to college, you see. I'd only ever waitressed, or worked at the drug store, or—believe it or not—worked as a debt collection officer. But I've always loved photography. Dabbled in it, you know? Taking pictures of family and friends. Not charging a lot. Then my friend sent me a link to your blog... and... well, I learned so much. I mean, I'd never run a business before, but I did what you told me to…and started believing in my own self-worth. And I went from making $100 dollars a shoot to $2000. I bought us a house… and a car!'

Tears pooled in Stella's eyes—another battle she was going to lose.

'So, I guess what I wanted to say,' the woman continued, 'is thank you. From the bottom of my heart. You changed my life.'

Stella pursed her lips and shook her head as moisture rolled down her face. She couldn't even speak.

'Can I give you a hug?' said the woman. Stella nodded.

The woman's arms wrapped around her, and Stella hugged her back, a sob escaping. The woman patted Stella's back and made shushing noises. Stella didn't mean to cry, but the woman's story and her kindness unlocked something inside of her.

The work she did was important. It wasn't only about teaching people to take pretty pictures. It was about all the women who needed independence. To make their own money. To be in control of their own lives.

Her sobs subsided and the woman stepped back. 'You okay?'

'I'm good. Sorry, I didn't mean—'

'Hey, we all have our problems. Even you. Just remember that you are amazing. You're Stella Knight!'

After the woman left, Stella leaned her hands on the counter and met her own steady, green gaze in the mirror. Her mouth was set into a firm line. Her red braid hung over her shoulder, battle ready like an Amazon warrior.

How much could happen in 24 hours? Yesterday seemed so long ago. Yesterday, she'd hoped for reconciliation with her husband. Yesterday, she made love to Connor for the first time in ages. Yesterday, she decided not to move to Los Angeles.

But this was today.

'You can do this, Price,' she said out loud, reverting to her maiden name. In her eyes, she saw determination. She saw strength. She saw capability. And she saw a decision made.

Blake said he'd changed. Well, she was going to follow her instinct and give him the benefit of the doubt. After all, there were always two sides to every story, weren't there? At least he'd been honest with her when she asked him about it, while Connor was the one caught in a lie. Again.

Reaching into her bag, she pulled out her phone for the third time since entering the toilets. She opened WhatsApp and started a new message to Blake. Her fingers were steady as she typed the words that would change her life, and her daughter's, forever:

The deal is on. We're moving to LA.

19

CONNOR

AT A TABLE IN A DARK CORNER OF THE BAR, WHERE NO ONE COULD SEE his screen, Connor retouched Stella's images. Twenty shots in total. He'd already been at it for two hours, taking his time. His hand ached from the work because he didn't have his Wacom tablet with him, but he wanted to do a meticulous job.

His retouching playlist pumped through his headphones. The original 'I Will Always Love You' by Dolly Parton came on, and the corner of his mouth shot up. Dolly Parton always made him think of Stella and how he'd dressed as the famous country singer to declare his love all those years ago.

He remembered the first time he realised he was desperately in love with Stella. They'd spent three days holed up in his flat, making love and exploring each other, mentally and physically. He'd shot a series of nude photos of her.

Later, for their first anniversary—the paper year—he'd bound those images into a book as a gift for her, combined with some she'd taken of him on another occasion. He called the book *Knight by Knight*. The cover was black linen, the title embossed in gold. There was only one copy in existence, and it lived in their bedroom at their house in London. He hoped her parents didn't find it while they were there. The thought of Stella's mother's face if she saw the mostly nude photos of them both made him shiver with mortification. She'd probably have it exorcised.

Anyway, his three-day tryst with Stella went sideways for a number of reasons. He couldn't recall them all, but the main one was that one of his other students from the chateau caught them shacking up together, and Stella had worried that he was going to tell everyone. She had a mortal fear of being the subject of gossip, thanks to her experiences with her ex-lover/old boss.

She'd returned to Wales to see her parents. As soon as she left, he felt strange. Like a part of him was missing. In the short time she'd been in his flat, she'd stamped her presence everywhere: the billiard table, the bath, his bed… especially his bed. It smelled like her. When his cleaner tried to change the sheets the next day, he'd asked her to leave them.

What did he love about Stella? Her determination, her humour, her talent, her kindness—and he'd be remiss if he didn't mention that she was also sexy as fuck. Her body drove him wild. But her other attributes outweighed the physical. After she'd left his flat, his heart ached to connect with her again.

He'd never felt like that before. After his mother passed, he'd been raised to be self-reliant. Needing somebody else was a foreign emotion. It took him a while to come to the obvious conclusion—which he eventually did, with a bit of help. He'd called Michael to talk about it, and Michael summed the situation up with, 'It sounds to me like you love her, you fucking idiot.'

From the moment Connor accepted that fact, he became hyper-focused on convincing her, thus dressing in drag as Dolly Parton and serenading her at her best friend's engagement party. As you do. Thankfully, Claudia and Magnus were on board with the plan.

Now, having finally smoothed things over with her, everything felt right again. The world was back on its axis.

He hummed along to Dolly as he saved and closed the image he was working on. Only a few left.

Connor's screen lit up with an incoming call from Angela Price, his mother-in-law. He quickly calculated the time in London. Ten o'clock. Was something wrong? Why was she calling so late?

With a sinking feeling, he hit the green button.

The video sprang to life on his computer. Angela was sitting in Connor's kitchen with Grace on her lap in her Peppa Pig pyjamas. His heart grew three sizes, as it always did when he saw his daughter.

'Hi, daddy!' she said.

He smiled like the besotted father he was. God, he missed her. 'Hi, Gigi. It's pretty late. Why aren't you in bed?'

Angela cut in. 'She said she would not sleep until she'd spoken with you. Something about a game you play before bedtime?'

Ah, the Three Things Game. Whenever he put Grace to bed, they'd recount three things from that day which made them happy. He'd read an article about how the practice promoted positive thinking and developed gratitude while encouraging reflection. And he found it was an easy way to get her to talk about her day. 'Okay, hit me with number one,' he said, with an indulgent grin.

'A lemur pooped on Nonno! At the zoo!' Grace giggled gleefully, covering her mouth with her perfect little hands.

'What?!' said Connor with exaggerated shock.

'This is true,' said Angela. 'We visited the lemur enclosure after school, and Nonno stood in an unfortunate spot.'

'It had dairy!' said Grace.

'Diarrhoea,' corrected Angela with a disgusted grimace.

Connor laughed, picturing it clearly along with Bill's reaction. Grace was obviously experiencing the joy of schadenfreude. 'Okay, that's one. Next?' he prompted her.

'Um…. my teacher gave me five house points for my reading.'

'Oh, well done! High five,' he said, holding his hand up to the computer's camera. She tapped her hand on her Nonna's phone.

'We have been doing the reading with her every night,' said Angela, as though reassuring Connor that they weren't slacking.

'Great. Thank you. We really appreciate your help, Angela,' he said. Her hand fluttered to her chest. *My pleasure*, the movement said. *All in a day's work.*

'And three,' said Grace, 'is getting to talk to you, daddy. When are you coming home?' Her voice turned sad.

How did kids know exactly how to skewer their parents with emotional swords? The question felt like a punch to his chest. 'Not for another week, Gigi. But we'll make sure to call you lots.' He missed his daughter, but nothing would make him give up the five days alone with Stella. They needed the time to reconnect before resuming their roles as parents.

'Okay, it's your turn!' Grace said, leaning forward and propping her head on her hands.

There was only one thing on his list, but he couldn't say 'I had sex with your mum'. The excitement and relief from knowing that he would soon be moving home filled him with giddy joy—a Gene Kelly tap-dancing 'Singin' in the Rain' type of euphoria. They could all put this period of their lives behind them and move forward, together.

Grace gazed at him expectantly, so he counted some alternatives off on his fingers: 'One. Uncle Michael and Grandad Armstrong are here, which was a nice surprise. Two. I ate a huge stack of blueberry pancakes—bigger than your head! And three. I've spent some quality time with your mummy.'

Angela raised an eyebrow at him. He widened his eyes at her. She nodded with approval. A whole conversation in gestures. 'All right, *cara*. It's time for bed now. You have school tomorrow,' she said.

'I'll call you again this weekend,' promised Connor.

'Love you, daddy.'

'Love you, too, Gigi.' He blew quick-fire kisses at her using his hands.

The call window disappeared. He sat back in his chair and replayed the mental video of Bill getting shat on by lemurs.

He glanced up to find the women at the next table watching him with enchanted smiles, like they'd never seem a dad turn soppy over his daughter before. He acknowledged them with a self-conscious nod and returned his attention to Stella's retouching.

A loud bark of laughter punched through the noise-cancelling setting on his headphones. He shifted his attention towards the bar, where a group of photographers were hanging out. He knew them all. Members of the old guard. Seasoned pros who had been coming to this convention as long as he had, if not longer. Damian was there.

And Blake Romero was with them.

Connor shifted in his chair. He stared as Romero passed around glasses of champagne.

What does that wanker have to celebrate? wondered Connor. He checked his phone for a message from Stella. Nothing yet, although she had seen his message earlier. He'd been so caught up in the retouching that he hadn't realised how much time had passed. Stella should have replied by now. He knew she had a class to teach right after her lunch with Romero, but still, she could have dropped Connor a quick line to let him know the deed was done.

He trusted her. He knew she would do what was right for their family.

So why was his heart beating like a gambler who'd just bet his entire fortune on red?

Romero clinked glasses with a wildlife photographer from Colorado. Connor slid his AirPods out of his ears and tried to listen in on their conversation. From fifteen metres away and with the bar's ambient chatter, it was nigh on impossible. The wildlife photographer laughed at something Romero said. Connor's lips curled down.

He must have stared a hole into Romero's back because the wanker squinted his eyes into the corner where Connor sat—and smiled. A slow deliberate smile that Connor did not like at all.

Shit. He shut his laptop. With a flute in each hand, Romero propelled himself off his stool and sauntered towards Connor.

His stomach clenched into a hard ball.

'Knight,' said Romero.

'Romero,' said Connor with obvious distaste.

Blake held out a glass of fizzing champagne. 'Peace offering?' he said.

Connor ignored it, narrowing his eyes. 'What's the occasion? Find someone else to fuck over, have you?' He didn't want to get into a fight in front of everyone, but Romero had it coming with what he'd tried to pull with Stella.

A look of confusion passed over Blake's face. 'You know what I'm celebrating.'

'I do?' A sour taste filled his mouth.

Blake put Connor's glass on the table and sipped his own. 'And I have to say thank you. I know it couldn't have been easy for you, with our past, to see this as a humongous opportunity for Stella. But she's a talented woman, and I think—'

'What the fuck are you talking about?' Connor shot to his feet, hitting the table. The flute of champagne fell onto the floor, dousing Blake's shoes.

He stepped away. Glancing at the spill then back up at Connor, Blake said, 'Our new venture in LA?'

'What fucking new venture? Stella told you she was out.'

'Hmmm. No, she didn't,' he said in an annoyingly confident voice.

Connor couldn't believe what he was hearing. Without thinking, he seized the lapels of Romero's expensive Italian-made blue suit. More champagne splashed onto Romero's shoes from his own glass. The chatter near the bar subsided.

'What did you say to her, you twat?'

'Put me down,' Blake commanded. Their eyes locked, a vein throbbing in Blake's temple. Reluctantly, Connor did as requested. He didn't want Stella to hear that he'd been fighting in the bar.

Blake set his champagne flute on the table and fixed the line of his suit. 'I didn't say anything to her. In fact, she said it was all off.'

Relief flooded through Connor.

'But then I received a text from her half an hour ago.'

Connor's spine stiffened. He swallowed hard. 'What text?'

Reaching into his suit pocket, Blake pulled out his phone. For Connor, time slowed as he tracked Romero's movements: the flick of his finger as he scrolled, the subtle noise of triumph when he found what he sought.

He turned his phone towards Connor, who snatched it. He saw his wife's name at the top of the chat. He read her words:

The deal is on. We're moving to LA.

Blake had responded:

Are you sure?

Yes. 100%.

Connor read the texts again and again, shocked by the proof before him. His fingers tightened around the phone. Blake tugged it out of his grip and returned it to his pocket. 'I wasn't lying.'

Static roared through Connor's head. What was going on? Last night, they'd been confessing their undying love to each other, and today, she was making huge decisions without him. It was as if last night never happened. It didn't compute. Something was wrong.

'Well, I'm telling you the deal is off,' said Connor, shoving his laptop into his bag and zipping it up. 'There's no way in hell she's working with you.'

Blake picked up his glass of champagne. 'If there's one thing I've learned about your wife in the short time I've known her, it's that she is a very determined and ambitious lady. I could make her a star.'

'She doesn't need you to do that. She has me.'

Tilting his head to the side, Blake said, 'But do *you* have *her*? I'm starting to think not.'

The urge to punch Romero in the face surged through him, pushing all other thought out of the way. His fists clenched. But then he sucked in a deep breath, pictured his wife and daughter, and imagined explaining to them how he'd beat up this waste of space and couldn't come home because he was in jail.

Not worth it. He unclenched his fist.

Taking it out on his satchel, Connor snatched it up and slung it across his body. 'Fuck off, Romero.'

As he stalked away, he heard Blake say, 'Nice to catch up with you too, asshole.'

He ignored the members of the old guard staring as he left the bar. He had to find Stella. Whatever had happened, he needed to fix it. After the story he'd told her last night, how could she even entertain the idea of working with Romero? There was no way they were going to uproot their family and relocate to California on the promise of that lying toe rag. Connor wouldn't allow it. She couldn't make that decision to rip their daughter away from her home. Not without at least talking to him.

Stella was teaching at the moment. He knew that for a fact. Connor opened the IPE app on his phone and searched the list of masterclasses to find out where. Studying the map, he charted a course to her classroom, even though the cacophony of his thoughts made it hard to concentrate. His thoughts kept shooting off in different directions, wily as snakes, trying to figure out what had changed. Memorising the route, he set off. The electronic choir of the gambling machines followed him as he raced across the casino floor. On the other side, he ran past the trade show doors, down the escalators, and into the educational zone. A security guard held up his hand when Connor tried to move past him.

'Pass?' said the guard.

Bugger. He'd only bought a trade show pass, not the full ticket. He didn't think he'd need it. 'I don't have one. I need to see my wife. She's talking in A5.' He stepped forward and an arm shot out in front of him.

'No pass. No entry,' said the tall, muscular man. Connor could square up to most men, but this guy looked like an ex-wrestler.

Connor grunted with exasperation. He reached for his wallet. 'How much is the pass? I'll pay for it right now.' He pulled out a wad of American dollars.

'I'm afraid I don't sell passes, sir.' The *sir* part rankled Connor. 'You'll have to do it online.'

'I don't have time—' he began.

'It's okay, Ralph,' said an authoritative voice. Connor looked past the guard and saw a woman with bobbed, dark hair and a big smile. It was Therese Asplund, the convention director. He'd known her for years. Originally from Sweden, she'd moved to the US after falling in love with a cowboy while on holiday at a dude ranch. He'd always had a lot of time for her. She ran a tight ship. 'Hello, Connor. Great to see you again.'

'Thanks, Therese,' he said. He didn't want to be rude, but he was also in a hurry. 'Do you know—?'

'Stella is in the room at the end of the hall on the right.' Connor set off. 'See you at the awards ceremony on Thursday?' she called after him.

He spun around whilst jogging away and said, 'Yep. See you there.' It was the last thing on his mind.

Stopping outside the door to room A5, he heard Stella's muffled voice carrying through the wood. The class laughed at something she said. He closed his eyes to steady his thoughts and calm down. As much as he'd love to run in there and insist that she speak with him right away, she'd be mortified if he caused a ruckus. Best to wait. He inched the door open and slipped inside. Thankfully, the lights were dimmed at the back.

The long room was packed with delegates—Connor estimated three hundred people. Similar to the rest of the convention centre, the decor came straight from the 70s: brown carpets patterned with beige circles, magnolia walls with white decorative moulding, and six crystal chandeliers hanging from the ceiling at even intervals.

Stella faced her model at the front of the room, readjusting the woman's purple tulle dress.

'It's important to make sure that the clothing is falling attractively before you take the picture,' she said. 'Trust me—you don't want to fix ruffles in post-production.'

Everyone chuckled.

To avoid distracting her, Connor hunkered down and extracted the only unoccupied chair from the back row. 'Sorry,' he mouthed as the leg snagged on a woman's bag. He moved the chair against the left wall behind a roller banner advertising AI software, dropped his satchel on the floor, and slid his bottom onto the seat.

Peeking around the banner, he watched his wife. To the others in the room, she looked perfectly composed: she explained her lighting set-up clearly; she gave direct verbal instructions to her model; and she entertained the room with an off-hand quip here and there.

But he could tell that she was flustered. It was the occasional tightening of her forehead, the minor hesitations, the redness on her face. Tucking her hair behind her ear. The way she stroked her chin.

She was a mess.

What had happened between leaving the suite this morning and now?

He settled into his chair and counted the seconds until he could find out.

20

STELLA

Applause echoed around the room.

'Thank you,' said Stella as she surveyed the audience with a wide smile. *Thank god that's over*, she thought. There was only one more engagement to bear before she could lock herself in her room and release the tears currently held at bay by sheer strength of will.

The show must go on. *Tits and teeth*, as she and Tristan used to say.

While the majority of delegates filed out, the usual queue of photographers who wanted a private word with her formed in front of the staging area. She didn't have much time to talk. The panel she was hosting started in thirty minutes, and she needed a short break to review her notes.

Stella thanked the model and promised to send her the images. Turning to the queue, she prepared herself for the onslaught.

'Hi! I didn't catch your camera settings for the shot using the two lights...'

And on it went. Stella tidied away her equipment as she answered as many questions as she could while maintaining a false veneer of calm. All she could think on repeat was:

Why did he lie to me?

Why did he lie to me?

Why did he lie to me?

After five minutes, she drew the Q&A to a close. Her head was throbbing with the exertion of not exploding.

'Sorry, I have to go,' she said, 'but if you still have questions for me, you can find me tomorrow on the AfterShoot stand from 10-11AM.' As the disappointed punters turned to exit the room, she had to do a double-take; Connor was standing at the back of the queue. Her stomach dropped and her jackhammering heart resumed work.

For a long moment, they stared at each other while people filed past him.

What was he doing here? From the thunderous expression on his face, he knew something was up. Seriously, was there a message board somewhere with notices of everybody's secrets? She'd only sent the text two hours ago.

Well, if he wanted a fight, then she was ready to give him one. But a short one. She had a panel to chair.

Clenching her jaw, she broke the tractor beam of his gaze and pretended to check the stage for any forgotten belongings while starting the fight with him in her head to save time.

The last delegate exited through the door, leaving Stella, Connor, and one of the IPE staff wearing the familiar blue shirt emblazoned with the convention logo.

Connor turned to the man and said, 'Can we have the room for a minute please?'

'Uh, sure. But literally only a minute. The next speaker needs to set up,' he said.

'Thanks.' Connor turned back to Stella and waited for the door to close.

Anger flooded her, even as her heart fluttered frantically. His eyes were flinty and hard, his forehead creased. The invisible wall that had separated them for the past six months was back—like last night never happened.

Hugging her bags close, she stepped off the stage and strode purposefully down the aisle. 'I don't have time to talk right now,' she said, her voice shaking. Those tears were a group of lemmings, heading blindly for the cliff. She pushed them back again.

'Too bad.' Stepping left, he positioned himself in her path and shoved his hands obstinately into his jeans pockets.

She dug her thumbs under the straps of her camera backpack and squeezed until her knuckles whitened. 'Connor, I need to go.'

'Not until you tell me what's going on. I ran into Romero, and he took great delight in telling me that we're moving to Los Angeles,' he said, the hurt plain in his eyes.

Her throat thickened with sorrow, but she'd made up her mind. When she said the words, it felt like they were being uttered by someone else. 'No, *we're* not moving to Los Angeles. *I* am moving to Los Angeles. Me and Grace.'

His nostrils flared. 'What do you mean *you and Grace*? I thought we were working things out.'

She swallowed hard before saying, 'That was before I found out you lied to me. *Again.*'

'What?' His handsome features twisted with confusion, and for a split second, she hoped that she'd misunderstood. Maybe Royale made it up. Connor held his hands out in entreaty, but didn't touch her. 'What did I lie about?'

'You honestly have no idea?' Stella crossed her arms.

'None.'

'Okay. In that case, I'm going to ask you a question, and you have one chance to answer it honestly.'

'Fine.' He mirrored her body language and waited.

She pinned him with a steely stare. Slowing down the words deliberately, she asked, 'Were you ever married before me?'

Connor shook his head no, but then a light dawned in his eyes, and his chin dropped to his chest. He winced. 'Betsy.'

It was true. 'You mean *Royale*?'

He made a noise of disgust. 'Whatever she calls herself these days. Stella, we were only married to get me a Green Card. It was Blake's idea. He's the one who introduced us.'

Stella clapped her palms together as though in prayer. She could feel her Italian hands raring to go. 'So let me confirm: you *were* married to her?'

'Yes,' he huffed, 'technically, but it wasn't real. Not like us. We were both seeing other people.'

She narrowed her eyes. He said it as though it was completely reasonable. 'So you weren't *sleeping* together?'

Connor stayed silent for a second too long. 'Well... yes, but she meant nothing to me.'

Unbidden, an image of Connor and Royale clenched together in passion flashed through her head. Jealousy ripped through her, and her hands shot into the air as though their leash had been dropped. Gesticulating, she shouted, 'You were sleeping with her! She was your *wife*. But she meant nothing to you?' Stella snorted. If there was one thing she took away from her conversation with Royale, it was that Connor had meant something to *her*. That's why she went to the trouble of telling Stella all about it.

Connor reached for her, and Stella took a step back. He sighed. 'We both knew the deal. The plan was to stay together for two years and apply for the card. But then Blake pulled his stunt, and I went back to London. We divorced straight away.' When she didn't respond immediately, he filled the silence with more excuses, desperation mounting in his voice. 'C'mon, Stella. I was 20! I didn't know what I was doing or even saying yes to. It didn't seem like a big deal. It wasn't marriage. Not what actual marriage is. What we have. I never even thought of it like that. Please believe me.'

'Connor.' She inhaled deeply and blew it out slowly. 'You were *married*, and you never told me. In fact, you lied to me about her last night. You said she was nobody. A wife is *somebody*, whether you want to acknowledge that or not.' Even though it happened twenty-five years ago, Stella recoiled at the idea that another woman had called Connor husband—especially a woman that looked like a siren from Old Hollywood. Stella had felt dowdy next to her.

'Stella, please—'

'No, Connor. I can't do this right now.'

The words burst out of him. 'I have ADHD!'

Her brow furrowed. Attention Deficit? What did that have to do with this? 'So?'

Connor ran his hand through his hair and rubbed the back of his neck. 'You know how I'm dyslexic?'

She nodded.

'Well, these things tend to come in twos. My therapist said—'

'Wait. *You're* in therapy?' She couldn't help the surprise in her voice.

'Why is that such a shock to everyone? Yes, I'm in therapy. What else was I supposed to do when my wife suddenly told me she wanted to separate?'

'It wasn't that sudden, Connor. I'd been hinting that things needed to change for over a year.'

'Yes! And now I see it! I was wrong. But it wasn't my fault. I mean, some of it was. But a lot of it was my ADHD.'

Her head was pounding now. Voice dangerously quiet, she said, 'You're blaming ADHD for lying about Valentina?'

'No, but also yes! It definitely impaired my judgment. I was so hyper-focused on the result that I wanted, and you know when I want something, I want it now and can't think of anything else. It's like tunnel vision. I set a goal. I achieve the goal. And I wanted that *Vogue* shoot. I know that you *forbade* me from ever working with Valentina again—'

'I didn't "forbid" you.'

He tilted his head to the side like *come on*. 'What would you call it then?'

'You promised!'

He rolled his eyes, which made her want to punch something. 'Semantics. Anyway, I *knew* I wasn't going to sleep with her, so I ignored my—as you say—*promise*, and I lied to you. For that, I will forever be sorry. But while I was in that obsessive hyper-focus mode, I couldn't see what I did was wrong. Now I do.'

She wasn't going to let him off the hook that easy. 'And all those times you were late when I specifically asked you to be home by a certain time? Was that ADHD, too?'

'Time-blindness. Well-documented in people with ADHD. I always meant to be there, but I'd get distracted.'

'And forgetting to call me when you were away on shoots for weeks at a time… also ADHD?'

'Object permanence. Basically, out of sight, out of mind. But *not* out of my heart. It's the same reason I always burn porridge whenever I make it. Again, well-documented.'

Was he comparing her to burnt porridge? 'You sound like a textbook.'

'I've been doing a lot of research.'

'Research. Great.' ADHD couldn't possibly be the explanation for everything problematic in their relationship. 'Connor. I'm sorry, but this sounds like a load of excuses to me.' He tried to interrupt, but she held up her hand. 'Is anything your fault? Or is everything you've ever done wrong due to ADHD?'

'What?'

'Is your research going to solve all our marriage problems?'

'Well, no, but Levi says—'

A loud knock sounded on the door.

'We're busy!' shouted Connor.

The door eased open, and a sheepish IPE employee shoved her head through. 'Um, I'm sorry to disturb you, Mrs Knight. I've been sent to find you. Your panel discussion started five minutes ago.'

'Shit!' She stepped towards the door.

Connor placed his hand on her arm. 'Stella—'

She shook him off. 'No, Connor. We have time set aside at the end of this week. We'll talk then. I have too much to get through to worry about this as well.'

'Goddammit, Stella. I love you. Don't shut me out.' His voice was thick with emotion.

Her heart pinched, but what choice did she have? She regarded the invisible, fortified wall between them. Sadness settled like a shawl over her shoulders, pushing them down. 'Goodbye, Connor.'

As she passed, those lemming tears started to fall.

Behind her, she heard him curse and kick a chair in frustration. She stepped out into the hall, ready to run for the room where her panel had already begun. But then she staggered to a stop, horror creeping up her spine: the hallway was full of people gawping, waiting to enter for the next class. Nobody spoke as blood rushed to her cheeks. Nausea stirred in her stomach. Unless they were all deaf, they must have heard the shouting. Everyone was looking at her, or rather—not looking at her. Most of them were examining the wall or their shoes. One person even giggled, in that way people do when they can't process how humiliating something is, so they laugh.

Stella's skin crawled with embarrassment. She dropped her head and followed the IPE lady down the pathway that miraculously opened up in the crowd like her condition was catching. She half-expected one of them to cry 'Shame!'

Great. She and Connor had just accidentally posted their marriage problems on the community secrets noticeboard.

21

CONNOR

As Connor made his way out of the conference room, he tried to ignore the whispers. This time, they weren't 'Is that Connor Knight?' This time, he heard words like *trouble in paradise* and *divorce* and *did he cheat?*

He wanted to yell, 'It's none of your fucking business!', but he didn't. The air thickened and he struggled to take a full breath. He had to get out of there.

Quickening his steps, he hurtled himself up the escalator two steps at a time and raced towards the front entrance of the hotel.

What had just happened?

Of all the scenarios he'd pictured for revealing his ADHD to Stella, that had not been one of them. When the moment arrived, the words spilled out all wrong. Normally, Connor was a smooth talker, but today he sounded like an ADHD website.

And why did Betsy tell Stella about their fake marriage? It was twenty-five years ago. They'd mutually agreed the terms. He knew for a fact that she'd been seeing other men while they were together, yet she apparently painted herself as the wronged party. The truth was that it had been an arrangement that suited both their needs.

The slot machines whizzed by him as he ran, but he barely saw them.

Connor had some theories about why Betsy did it. One: knowing her as well as he did, he could imagine her acting due to professional jealousy. Betsy had always been ambitious. What if she was trying to influence Stella to turn down Blake's deal, so that he'd offer it to her instead? Connor wouldn't put it past her. Though if that was Betsy's aim, the joke was on her; her meddling had pushed Stella the exact opposite way.

Two: what if *Blake* had put her up to it? What if he had plans for Stella that went beyond working together?

What if he wanted to blow up their marriage?

The very thought of Blake touching Stella was enough to make Connor want to destroy something. He stalked through the plant-filled atrium and the white marble lobby, out the double sets of glass doors, and into the open air. He stopped in front of a poster advertising Chris Seals' concert tour and gulped in a deep breath, leaning his hands on his knees.

Thoughts ricocheted around his brain. What should he do? How could he show Stella that it had been an honest mistake, not a conscious deception? What if she never forgave him? What if she moved with his daughter halfway across the world?

Standing straight, he wove his hands together behind his head, opening his chest so he could breathe. What a fucking mess.

A giant motorhome pulled up in front of the hotel with 'Live Free or Die' emblazoned on the side above a stylised illustration of the American flag. The door opened, and to Connor's surprise, Michael jumped out, followed by Tristan. They were both smiling.

'Best of luck with your trip,' Michael called over his shoulder, to which a voice from inside the motor home said, 'You too, sugar!' before Tristan waved and closed the door, readjusting his hat and sunglasses.

For a moment, Connor forgot his own woes. He had so many questions.

The RV pulled off.

Michael and Tristan sauntered towards the hotel, chatting and laughing. They didn't notice Connor. 'Um, did hell freeze over?' he said to get their attention.

'Oh! Hey, Con,' said Michael.

'Why were you two in an RV?' That seemed the easiest question to start, instead of diving in with, 'Why aren't you at each other's throats?'

'Funny story,' started Tristan. 'Do you want to tell it?'

Michael held up his hands like he was about to set the scene for an epic tale. 'We went for a walk in Red Rocks Canyon, but then we couldn't get any phone signal to call a taxi to bring us back, so Tristan—'

'I approached this older couple in the car park to ask if we could hitch a ride—'

'At first they were suspicious—'

'I suppose we're a bit imposing.' They laughed. Oh, how they laughed.

'But they couldn't resist his posh accent,' Michael pointed at Tristan with his thumb. 'The King himself has never sounded so fancy—'

'Excuse me, darlings,' Tristan said, laying on said accent and pretending to doff his cap, 'but could we possibly bother you for a lift into town. I'm afraid we're in a terrible predicament thanks to our silly mobile phones.'

'She practically curtsied to you.' Michael chuckled, touching Tristan's arm. Connor looked on, bemused. When had they become friends? Why were they both covered in dirt smudges? And why was Michael wearing a Fedora?

After a moment of joviality, Michael wiped an actual tear from his eye and continued, 'Anyway, they offered to give us a ride. Merv and Jenny. They've been married for thirty years and sold everything they own.'

'Now they're travelling the US in an RV.' Tristan frowned. 'Sounds ghastly if you ask me.'

Michael shoved Tristan flirtatiously. 'Oh, come on. It was romantic. And that RV was rather luxurious inside—'

Another voice cut in. *'Prynhawn Da! Sut wyt ti?'* said Armstrong from behind.

Connor turned towards the glass doors to see his father walking towards them hand-in-hand with Liliwen. The newlyweds glowed with vitality. With a shudder, Connor tried not to surmise what they had been doing to encourage such a radiant shine. 'Excuse me?' he said.

Wearing a cute pink tennis dress and visor, Liliwen cuddled into her new husband. 'Oh, I'm teaching Armie some Welsh.'

Armie???

'Popty ping! Isn't that adorable? It means microwave,' said Armstrong.

'Wyt ti wedi bod yn fachgen drwg?' Liliwen asked with a fiendish gleam in her eye.

Tristan coughed with laughter and Michael said, 'Do we want to know?'

'She's asking if he's been a naughty boy,' said Tristan, scratching at the back of his neck.

Michael and Connor blinked at each other as if trying to send help messages with their eyelids. *'Anyway,'* said Michael, drawing out the word pointedly. 'We just arrived back from the desert.'

'Sounds fun,' said Armstrong. 'We were about to go to Fremont Street to do the zip line before dinner. Anybody want to join us for Chinese later?'

The last thing Connor wanted was dinner. His usually healthy appetite had shrivelled up.

Liliwen was studying him, head tilted to the side. 'Connor, lovely, are you feeling well?' She reached up to pat the back of her hand against his forehead. 'You're a bit peaky.'

'Yeah, you're not looking great,' added Michael with concern. All eyes turned to Connor.

He waved his hand dismissively. 'I'm fine. It's just... Stella and I had a massive fight.'

'Oh, love. I'm sorry. The two of you...' Liliwen shook her head. With genuine concern in her eyes, she asked, 'What happened?'

His shoulders slumped. 'She found out I'd been married before her.'

'Holy mother of Richard Burton!' Liliwen clasped her hand to her chest.

'Whoa,' said Michael at the same time Tristan sucked through his teeth. They exchanged a surprised look before Michael asked, 'Why don't I know about this?'

Connor threw his hands in the air. Why did everyone think they had the right to his life story? 'Because I didn't tell anybody! We only did it so I could get a Green Card.'

'The legal professional in me will pretend I didn't hear that,' said Michael.

'I never thought of it as a real marriage. It would be like counting whatever this is between you two as a real marriage.' He indicated his father and his 'wife'.

'Hey, son. This is a real marriage,' protested Armstrong as he pulled Liliwen closer.

Connor ran his hands through his hair and scrubbed them over his face. Panic flared in his core. 'Now she says she's moving to Los Angeles without me and taking Grace with her.'

'What? She can't do that,' said Armstrong. 'I mean, it seems an extreme reaction. Why Los Angeles?'

Connor realised that they probably didn't know about her offer. She must have kept it close to her chest—a very Stella thing to do. 'She's been approached with a crazy scheme to move to the US and start a new online education platform under her name.'

'Hmmm,' objected Tristan, crossing his arms. 'When she told me about it, it sounded more like an opportunity, not a crazy scheme, darling.'

'Well, did she also tell you about how Blake Romero screwed me over?' exclaimed Connor angrily before explaining exactly what Blake had done to him twenty-five years ago and Betsy's involvement in the whole situation.

'I never liked him, me,' said Liliwen afterwards.

'So, let me get this straight, darling,' said Tristan. 'Because you didn't tell her about your marriage to this Betsy person, she's accepted the offer to move halfway across the planet to work with a proven crook.' He considered this information for a second. 'Yes. That sounds like Stella.'

'But Connor! You can't let her!' said Liliwen in distress, stepping forward and grabbing his shirt. 'What are you going to do about it?'

If only he knew. 'She's so mad at me right now... I can't talk to her.'

What *was* he going to do about it? The question pounded so loudly in his head that it was hard to think straight. Liliwen was right—he couldn't let Stella make this mistake. He didn't want her to get taken for a ride by Romero, but by the same token, he didn't want to get into a custody battle that would hurt Grace because he *would* fight for access to his daughter. He would never allow himself to be cut out of his wife and daughter's lives. They were his family.

He needed a plan. He needed to prove to her that Romero was a bad bet. What he needed was information. Facts. An argument she couldn't refute.

Scrutinising the people around him, he had the stirrings of an idea. 'Armstrong, do you have any contacts skilled in digging up information?'

'Of course, I work in government,' he said, as though Connor had asked if Christmas was on December 25th every year.

Connor snapped his fingers and pointed. 'Great. I need you to make some calls. See what you can find out about Blake Romero.

Trouble with the law, questionable social media posts, has he ever kicked a puppy. What about his family? Dodgy uncles. Go deep. But be quick. I need to know by tomorrow. Time is of the essence! Michael?'

'Reporting for duty,' Michael said with a salute.

'Do you know any forensic accountants? Somebody who could sift through his money story. See if he's evaded his taxes. Find out if he's hiding anything? I can pay, of course.'

Michael screwed up his face in thought before saying, 'I know a guy. Or actually, a gal. I can call in a favour.'

'Great.' He turned to Liliwen. 'Do you have access to Stella's calendar?'

Liliwen bit her lip. 'Well, yes, but I'm not sure I can show you. Wouldn't be ethical. Why do you want it?'

'I need to get her attention. Convince her that I'm still the man she married. But I need to know where she'll be first.'

'Hmmm.' Liliwen scrunched up her nose and shook her head. 'I don't feel right about giving you access. Besides, from memory, she's booked up most of tomorrow. However, I can give you a hint about one place she'll definitely be, if that helps.'

'A hint?' said Connor, brow furrowing.

'Yes, I can't say it, but maybe I could... you know...' She started bucking her chin and widening her eyes.

'Are you okay, *fy nghariad bach*?' Armstrong asked. 'Are you having a fit?'

'No!' she said, continuing the strange movement, her whole body getting into it now. 'I'm giving a hint...!'

Connor rubbed his chin, completely flummoxed. 'The rodeo?'

'Watching... seals at the zoo?' said Michael.

'Electric shock therapy?' suggested Tristan.

Liliwen made an infuriated noise and moved to stand in front of the Chris Seals poster. The singer was pictured surrounded by female sailors. She jerked her head towards it.

'Chris Seals... She's going to the Chris Seals concert!' shouted Connor with excitement.

She placed a finger on her nose and pointed at Connor with the other hand.

'Okay, when?' he asked.

She pointed to the ground, then put her hands together in prayer and mimed a hump in the air over and over again.

Everyone tilted their heads at her in confusion.

Finally, she exhaled like she'd been holding her breath. 'Tomorrow night, love! By the light of Catherine Zeta Jones, I hope I'm never stuck on a charades team with any of you lot,' she said, putting one hand on her chest and one on her waist as though she'd just run a great distance.

It felt like fate was stepping in. 'You're sure she's going to the Chris Seals' concert *tomorrow night*?'

'Yes! Oh, I do love his music. My Gareth and I went to see him play live in Cardiff some twenty years ago. He's lush. One of Stella's suppliers is taking her.'

A plan began to form in Connor's head. A crazy plan. It would require many stars to align, but it might just work. He needed to make some calls, ask for some favours, and keep *everything* crossed.

He hugged Liliwen and planted a kiss on top of her pixie head. 'Great. That's perfect, Liliwen. Thank you.'

'Well, you are my stepson, lovely. I feel a loyalty,' she laughed.

'Okay, so does everybody know what they have to do?' said Connor, like the chief of police briefing his team on a complex sting operation.

They all nodded. Tristan stepped forward. 'What should I do? Everybody has a job. I want one, too.'

Connor clapped his hand on Tristan's shoulder. 'Pray.'

22

STELLA

THE VENUE THRUMMED WITH THE LOW CHATTER OF EXCITED CONCERT goers. Massive Jumbotrons on either side of the stage played AI-generated dreamscapes that were hypnotic to watch. From her top-dollar seats in a box directly in front of the stage, Stella found herself entranced by the graphics as they coalesced and changed like ginormous lava lamps. A sense of peace washed over her for the first time since she arrived in Las Vegas. Over the next few hours, she didn't have to talk to anybody or think about Connor, Los Angeles, or anything else. She could simply sit back and be entertained.

'One red wine,' said Joey, the moustachioed CEO of Podacious, as he handed her a plastic cup and settled into the chair next to her. Other company employees filled the remaining ten seats in the box. The Exhibition Manager, a woman in her twenties with blue hair, sat to Stella's right.

'Thanks,' she said. Stella had been looking forward to this night ever since Joey emailed the invitation. They were celebrating her coming on board as a brand ambassador. Podacious sold affordable camera accessories. She liked the durability and ingenuity of their products and had no qualms about recommending them to her fans.

'Are you a Chris Seals aficionado?' Joey asked as he sipped his beer. Light briefly reflected off the barbell piercing in his tongue.

'Oh, he's great! *Love Songs for My Plants* is one of my favourite albums.' Chris Seals had recorded this 90s ballad-heavy album in a greenhouse.

Joey countered with, 'I'm more partial to *Karaoke Night with the Devil.*'

'Another classic,' Stella conceded. Seals had used real people he'd found performing in karaoke bars across America as his back-up singers on this album, produced in the early Noughties. 'I love how he's always surprising us,' said Stella.

Joey agreed. 'His best—' he started saying when his mobile phone rang. 'Sorry, do you mind?'

'No! Go ahead.' She went back to staring at the Jumbotrons. Thankfully, the Exhibition Manager didn't try to engage her in conversation. Stella had done so much talking this week that her jaw ached.

Podacious and Stella had been discussing a working relationship for a while, but the timing hadn't been right. Their marketing team already had an established relationship with a different female glamour photographer. But then that photographer had accidentally been filmed holding a competitor's product, and one of her students posted the video on social media. The contract strictly embargoed handling rivals' accessories. Even though it hadn't been the photographer's fault or her video, Podacious terminated their agreement.

Her loss was Stella's gain.

At present, Stella had relationships with a lighting company, an album company, an AI-software company, and Podacious, plus she was a Canon Ambassador. These relationships were a profitable way to supplement her income and receive free kit, but it could also be a headache remembering each companies' contract clauses to make sure she stayed compliant.

But tonight, she didn't want to think about any of that. She'd never seen Chris Seals live, and she heard he put on a spectacular show.

The lights dimmed, and the voices around the venue hushed. One excited fan yelled out, 'I want to have your babies, Chris!' and a wave of laughter rippled over the audience. Even though he was in his sixties, his latest wife had recently given birth to twin girls.

Expectation hung in the air.

One drum beat. Two drum beats.

Behind a scrim, a chorus in silhouette started singing, 'Yo-ho-ho. Yo-ho-ho.'

A shiver of anticipation ran up Stella's spine. The show was starting with one of her favourites from his last album, a rousing song called 'Mermaids and Rum'.

On the stage, a lone dancer appeared, dressed in a white and blue sailor's costume. She stood ramrod straight with her arms glued to her side, only her feet moving, tapping out a beat in Irish style.

The hee-haw of an accordion joined in, and more dancers dressed like the first flooded the stage—forty of them in total, all bouncing like sticks, cracking their shoes against the dark floor in unison.

Joey and Stella exchanged an excited look.

Chris Seals's voice echoed around the auditorium. 'Are you ready to swim on the wild side, Las Vegas?'

The crowd roared. Stella joined in, letting go.

He began to sing in sea-shanty rhythm as the dancers stamped out the beat:

'There once was a woman. I loved her well.
'Ere she turned to a fish and we went to hell.
She called me captain. I called her Love.
Ne'er mix mermaids and rum.'

The scrim lifted. The prow of a pirate ship slid into view, slicing through the middle of the chorus, with Chris Seals clinging to a mast doing his best Captain Jack Sparrow imitation. His face appeared on the Jumbotron at 10,000 times magnification; Stella couldn't imagine being that big on a screen. Terrifying.

His eyes were kohled along the edges which made his twinkling Irish blues pop. Although he was no longer the fresh-faced teenager discovered while singing in a wedding band, he still had it—whatever 'it' was. The crowd screamed for more. He slid down the mast as the dancers ripped off their sailor costumes to reveal green sequin leotards with shimmering mermaid-tail half-skirts at the back.

Seals launched into the song with gusto. The dancers transitioned from Irish dance to hip-hop. What a way to start the show! For a sixty-year-old entertainer, he moved like a man half that age.

All the people in Stella's box were on their feet, their bodies moving to the music. It had been ages since Stella really danced. She used to love it. Back in the days when she and Tristan competed, she enjoyed the intense physicality of it, being in tune with her body in a way that she'd lost since she quit to attend university.

As her hips swayed, she felt her problems temporarily peel away, allowing the music to transport her. For the next couple of hours, her only commitment was to have fun and surrender to the beat.

THREE-QUARTERS THROUGH THE SHOW, Stella sported a healthy sheen of sweat after rocking out to 'The Bastards of Ballygriffin'. The concert had been unreal so far. An unexpected guest appearance from Dave Grohl saw them performing Foo Fighter's 'The Pretender' together. Stella's heartbeat must have touched 150bpm while they banged their heads to that one.

'I'm heading to the bar. Want another drink?' asked Joey.

'Just water, please,' she said. She'd already completed an aerobic workout and needed hydration.

After a quick costume change, Chris Seals swaggered out on

stage alone. He wore all white, and Stella wondered what hit he'd perform next. Considering his outfit, maybe 'Queen of Angels'?

He addressed the crowd, his Irish accent faded from living abroad for so many years: 'I'm going to slow things down for a wee moment. How many lovers do we have in the house?'

Whoop, whoop, whoop went the crowd.

'This one's for you. You know, marriage is a tough old game. I should know. I've weathered four of them myself.' The audience tittered. 'Just this morning, a mate of mine rang, needing my help. He and his wife, who's here tonight, had a wee kerfuffle! And, well, we just want to let her know that she's the only woman for him.'

Stella put her hand over her heart. How sweet!

Chris Seals continued, 'We only cobbled together this song and dance routine today, so go easy on us, will ye? And it's a departure from my usual fare... but you know me! I'm mad for a bit of variety. With that in mind, I'm bringing my friend out here in a moment, and we're going to belt out a song made famous by the Backstreet Boys. Please put your hands together for Connor Knight!'

Stella blinked and shook her head. *What did he say?*

The employee sitting to her right elbowed her in the ribs. 'Wait, isn't that your husband?'

She couldn't speak, only watch in disbelief as Connor ran onto the stage, also dressed in white. His face appeared on the Jumbotron. Of course, he looked hot AF; the camera always loved him. The tank top he wore accentuated his muscles. On top of that, a loose, unbuttoned cotton shirt flowed with his movements. Like the natural entertainer he was, he waved at the crowd, and they cheered louder.

Her heart pumped faster as her head filled with static. Was this actually happening? Her time away from her problems disintegrated before her eyes. Her biggest problem was standing on stage, about to serenade her in front of thousands of spectators *after* Chris Seals announced they'd had an argument? It was cute when the 'wife' was some other faceless woman in the crowd, but now it was *her*, and she didn't like it. Not one bit.

Did Connor really think that a song and dance would make her forgive him?

Throwing his arm over Connor's shoulders, Chris said, 'Are you ready for this then?'

And Connor replied, 'Chris, I was born ready.' He was clearly enjoying himself. Stella wondered if this was more for her benefit or his.

'Okay, then, let's do this!'

Three of the back-up singer/dancers in white joined them to make up their numbers. Connor stood at the front of their V-formation with Chris Seals to his left. A spotlight circled each of them from above.

Could the floor possibly open up and swallow her? Stella prayed hard for it to happen. When the hell had Connor become best mates with Chris Seals? She knew that Connor had shot Chris for an Omega campaign, but there was a long road between that and *this*. Connor had an innate ability to charm people into getting what he wanted. No one seemed to be immune.

Except her.

The guitar notes of a song Stella vaguely recognised echoed through the arena. 'Hmm. Yeah, yeah!' sang Connor, pitch perfect through a cordless hand mic that appeared from nowhere. The audience went wild, excited that he didn't suck. Stella remembered the first time she heard his voice during that karaoke night on the course in France. He'd covered her favourite song, 'Jolene', and it was practically a religious experience for her.

But that was ten years ago.

Connor's deep voice caressed the opening words, asking for his 'Baby' to forgive him.

The other dancers/back-up singers stayed still for the first couple lines, then Chris Seals stepped forward. Connor slid back into the standard boy-band V-configuration behind Chris. Stella still couldn't recall the name of the song.

Joey sat down in his chair and handed a bottle of water to Stella. 'Wow. Did you know he was going to do this?'

'Nope,' she said through a rigid smile, afraid to betray her inner turmoil by saying more. She unscrewed the bottle cap and gulped down half its contents.

As Chris Seals and his crew reached the chorus, the choreography began. In perfect unity, all five of them circled one foot, then the other on the ground before popping their bodies, and pumping their hands over their chests. 'Shape of My Heart'—that was name of the song.

The crowd ate it up, screaming like teenagers. If she wasn't so angry, she would have loved it. Connor was a talented performer, and the Stella who adored him was proud of him deep, deep, deep, *deep* down.

But the Stella who was angry with him wanted to scream.

Would anyone notice if she crawled under her chair? Everyone in the box kept touching her shoulder and saying things like 'You must be stoked!' and 'This is so awesome!'

She was not 'stoked'. This was not 'awesome'.

On stage, the dance routine continued. The camera was on Connor again as he sang out the third verse.

Many years ago, he'd dressed up as Dolly Parton and serenaded Stella to declare that he had fallen in love with her. It was one of her favourite memories. With his reputation for dating around, it had shown her that he didn't care who knew that he had lost his heart. The act was touching and funny and personal.

But this... She imagined it had taken a lot of work to make it happen, but it felt like an ambush.

They were approaching the end of the song. There was only one more chorus left. Thank goodness. She couldn't wait for this to end.

And then it happened.

As Connor began the final verse, her face appeared on the Jumbotrons.

Her sweaty, frowning face.

With supreme effort, she pushed the corners of her mouth upwards. Her skin felt like it was on fire. Sure enough, Jumbotron Stella was growing redder by the second. *This must be what hell feels like,* she thought.

'OMG! We're on the screen!' said the Podacious Exhibition Manager sitting next to her, waving like a maniac and making sure the logo on her shirt was in the picture.

Stella held her breath, counting the seconds until the song finished and her lobster face came off the Jumbotron.

Finally, Connor sang the last line: '...the shape of my heart.'

As the notes ebbed, the crowd erupted in applause and hoots. Stella also clapped and smiled, so she wouldn't look like a complete arsehole. Most women would be thrilled if their husbands did what Connor had done for her.

Guess she wasn't most women.

Chris threw an arm around Connor, who was grinning from ear-to-ear. 'Connor Knight, everyone!' The camera finally switched from Stella to the stage. She sagged like a string had been cut. Her husband waved at the crowd, soaked in the applause, and ran into the wings. Seals segued straight into 'Queen of Angels'.

So much for the momentary escape from her problems. Now Stella had new ones to add to her pile. Why couldn't Connor wait until after the convention for the five days they'd mutually put aside to discuss everything? *Argh,* she screamed silently.

After Connor's act, she couldn't enjoy the concert. Everyone else in the box was high on the excitement of their brush with Jumbotron fame while she struggled to maintain a jovial appearance.

'I filmed it for you!' said the Exhibition Manager before airdropping it to Stella's phone. 'You two are my couple goals!'

Stella bit her tongue to stop herself from disagreeing. She needed to escape, find somewhere she could take a few deep breaths without fear of having her face projected anywhere.

She stepped past Joey and headed for the door at the back of the box. Before she arrived, a business-like knock sounded, and the door was pushed open.

A woman in black with green glasses and a clipboard stepped through. 'Oh! Hello, Mrs Knight. Just the person I was looking for.'

What now? 'I was heading to the toilets,' Stella replied lamely.

'I won't be long! I just wanted to extend an invitation to you and all of your friends here to join Mr Seals backstage after the show. Somebody will come to escort you during the finale.' The woman beamed benevolently at them, like she'd given them the gift of fire, and left.

Behind Stella, the Podacious employees high-fived and whooped.

Stella slipped out to hide in the toilet. She seemed to be making a habit of that.

23

CONNOR

WHAT A BUZZ!

Connor had been on many stages in his life, but nothing like *that.* And to perform one of his favourite BSB songs with a legend like Chris Seals—it was a dream come true. The only thing that might beat it would be to do it with the Boys themselves.

His brain seeped out dopamine in bucketloads. It was like being high. His heart was pumping overtime, and he couldn't keep still.

Thanks to his work with Chris in the past, Connor had his publicist's number. When he'd called her with the idea, she seemed dubious, but after some persuasion, she promised to fly it by Chris. After an hour of waiting for her to call back, Connor feared it was a nogo. But then she rang to say that Chris wanted to help. He thought it sounded fun and completely out of left field—his favourite sort of idea.

After that, Connor had headed to the venue to learn the simple routine that Chris' choreographer put together, practicing it a few times. Then it was showtime. The whole three minutes and fifty seconds he was performing, he'd been shaking.

But it had been worth it.

He hoped that Stella understood the message. He'd chosen the song carefully. It conveyed that he was sorry, that he'd been a different person, and that he was willing to change. For her and Grace.

Backstage, a banquet had been laid out for the performers, the crew, and Chris' guests. The black brick room was lined with posters of past acts, all the way back to Sinatra and Sammy Davis Jr.

Chris was currently holding court with a gaggle of fans near the bar. Connor grabbed a quick beer with Dave Grohl—great guy. After Dave excused himself to take a call, a few of the dancers surrounded Connor, complimenting him on his performance, but his eyes kept wandering to the door. When would Stella arrive? Every time it opened, his heart sped up.

Liliwen had discovered where Stella was sitting so that one of Chris's assistants could show her backstage after the show. Connor hadn't expected them to project Stella's face on the Jumbotrons; he knew she'd hate that. But hopefully, she'd see the bigger picture—no pun intended.

He couldn't wait to see her. He pictured a romantic reunion: maybe they'd get a bite to eat before heading back to hers for dessert. As far as grand gestures went, tonight should score high. Hopefully she'd listen to him now when he told her that he loved her and hadn't lied to her on purpose.

Finally, the door opened, and a crowd of people from Podacious came in, followed at last by Stella. Their eyes met, and her gaze flicked over the company he was keeping. He couldn't read her face. Excusing himself from the dancers, he crossed straight to her.

'Thanks for setting this up,' said the CEO of Podacious, holding out his hand. Connor couldn't remember his name.

'No problem.' Connor shook it while keeping his eyes on his wife, her expression still blank. 'Help yourselves to drinks and food,' he said to the CEO, hoping that would move them on, so he could be alone with Stella.

The Podacious group swarmed the refreshments table like they hadn't eaten in a decade.

'Hey,' he said to Stella and smiled.

'Hey,' she said back, her voice neutral. No smile. His dopamine rush dipped.

'What's wrong?' he asked, grasping her hand to pull her towards a private corner.

She extricated her hand from his grasp. 'Nothing. I just thought we agreed that we'd talk at the end of the week.'

Fuck. His performance obviously hit the wrong note. 'Stella, what—'

'Here are the lovebirds,' called out Chris Seals as he walked towards them, arms open. He defined 'rockstar' in his ripped jeans, black leather jacket, worn cowboy boots, and loose t-shirt. He took Stella's hand in his and kissed it.

Connor noticed she was smiling now. So her lips weren't broken.

'Mr Seals, thank you for such an amazing show,' Stella said.

'Please, call me Chris. Your husband's quite a fine singer, eh?'

'I'm a lucky woman,' she said. Connor detected the tiny sliver of sarcasm in her voice.

Chris ushered them further away from the others until they were in a corner near a Rolling Stones poster, out of hearing distance. He fixed them with a fond stare. 'As you might know, I've walked down the aisle more than my fair share of times. And this is what I've learnt: the most important thing is to learn how to fight well. When I married my first wife, I didn't know how to fight properly. Every argument was armageddon. I'd learnt from my ma and da, you see, who were all feck this and feck that and plates flying. Took me four wives until I realised that wasn't normal.'

He reached out and took both their hands in his. He clasped them all together. Connor couldn't believe he was getting marriage advice from Chris Seals. It was almost more surreal than being on stage with him earlier.

'I have a good feeling about you two,' Chris continued. 'I hope whatever it is that's ailing you, that you can work it out. Don't be too stubborn,' he said to Stella. 'My second wife was a redhead, so I know what you're like. And you—' He turned to Connor. 'Never be too proud to admit when you're in the wrong.'

Releasing their hands, he clapped and said, 'Now if you don't mind, I'm gasping for a drink. Stella, it was a pleasure to meet you.'

'Thanks again, Chris,' said Connor.

Chris flapped his hand and said, 'I can't resist a good love story. Maybe I'll write a song about it.' He laughed. 'Now, no fighting tonight. I want to see you two playing nice.' He winked and moseyed towards the food and drink, calling out, 'Grohl, I want that Scrabble rematch!'

As soon as Chris was out of earshot, Stella leaned towards Connor and said under her breath, 'You told Chris Seals about our separation?'

'How else was I supposed to convince him to let me sing with him? Does it matter?'

'Yes,' she hissed.

'He's watching us.'

They both replaced their frowns with smiles and waved.

'You can't razzle dazzle your way out of this,' she said.

Keeping the grin on his face, Connor said, 'So you didn't like the show?'

Chris Seals looked away as someone brought out the Scrabble board, and they both dropped the act. Stella poked Connor in the chest. 'I loved it right up until my husband turned into Justin Timberlake and my face was huge on a screen.' She gesticulated towards an imaginary Jumbotron.

'To be fair, I didn't know they were going to do that.' Also, Justin Timberlake was in rival band NSYNC, but Connor didn't think she was in the mood to be corrected.

'What did you hope to accomplish tonight?' Stella crossed her arms.

Connor leaned his shoulder on the brick wall and shoved his hands into his pockets. 'I don't know. Maybe I just wanted to make you smile.' He missed the Stella who used to have a laugh with him.

'Well, mission *not* accomplished. In fact, I felt embarrassed in front of all the people from Podacious.'

His brow drew down. 'Embarrassed? Why?'

'Because on top of all the people outside the classroom yesterday, everyone in that venue now knows that we're having issues.'

'Do they? I bet they thought it was romantic. Like any *normal* person would.'

'I just... wish you'd leave it. It's only twenty-four more hours until we have five whole days together to hash everything out.'

He didn't like the way she said that: *hash everything out*, like the details of a divorce. 'I feel like every second I *leave it*, you move further away from me. Like, to Los Angeles.'

She shrugged. 'What do you want me to say?'

Thank you? I love you? He frowned as he studied her face. He was getting tired of being the constant bad guy. If Stella didn't want him chasing her, fine. He'd give her the space she so desperately wanted. 'Okay, I get it. You want me to back off? You have your wish.'

Stella closed her eyes and said sadly, '*I have my wish?* Connor, this isn't easy for me either.'

Not easy for *her*? She was the one who had insisted on the separation in the first place. He was the one that had to relocate to a badly furnished flat on his own for six months, seeing his daughter only occasionally. He had gone along with it for Stella—not because he wanted to do it, but because he hoped that at the end of this path lay a future with his family.

He thought of the hours he'd spent with Levi, the wounds he'd picked open trying to become a better person, the discussions about his mother, his father, his relationship with his wife, his daughter, his brother, women in general. Ultimately, he'd done it all for himself, but also because he believed in their marriage and wanted to save it. He was trying to be the man she wanted, but it was exhausting. Even he had his limits.

'I've tried to show you how much I love you—'

'By singing a song with Chris Seals?'

'No, Stella. By going to therapy, by doing the work, by learning how to handle my ADHD. I even called that marriage counsellor you wanted me to talk to.'

That brought her up short. 'Oh. You did? Well, *finally.*'

He ignored her sarcasm. 'And what have you done? Because if there is one thing I've learned in therapy, it's that it takes two people to make a marriage. I'm not the sole cause of all our problems.'

She bristled. 'You think I'm part of the problem?'

'You refuse to forgive me for the Valentina mistake despite the fact I've spent four years apologising. I know—I get it. I was wrong. I was an arsehole and I acknowledge that. But people make mistakes, Stella. *You've* made mistakes. They help us grow and change.' That was the closest he would come to mentioning her affair with her boss. The surprise on her face told him she knew exactly what he was referring to. 'But... it's hard to evolve when you keep throwing it in my face. I mean, do you even *want* to forgive me? I feel like you're always assuming the worst about me. Like with this Betsy issue. I honestly never thought of it as a real marriage. That's why I didn't tell you. But in your eyes, it was a calculated deception.'

'Connor, I—'

'I'm tired of it, Stella. I'm willing to make changes, but you need to meet me halfway.' He ran a hand through his hair and inhaled deeply. 'I believe we're strong enough to get through this, and I will continue to fight for you. For us. But you're right—let's leave it until after the conference. I'll pick up the rental car for us. See you on Saturday morning.'

Her head snapped up. 'Aren't you coming to the awards ceremony tomorrow night?'

Why should he bother? His wife didn't want him there. All the people who used to be his IPE family didn't seem to care whether he was there, either. 'I'll give it a miss. Look, I wish you the best of luck, and I'm sure you'll win. You know I'm always proud of you. But I think you're right. We both need space. My presence won't be missed, and you can relax and enjoy yourself.'

She reached out to touch his arm and he pulled away. 'That's not what I—'

'Goodbye, Stella,' he said and stalked out of the party.

When he finally managed to find the exit, he pushed the door open so forcefully that it bounced against the wall, startling the security guard outside. Connor apologised, then stalked towards the main road. The night air cooled his temper, and he came to a standstill, dropping his head into his hands. This evening had not gone as he'd hoped.

Who did Stella want him to be? Whoever it was, it didn't seem to be Connor Knight. He'd done a lot of growing in the past six months, but she refused to see it.

What if he couldn't win this fight? His chest spasmed with sorrow. With Stella and Grace, he thought he'd finally discovered what family meant, but maybe he wasn't cut out for this life. Maybe he was too much like his father after all.

No. He stood up straighter. *I won't believe that. I'm my own man.*

His phone rang, interrupting his inner monologue. It was Michael.

'Hey, how did the concert go? Are you back yet?' Michael said, sounding impatient.

Connor cleared his throat. 'Just leaving now.' He'd return to the hotel and head straight to his room. He wanted to go to bed and pretend none of this had ever happened.

However, Michael had other plans for him. 'Good,' he said, 'because dad and I need to talk to you now. It's about Blake Romero.'

24

CONNOR

THE THWACK OF CLUBS AGAINST GOLF BALLS PUNCTUATED THE NIGHT air. Connor had never been to a place like this before—sort of like a bowling alley, only for golf. He sat in a cubicle that faced out over a spacious green littered with balls. There was no ceiling, just the open, light-polluted Vegas sky. Waiters flitted between booths, delivering food and drink orders while music blared from hidden speakers.

Tristan was hitting balls into the green while Connor faced his father and brother across a low table covered with beer bottles and baskets of fries.

'So... you didn't find *anything*?' Connor asked, incredulous.

'Sorry, man,' said Michael. His knee bounced as he talked. 'Romero's finances are all above board. No bankruptcies. No hidden bank accounts. Taxes filed. Everything checked out.'

'Shit,' said Connor. 'Are you sure your person was thorough?'

'She's one of the best, Connor.'

'Same with my contact, son,' said Armstrong. 'He couldn't find anything dodgy on Romero's record. In fact, quite the opposite. Did you know he chairs a charity for orphaned animals?'

Connor slapped the table. 'Fuck.' And then realising what it sounded like, he added, 'I mean, that's great for the animals.'

Michael leaned back on the sofa. 'Isn't it a good thing, really? Sounds like he's not trying to take advantage of Stella.'

'I was convinced he was up to something,' grumbled Connor.

'Son,' said Armstrong, and Connor had the uncomfortable feeling that a hard truth was incoming, 'Is it possible that Blake has changed? That he learned a lesson from what happened with you?'

'I suppose it's possible.' Connor shrugged. He thought back to his conversation with Stella only an hour ago, telling her that people could change, that *he'd* changed.

'It's been twenty-five years since you had... your *experience* with him. That's a long time,' said Armstrong. 'Hell, twenty-five years ago, the world was a different place. I was a different person. Your brother wasn't even gay yet—'

'Dad, I was always gay,' Michael said, rolling his eyes.

Armstrong held his hand out, palm up. 'What I'm saying is, perhaps it's time to forgive Blake Romero for what he did. If only for the sake of your wife who seems to have a great opportunity in front of her.'

Michael sat forward again. 'Yeah, that MuseTV is actually quite slick. Have you had a look at it?'

'Of course, I have,' said Connor. He'd done his due diligence, spoken with some of the other photographers featured on the site. They had nothing but good things to say.

'Are you worried she won't... come across well or something?' asked Michael.

Connor shook his head. 'Are you kidding me? She'd be brilliant. She's one of the most talented photographers and teachers I know, and I know a lot of them.' Even the first time he'd seen her work— some chicken project she'd photographed for a breeder—he'd noticed she had a good eye. Stella had always been one of his best pupils. He'd watched her grow and develop over the years into the shooter she was today, and he was her biggest cheerleader. If this offer had come from anyone but Blake Romero, he'd be telling her to grab it with both hands.

'Well then... I'd say she should go for it.' Michael swigged from his beer bottle. 'I'm happy to recommend someone to go over the contracts for her.'

Connor studied his father. 'What about you? You were about to move to London.'

Armstrong waved his hand. 'London... LA. It doesn't matter to me.'

'What about your new *wife*? Have you spoken with her about it?' Connor raised an eyebrow. His father had probably forgotten about that one tiny logistic.

A flicker of concern passed over Armstrong's face. 'Oh... ah... of course, I need to discuss it with her.' Connor huffed. Armstrong wasn't used to thinking about anyone's desires except his own. Must be a shock to the system realising that he wasn't a free agent anymore.

Tristan interrupted, '*Nil pois* for me. Your turn, Armstrong.' He crumpled onto the sofa next to Connor, across from Michael. 'I thought I'd never meet a small ball I didn't like, but that was until I tried golf.'

'Not a fan?' said Michael.

'I'm too tall for this game. Or the clubs aren't long enough.'

Michael said flirtatiously, 'Blaming the equipment?'

'Of course, darling. It's obviously not *my* fault.'

Connor suddenly felt like he was intruding. What had happened in the desert to make these two friendly again? Did they encounter a shaman with an endless supply of ayahuasca? Get bitten by a spirit animal? *Note to self*, he thought. *Take Stella into the desert.* To be fair, they were about to spend five days in Joshua Tree—as desert as it could get.

Shifting his attention back to Connor, Michael said, 'You never told us how the concert went.'

He groaned, Stella's reaction fresh in his mind. 'Not well. I mean, *great* in that I performed on stage with a rock legend. But not well for my marriage.'

'She didn't fall at your feet?' Michael made doe eyes.

'Far from it. In fact, she was angry that I discussed our marriage issues with Chris Seals.'

Tristan laughed. 'Watch out, darling. He'll probably write a song about it.'

Chris saying exactly that flashed through Connor's head. 'I don't know what she wants from me. She seems to have high expectations that I'm not sure I can reach.' He pinched the bridge of his nose, the beginnings of a headache threatening to descend on him.

Tristan hummed like he had thoughts on the subject and Connor's head snapped up. 'What?'

Stella's oldest friend was regarding him, as though deciding whether to impart some knowledge. Connor looked him dead in the eyes. 'I love her, Tristan. With all my heart. If there's something you know that can help me, please... tell me. I'm desperate.'

Tristan gave a curt nod. 'I know you love her. I can see that. And to be honest, you're the only one of Stella's romantic entanglements that I've ever liked. So I'm going to tell you what I think.'

Connor leaned in, desperate for whatever pearls of wisdom Tristan had to give.

'You say she has high expectations,' Tristan said, and Connor nodded. 'You know why that is, right?'

Throwing his hands in the air, Connor said. 'I have no idea.'

'Her parents, of course,' Tristan said, picking up his beer, leaning back on the sofa, and crossing his long legs at the ankle.

'Angela and Bill?' Connor had always enjoyed a good relationship with Stella's parents. Angela loved to mother Connor whenever they visited, treating him like the son she never had. And Bill was a funny man. He always insisted on taking Connor to the pub to share stories about every woman he dated before he married Angela, as though this were a bonding rite. Thankfully, there weren't that many, so Connor heard the same stories repeatedly.

With Grace, they were picture-perfect grandparents, giving her the kind of loving attention that Connor never had from his.

Tristan continued, 'I love them like they were my own, but they were intense. Both Stella and I are only children—probably why our partnership worked so well—but whereas my parents were laid-back hippies, hers focused all their attention on her. Good and bad. They always put pressure on her to be the best, to be perfect. My least favourite part of being her partner was the rides home from competitions. Bloody hell. Bill would spend the whole journey critiquing our performance like he was Craig Revel *effing* Horwood, telling us what we needed to change to win in the future. In his *non-professional* opinion.'

'Hmm, she's mentioned that they had high standards for her, but he's not like that at all now. Grace has him wrapped around her little finger,' Connor said.

'That's because grandparents have no skin in the game,' Tristan explained. 'They already poured all their crazy into their kids. Did Stella ever tell you about her mother's pre-performance ritual?'

'No.' Connor put his beer down and leaned in further, intrigued.

'I refused to take part, but Angela used to make Stels pray for spiritual integrity and God's guidance before every competition, followed by twenty Hail Marys. Twen-ty!' He said it like it was two words. 'The pressure for her to remain pure-of-heart and yet she-devil competitive was intense. Stels used to beg my mother to drive us instead. And...' He winced and shuffled in his seat uncomfortably. 'Well... I'm not sure I should tell this story...'

'Now you have to,' said Michael, reaching over the table to slap Tristan's knee.

'Uh, okay, but you didn't hear it from me,' he said as he uncrossed his legs and shifted forward, drawing them in. Connor and Michael obliged by tipping closer. Tristan lowered his voice. 'She never admitted to doing this, but I remember this one time when we were sixteen. Bill and Angela were supposed to drive us to Bournemouth for a competition, but when they woke up, somebody had slashed all the tires on their car, so my parents had to take us instead.' He paused for a moment. 'I always suspected it was Stels. When I asked her about it, she had that ducky-faced look she gets when she lies.'

Michael tsked. 'Poor Stella!'

Connor's heart hurt for the woman he loved.

Tristan shook his head sadly. 'Regardless of what she says, she's still that little girl, looking for attention and trying to be perfect for everyone around her.' He sat back again. 'I swear, if it wasn't for my steadying presence in her life, she would have turned to drugs.'

Michael barked a laugh.

'It's true,' protested Tristan. 'Stella has *always* been a perfectionist and has *always* found it hard to forgive mistakes. Even her own. *Everyone* is held to the same high standards.'

This gave Connor so much to consider. Why had he never thought to talk to Tristan about Stella? He knew her in a different way from Connor—in the way that only came from experiencing puberty together.

Connor clapped Tristan on the knee. 'Thanks, mate. I really appreciate you sharing this. It... helps.' Turns out there were things that his wife hadn't told him, too. They both had scars from their childhoods: he had too little parental guidance, and Stella had too much.

'One hundred and ninety-two points for me!' Armstrong said, swaggering back to the group. 'All those years schmoozing at golf clubs has finally paid off. Connor, you're up.'

Perfect timing. He needed time to think, and mindlessly hitting balls sounded like a good way to keep his body occupied while letting his thoughts spool. After that, he planned to drink too much beer, then fall into a dreamless sleep.

It wasn't like he had any plans tomorrow.

25

TRISTAN

TRISTAN HAD BEEN FRIEND-ZONED.

Since their strictly platonic bonding session in the desert, Tristan and Michael had palled around all over Vegas: seeing shows, zip-lining with Liliwen and Armstrong, and checking out the fringe eateries and bars on the outskirts of town.

But that was it.

When Tristan let his leg touch Michael's under the dinner table, Michael slowly moved his away. When Tristan suggested they go dancing at a gay club like they used to, Michael begged off.

Tristan got the hint. And he was fine with it. He was enjoying being Michael's friend again.

That said, he wouldn't mind bending him over the sofa and having mad, passionate sex with him.

From the safety of the sofa in the golf bar, Tristan feasted his eyes as Michael swung his club, his body twisting when he flowed into the arc of the shot. His calves bulged with muscle; his slim hips whipped around to the front; his arms flexed as they raised the club high. He was much better at golf than Tristan.

'Sixteen points!' Michael exclaimed before glancing over his shoulder. Tristan quickly averted his gaze to the green so that Michael wouldn't accurately surmise that he'd been staring.

'Aren't you a regular Tiger, darling,' said Tristan in his usual blasé tone.

Their eyes connected for a milli-second longer than necessary, and a brief flicker of hope flared in Tristan's belly. But then Michael laughed, shook his head, and went back to beating balls.

The hope sank like a rock.

Armstrong had already left for the hotel. Apparently, Liliwen gave him a pass for boys' night, but Armstrong missed her and wanted to crawl back into her loving arms. Tristan laughed to himself. Liliwen had Armstrong 100% pussy-whipped. Good for her.

Connor had disappeared to the toilet some time ago. That man was in bad shape. Tristan genuinely hoped that Stella and Connor could work things out. Whether Stella realised it or not, Connor was good for her. She needed a man with a personality as strong as hers, and Connor definitely had that.

If he was honest with himself, part of Tristan was a little irritated with her. Anyone with eyes could tell that Connor loved Stella. She was so lucky and she didn't even know it. Tristan doubted he'd ever find that kind of devotion. The words *artificial* and *shallow* flitted through his thoughts, and he pursed his lips to keep from frowning.

It didn't help that he had to keep shifting his seat because Michael's golf form was giving him an inconvenient boner.

'Whoa! Did you see that?' said Michael, shielding his eyes as he studied the field. 'I sank it in the farthest hole!'

'Splendid,' Tristan squeaked, very much picturing which hole he wanted Michael to sink into.

Everything had changed between them in the desert.

After Tristan told Michael about his diagnosis, they'd discussed it for hours on that ledge. Michael was more educated about HIV than Tristan had been when he first heard his diagnosis: HIV was no longer a death sentence. In fact, with medication, the virus practically disappeared. U=U. Undetectable equals Untransmittable. As long as Tristan kept up with his anti-retroviral treatment, he couldn't transfer the virus to a sexual partner.

Tristan took his medication every night before going to bed and said a little prayer. Not to any god, but to everyone who had ever donated to an AIDS charity and to every scientist who took that money and turned it into that one little pill that saved Tristan's life on a daily basis.

That being said, he still felt embarrassed for having caught HIV. He hadn't touched another man since he found out.

'Why did you move to Mexico City?' Michael had asked on the ledge.

Tristan pulled the hat down to cover his face. 'You're going to think I'm ridiculous if I tell you the truth.'

'Go on, then.' Michael turned on his side and grinned his contagious grin.

'Uh. Okay. It's because I dated a Mexican footballer for a week, and he talked about it. A lot. I remember thinking it sounded like a nice place to live.'

'Okay, that is ridiculous,' Michael laughed.

Getting serious, Tristan said, 'My diagnosis was a wake-up call. I realised I wanted to... to do more with my life than worry about getting regular coverage in the tabloids. I wanted to make a difference.'

'I can understand that,' Michael had said.

They'd talked about Tristan's work at Sin Pecados, about the boys he'd helped who had run away from their homes in rural Mexico because their families didn't accept them. Mexico City was much more gay-friendly. For men, at least. Lesbians still struggled in the machismo culture.

'How long are you planning to stay there?' asked Michael.

'Until I'm ready to leave,' was Tristan's honest answer.

Since then, the subject they avoided most was their love lives. Tristan didn't mention that he had sworn off meaningless sex, and he didn't ask Michael if he was involved with anyone special.

But of course, sex with Michael would never be meaningless. He was The One That Got Away.

'Two-hundred and eight points,' said Michael triumphantly when he finished hitting his balls.

'You beat your dad,' said Tristan.

'Shame he's not here for me to rub it in.' Michael snapped his fingers like 'oh, rats!'

He was so damned cute.

Connor returned from the toilets, looking like a man ready to call it a night. 'Our Uber is here.'

'I guess we're leaving.' Michael extended a hand to help Tristan up from the low sofa. He pulled a little harder than Tristan expected, and next thing he knew, they were standing toe-to-toe, their hands trapped between their bodies, Tristan's hard-on pressing where it shouldn't be pressing. Their eyes met. Michael swallowed, his Adam's apple making a quick down and up motion. Tristan thought he saw Michael's blue eyes darken with desire.

And then Michael stepped back, practically tripping over himself in his haste to get away. 'Right, let's get out of here.' He walked briskly towards the exit.

Tristan followed behind, cradling the hand that Michael had touched like it was as valuable as Madonna's cone bra.

In the taxi, Connor sat between them. It was safer that way. But then at the hotel, Connor said, 'I'm heading straight to bed. See you later,' and disappeared in the direction of the lifts.

Tristan and Michael stood in the lobby, each with their hands shoved in their pockets, like kids looking for mischief.

'You tired yet?' asked Michael.

'Not particularly.' Tristan's heart was pumping too much adrenaline through his body.

Michael pulled some quarters out of his pocket. 'Shall we go see the Girls?'

At *The Golden Girls* machine, Tristan perched on the stool and Michael pulled one over from another machine. Their legs brushed.

This time, Michael didn't move away. For Tristan, that one point of contact radiated heat all over his body.

They sank their first quarter down the slot.

Blanche, Dorothy, Sophia, Blanche.

The next ten quarters also failed to win, but Tristan didn't care. He was having fun being with Michael, chatting about nothing important. By sharing his secret with him in the desert, some of their old camaraderie had returned, and Tristan wanted to enjoy it while it lasted.

On Saturday, he'd head back to Mexico, Michael would return to New York, and this week would become a distant memory.

When their last quarter produced no win, Michael said, 'Oh, well. Next time.'

They were both silent for a moment.

Michael started twisting his seat back and forth, like a child discovering the joy of a swivelling stool. Every time he wheeled left, their legs touched for a brief moment. 'Thanks for what you did for Connor earlier. I really appreciated that.'

Tristan was having trouble concentrating on what Michael was saying. Whenever their legs touched, an electric shock of awareness shot through him, straight to his dick. 'Um, no-no problem. I hope they sort things out.'

'Yeah. Me, too,' said Michael, nodding. Then all of a sudden, he stood up. Stretched. 'I think it's time for bed.'

Uncharacteristically inarticulate, Tristan said, 'Yeah. Okay.'

He didn't want the evening to end. They only had one more left. He'd happily give up sleep to spend every second of tonight hanging out with Michael.

The lifts were empty this time of night. On the weekends, there were so many people checking in that there were always queues, but on a Thursday at midnight, everyone was out having a good time.

They walked into an empty lift and pressed their respective buttons.

Both of them leaned against the back wall, arms crossed, quiet.

Near each other, but not touching. The lift ascended, along with Tristan's heartbeat. He could hear Michael's steady breathing above the muzak. The hairs on the right side of Tristan's body stood on end, reaching towards Michael's. Could he feel this tension, too? Or was it only Tristan going through sensory hell?

He remembered how they'd been as a couple. They couldn't keep their hands off each other. Tristan closed his eyes for a moment, recalling the feel of Michael's soft lips on his.

But Tristan was too scared to make the first move. What if Michael rejected him? Would all their newfound friendship disappear in a puff? He couldn't take the chance. Tristan's delicate confidence was at a low after a whole year without another's touch. Besides, he was no longer the hot, party-ready model that Michael had dated all those years ago. The new Tristan Hughes was less exciting, more lost—whereas Michael was still an amazing human with a bright future. What did Tristan have to offer?

The lift pinged and his eyes opened.

Michael glanced at Tristan and shrugged, 'This is my floor.'

'Yeah. So it is.' A beat. 'I guess this is goodnight then,' said Tristan with a lame smile that quivered from the effort of lifting the corners of his lips. Michael stepped into the hallway without looking back.

Fuck it, thought Tristan, kicking the wall behind him with his foot. He hated himself for being a coward. They were both leaving on Saturday. Opportunity was slipping through his fingers.

He watched as the lift doors began to close. He pictured a beating love heart hanging between them, waiting to be squished.

Just before they sealed, a hand reached in, and the doors stalled.

Michael pushed the doors apart again. Neither of them spoke as they stared at each other. 'Well, are you coming?' Michael said with a hungry grin.

Tristan's heart pounded so forcefully in his chest that he was surprised Michael couldn't see the outline of it through his shirt.

'I thought you'd never ask,' Tristan said, stepping forward and taking Michael's head between his hands, kissing him passionately.

His lips were as soft as Tristan remembered, yielding and eager. Their tongues lashed together, teeth scraping in their haste to taste each other. Michael squeezed Tristan's hips and groaned.

Huzzah. At least Tristan remembered how to kiss.

They stumbled out into the hall. 'Where's your room?' Tristan asked as he pushed Michael against the wall. He could feel Michael's excitement, strong as his own, their bodies independently acting like they were greeting an old friend.

It had been so long since he'd touched anyone. Tristan had to concentrate so he wouldn't embarrass himself by finishing too soon. There were many things he wanted to do tonight, and ejaculating like a horny teenager wasn't one of them.

Taking Tristan's hand, Michael led him down the hall. At his door, he fumbled in his wallet for his key card as Tristan nibbled on his ear from behind, enjoying the plains and hills of Michael's back pressed into him. Finally locating the card, Michael slapped it repeatedly against the lock. 'Fucking *open*,' he laughed. When the electronic buzz sounded, they fell through the door together, the tangle of their bodies slapping against a closet door.

'Ow,' said Tristan, smiling.

Michael kissed his shoulder. 'All better?'

'Much,' whispered Tristan. And he meant it. Whether Michael knew it or not, his touch was healing so many things within Tristan's broken soul.

Inside the room, they set an Olympic record for undressing. Entwined, they fell onto the bed, chuckling at their mutual desperation.

Tristan's whole body was on fire, stoked by the sensation of Michael's warm, perfect skin against his. Taking the lead, Michael flipped Tristan onto his back and sat on his chest. Lacing their fingers together, he pinned Tristan's hands above his head and leaned down to whisper in his ear, 'When did you realise you still fancied me?' He trailed kisses along Tristan's jaw and down the column of his neck, sending shockwaves of pleasure down his body.

With a wicked grin, Tristan said breathily, 'When I saw you in that restaurant wearing that ridiculous sombrero. You?'

'When I saw that sexy as fuck phoenix on your back.' His knees squeezed Tristan's torso.

Freeing his hands, Tristan reached behind Michael and palmed the cheeks of his firm arse. 'It really took you that long to realise you still wanted to fuck me, huh?'

Michael's lips lifted cheekily. 'Okay, it was the restaurant for me, too. Moment I saw you. Took all of my willpower not to drag you under the table and fuck you senseless.'

Tristan loved it when Michael talked dirty. 'That would've been delightful.'

Throwing an arm around Michael, Tristan flipped them, so that he was now on top. Skin-on-skin, their hands and mouths rediscovered the intricacies of the other's body. Tristan tapped into his Michael-shaped memories. His soft sighs when Tristan ran his tongue along the shell of his ear, the way he bucked when Tristan bit his nipples, the sweet, up-close scent of Michael himself, his unsteady breath when he was ready for more.

Tristan pulled back for a moment to look Michael in the eye. 'I'm safe, so you know.' He made sure to get his viral load tested regularly, as well as a full health check every six months.

'I'm on PrEP anyway,' Michael said. PrEP was a daily oral medication that stopped sexual partners from contracting HIV, even when exposed.

'Great, because I don't think I can hold out much longer,' said Tristan.

Thankfully, Michael felt exactly the same.

AFTERWARDS, Tristan lay on his front while Michael stretched out next to him, their legs entwined, his fingertip tracing the lines of Tristan's tattoo.

'That was even better than I remembered,' Michael said, leaning over to kiss Tristan's temple.

'No complaints here, darling. I'm just glad I haven't forgotten what to do.' From the way Michael screamed his name when he came, Tristan figured he'd fulfilled the job description well enough.

'Oh, you definitely haven't.' Michael's hand moved lower, causing goosebumps to break out all over Tristan's arse.

His dick was perking up again, but before they started round two, there was something Tristan needed to know. He rolled onto his side so they were facing each other. 'Why did you break up with me?'

Michael's finger stopped moving.

Deep down, Tristan had always believed that what Michael said that night was a lie—his line that their 'lifestyles didn't align' and Tristan was too 'shallow and artificial' for him. In hindsight, Tristan had been both of those things, but not when he was with Michael.

He tipped onto his back and shoved his hands behind his head, studying the ceiling. He sighed and said, 'Just before we started dating, I won a landmark case in Kenya. Key members of an LGBTQ advocacy group were arrested for protesting, and I spearheaded a campaign to free them. Amnesty International was involved. It was a big win.'

'Mmm. Yes, I remember you mentioning it.' Michael had more than mentioned it. Tristan could have named all the defendants in the case.

'Well, six months later, I received news that their leader had been murdered in Nairobi. It was no random act of violence. He'd been killed because he was gay.' He took a shaky breath and turned his head towards Tristan. 'I felt guilty that I was busy having... having the time of my life with you while there was still so much work to be done. You were too distracting.'

Warring emotions spread though Tristan. On one hand, his sadness at the story Michael had shared was overwhelming. It was a tale they heard all too frequently. On the other hand, warmth radiated through his chest like he'd been cracked open, and the sun came out. Michael hadn't broken up with him because of anything Tristan did.

He placed his palm over Michael's heart. 'You can't save everybody... but I love that you feel you have to try. And... I wish you'd *told* me what happened instead of shattering my heart into a million pieces.' He scooted forward and laid his head on Michael's bent arm.

His head turned towards Tristan so they were almost nose-to-nose. 'Did I really?'

'Did you really what?' Tristan's brow furrowed.

At the end of the bed, their feet absentmindedly rubbed each other's. 'Shatter your heart into a million pieces?'

Tristan closed his eyes, realising he'd basically told Michael that he'd been in love with him. He swallowed hard. Life was too short. 'Yes... you did.'

With the speed of a professional athlete, Michael pushed Tristan onto his back, swung his leg over, and straddled him. Leaning down, he worked his mouth up Tristan's jaw to his lips. 'It shattered mine, too,' he said before kissing him with years of pent-up desire.

When he pulled away, Tristan said breathily, 'Well, darling, I think this is the beginning of a beautiful friendship.'

Michael chuckled deep in his throat at the quote from *Casablanca*, the movie about ill-fated lovers Rick and Ilsa, which they used to watch curled up in bed together. 'Indeed it is.'

As they began round two, Tristan's entire body smiled. He was happier than he'd been in a long time.

26

STELLA

At around 1AM, Stella returned to her room at the hotel.

After Connor left the party, she'd stayed, loathe to abandon the Podacious crowd as she was the reason they'd been invited backstage in the first place. Plus Chris had asked her to play a game of Scrabble with him and Dave Grohl, and she couldn't say no to that. It was the bucket list experience she never knew she wanted—especially because she won. Her parents would be so proud.

'Hello?' she shouted into the dark suite, suspecting that nobody would answer. Both Tristan and Liliwen's doors were wide open, their rooms empty. She frowned. She wished they were here to talk her down from her mental ledge.

If she moved to LA, she'd have to get used to this loneliness. Except for Grace, everyone she loved would be in the UK. Her stomach soured at the realisation.

She switched on a lamp in the common area and crumpled onto the grey sofa.

What a week.

Tomorrow was the last day of the convention, with her usual full-on schedule of meetings and appearances, followed by the awards ceremony in the evening.

She groaned, Connor's parting shot echoing through her head. How was she going to convince him to come tomorrow night? He had no idea he was receiving the Lifetime Achievement award, and so many people would be disappointed if he didn't show: Damian, who had nominated Connor in the first place; Therese, who'd helped with organising it; and Armstrong and Michael, who travelled all this way...

As she slid her high heels off and reclined on the cushions, she replayed her discussion with Connor at the party. Was there some truth to what he'd said? *Was* she too hard on him?

She'd been so *angry* at the concert. She hadn't been thinking straight. She'd been looking forward to the night as an escape, an opportunity to get away from her problems. Then Connor had appeared—a reminder. She felt blindsided, and her temper had gotten the better of her. Maybe Chris Seals was right: she was too stubborn.

And now Connor was upset, and she somehow had to convince him to come to the ceremony without ruining the surprise.

Should she text him? Simply... beg him to come? She pulled out her phone and stared at it for a minute, trying to work up the bravery to ask him. Her thumb flicked across the screen, but instead of opening WhatsApp, she tapped her photos folder.

Sitting at the top was the video that the Exhibition Manager had sent her. She played it. 'The Shape of My Heart' rang out from her iPhone. In hindsight, what Connor accomplished was quite impressive. A small smile played at her lips as she watched him this time, really listening to the words, taking his message on board.

He was asking for her forgiveness.

He had asked for it in front of 20,000 people, but still...

What she'd also missed in real time was how utterly happy and natural he looked on stage, dancing his wanna-be boyband heart out to the Backstreet Boys. She laughed softly. Connor thought she didn't know about his obsession with the band, but of course she knew. She'd heard him singing in the shower hundreds of times, belting out 'I Want It That Way' or 'Quit Playing Games With My Heart'. She'd been married to him for seven years; it was impossible not to notice how excited he became when one of their songs played. He might not realise it, but whenever that happened, he would stop what he was doing, grab something to act as a microphone, and sing into it. And he knew *all* their moves. He also had a playlist on his phone called 'BSB 4ever'.

It was one of the many, many surprises of Connor Knight. On the outside, he appeared all cool and sexy, but on the inside, he was a BSB-loving dad who enjoyed watching Peppa Pig with his daughter and singing karaoke.

And Stella loved that about him.

On a whim, she went onto Instagram to see if anybody had posted the video from other angles. Using hashtags to search, it didn't take her long to find them. One was taken by someone in the front row, Connor's sheer delight zoomed in. And when Stella's face flashed onto the Jumbotrons at the end, she looked so grumpy. Ugh! When had she become that woman?

There were loads of comments like 'This is so cool!' and 'Who is this guy?' and 'Why doesn't my husband do this for me?' But there was one comment that got her attention: 'His wife looks pissed off. If she doesn't want him, I'll take him!'

Stella dropped her head into her hand.

What was wrong with her? The whole point of the separation was to shock him into realising that they needed change. At this point, Connor had gone to therapy, called the marriage counsellor, and serenaded her on stage with a famous rockstar, singing about becoming a new man. What more did she want?

Her parents had always pushed her to be perfect, and she'd hated it because it made her feel constantly inadequate. Was she unconsciously repeating the same pattern with Connor and their marriage?

And what about his ADHD? She'd dismissed it when he told her because she thought it seemed too convenient. But it deserved attention. She needed to do some research and see if she could find ways to help him. That's what she would want if she were in his situation.

And maybe his ADHD *was* part of the reason he'd 'forgotten' to mention his marriage to Royale. As he said: out of sight, out of mind. What if Stella gave him the benefit of the doubt?

It was entirely possible that what he said about his marriage to Betsy/Royale was true—that he never considered it a real marriage and so never considered it newsworthy. It showed a lack of consideration to Royale and smacked of a 20-year-old man's self-interest, but that didn't make it false.

Added to that, something he'd said replayed through her head: *You're always assuming the worst about me.* Maybe he was right about that, too. Wasn't that what she had done all those years ago when she made him promise not to work with Valentina? Stella had assumed the worst about Connor—that, if tempted, of course he would cheat.

Because, deep down, Stella worried she wasn't enough for him. He'd never given her cause to think that, but her own mind wouldn't accept that Connor Knight had chosen *her*, out of all the women in the world. Even now, seeing him even near other women sent her loopy. *Look at how you reacted to him talking to Royale.*

By forbidding him to work with Valentina, she'd put Connor in a difficult position: anger his wife or lose a huge opportunity, so he'd tried to avoid both. His solution wasn't ideal, but she understood his choice better now. And she finally felt ready to forgive him.

If she could go back in time, she'd handle that situation differently. She'd make him aware of her insecurities but also tell him that she trusted him. She should never have tried to clip his wings. After all, she didn't like being on the reverse side of that, did she?

Now it was *her* with the opportunity and Connor who would be hurt by her choice to pursue it. Was he right? Was she part of the problem, too?

The creak of the door opening surprised her, and she leaned

forward to see who it was. Liliwen tiptoed into the suite, wearing another pink dress and a pair of golden sandals. 'Oh, hello, lovely!' she said when she spied Stella.

'Hey, stranger. What are you doing here? I thought you'd moved to Armstrong's room?' She still couldn't get used to that, but if it made Liliwen happy, who was Stella to judge?

'Oh, I fancied sleeping in my own bed tonight. No word of a lie, Armstrong snores like a flock of bleating sheep.' Liliwen made herself comfortable on the sofa next to Stella. 'Anyway, I wondered if you'd be up. How was the concert?'

'I assume you were in on Connor's impromptu performance?' she said.

Liliwen shrugged. 'He is my step-son.'

Stella bit down a sigh. They'd only been related for three days. Stella had been one of Liliwen's closest friends for ten years. 'I'm afraid I didn't react as he expected.'

'Oh, love! What happened?'

'We had a fight. I accused him of ambushing me, but... I think I may have pushed him too far this time.' The memory of their conversation hit her full force: the way she'd pulled away from him, the hurt on his face, how he'd been so excited about his performance before she opened her mouth. Unexpected, fat tears rolled down her cheeks.

'Don't cry, lovely!' Liliwen scooted over and put her arms around Stella so that her head rested on Liliwen's shoulder. 'Oh, now I'm sorry I ever told him you were going to that concert. We were all so concerned after Connor told us what that *coc oen* Blake Romero had done to him.' Stella's Welsh wasn't as good as Liliwen's, but she was pretty sure that *coc oen* meant *lamb's willy*. 'Are you really moving to LA?'

Stella nodded. 'I... I think I am, yes.'

'Without Connor?'

'I don't know,' she sniffed and wiped at her eyes. 'Everything is such a mess.'

'Actually, these things are often simpler than you think. The only question is: do you still love him?'

If there was thing Stella had learned through this separation process, it was this. 'Of course I do.'

'Then you need to fight for your marriage.'

Stella threw her hands in the air. 'What's the secret, Liliwen? You were married for forty years. We couldn't even make it seven without imploding. I know it wasn't always smooth sailing for you either, but—tell me. How did you do it?'

Liliwen sighed and took Stella's hands in hers. 'I don't think there is a big secret. What I learned being married to one man for most of my life... well, it's like the longest game of pass the parcel you'll ever play. You keep passing the parcel back and forth, back and forth. With every layer you unwrap, you learn something new about the person you married. And it changes over time. Just when you think you've got the measure of him and you're expecting to unwrap a packet of gummy bears, he serves you a diamond. And when you're expecting the diamond, he gives you the gummy bears. But let me tell you, there is no greater privilege than growing old with somebody you love—' She paused for a moment as tears filled her eyes '—and getting to see what's at the centre of that parcel at the very end.'

'Oh, Liliwen, I'm sorry,' wailed Stella, hugging Liliwen tight. Her friend put on a brave face, but the death of her husband had hit her hard. It must be horrible to have lost the person that she thought she was going to grow old with.

Stella wanted to grow old with Connor.

She thought back to when they first fell in love. Stella had been broken after a relationship where she'd been somebody's dirty little secret. Her self-confidence was so low that she thought that was all she deserved. Then she'd met Connor, and he helped her believe she was worth more than that.

In the years since, he'd been her husband, her lover, her teacher,

her friend, her co-parent, and her business partner. She needed him in her life.

They'd lost their way, but hopefully they could work together to fix their relationship. Their daughter was named Grace, and maybe that was exactly what they needed: to give each other more *grace*.

Liliwen and Stella continued to sob in each other's arms. They were so loud that they didn't even realise Tristan had returned until he said, 'Have you ladies been watching *A Star is Born* or something?'

'Hey, you,' said Stella, wiping at her eyes. 'Where have you been?'

'Golfing.'

'*You* went golfing?' asked Stella. The only clubs he usually liked were the kind where dancing happened. 'Why's your hair wet? Is it raining?'

Tristan shoved his tongue into his cheek. 'Because I took a shower with Michael.' An unstoppable, ear-to-ear grin tore across his face.

'What?!' Stella lunged forward to pull him onto the sofa, sitting him between her and Liliwen. Both women angled their bodies towards him. 'When did this happen?'

'Tonight.' He laughed and hid his mouth with his hands, appearing every inch the excited school boy. Stella hadn't seen him this happy in far too long.

She clapped her palm on his leg. 'I thought you two hated each other.'

'Oh no, lovely,' said Liliwen. 'I predicted this from day one.'

Tristan raised an eyebrow. 'How's that?'

'Because at that dinner, whenever the other wasn't looking, you two were gazing at each other like Mr Darcy and Elizabeth Bennett.'

He laughed dirtily. 'I'm surprised you noticed much of anything at that dinner, occupied as you were by Knight Senior.'

Liliwen shrugged noncommittally, as if someone had asked whether her steak was cooked to her liking and the answer was meh. Stella wondered if something was amiss.

They'd deal with that later. At the moment, she wanted to know all about Tristan and Michael. 'So why are you here instead of snogging my brother-in-law?'

The grin slid from his face. After a moment's pause, he said, 'Because I need to take my pill.'

'Your pill?'

He nodded and fixed his brown eyes on her, suddenly serious. 'There's something I need to tell you. It's linked to why I moved to Mexico City and... everything else.'

'Shall I go?' asked Liliwen.

He reached out and touched her knee. 'No, stay. It's fine. I trust both my Welsh ladies.'

The jovial atmosphere from a moment ago died completely as Stella held her breath. Ever since Tristan left the UK, she'd wanted to know why he blew up his life, but she also didn't want to pressure him. She had a sinking feeling she wasn't going to like what he had to say.

Taking a deep breath, he started, 'Just over a year ago, I went for a blood test. I'd been feeling tired, so I went to get my iron checked. The nurse asked if I wanted an HIV test while I was there—you know, because it had been four months since my last one—so I thought might as well.'

Stella's heart thumped in her chest, afraid of his next words.

'Much to my surprise, two dots appeared.'

She closed her eyes and squeezed his arm, her breath sticking in her throat.

'I'm HIV positive.'

Both Stella and Liliwen gasped.

'No!' whispered Stella, throwing her arms around his neck and burying her head in his shoulder. This made all her problems dwindle in comparison. Her best friend had HIV! All she could think of were videos of Princess Diana visiting AIDS patients in the 80s, the constant news of how it ripped through the gay community. Fresh tears streamed down her face.

'Ah, love.' Liliwen rubbed her hand up and down his leg in a motherly gesture.

He covered her hand with his. 'It's okay. I'm fine.'

Suddenly, Stella remembered what he'd said earlier, about being with her brother-in-law. 'But... but what about you and Michael? Will he...? Does he...?'

'He's safe. My viral load is undetectable and therefore untransmittable. I know... I was shocked when I first heard the diagnosis, too. I kept replaying *Angels in America* in my head. Remember when we saw that production at the National... with Andrew Garfield in the lead?'

She nodded, unable to speak. That show had been terrifying.

He continued, 'Anyway, you shouldn't worry. I can live a happy, *normal* life as long as I'm taking my pill every day.'

Slowly, fear gave way to relief and Stella's crying subsided. Tristan was okay. 'Thank god. I didn't realise treatment had come so far.' She hugged him again.

'To be honest, I barely think about having HIV anymore—it has that little impact on my life.'

Liliwen cut in, 'So that's why you moved to Mexico?'

Tristan stared into the middle distance. 'It was the wake up call I needed. Who had I become? And was it who I wanted to be? I'd fallen down a celebrity rabbit hole where nothing I did really mattered. So I decided to have a fresh start. I went somewhere I could make a difference to regular people. Gay men like me who needed help.'

'What will you do now?' Stella asked, sitting up to look him in the eye. She wanted to ask if this thing with Michael was serious, but what she said instead was: 'Will you ever move back to the UK?'

He lifted a shoulder and stuck out his bottom lip. 'No idea. Thankfully, I have enough money saved that I don't need to worry about work. But I don't feel done in Mexico yet, so...'

She wondered what it would mean for Michael. Maybe this was

just a Vegas fling, but remembering how devastated he'd been after the break-up, she doubted it.

'Well, I'm done in, me. Off to bed.' Liliwen stood and stretched her tiny hands in the air before heading into the kitchen to fill a glass of water.

'And I'm going to head back to Michael's room,' said Tristan, unfolding his long body. Then he laughed. 'Look at us... all three sleeping with Knights.'

Stella frowned. She wished she was sleeping with her Knight tonight. She regretted how things had gone at the concert and wished Connor was with her now, so she could take him in her arms and show him that she believed in them, too. If she were a more courageous, confident person, she would've sent him a booty call text inviting him to come over. She imagined Betsy/Royale would send that message, no problem. But despite what Liliwen said, it wasn't that simple for Stella.

They'd already made the mistake once of making love before talking. She couldn't fall into that trap again with the question mark hanging over their future. Connor said they were strong enough to get through this... but did that mean he would be willing to put aside his past with Blake and relocate to Los Angeles with her? *For* her? If he wasn't, what did that mean for their marriage?

It wasn't a conversation she felt alert enough to have with him tonight.

Liliwen emerged from the kitchen, heading to her room with a water glass in hand. 'Yes, we're all jousting with Knights, but I bet mine is the only one that needs Viagra to stiffen his lance. Anyway, *nos da!*' she yawned as she closed her door.

Tristan and Stella looked at each other and broke out laughing. She put her arms around him and squeezed.

'I love you, you know?' she said. 'Are you happy?'

He nodded. 'More than I deserve.' Turning philosophical, he said, 'If there's one thing I've learned this past year, it's that life is short, happiness is a choice, and second chances are life's way of letting you rewrite the story with a better ending.'

Stella laughed, 'That's three things.'

'Still shit at maths, I guess.' He leaned down and rested his forehead against hers. 'Tits and teeth, Stels.'

'Tits and teeth,' she repeated.

After Tristan took his pill and returned to Michael, Stella thought about second chances. She already knew the ending she wanted with Connor, and divorce wasn't it. She wanted Liliwen's vision: to unwrap the Connor Knight parcel until the end of their days.

And the first step was making sure he came to that ceremony. She picked up her phone and typed a message:

> Please come tomorrow night. I really want you there. Sx

Stella sighed. One step at a time. After that, they'd talk about Los Angeles.

27

CONNOR

AT 7AM ON THE DOT AND WITHOUT THE ASSISTANCE OF AN ALARM, Connor jumped out of bed, sure that there was something he needed to do. Unfortunately, as he looked around his empty room for inspiration, he had no idea what it was.

He picked up his phone, hoping to find a clue there. A message from Stella waited for him, asking him to come to the awards ceremony that night.

Connor sighed and sat back down on the bed. He regretted telling Stella that he wouldn't go. Hopefully she'd win some awards, and he would have liked to be there to witness it. But there were also many reasons to avoid it. First, he knew his wife. Most likely, she was feeling guilty about their fight yesterday, thus she sent the text. The fact that she'd asked him for space and he'd ignored her filled him with regret. In hindsight, it had been the wrong move.

Now, he had the opportunity to do the right thing; let her have her night with her friends without the shadow of their broken marriage in the room. Tomorrow, they'd drive to Joshua Tree together. He just needed some patience—not usually his best quality.

Second, sitting in that ballroom would be painful. Not only because of feeling emotionally cut off from Stella, but because of the nostalgia that had been churning within him all week for the good ol' days, the days when he'd been 'the future of weddings' and his wife looked at him like he could do no wrong.

Sure, he had achieved the greatest heights as a photographer, but it was lonely at the top.

He put the phone down. He'd think about it and decide later.

The feeling of missing something important persisted.

While stirring his morning coffee, he stared into space, mentally cataloguing possibilities. Call Grace? He'd already FaceTimed her two days ago, plus she was still in school at that moment. Respond to an important email? He couldn't think of anything outstanding. Pay a bill? It all happened automatically these days.

He circled his shoulders and stretched, hoping that would shift the strange sensation plaguing him. It felt like tiny bugs crawling all over his body, making his skin itchy with inertia. He needed to be moving.

Maybe that was it! He picked up his phone and sent a text to Michael.

> Ready for that squash rematch?

A few moments passed and the reply came:

> Can't. Busy.

Connor wondered what might be keeping his brother occupied at this time of the morning. Recalling his suspicions from last night, he grinned and typed:

> Busy as in you're currently getting busy with Tristan?

Michael replied with a winky face.

Surprise, surprise. The sexual tension between those two had been thick from the beginning. Connor just hoped that Michael wouldn't get hurt. The pair didn't exactly live near each other, and long distance relationships seldom worked out, so he'd heard.

He swore as the fact that Stella was about to relocate to Los Angeles crashed down on him. It was a very long way from London —and from what she'd said last night, he wasn't invited.

The thrumming in his mind and body intensified when he thought about LA. And whenever he thought about LA, that path inevitably led to one thing: Blake Romero.

Bingo. Like a tuning fork finding its perfect pitch, his brain vibrated with purpose.

'Fuck.' He dropped onto the bed and sunk his head into his hands.

Last night, he'd told Stella that he'd continue to fight for her. That involved laying down his fight with Romero.

A grudge like his was a heavy load to carry for twenty-five years. Whether he liked it or not, his path had crossed with his arch nemesis again, and letting the wound continue to fester would only lead to rot. He knew what he had to do: he needed to talk to Blake Romero. Clear the air. Forgive him. For Stella's sake, but also for his own.

Holding onto the grudge was exhausting. The way his blood pressure shot up every time he thought about Romero couldn't be healthy, especially for a 45-year-old man. Connor wouldn't let his feud with Blake ruin Stella's opportunity or—more importantly— his family.

He picked up his phone and shot off a message to a couple of his old photography mates. Five minutes later, he had Blake Romero's number. He stared at it, wishing he didn't have to do this but knowing he had no choice if he wanted to save his marriage.

And his sanity.

Before he could change his mind, he dialled the number and lifted the phone to his ear. It rang once. Twice.

'Hello?' answered Blake groggily.

'Romero. It's Knight. Meet me in the hotel gym in thirty minutes.'

. . .

THE GYM WAS RELATIVELY empty at this time of morning. From experience, Connor knew that the convention parties ramped up as the week progressed: late nights layered with alcohol layered with more late nights. Most people would be lying in today or dragging their hangovers to the trade show for final-day deals.

Only two other people were in the gym: a man Armstrong's age on the treadmill and a woman using the fitness ball in the corner. Connor had chosen the gym as the location for their meeting because it served as neutral ground. Additionally, his body wanted to move, shake off the residue of that morning's agitation.

He crossed to the rowing machine, straddled the metal beam, and sat on the black leather seat. He hit the 'Just Row' button on the display and wrapped his hands around the oar grip. He began to glide his body back and forth, setting an easy 2:00 minutes per 500 meters pace.

The gym door opened, and Romero walked in, dressed in top-of-the-line workout gear—the type of high-performance sweat-wicking material that was probably developed for astronauts.

Their eyes met in the mirror. Connor kept rowing.

Romero sauntered over and mounted the machine next to Connor.

Without speaking a word, Blake slipped his feet into the straps and tightened them. He started to row.

Their paces synced. It didn't take long for their breathing to speed up to match their effort. Connor glanced over at Blake's metrics: 1:56 per 500 metres. Connor tugged harder, his time inching lower by a few seconds. The force of his row made him grunt like a bear on the pull stroke.

Knees bent and unbent. Shoulders hunched and then rolled back.

Eyes narrowed. Hearts pumped.

The machine itself trembled underneath him, as though it might shake apart at any moment.

Sweat poured down Connor's face, blurring his vision slightly. His gaze cut to Blake's screen again.1:48. *Fuck!* Pushing faster off the foot stretchers, Connor focused on increasing his pace. He crested 1:45, but his lungs were burning, and his shoulders ached. The calluses on his hands pulsated with fire.

From the panting next door, Connor could tell Blake was also struggling as he pushed his stroke time to 1:42. Connor gritted his teeth. Digging deeper, he drove to shave off a couple seconds more. Even though Connor had more muscle, Blake was leaner than him, which gave him an advantage when it came to speed. *The bastard.*

The noise of their quivering rowing machines, the swish of the ERG, and their extreme grunting overwhelmed the pop music playing on the gym sound system.

In a moment of triumph, Connor touched 1:40, but he couldn't keep it up. The oar grip slipped from his slick hands, and he slid to a stop, dropping his forearms to his knees, head bowed and shoulders heaving.

Romero was still going, his body flying back and forth. Connor reluctantly lifted his head and saw that Blake had reached 1:38/500m. A second later, he also relinquished his oar, his hoarse panting louder than Connor's.

A wave of nausea exploded through Connor. He stayed still and waited for it to pass. When his breathing slowed to a less frantic rate, he emptied his water bottle down his throat. With shaking hands, he loosened the strap securing his feet to the stretcher. They fell to the floor with a thud. He barely had the energy to move them.

'I won,' rasped Romero. If Connor had any strength left in his arms, he probably would have punched him.

'Fuck off.'

Blake waited for a beat, still panting. 'So why are we here?'

Connor turned his head away for a moment, gathering his thoughts, before swinging it back to pin Blake with his steady gaze. 'Remember that place we loved to eat? The one that did the great breakfasts with the fried pickles?'

'And the cactus salad? How could I forget? I cried like a baby when it shut down.'

'It did? What happened?'

'Pedro died.'

'Oh.' Pedro was one of the two owners. The other was Rosco. Both men were in their sixties, and they'd been friends since their army days, met when they were twenty years old. They opened the restaurant because they wanted to do something together and they both loved to cook. And fight. They looooved arguing with each other.

Connor continued, 'I used to think that Rosco and Pedro were what we would be like when we were older. Friends for life. Bickering about nothing, hanging out, doing what we loved.' He picked up his water bottle and turned it around in his hands. 'It threw me when you betrayed me. I thought I knew you like a brother, and then—'

'I'm sorry, Connor,' Blake cut in, taking Connor by surprise.

Running his hand through his sweaty blond hair, Blake swivelled so they faced each other. 'I'm sorry about what I did, and I'm sorry I never apologised. I was young and stupid and full of my own self-importance. Didn't like being told I was in the wrong. But... we were boys. I'm not the same man anymore.'

'Huh. Me either.' The Connor of twenty-five years ago was so sure of himself. The Connor of now wasn't sure of anything.

Shaking his head, Blake said, 'After you left, I did a lot of soul-searching. I didn't like what I saw. On top of that, I was mourning a friendship that meant a lot to me.'

It seemed the incident had served as a sharp lesson for them both. 'At least you had Betsy there to console you.'

Blake laughed without mirth. 'You're kidding, right? She was in a worse state than I was.'

That *really* took Connor by surprise. 'Why?'

'She was a wreck! You divorced her with barely a goodbye.'

Connor repeated what he'd been saying all week: 'But it wasn't a real marriage!'

'It may not have been a real marriage. And you may not have felt like a real husband, but at the very least, Betsy thought of you as a real friend. And, yeah, maybe she was also a little bit in love with you.' Blake reached down and retied his shoelace. 'When you left like you did, you made her feel like your entire relationship didn't matter. That *she* didn't matter.'

'Wow. Shit. Okay.' Connor rubbed the back of his neck, trying to parse the information Blake had just dumped on him. Self-reproach settled uncomfortably on his shoulders. It was disorienting to realise he wasn't the only wronged party in this whole disaster—that he'd done something bad, too.

He thought about the rejection sensitivity that was part of his ADHD and how he would have felt in this situation. The answer: not good.

Blake added, 'You know she avoided this conference for ages to make sure she didn't run into you. She only started coming again after you stopped.'

'I didn't think,' he said, guilt coating his stomach with acid. He hadn't meant to hurt Betsy, but as Blake said, they'd been young and stupid and full of their own self-importance. He'd cared about her— as a friend, at least. They'd had some good times together. It didn't make him proud to realise how badly he'd treated her. That wasn't the kind of person he believed himself to be. He valued loyalty.

'So...' said Blake, holding out his hand. 'Friends again?'

He wasn't going to get absolution that easily. 'That depends. This thing you have planned for Stella... is it legitimate?' Despite the apology, he couldn't quell the lingering doubt that Blake might be up to his old tricks.

Blake dropped his hand. 'Connor, your wife has become a major influencer in the lifestyle photography industry. She has fans all over the world. What we have planned for her... it's bigger than anything you or I ever dreamed of way back when.'

Connor knew this. Stella always had potential to be a star. He'd realised it the first time he met her, confidently challenging him to that thumb war in the bar. Maybe that's why he acquiesced and gave her a spot on his sold-out course in France.

But he wanted guarantees that Blake wouldn't mess up her career like he'd messed up Connor's. He leaned towards Blake. 'Promise me you'll take care of my girl,' he said with iron in his voice. 'If I hear that you've done anything remotely dubious, I swear to all the gods, I will make you pay. Understood?'

'Understood,' said Blake. 'Shake on it?' He held out his hand again.

Connor guardedly looked at the hand extended towards him. He slapped his palm against Blake's, and they shook. Connor's shoulders relaxed immediately, like a weight he'd been carrying had sloughed off. It felt good. Right.

'Guess I'm moving back to LA,' said Connor. Whether Stella wanted to be with him or not, nothing would keep him from living in the same city as his family.

Blake grinned, showing off his annoyingly perfect teeth. 'Great. I look forward to taking you on a tour of all the best restaurants in LA.' He'd always been a foodie.

And for the first time, eating a meal with Blake didn't sound like the worst idea in the world. 'Yeah,' Connor said. 'Maybe.'

They parted ways. Blake headed for a meeting, and Connor finished his workout. The antsy feeling he'd woken up with had resolved, although now there was a new feeling in its place: he should apologise to Betsy.

As he left the gym, he reread Stella's message. Part of him still wanted to go to the awards ceremony, but his earlier reasoning held firm. Besides, if he saw her tonight, he'd reveal that he'd decided to move to LA whether she wanted him there or not, and that would lead right back to the subject she said she didn't want to discuss until tomorrow. Making a decision, he wrote back:

Good luck tonight. I know you'll smash it. Think it's best if I see you in the morning, as planned. Cx

He hit send.

The lift doors opened, and a young woman ran out, crashing into Connor and making him drop his phone. It cracked against the hard tile floor.

'Sorry!' she said before her eyes flew to the device at their feet. 'Oh, shit! Is it broken? I'm late for my massage appointment, and I didn't see you.'

Connor picked up his phone. The screen was smashed, covered in shards and cracks like frost studied under a magnifying glass. He took a deep breath. 'It's fine,' he said. 'Don't worry about it.'

'I should pay for a replacement,' she insisted.

He didn't want to get into all that. Easier to sort it out himself. 'I have insurance, it's fine.'

'If you're sure…' she said, already backing towards the spa door.

'It's fine,' he repeated, giving her a tense smile. He'd locate a shop later to get it fixed.

At least it gave him something to do.

28

TRISTAN

THE CRISP DESERT LIGHT STREAMED ONTO THE CRUMPLED BED.

Tristan lay on his front, eyes closed, luxuriating in the lick of warm sun on his skin. In contrast, goosebumps peaked all over his back as Michael delicately traced the outlines of Tristan's tattoo again.

They hadn't left the room all day. Room service kept them fed and watered. If they didn't have this award ceremony to attend tonight, Tristan suspected they'd order dinner, too. Both of them wanted to squeeze every last second out of the time they had left.

Only one more night together... they'd wasted so much time this week, and now Tristan was less than 24-hours away from a return flight to Mexico City.

And what happened after? He didn't know. Didn't want to think about it. In the words of the inimitable Scarlett O'Hara: *Tomorrow is another day.* Cue the music.

Michael's finger lazily crested the right wing of the phoenix.

'Would you ever get a tattoo?' asked Tristan, turning his head towards his lover.

'Hmmm. I used to think the answer was no... but after seeing yours, I'd reconsider,' Michael said, trailing kisses down Tristan's shoulder.

Shifting onto his side so they faced each other, Tristan smiled. 'Oh yeah? What would you get?'

'Well, I *wouldn't* get matching Pac-Mans like dad and Liliwen.'

'What were they thinking?' Tristan laughed. 'What about Kit from *Knight Rider?* Or maybe David Hasselhoff's head?'

Michael snorted. 'Sounds perfect, right above my cock so you'd have company while you were down there.'

A shot of joy ping-ponged through Tristan. Not at the idea of staring at David Hasselhoff's face while giving Michael a blow job, but because Michael's words implied some sort of future.

Turning so that his back spooned into Tristan's front, Michael tangled their legs together. 'Seriously…. maybe I'd get a dahlia? It was my mother's favourite flower. Just a small one. Here.' He touched his bicep, and Tristan leaned forward to kiss the spot.

Pressed together like this, Tristan felt at peace, like this was exactly where he should be. He would never be able to get enough of Michael Knight.

The sound of a phone ringing threatened to break the mood.

'Don't answer it,' whispered Tristan as he pulled Michael closer to his chest and nibbled at his ear. His dick stirred with renewed interest.

Michael groaned and reached for his phone charging on his nightstand. He checked the screen and said, 'Ugh, sorry, I have to take this. My assistant never sleeps.' He sat up in bed and pressed a button. 'Hey, Ricky. What's up?'

Ricky? Tristan thought. Ricky Gervais, Ricky Ricardo, Ricky Martin… not a very professional law-firm kind of name. *Just sayin'.* He wondered what Ricky looked like.

'Yes, I saw it. Tell them I'll go over everything on the plane Monday. I'll have plenty of time then.' He laughed nervously. 'Is all the paperwork for our trip in order? Visas stamped?'

Tristan wondered where Michael was going. They hadn't really spoken about Michael's day-to-day life, avoiding the subject, probably because it was too much like reality when what they wanted was to remain in this fantasy. All Tristan knew was that tomorrow, Michael was flying back to New York a few hours after Tristan left for Mexico. He pictured a map of the world with lines following the trajectory of their separate planes heading away from each other.

His whole chest seized with sadness.

'Thanks, Ricky. See you at the airport. Don't forget to bring your sun cream this time.' He hung up.

Sun cream? What kind of work trip was this? 'Going somewhere?' asked Tristan.

'Trying not to think about it. We're off to Yemen for a case.'

'Oh?' Tristan felt like he'd been punched in the stomach. As a gay man, he knew which countries to avoid. Yemen was at the top of the list. 'Why are you going there? Is it safe?'

Ignoring his second question, Michael said, 'I'm arguing for a 17-year-old boy who's been condemned to death for homosexual activities. Unfortunately, I have to be present in their court. It's not ideal, but that's where the work is.'

'But is it safe?' Tristan repeated, pulling Michael down until their eyes were level again.

Michael took Tristan's face between his hands. 'It's where the work is,' he said again, quietly.

He kissed Tristan, a deep kiss intended to allay Tristan's fears, though it only made him more apprehensive. But what could he do? He wasn't Michael's life partner. They weren't in a relationship. He couldn't forbid Michael to go, much as he'd like to.

And even if he could, Michael would go anyway.

The real world was encroaching and Tristan didn't like it.

Ending the kiss, Michael said, 'Come on, let's not think about it. There are other things I'd rather be doing.'

Tristan blew out a shaky breath. 'You're too good for this world, Michael Knight.'

'Damned straight. I'm *very* good,' he said with a saucy wink. His mouth began to make its way down Tristan's torso—

The phone rang again. Michael broke away sharply, sitting up. 'Fucking hell, Ricky. Timing!' But when he looked at the phone, it wasn't Ricky. 'Stella, what's up?' As he listened to her answer, his eyes slid to Tristan, brow tensed. 'Hold on. Tristan's here. Let me put you on speaker.'

'Hi, Stels,' said Tristan as Michael held the phone between them.

'I can't find Connor anywhere,' she said, panic clear in her voice. 'He's not answering his calls or his texts. He's not even reading them. That's not like him.'

'Calm down, darling. Maybe he's in a show or something. Somewhere he can't use his phone?' suggested Tristan.

'For *five hours?*' Stella said. Tristan looked at his watch. *Shit, almost three o'clock.*

Michael said, 'I texted with him this morning.'

'Me, too!' she said. 'The last text I had from him was around ten o'clock. I sent him another text, but then I went into a two-hour class, thinking he'd reply while I was in there. He didn't. I called. No answer. Texted again before heading into a meeting.' The desperation in her voice ratcheted up a notch. 'We have to find him. We had a fight after the concert and he... he said he's not coming to the awards tonight.'

'But he *has* to come,' said Michael, running his free hand through his hair and sharing a worried look with Tristan.

'I *know!* That's why I'm trying to find him. I just came out of a panel and found he still hadn't replied. I'm not free until just before the awards...'

Tristan's shoulders slumped. There went their afternoon of torrid love making.

'No worries,' said Michael. 'We're on it.'

'Thanks, I owe you one,' she said. 'See you at the awards. Please let me know when you find him!'

29

TRISTAN

MICHAEL BANGED ON CONNOR'S DOOR, THEN PRESSED HIS EAR TO THE
wood.

No answer.

He banged again.

'Should you call him? Check if you can hear it ringing?'
Tristan said as he rolled up the sleeves on the same navy
button-down shirt he'd worn last night. Annoyingly, he'd
forgotten his baseball cap and sunglasses in their haste to leave
the room.

'Good idea.' Michael pushed a button on his phone. He waited,
then said, 'Still going straight to voicemail.'

He sighed and pressed another button. 'Dad? Yeah. I'm at
Connor's room. He's not here... okay, we'll meet you downstairs.
Start making a list of places he might be.'

In the lift, Michael jiggled his hands in his pockets the whole way
down. 'Where do you think he is?'

'Should we check the roof?' Tristan joked, trying to lighten the
mood. But when Michael didn't laugh at *The Hangover* reference,
Tristan cleared his throat. 'I'm sure he's fine. Maybe he lost his
phone. Lots of pickpockets in Vegas.'

'Hmmm. He didn't seem himself last night. I hope he hasn't done anything impulsive.'

Tristan tugged Michael to him and kissed him. 'It'll be okay. He can't have gone far.'

Michael blinked up at him like Tristan could fix all his problems. In that moment, Tristan wished he could. He wished he could make the world a better place for Michael, who tried so hard to make the world a better place for everyone else.

Shit, he fucking loved this man.

His heart thumped faster. Michael could probably feel it through his shirt.

The lift doors opened. Michael's hand crawled into Tristan's, who squeezed it tightly and pursed his lips to hide how pleased that one gesture made him. This was the first time they'd held hands in public. Back when they'd dated, Michael wanted to avoid any press lest it affect his career. They rarely displayed signs of being together in case the paparazzi were waiting, even going to the extremes of arriving and leaving restaurants separately. The one time they'd let the facade slip at some society party, their photo was in the next issue of *Hello!*, although thankfully they cited Michael's name wrong.

'Where's your dad?' asked Tristan, as he searched the lobby for Armstrong's distinctive silver head.

'Waiting in the bar.'

They found Armstrong huddled on a stool, nursing a whiskey. 'Dad, what are you doing? Where's Liliwen?' asked Michael.

'She went shopping,' Armstrong said with a sad tone that begged for a follow up question.

Michael closed his eyes as though asking a divine power for help. 'What's wrong, dad?'

'Was I a good father?' Armstrong rested his elbow on the bar and supported his chin with his fist.

'Are you serious? Is this really the right time for an existential crisis?' said Michael, putting his hands on his waist. Tristan saw a vein stick out on his neck.

'One of my sons is missing. Both of them are workaholics. Connor is having marriage problems. You haven't had a boyfriend in two years...'

What was that? All of a sudden Tristan found the conversation extremely interesting.

Someone tapped him on the shoulder, dragging his attention away. He whipped around to find a man in his 20s standing behind him, dressed in tight jeans and a Lady Gaga t-shirt.

'Hi,' said the man. 'Aren't you Tristan Hughes? Oh my god, I can't believe you're alive! I thought you'd been eaten by a tiger while on safari in Africa! Can I take a picture with you?' He lifted his phone before Tristan could say yes or no.

'Sorry,' Tristan said, holding up his hand, palm facing the man. 'Now's not a good time.' He turned back towards Michael and Armstrong.

'I just want one picture,' said the man, his voice peevish.

'I said no.'

'Well, fuck you very much,' the man said before trouncing off. Tristan caught him snapping a revenge picture from a distance. *Great. When it rains, it pours.* He could see the social media post now: *OMG Tristan Hughes spotted ALIVE in Vegas. Such an asshole IRL!* He returned his attention to Michael and Armstrong, pushing the encounter with the disgruntled fan out of his mind. Regrettably, they'd moved on from discussing Michael's love life.

'We need to come up with a plan for finding Connor,' said Michael. 'Did you make that list, dad?'

'No, I did something better. I called a guy,' said Armstrong, swirling his drink and appearing very pleased with himself.

'You *called* a guy?' said Michael. 'What are you? In the mob?'

Armstrong rolled his head to the side and gave Michael an unamused look. 'No,' he scoffed. 'I'm in government.'

Armstrong's phone pinged.

'And there it is now.' He swung his stool around and showed Michael and Tristan the screen.

They squinted at a Las Vegas address. 'What's that?' asked Michael.

With a cocksure grin, Armstrong said, 'That, my son, is where Connor's phone is right now.'

FRIDAY AFTERNOON WAS the wrong time to drive across Las Vegas. The taxi crawled through the traffic at an excruciatingly slow pace as the tourists arrived and the locals escaped. They probably could have walked it faster. Michael's knee bounced the whole way, even with Tristan's reassuring hand on his thigh. They'd left Armstrong at the hotel in case Connor turned up there.

On the way, Tristan pondered where this journey would lead. Was Connor wallowing in a seedy strip joint? Hiding his woes in the shadows of a Vegas magic show? Gambling away his worries at a high-stakes casino?

It had better be something good, because being stuck in a taxi listening to country music was *not* how he would have liked to spend his last afternoon with Michael.

'So... two years, huh?' said Tristan with a gentle elbow to Michael's ribs.

Wagging his pointer finger in the air, Michael said, 'You see, I knew you were going to bring that up.' He pinned Tristan with his innocent blue eyes. 'He said two years since I had a boyfriend. Not two years since I had sex.'

'Oh.' Tristan no longer wanted to have this conversation.

An hour later, they stopped outside of a run-down phone repair shop on the outskirts of town that promised 'same day service with a smile'—a disappointingly ordinary end to their sleuthing.

'What do you think he's doing here?' said Tristan. Then he had a thought. 'Do you think it's a front for an illegal high-stakes poker game or something?'

'You watch too much TV,' said Michael. 'I find that the simplest answer is usually the right one.' He pushed the door open.

Tristan asked the driver to wait and followed Michael inside.

A bell dinged as they entered the shop. One wall was lined with a paltry selection of phone accessories available for purchase, displayed in untidy rows. Opposite, a Latino youth sitting behind the counter looked up from his comic book. 'Can I help you?' True to the promise on the window, he was smiling.

Tristan wasn't ready to give up on his poker game theory and eyed the shop for hidden doorways. But Michael held up his phone, showing a picture of Connor on the screen. 'Did this man come in earlier today?'

The employee examined the screen. 'Oh yeah. Are you the couriers?'

Just as Michael was about to say no, Tristan stepped forward. 'Yes. Yes, we are.' Michael might be too lawyerly to lie, but Tristan had no issues impersonating a courier.

Michael threw him a sharp look, but kept his mouth closed.

'Great! I'm closing up early, and he said he'd send the courier by five. It's my sister's *quinceañera* tomorrow, and I need to get home to help.' He rummaged under the counter and pulled out a box containing a shiny black phone, receipt secured to it with a rubber band. 'Here you go. Just need your signature.' He detached the receipt and indicated where to sign. Michael scribbled something on the line that looked nothing like his name.

The employee handed the phone over. As they turned to leave, he said, 'Hey, dude. Has anyone ever told you that you look like that Tristan Hughes guy?'

'No. Never,' said Tristan straight-faced.

The youth shrugged. 'You should try modelling, man. Pays better than being a courier.' Then to Michael: 'No offence.'

Tristan had to bite his tongue to stop himself from laughing at Michael's comically outraged face. 'Thanks for the tip. I'll think about it,' Tristan said. 'And *feliz cumpleaños* to your sister.' They hurried out of the shop. A real courier was pulling up on a motorbike, and Tristan walked faster.

'No offence?' Michael laughed as they got into the taxi. 'What was he implying?'

'Well, baby, when you've got it, you've got it,' said Tristan.

ANOTHER HOUR PASSED in the taxi before they finally reached the hotel. As they pulled up, Tristan received a text from Stella:

Have you found him yet?

Still looking. But we know why he wasn't answering his phone. It was at a repair shop.

?????????

Tristan tucked his phone into his pocket and exited the taxi, slipping his hand into Michael's like they'd been doing it for years. A crease dented the area between Michael's eyebrows. He seemed so worried about Connor. The laughter after their exchange at the phone repair shop had slowly morphed back into concern in the taxi.

'We'll find him,' Tristan said, hoping it was true. He leaned down to kiss Michael quickly on the lips.

'Tristan!' called a voice.

He looked up.

A flash bulb went off, followed by a steady stream of fast, bright lights.

'What the fuck?' said Tristan, holding up a hand in front of his face.

'Tristan, over here!' called a paparazzo.

'Tristan, where have you been?' yelled another.

'Tristan, who are you with?'

Michael yanked his hand away. Tristan immediately mourned the loss.

'Bugger off!' he shouted before chasing Michael into the hotel where the paps couldn't follow. 'Wait!' He caught up halfway through the lobby.

'How do you put up with that?' asked Michael, his eyes spooked. 'They just... appeared. It's so invasive.' The horror on Michael's face tore at Tristan's heart.

He remembered a time when he didn't just put up with it; he encouraged it, his publicist tipping off the paps so they could shoot him outside restaurants, gyms, and parties. His whole life had been one big photo op. If a week went by when he wasn't in the tabloids, he'd worry about being forgotten by the fickle public.

Now, he no longer wanted that, especially if Michael didn't like it. He cursed himself for forgetting his baseball cap and glasses earlier. He should have gone back for them. 'I'm sorry—' he said.

'It's fine. I don't have time to worry about it now,' said Michael, taking a step back and checking his watch. 'We need to find Connor. The awards start in less than an hour.'

Tristan was tempted to go back outside and rip the memory cards out of each of those cameras, one by one. But that would just land him in jail. Instead, he took a deep breath and said, 'Where should we search next?'

They met up with Armstrong where the food court adjoined the leafy atrium. He'd walked all around the casino floor and through the arcade of luxury shops. 'No sign of him,' he said. 'But I did pick this up for Liliwen. What do you think?' He flipped open a red box to reveal a pricey silver Cartier watch.

'You stopped searching to go shopping?' said Michael with dismay.

'It was quick. I knew which one I wanted.'

'Whatever. I think she'll love it, dad,' said Michael, hands on his hips. 'Now can we get back to finding Connor?'

'There aren't many places left to search here. Just the theatres, restaurants...? He might be off-site. Should I start searching strip clubs?' Armstrong sounded hopeful.

Michael pulled a face. 'You know Connor wouldn't go to a strip club, dad.'

Armstrong held his hands up. 'Merely a suggestion.'

Just then, Michael perked up like a meerkat. 'Wait! Shhh! What is that?'

They stood still for a handful of seconds, listening.

'What are we listening for?' asked Tristan.

Without answering, Michael jogged into the food court, where the smells of all the fast-food restaurants coalesced. Armstrong and Tristan had no choice but to follow. Michael stopped outside the Ramen/Bubble Tea/Karaoke place, where somebody was singing 'I'm Just Ken' loudly and with great feeling.

At first, they couldn't see Connor, but as they walked past empty booths, further into the white-and-red tiled restaurant, a pair of trainers appeared, sticking out from a bench seat towards the back. Aside from two bored servers waiting with arms crossed behind the counter, there were no other punters.

'Welcome to Sing'n'Slurp! Chicken, beef, or veg?' asked the male server.

'Uh, we're here for him,' said Michael, nodding towards Connor's feet.

'Thank God!' said the male server. 'He's been hogging the mic for three hours.'

'I'm not complaining,' said the girl.

At the sound of their voices, Connor stopped mid-chorus and sat up, his head popping up above the booth. 'Hey! It's my boys! Why don't you come over here and sing with me?' He scooted forward off the red bench and stood up.

'No, thanks,' said Michael and Tristan at the same time.

'Son, what are you doing?' asked Armstrong.

Connor threw his arms open like he was Julie Andrews on a mountain. 'What does it look like I'm doing? I'm singing!'

Armstrong readjusted his jacket. 'There, we found him. I'm going to pick up Liliwen. See you soon.' And he left.

'What's his problem?' asked Connor.

Frustrated, Michael stomped up to his brother. Tristan had never seen Michael so agitated, except because of him, of course. 'Connor, we have to go. We're late for the awards.'

Shrugging off his concern, Connor said, 'I'm not going.'

'Yes, you are,' insisted Michael, taking hold of the mic and handing it off to Tristan.

'Stella doesn't want me there.'

Michael groaned. 'Stella's been worried sick about you. Who do you think sent us to find you?'

'Why is she worried? I'm giving her the space she wanted.'

In a sharp, commanding voice that Tristan had never heard Michael use before, he bellowed, 'Well, she doesn't want space. She wants *you* at the awards. Now!'

Was it weird that Tristan was suddenly turned on by this new, forceful Michael? He realised he was absentmindedly stroking the microphone. He put it down on the counter.

'Shit. Is she angry with me again?' Connor sat down heavily in his booth. 'I can't seem to get anything right.'

'Just come with us, and I'm sure she'll forgive you.'

Tristan examined Connor. He did not look well. His white shirt was untucked, his jeans stained. His eyes had a manic glaze, and he couldn't seem to sit still, even though his movements were sluggish. If Tristan didn't know better, he'd say that Connor was drunk or even *high*. That was an unexpected complication.

He didn't want to be the bearer of bad news, especially after the paparazzi incident, but...

'Michael,' interjected Tristan. 'Do you think we should sober him up first? He looks like he's...' He leaned towards Michael so that only he could hear, '...at cruising altitude, darling.'

Eyes scouring his brother, Michael said, 'Connor...' He lowered his voice. 'Have you been taking *drugs*?'

'What? No!' He pointed towards his table, which was obscured from their view. 'I've just had *those*.' Stepping forward, they found the table littered with empty cups of bubble tea—at least ten. Connor touched a hand to his temple. 'I—I think I have a headache. And I really need to pee.'

Michael threw his hands up in the air. 'Seriously, am I the only sane one in this family? Let's sort you out. You can't go to the ceremony like this.' Turning to Tristan, he said, 'Can you text Stella and let her know we found him?'

30

STELLA

THE HOTEL BALLROOM OVERFLOWED WITH PHOTOGRAPHERS IN THEIR best attire. Most of them congregated around the bar at the back, but some were already sitting at the round-top tables facing the main stage. Waiters in crisp black trousers and white shirts served canapés from dainty trays.

This was the final night of the convention. The final night to hang out with their peers, celebrate the excellent work they all strived to create on a daily basis, and party like kids on spring break —before returning to their normal lives: the emails, the clients, the constant worry about their bottom line.

Stella arrived alone, self-consciously smoothing down the off-the-shoulder lilac gown that Claudia had helped her purchase a month ago. It cost more than she'd normally spend on a dress, but tonight was a special occasion. She wore her red hair down, wavy but tamed into a sleek bunch and swept to one side of her neck to cascade over her shoulder. Classy.

Award ceremonies still held a modicum of terror for her. Her mind flitted back to another night eleven years ago, when she was attacked on stage by her lover's wife—an experience that ended one career and started her on the path to this one. Although she wouldn't change the outcome and she loved being recognised for her work, nerves still plagued her every time she sat at a round table where trophies were involved.

She hoped they found Connor. Having him next to her always made these nights easier.

At the entrance, she checked the table plan. Theirs was right in front of the stage, which made sense, given Connor's award. He'd have a good view of the screen from there.

She weaved through the crowds, smiling and stopping along the way to speak with friends, admirers, and well-wishers. A few asked for selfies. Tonight, she was a finalist in four portrait categories: maternity, individual, boudoir, and creative. In the first two, she was competing against herself, all her images in the top slots. But in boudoir, she was competing against none other than Royale Lefevre.

Up ahead, Stella could see Royale, swathed in a tight green sequin gown worthy of the Oscars, hair swirled up in a configuration only a professional could achieve. She was surrounded by a crowd of admiring men.

The usual burning itch of jealousy kindled in Stella's belly. Knowing that this woman had also been married to Connor, *her* Connor, ate at her.

But why?

Connor had chosen Stella. He'd made it clear that Royale wasn't a threat.

She couldn't go through the rest of her life being jealous of every woman who spoke to him. Stella was a beautiful 38-year-old woman who had achieved so much. She had a gorgeous child, a talented husband, good friends who loved her... when would she stop feeling like she wasn't enough?

Now, that's when, thought Stella. It was time for her to own her power and stop competing. Squaring her shoulders she approached Royale. 'Hello,' Stella said, her pink lips stretched into a genuine smile. 'I just wanted to say good luck tonight. I love the image of the woman in the glass slipper. It's amazing.'

'Thank you,' purred Royale, quickly hiding the momentary spark of surprise on her face. 'Good luck to you, too.'

'Thanks.'

As Stella turned to leave, Royale stopped her with a hand on her arm. 'And... let me know if you want to have a chat about the best places to live in LA. I've been there a long time, and I used to date a reliable realtor. I can pass on her number.'

Her number? Interesting.

'That would be great,' said Stella. 'I'd love that.' They might not end up the best of friends, but it didn't mean they couldn't be kind to each other.

Glad that she'd made the effort, Stella found her table. The ones nearby had already filled up with fellow photographers. Hers... was empty aside from herself. Embarrassing! She pulled out her chair and sat like she was expecting her friends to arrive at any minute.

Taking her phone out, she checked her messages. Nothing from Tristan, Michael, or Connor. With dismay, she noted that the wifi had dropped out. When she refreshed her WhatsApp screen, a circle appeared at the top with the words *waiting for network*.

What if they didn't find Connor tonight? Where could he have gone? Was he okay? So many people worked hard to organise this award. If he didn't turn up, he'd be missing out on a special evening of well-deserved recognition, and it would be all her fault.

Thinking back to the Chris Seals concert, she wished she could have a do-over.

Thirsty, she reached for a bottle of still water in the middle of the table and poured herself a glass. There would be no dinner at the event; people knew to line their stomachs generously beforehand because the alcohol always flowed. Stella herself had woken in the past with a woolly head on Saturday morning. Nonetheless, she didn't want to drink too much tonight. She wanted to remember every second... unless, of course, Connor never turned up, in which case, she'd happily forget it.

Where was he?

The noise of conversation surrounded her, overlaid with a rousing mix of pop music. Stella struggled to appear serene and unworried as she continued to sit alone. It felt like she'd been sitting for an hour, when a quick glance at her phone showed it had only been two minutes. The loneliness that she'd experienced last night washed over her again. In Los Angeles, she'd be starting over without her entire support network. And if she and Connor failed to work things out, then she'd also be solo parenting.

She knew she could do it if she had to, but she didn't want to. She loved Connor. He was the only parcel she wanted to unwrap. She only hoped she hadn't pushed him too far. Why hadn't he replied to any of her texts today?

Speaking of which, she checked her phone again. Still no service. Bloody hotel wifi.

'There she is,' said Blake, seizing the chair next to her and sitting down in his tailored, light blue suit. His eyes briefly registered the lack of other people. He placed his wine glass on the table. 'Do you need a drink?'

'No, thanks. I'm fine. Trying to keep a clear head.' She tapped a finger against her temple.

'I imagine you'll be up on stage a few times tonight.'

'Fingers crossed.' She demonstrated the gesture.

His gaze grazed the table again. 'Is anyone else... joining you?'

'Yes! They're just...' For a second, she considered making up some lame excuse, but she decided to just come out with it. 'They're looking for Connor. He went missing today.'

'Missing? But I saw him this morning.'

'You did?' She couldn't hide her surprise.

'Yes, believe it or not. He called me. Asked me to meet him in the gym.'

She scanned Blake's face to make sure he hadn't covered up a black eye with concealer. The man seemed intact. 'And?'

'And... we talked.' He shrugged. 'I apologised. He forgave me.'

'Wow.' She thought back to three days ago, when Connor shared

JULIA BOGGIO

his story about Blake. If anyone had asked her then whether reconciliation was imminent, she'd have said *no way*.

Blake added, 'And he threatened my life if I screwed you over.'

She barked a laugh. That sounded about right.

Narrowing his eyes, he considered her and said, 'He really loves you. I can tell. If there is one thing I know about Connor Knight, it's that he's intensely loyal. I had that loyalty once and I blew it. But I'm hoping, maybe, when we're all in LA, maybe we can repair some of the damage.'

She grabbed his arm. 'Wait—did he say he's coming to LA?'

'Uh, yes?' Blake seemed confused by the question. 'You and his daughter will be there, so...?'

Happiness bubbled up inside of her. Connor was moving to LA! She knew it was a sacrifice for him, just like reaching out to Blake had been. But he was willing to do these hard things—for her.

And if he was willing to do these things for her, it meant that he really did believe in them; he was still committed to making things work. Her entire body relaxed. She hadn't realised how much tension she'd been holding with the stress of worrying about their marriage and the thought that she'd pushed him too far. Stella took a deep breath and pursed her lips to contain the shriek of joy she'd otherwise let out.

Now she just needed Connor to turn up.

'Hello, lovelies!' said Liliwen, plonking an empty ice bucket on the table. She looked amazing in a pink chiffon cocktail dress. Something shiny caught Stella's eye: a brand-new silver watch. Cartier, no less.

'Anyone need a drink?' said Armstrong, brandishing a bottle of champagne and six slim flutes stuck between his fingers like some sort of party-ready Edward Glasshands.

'Blake,' said Liliwen coldly, her smile dropping.

'It's okay,' said Stella, red colouring her cheeks. 'Everything is sorted.'

'Thank goodness,' said Liliwen with relief. 'I couldn't stay angry at such a handsome devil.' She winked at Blake and he chuckled. 'My turn to buy you a drink later, lovely.'

Armstrong frowned at the exchange and put an arm around Liliwen's waist.

Noting it was almost showtime, Blake stood up. 'I'll see you later. Good luck tonight.' He kissed Stella on each cheek before returning to his table.

Stella addressed her father-in-law. 'Did you find Connor?' Her heart pounded as she waited for the answer. He'd be so disappointed if he missed this.

'Of course we found him,' Armstrong said as he poured champagne. 'Tristan and Michael are just cleaning him up and getting some food into him before bringing him here.'

His turn of phrase alarmed her. 'Cleaning him up? Where did they find him? In a dumpster?'

He passed her a glass. 'No, singing karaoke. Ghastly business.'

Actually, that made perfect sense. She chuckled to herself.

The lights dimmed, and the music grew louder, signalling that the show was about to start. Three seats at their table were still empty.

On stage, Therese Asplund, the IPE director, approached the podium, resplendent in an orange, long-sleeved dress edged with yellow and black flowers. She always wore Swedish designers and looked immaculate.

Therese leaned towards the microphone. 'Welcome to this year's IPE Awards!' she said, and the whole room broke out into raucous applause. Her eyes flicked down to Stella's table, and then up to Stella with a question in her gaze: *Where's Connor?*

Stella held her hands out reassuringly to signal that he was on his way.

Therese nodded and addressed the room again. 'Every year, we come together to recognise the best of the best at this, the world's greatest convention for photographers!' More applause. More hooting and whooping. The Americans could give a masterclass in hooting and whooping.

'IPE is more than just the place we all go every year to buy more photography gear and drink a lot of booze,' she said, scrutinising the audience. 'It's where we come for inspiration, to learn, to improve our craft, and most importantly, to connect with our IPE family.' Behind her, on a large screen, shots scrolled of delegates laughing together, hugging, watching demonstrations. Stella saw a picture of herself go past, teaching on the Canon stage.

This year, she'd been so frantic with work and so distracted by her marriage issues that she didn't really get a chance to enjoy the convention. She remembered the first time she came here with Connor, after they'd been dating for six months. He was the hottest wedding photographer in the world, in more ways than one, and hearts broke when people saw him strolling around the conference holding her hand. She'd felt like a queen by his side.

Now the hot wedding photographer was Ali Kazan, and in a few years, it would be somebody else.

Who knew what the next twelve months would hold for her? After they'd launched her platform, she'd probably have her own stand in the trade show. The only constant was indeed change.

But this year wasn't over yet. She checked the time on her phone again.

Where was Connor?

31

CONNOR

WHEN MICHAEL REUNITED CONNOR WITH HIS PHONE, HE RECEIVED A string of messages from Stella sent throughout the day:

> Please reconsider. I really want you to come to the awards. Sx

> Connor, please. I'm sorry about what I said after the concert. I really want you with me tonight. Sx

> Connor?

> Would it help if I offered sexual favours afterwards...?

> Okay, stop twisting my arm. You can get a dog. A small one though.

> Connor?

> Getting worried now. Combo of dog and sex should have elicited swift response.

> Really worried now. Calling the police. And your brother.

He found it interesting that the offer of sexual favours came before the dog. He knew she had a childhood fear of getting bitten, so he supposed a dog ranked as a rarer prize. The one-sided exchange warmed his heart. When they returned to London, he'd probably print it out and frame it. Not only because he fully planned to hold Stella to both promises, but also because, for the first time in a long time, he knew that everything between them would work out. These were not the texts of a woman who wanted to end their marriage. After all, a dog meant commitment.

'Come on,' he called to Michael and Tristan, who were lagging slightly behind.

'I can't run in pleather!' objected Tristan, pointing to his trousers. 'And I don't want to get sweat stains on my shirt.'

'Your shirt's practically air conditioned,' Connor said to Tristan's billowing, Zorro-style blouse undone halfway to his navel—although even as a straight man, Connor had to admit that Tristan did look hot tonight.

Perhaps Connor should wear black more often, instead of his white button-downs and the grey trousers that he knew Stella liked because of the way they hugged his arse.

Michael had also made an effort, breaking his usual pattern avoidance by donning a short-sleeved floral shirt and off-white trousers. The shirt was purposefully one size too tight and showed off Michael's gym body.

As a couple, they were like ying and yang. Dark and light. But somehow, they fit. And they were holding hands—which was very cute, but Connor really wished they'd hurry the fuck up.

He cursed the size of Las Vegas hotels. It took half an hour to get anywhere. By the time they'd eaten something, returned to their rooms to shower and change, and hauled themselves across what felt like ten miles of corridors, casinos and arcades, over ninety minutes had passed. The awards show would be half over by now, but he really wanted that dog.

Finally, they reached the ballroom. He checked the table plan outside. Of course, their table had to be right in front of the bloody stage.

From outside, he heard Therese begin to announce the Photographer of the Year, which meant the category awards had already finished. *Shit.* He opened the door quietly while holding his breath, hoping to hear Stella's name.

'The Photographer of the Year...' Therese said then paused dramatically.

Connor, followed by Tristan and Michael, wove through the darkened auditorium towards their table.

'...is Steve Scalone!' announced Therese as the room erupted in applause and everyone rose to their feet.

Aw, bad luck, thought Connor, disappointed for Stella. But Steve was an amazing architectural and landscape photographer from Australia and equally deserved the award. It would be Stella's turn another year. That was the way of awards: you won some, you lost some.

As he approached the table, he could see that Stella had already won some. Four pieces of glass sat in front of her, which meant she'd won every one of her categories. His heart swelled with pride, even as he regretted missing her moments.

He knelt next to her chair and leaned towards her ear. 'Congratulations! Sorry I'm late,' he said under his voice, so only she could hear.

She turned to him, her face lit up by a massive smile. 'You're here!' she whispered loudly, throwing her arms around his neck and kissing him. She tasted like champagne. His hands slid around her waist, loving the smoothness of her silk dress. It was the kind of kiss that made him wish they could go back to her room right now and skip this award show. For the first time in a long time, they were acting like the real Connor and Stella again.

When she pulled away, he joked, 'I'm going to break my phone more often if that's the response I get.'

'Don't you dare,' she said with a nip to his nose. He stood up and pulled his chair so it nestled beside hers, both facing the stage.

Tristan and Michael sat opposite. Stella waved at them.

Steve Scalone collected his award and everyone applauded again. Therese went back to the microphone. Covering it with her hand, she leaned around the podium and said to Connor, 'Nice for you to finally join us, Mr Knight.'

He smirked and swirled his hand next to his head like a royal greeting. She laughed.

Clearing her throat, she moved on. Only half listening, Connor squeezed Stella's hand, which he held like a precious artefact sandwiched between his palms. God, she looked beautiful tonight: her hair swept mermaid-like over her shoulder, the lilac of her dress complimenting her pale skin and freckles. Her bare neck called to him.

She mouthed, 'What?'

'I love you,' he mouthed back.

'I love you, too,' she whispered, then pointed at the stage.

Therese readjusted the mic. 'Every year, we honour a photographer who has made an extraordinary contribution to the field. This person has been selected by our entire pool of judges and—I have to say—everyone was unanimous in their choice this year.' She turned over her notes. 'This man has been among us for more than two decades. Those who have been coming to IPE for a while remember him as an eager boy, milk still behind the ears and convinced that he would one day be running the show. Well, he's not running this show, because *I* am, but he is running circles around an industry where creativity and originality are prized.

'There are probably very few people in this room who haven't learned something from him. But enough from me. Let's hear what others have to say about him.'

The screen behind her flickered and an old-style black-and-white cinema countdown appeared. Connor yawned behind his fist even though he'd drunk ten bubble teas. He probably wouldn't be able to sleep for a week. He had no idea what had possessed him to have so many. The girl just kept bringing them to his table, and he kept drinking them. His teeth ached from the sugar overload, even though he'd brushed them thoroughly back in his room.

Five... four... three... two... one...

The screen went blank and the first notes of 'In My Life' by the Beatles played. A video faded in of Grace sitting on the floor of her bedroom, surrounded by Squishmallows.

Speechless, he twisted towards Stella, eyebrows raised, jaw dropped.

She had tears in her eyes. 'Watch!' she said, pointing him forward again.

'What do I say, mummy?' Grace asked in her high-pitched voice.

Stella giggled off-screen. 'Just say congratulations, daddy!'

Grace broke out in a toothy grin and threw her arms in the air. 'Congo-lations, daddy! I love you!'

The whole room went 'awwwwww!' Emotion inflated inside him, practically cutting off his oxygen. His eyes grew moist. Stella squeezed his hand to say *I'm here*.

After that came messages from Damian McGillicuddy saying he took credit for all of Connor's greatness and Therese, plus a few other photography industry professionals he'd worked with over the years and students from classes past, like Karen and Gunner, who attended the same chateau course as Stella. Connor's unstoppable smile was using muscles he didn't even know he had.

A photography studio faded in. Ali Kazan sat on a stool, surrounded by lighting stands. To his knowledge, Connor had never met him. 'I remember the first time I saw Connor Knight speak at IPE. It was... electric! I was shook. I knew from that moment what I wanted to do with my life. So thank you, Mr Knight, from all the countless photographers whose lives you've touched.' He tapped his heart with his fist and made a peace sign at the camera.

Blake Romero came on next, filming in a conference room. 'I first met Connor Knight at my very first IPE conference... too many years ago to mention. I knew right away that he had more talent in his pinky finger than most people have in their whole body. It's been amazing to watch what he's achieved in this industry, not just as a photographer, but as a teacher.' He stuck his tongue in his cheek. 'Connor... is this a good time to ask you to do a class for MuseTV?'

The room chortled. Connor pretended to be grumpy and crossed his arms. 'Not bloody likely,' he called out loud enough to be heard above the Beatles backing track.

'Too soon?' yelled Blake.

Surprisingly, Betsy/Royale came on. She was sitting on a sun lounger in a red bathing suit, large sunglasses covering her eyes. Without moving his head, Connor shifted his gaze towards Stella, worried what her reaction would be. But she was watching the screen with open interest. No tight-lipped scowl. No stroking her chin with angst.

'Connor, Connor, Connor,' said Royale, and he dreaded what she might say. 'When I knew you... and I knew you well... you were full of dreams and possibilities. It's been a pleasure to watch your career grow over the years. As Edgar Degas said, "Everyone has talent at 25. The difficulty is to have it at 50." Well, you're 45, close enough. And from where I'm sitting, your talent is showing no signs of stopping. Congratulations.'

He nodded his head in appreciation. Usually, when he thought about his time in LA, he couldn't get past the anger. It painted everything in a foul wash. But forgiving Blake had unblocked his memories. Blake, Royale, and Connor had enjoyed some wild times together. Now he could remember them without the bitterness of disappointment and rage.

In a surprise dash across the Atlantic, Krish, Francesca, and Soraya appeared, sitting on a bench in their garden. Norman, their Golden Retriever, sat like a sentinel next to the family.

Looking into the camera, Krish said, 'Where would I be without

Connor Knight? He taught me everything I know. Not just about being a photographer, but about business, and most importantly, about going for my dreams. The years I worked with you were some of the craziest, most inspirational times of my life. I love you, Boss.'

Francesca played it straight. 'He's all right, I guess.' Soraya chose that moment to fill her nappy loudly, the fart startling both parents before they hooted with laughter. The dog howled.

A wide grin split Connor's face. This was astonishing. He couldn't compute how much work had gone into making this video.

Next came Claudia with her husband Magnus in the living room of their house. She went first: 'Connor, you're a BLEEPin' legend. BLEEP. Sorry. Am I allowed to swear?'

When she finished, Magnus spoke, 'I think what my wife is trying to say is that you've been setting the standards in this industry for as long as we've been in it. And I BLEEPin' hate you for it, you BLEEP,' he said with a cheeky grin.

Connor barked. Magnus and he used to dislike each other, but since they married best friends, they'd learned to get along.

The image shifted to Armstrong, being interviewed in his hotel room. Usually so collected, Connor was surprised to see him wringing his hands. 'I don't think I say this enough, son. But I'm proud of you. And your mother would be proud of you, too. What you can do with a camera... it's incredible. Who knew we had such genius in our blood? I may have trouble showing it, but son... I'm your biggest fan.'

Tears moistened Connor's eyes again. Stella handed him a tissue, like she'd expected this to happen. He leaned back and glanced over at his dad, who was nodding his head, eyes shining with pride. 'Thanks, dad,' Connor mouthed.

Michael came next. He was sitting near the hotel pool, holding the Fedora in his hands, fidgeting with the rim. 'Hey, big brother. Congratulations on your Lifetime Achievement award! You deserve it. For me, you've always been the easiest person in the world to look up to, so I'm glad to see that others recognise how great you are, too. Well... at everything except squash.' He winked and smiled.

Connor laughed and turned to Michael, narrowing his eyes with challenge. 'I want a rematch soon.'

'You're on,' said Michael.

He assumed that Stella would be last, and sure enough, her face finally filled the screen. She was in her hotel room, with the bright poppies and oranges on the table behind her. He recognised the outfit she wore to the concert last night, which meant that she'd recorded it recently.

She spoke directly to him. 'I remember the first time I saw you on stage.' She placed her hand on her chest. 'You took my breath away. Whether I knew it or not, our lives were linked from that moment, and I... I am a better person for it. Your fingerprints are all over me.' She smiled and looked up. 'Okay, that sounded weird. What I meant to say is that because you're in my life, I am the photographer I am today... the wife, the mum. Connor Knight, you are the shape of my heart.'

He could feel her shaking next to him and knew she was crying. He turned to her and cradled her face between his hands. Her lashes glistened with tears. He kissed her, tasting salt on her lips. How lucky was he that this woman had sought him out all those years ago and inserted herself into his life? Never had he been so happy to lose something as he was losing that battle of thumb wars (even if she cheated).

'I love you,' they both said at the same time and laughed.

'There's one more,' she said, drawing his attention back to the screen. The image shifted again. Suddenly, they were in a music recording studio, and Kevin, Brian, AJ, Howie, and Nick were smiling into the camera, no longer boys, but men.

'Holy shit!' said Connor, then covered his mouth with his hands, shocked.

Brian said, 'Connor, we heard you're getting a Lifetime Achievement Award today.' Then Kevin: 'And we just wanted to say a huge congratulations from your friends, the Backstreet Boys.' AJ then added with a wink: 'A little birdie told us you're a big fan.' Then all together they sang a few lines from 'Larger Than Life', their voices still blending seamlessly after all these years.

Connor couldn't believe it. He leaned forward and looked past his wife to Michael. 'Was this you...?'

Michael shook his head and pointed across the table. 'Stella.'

How did she know?!

When he looked at her, she was smiling like she'd pulled off the surprise of the century. She lifted her eyebrows. 'Well, I *have* been married to the sixth Backstreet Boy for seven years.'

He threw back his head and laughed. She knew him better than he'd thought.

Therese's voice cut in, saying, 'Please let us all welcome Connor Knight, the recipient of this year's Lifetime Achievement award, to the stage.'

Stella kissed him quickly and said, 'Go!'

His head was spinning—a combination of the shock and the residual effects of bubble tea. Up on stage, Therese greeted him with a peck on each cheek before handing him an angular glass IPE trophy. He took his place in front of the podium and scanned the ballroom. Everyone was on their feet, clapping and whooping for *him*.

He'd been foolish to think he was no longer part of this family.

'Wow,' he said. 'This is a surprise. I had no idea. Unaccustomed as I am to public speaking...' Everyone laughed. They all knew he loved a stage. His body zinged with dopamine. 'I'm absolutely honoured to be recognised by my peers like this. And of course, the Backstreet Boys.' He paused for a moment. 'Everybody has their own feelings on what family means to them. I've been in therapy recently—' Somebody cheered. '—thank you. So I probably have more recent feelings on it than most. I had an interesting childhood. My father worked in diplomatic services. We moved around a lot— every three years, to be exact. My mother died when I was eight, leaving us three boys to fend for ourselves.' He found Michael's eyes and gave him a small smile. He was gratified to see Tristan had his arm around Michael's shoulders.

'Because of that, we were raised to be independent... which is great in many ways—as my father used to say, "There's only one person you can truly rely on in this world." But, in other ways, it falls short of the reality, which is that *no man is an island unto himself.* We need each other. That's what being human is about. Not independence, but *inter*dependence. I think the first time I truly learned that lesson was when I came to IPE.

'Many of you in this room were my second family. And I'll be eternally grateful for everyone who took the time to teach me or critique my work so I could improve, who laughed with me, believed in me, and welcomed me back year after year despite the fact that I was probably a bit of an arrogant prick.' He smiled with self-deprecation as some in the audience hooted their agreement. 'I think it was from your example that I became passionate about teaching others. It's something I haven't been doing much of lately, and I think it's time to get back to it. I forgot how connected it makes me feel to all of you. So... yeah, Blake, what the hell. I'll do a course for MuseTV.'

A resounding cheer bounced off the walls, and Blake stood up, put his hands together in prayer, and bowed. 'You heard him say it!' he shouted to the room.

Connor continued, 'The second time I learned that I needed others was when I met my beautiful wife, Stella. Her fingerprints are all over me, too. Behave!' he growled playfully in response to some wolf whistles. 'She taught me, too. About love and vulnerability and how you should never mix colours with whites in the laundry.' More laughter. 'Now, I genuinely cannot live without her. By the way, she's going to do great things! And I'm going to support her every step of the way, because that's what family does. I'm so proud of you.' He blew her a kiss. She caught it and cupped it over her heart.

'Okay, that's enough from me. I'm getting soppy in middle age.

Just... thank you! I really appreciate this.' He held up the trophy and the photographers got to their feet again for another roaring ovation.

Afterwards, friends old and new crowded around him. It felt like the good old days again. As he chatted with somebody reminiscing about one of his courses, he spotted Royale nearby, holding court with her own adoring crowd. There was unfinished business between them.

He excused himself, dragging Stella with him. 'Do you mind if I talk to Royale for a minute?'

'Of course,' she kissed him, and he understand her message: *I trust you.*

His heart swelled with gratitude. How long had he waited for this? For her forgiveness? 'I'll be right back.'

Approaching Royale, he touched her elbow lightly to get her attention. 'Can I have a word?'

'Sure. Excuse me, boys.' She followed Connor into the hallway, where there were fewer people vying to talk to him. Her green sequin dress reflected the tungsten hotel lights. 'Congratulations on your award.' She gestured towards the crystal tower he was clutching.

Connor readjusted his grip on it. The glass was heavier than it looked. 'Well, thank you for your kind words. I have to say, I don't think I deserved them.'

She lifted one of her elegant shoulders. 'It was all true.'

'Even so... I owe you an apology.' He made sure to look her in the eyes when he said, 'I realise now that I... that I didn't treat you very well, when we were... when we were—'

'Married?'

'Yes. I shouldn't have run away without a proper goodbye. It was wrong of me, and I was a terrible friend. You deserved better.'

She sighed. 'I did, yes.'

'I just wanted you to know, it wasn't your fault. And I truly am sorry.'

Royale smiled, not a bright happy smile, but one that acknowledged their shared past. 'It was a long time ago. We've both done a lot of growing up since then.'

'I suppose we have,' he said, thinking back to the arrogant know-it-all he used to be.

'Apology accepted,' she said, touching his cheek affectionately with her manicured hand. Then with the speed of a striking snake, she reached down and twisted his nipple between her fingers. The pain shot through him, straight to his toes.

'Ow! Ow! Ow!' he said until she released him, a satisfied smile on her lips. 'What was that for?'

'It's called a Purple Nurple, and that's how we punish bad boys where I come from.' With a shrug, she said, 'Sorry. Just had to get that out of my system.'

When Connor returned to Stella's side, she asked, 'All sorted?' while watching him rub at his sore chest.

And Connor said, 'Yep.'

32

TRISTAN

Wow, photographers knew how to party. Tristan thought fashionistas and socialites had it well sussed, but photographers were like wild animals. He hadn't danced that energetically in ages.

When he and Michael had returned to the hotel room, Tristan insisted on a shower before they did anything else. Pleather was not a breathable fabric. And as their damp bodies sank onto the bed for one last night of passion, they had both promised to stay awake all night, eager to take advantage of every second.

That was five hours ago. Now, Michael snored next to him.

Tristan smiled sadly, tracing his lover's profile with his eyes. He couldn't sleep. There was too much noise in his head.

These past couple of days had been amazing. Part of Tristan had come alive again: not only one *specific* part of him, but also the part of him that believed he was worthy of love. For the first time, Tristan understood the concept that another person could complete him. Michael did that. Together they could be whole.

However, the few times that Tristan had tried to ask Michael the question *what next?*, Michael didn't seem to want to talk about it, which made Tristan think the answer wasn't one he wanted to hear.

He sighed. He'd only just sewn his heart back together. It was too soon to rip it apart again.

His thoughts strayed to when they had returned from the phone repair shop, the way Michael tore his hand out of Tristan's as the flashes went off instead of staying staunchly by his side. There'd been a spooked look in his eyes when he railed against how intrusive the paps were. Mad *at* Tristan or *for* Tristan?

On a whim, Tristan picked his phone up from the bedside table and typed his own name into the search engine. Sure enough, their photo was already on the TMZ website with the headline, 'Tristan's Tryst in Vegas Love Nest.' The picture clearly showed him kissing Michael. Although the copy indicated that they didn't know who Tristan's mystery lover was, it would only be a matter of time before they figured it out. Technology was too clever these days. Besides, the paparazzi would probably be waiting for them again tomorrow. Once they had the scent of celebrity, they were tenacious.

Fear like nothing he'd ever felt before slithered through him, paralysing him from the top of his head to the tips of his toes. He couldn't move.

Michael was about to fly off to one of the most dangerous countries in the world for gay men. What if somebody in Yemen found the picture? What if they put Michael in jail or arranged for an unfortunate accident? Tristan had absolutely no concept of what was possible or probable in this situation, but his imagination fired in all directions, the opposite of his petrified, immobile body.

He would die if anything happened to Michael.

But Michael had made it clear that his work was more important than any relationship. *That's* why he'd broken up with Tristan seven years ago. That's why he didn't want to talk about their future.

It was because they didn't have one.

The thought of being without Michael broke him. Tristan was ready. He'd move to New York. Move wherever Michael wanted him to be. Life was too short to waste time.

But if they were together, how would Tristan deal with Michael flying into dangerous situations again and again, putting other people's needs before his own safety? It was one of his qualities that Tristan both loved and hated.

Tristan's chest grew thick as he struggled to breathe.

He remembered Michael's words last time they broke up: *'you're too shallow and artificial for me.'* Tristan knew now that Michael had spoken out of desperation, wanting to sever ties completely. Leave no room for doubt.

Tristan didn't want to force that situation again. He wouldn't make Michael fabricate a reason to walk away. Tristan loved him too much to get in the way of the work Michael felt he was born to do. His unshakeable belief in his higher purpose was so strong that nothing would convince him otherwise. It was hard-coded in him by his mother's death.

So Tristan would make it easier for him this time.

Again, the pain of Michael tearing his hand from Tristan's scissored through him.

Slowly, so slowly, he untangled himself from the sheets. Using the light from his phone, he located the hotel notepad, picked up a pen, and wrote to Michael, pouring his heart onto the 7x5 inch pages:

Dear Michael,

Let me start off by saying I love you, in case you didn't know. You are a Knight in all ways, and you're probably too good for me.

Which is why I don't want to make this hard for you. The past couple days have been idyllic, but I understand you have your work to do. I will **not** get in the way of that.

Instead of putting us through a painful goodbye,

I thought this would be easier... more romantic, right?

Remember Casablanca? Well, I'm Rick, and you're Ilsa, and our problems don't amount to a hill of beans in this crazy world.

All I ask is that you stay safe. My heart wouldn't survive if anything happened to you.

All my love,
Tristan

Tenderly, he placed the note on his pillow and stood for one more minute, looking down at Michael's beautiful sleeping form, his blonde hair curling at the ends, his chest rising and falling peacefully. Tristan gathered his clothes. He slid into his briefs and shirt but held the pleather trousers at a distance. They would make too much noise if he tried to put them on. He picked up his hat and sunglasses and the other things he'd left strewn about the room.

With one last glance behind him, Tristan quietly opened the door and tiptoed into the hallway, leaving his heart behind in Michael's bed.

33

STELLA

'OH MY WORD,' SAID STELLA AS CONNOR PULLED UP TO THE HOTEL IN a yellow Ferrari convertible, the roar of its engine thundering through the carport. The paparazzi who'd been leaning against the wall smoking cigarettes all morning turned to check out who it was.

Connor cut the engine and flicked his Ray-Bans onto his forehead. The paps squinted at him and shot off a few snaps, just in case he turned out to be famous. 'I upgraded,' he said with a cocky grin. She approached and leaned on the door like she was a Pink Lady and he was a T-Bird.

'I love it,' she said, bending down to kiss him. 'Can I drive it first?'

'Tell you what. Let's thumb wrestle for it. Winner takes the first hour.'

'You're on,' she said, holding out her hand. She was still an undisputed champion at Thumb Wars.

'Hey!' called Michael. Stella turned to see him running out of the hotel in shorts and a t-shirt, hair dishevelled and a small notepad clutched in his hand. 'Have you seen Tristan this morning?'

Out of the corner of her eye, Stella caught the paps perking up at Tristan's name.

'He left for the airport hours ago,' she said so they couldn't hear.

'Didn't he say goodbye?' He'd left a note for her in their room, saying he'd call her soon. She was sad that they didn't say their farewells in person, but perhaps she'd see more of him when she lived in LA. It was only a four-hour flight!

'Fuck,' said Michael, his head dropping into his hands.

Connor slammed the car door and tossed the keys to a concierge. 'We'll be leaving within the hour,' he said. To Michael: 'What's going on?'

'He left me.' Michael started heaving like he was struggling to breathe.

'Shhh. It's okay,' said Connor, putting his arms around his brother. 'I've got you.' Over Michael's shoulder, his eyes connected with Stella's. 'Panic attack,' he mouthed, and she nodded, familiar with the symptoms herself. Poor Michael. Anger at Tristan bubbled within her. She thought he'd changed. What kind of game was he playing?

Seeing them together last night, it seemed like the beginning of something, not the end.

The pad in Michael's hand dropped to the floor, so she picked it up. Inadvertently, she read the first line: *Let me start off by saying I love you, in case you didn't know.*

Oh. Guilt replaced her anger. Shame on her for jumping to conclusions. She of all people should know better. There was more to this story than she'd thought.

Michael slowly calmed down, his breathing returning to normal.

Connor pulled away but held onto Michael's arms. 'I have a fast car. Do you want me to get you to the airport?'

With a huff, Michael said, 'This isn't a romcom. I wouldn't be able to just fly past security and catch him at the gate. That only happens in the movies. Besides his plane leaves soon.' Suddenly angry, Michael looked up and shouted, 'What are you looking at?'

Stella followed his gaze to the paps resting against the wall.

Shaking Connor off, Michael launched himself at the nearest

one. 'This is all your fault! You people are vultures!' he yelled as he grabbed the pap's shirt. She'd never seen Michael so furious.

'Just doing my job, asshole,' said the man.

Connor intervened, diffusing the situation. He pulled Michael away and inserted his body between them. 'Mikey, stop. You can't beat people up.'

'I could sue you!' said the man.

'Leave it, mate!' said Connor over his shoulder while guiding Michael towards the entrance of the hotel.

Stella followed. This was a lot more drama than she expected this morning.

Once inside, Connor led his brother towards a sofa in the lobby. He settled Michael onto the cushions and hunched down in front of him. 'So you're the guy who punches people now?'

'I'm just so... enraged. They took our picture yesterday, and I freaked out a bit. I think that's why Tristan left.'

'Because you don't like paps?'

'No! Because *he* thought that *I* thought our lifestyles weren't mixing again, like oil and water. But I don't care if my picture is in the tabloids with Tristan. I just don't like the way those piranhas go about it. It should be illegal.' He kicked at a spot on the floor like it was his injured sense of right and wrong. 'I'm also angry that Tristan didn't trust me enough to have the conversation *with me*.'

'Did you call him?' asked Stella.

'Went to voicemail,' Michael said miserably.

Stella sat down next to her brother-in-law and put her arm around his shoulders. 'He probably thought he was doing the right thing. I've known Tristan a long time, and I have *never* seen him be with anybody like he is with you. And... with his diagnosis—'

'What diagnosis?' asked Connor.

'I'll tell you later,' said Stella. 'With his diagnosis, it's obviously made him question everything. He's literally been hiding in Mexico. He's probably worried that he's not worthy of you.'

'That's ridiculous,' said Michael.

'It can be both ridiculous and true,' she said. She reached out for Connor's hand and squeezed. 'Trust me, insecurity can do a lot of harm.' She'd almost let her own insecurities ruin her marriage.

'There you all are. Is nobody answering their phones?' said Armstrong as he stormed up to the group.

'We're a little busy, dad,' said Connor, tipping his head meaningfully towards Michael.

'Well, I'm having a catastrophe.' Armstrong plonked down in the chair next to them.

Michael and Connor's eyes did the what-is-it-now dance.

'Liliwen wants a divorce,' Armstrong said, catching his head in his hands.

'Oh dad,' said Michael. 'Sorry to hear that. Break-ups are never easy.'

Armstrong looked up, tears glistening in his grey eyes. 'Oh, she doesn't want to break-up completely. She wants an "open relationship".' He mimed quote marks with his fingers.

Of course she does. Stella had to purse her lips to keep from laughing.

Ever the peacemaker, Michael said, 'Well, dad, she *has* just lost her husband of forty years. She might not be ready to settle.'

'I know. But I thought... I wanted...' he sighed heavily. 'It was nice to have a person of my own, if only for a few days.' His shoulders slumped.

Connor stood and sat on the arm of Armstrong's chair. Pulling him in for a side hug, he said, 'Dad—*we're* your people. Michael, Stella, Grace, me... all of us.'

'Thank you, son,' Armstrong said, patting Connor's knee.

Stella wished she had her camera. This was a moment worth capturing.

'Hello, lovelies! Look who I found in the lifts!' said Liliwen as she approached the group, arm threaded through Blake's.

'Everyone all packed and ready to get out of here?' said Blake, not noticing the dirty look that Armstrong threw him.

'Actually,' said Stella, standing up, 'Connor and I were just getting ready to leave. We're heading to Joshua Tree for a few days, then we'll pop into LA to house hunt before we fly back to London.'

'My ex-wife is a realtor. I can put you in touch,' said Blake.

'I could head to LA today and start scouting for you,' offered Armstrong. 'When you come, I can show you some options?'

'Wow, that would be so helpful,' said Stella. 'Are you sure you don't mind?'

'Of course not. You're my people.' He squeezed her hand and winked. 'Besides, I need you to rent a place with an adequate-sized pool house for me.'

Connor and Stella exchanged a concerned look.

'Great. I'll text you her number,' said Blake. 'And, Stella, I'll be in touch soon to talk timelines, contracts, etcetera.'

'Can't wait,' she said. It was all starting to feel real. They were doing this. Was it the right decision?

As if detecting her nerves, Connor put his arm around her and squeezed. 'You have star material here,' he said to Blake, but really it was a message for Stella: *You can do this. I've got your back.*

'Well, *ci vediamo*,' Blake said before the usual farewell kisses and handshakes. He left to make a phone call.

While Connor talked to his father about LA neighbourhoods, Stella pulled Liliwen aside. 'Are you okay?'

Liliwen flapped her hand. 'Me? I'm fine, lovely. I'm excited. Life seems full of possibilities again. Armstrong helped me remember a part of myself that I thought had died with Gareth. I'm ever so grateful to him.' She glanced over her shoulder at her soon-to-be-ex-husband and asked with genuine concern, 'Do you think he'll be okay?'

Stella thought about it. 'I think so. I think you helped him realise that he'd been missing out on something all these years. A lesson he probably needed to learn.'

'He'll make some lucky lady very happy,' said Liliwen, 'but I'm afraid it won't be me. I'm in a different place. Ready for adventure.'

'What will you do?'

'Travel, I think. See the world. Experience new things. New people,' she laughed, the familiar tinkle warming Stella's heart. 'I'm so glad you've worked things out with Connor. You two belong together.'

'I'll miss you,' said Stella, putting her arms around Liliwen.

'I'll visit,' she said, squeezing Stella tight.

Breaking away, Liliwen clapped her hands. 'I'm peckish. Armstrong, shall we get some lunch, lovely? My flight isn't until this evening.'

'I guess so,' he said, his eyes on the floor.

'Oh, lovely, don't look so glum. It's not all that bad,' Stella heard Liliwen say as they strolled away, arm-in-arm. 'Besides, I was wondering... Have you ever tried a threesome?'

Stella snorted. Lord help poor Armstrong.

Michael stood up. 'I guess this is goodbye then,' he said, slapping Connor on the back.

'Never did get that squash rematch,' said Connor, leaning into the hug.

'Next time,' said Michael.

'You sure you're okay? We can stay a bit longer?' said Stella.

'Don't worry. I need to leave soon for the airport anyway. But... I'll try to come see you in LA soon, okay? Or you could come to New York. Either way, I'd love to see more of you all. We can't have Grace missing out on quality time with her guncle.'

'You're welcome whenever you want. We'll make sure to get a place with guest rooms,' said Connor, sounding excited by the possibility of more family time.

Michael hugged them both again before heading for the lifts. Stella watched him go. This week had been equal parts exhilarating and exhausting for all of them in different ways. She was glad to see the back of it.

'Well,' she said, as Connor slid his arm around her and they ambled towards the luggage room to collect their bags. 'That was an emotional send-off.'

'Looks like we're the only ones who got their happy ending,' said Connor, kissing her on the head.

We're the lucky ones, she thought. 'Yeah, and how did we turn into everyone's relationship counsellors?'

'I don't know,' he laughed. 'We haven't even had our first session yet.'

Stella checked her watch. It was already 10:30, and they had a four-plus hour drive ahead of them. 'Can we please get out of here?'

'Oh my god, yes. But first,' he turned to her, face serious. 'We have some unfinished business.'

Her head fell back as she groaned, 'What now?'

He held out his fist, thumb sticking up in the air. Steady. Ready. 'Winner drives first.'

EPILOGUE

THREE MONTHS LATER

Tristan

THE JUNE HEAT WAS ALMOST UNBEARABLE.

Thankfully, it was dusk, when the sizzling downgraded to gentle frying. All of Tristan's windows were open, and he had ten fans on full blast. Outside, the Mexico City noises persisted. People laughing in restaurants. Children playing in the street. Dogs barking. The tinkle of cutlery tapping on plates. Music. Always music.

When Tristan eventually moved away, he'd find it hard to sleep without this noise.

Lying on the L-shaped sofa wearing only shorts, he closed his eyes, enjoying the whisper of wind against his bare skin as the fans oscillated. He considered a trip to the department store, just for the air conditioning, but he was too tired to move. It had been a long day at Sin Pecados. A couple of new boys had arrived from out of town, and they always needed extra attention in the first week. Tristan's Spanish was now at a passable level, so he could talk to them, listen to them without forgetting that *constipación* meant a cold and *exitó* meant success, not where to leave the building.

Everyone at the charity affectionately called him *Güerito*, which meant a light-skinned or light-haired person. Although Tristan was neither and, in fact, was deeply tanned, being European was enough to earn him the term.

Like Thing from *The Addam's Family*, his hand lumbered towards the TV remote, and he switched on the latest episode of *Amor en Sombras*. Last time, they found out that Marisol was actually the long-lost daughter of Alejandro's aunt, which made her his first cousin. But their wedding was only one week away. The drama!

His doorbell buzzed.

It was probably some kids having fun; he wasn't expecting anybody. Maybe if he ignored it, they'd go away.

It buzzed again.

Groaning, Tristan rolled off the sofa. He trudged to his window, so he could lean out and see who it was. He lived on the third floor overlooking a busy pedestrianised street. He squinted at the entranceway to his building but couldn't see anybody at the bell—

Only a five-man mariachi band standing below, blinking up at him.

They were all dressed in black boleros and trousers, with white shirts stretched across their paunches. Tristan imagined they must be boiling.

'*Puedo ayudarle?*' Tristan asked. *Can I help you?*

'Uno, dos, tres!' counted their leader.

The man holding the violin started sawing his bow across the strings, then the trumpeter joined in, along with the two players on guitar. Tristan recognised the beginning of 'Can't Take My Eyes Off of You' by Franki Valli. A moment later, the leader began to sing.

Tristan had no idea what was going on. Was this a singing telegram or something? He glanced left and right down the street, expecting to see his friends from Sin Pecados laughing at him.

Then he had a sobering thought. Maybe it was a stalker. Somebody who'd been watching him from afar and now wanted to woo him through the medium of mariachi.

As the band approached the first chorus, Tristan was none the wiser. His face didn't know how to look. Pleased? Confused? Entertained?

He settled for confused.

As the singer warbled out the refrain, somebody in a Fedora stepped out from under a nearby jacaranda tree. When the mysterious stranger tilted his head back and their eyes met, Tristan's heart fumbled for a few beats.

'Michael?!' he said incredulously, his jaw slackening with shock. A white t-shirt clung to Michael's upper half, and a battery-operated fan circled his neck. His outfit cried 'tourist', and it was not the sexiest of looks, but to be honest, Michael could wear a plastic bag and Tristan would be all over him.

Michael was here.

They'd had zero contact since that morning Tristan left Las Vegas. Not even a text to say *fuck you*. Nothing.

Tristan had grieved. His heart broke anew every morning when he woke up and realised Michael was no longer in his life. But it had been the right decision, and obviously, Michael must have agreed, otherwise he would have been in touch, right?

Through Stella, he knew that Michael had survived Yemen unscathed, even though he'd lost his case. Tristan worried that Michael would be a mess over it and would have flown to New York to comfort him if he thought Michael would welcome him with open arms. That had been over two months ago.

Time marched forward and, with every day that passed, the distance between them grew.

But now Michael was here.

'Wait there!' he yelled to Michael, who was smiling that smile that visited Tristan in his dreams.

He ran to his flat door, slid his feet into flip-flops, grabbed his keys, and stumbled down the stairs as fast as he could. Reaching the entranceway, he pulled himself up short and took a few deep breaths. Hyperventilating in Michael's face would hardly be a charming welcome.

Calmer, he opened the door and stepped out into the sticky night air.

As the mariachi band sang the final verse, Tristan approached Michael. Up close, Tristan could see that the poor man was sweating profusely. With his fair skin and blond hair, he would suffer in the soaring Mexican temperature.

On the plus side, Tristan had plenty of sun cream.

Tristan smiled shyly. Shy wasn't normally his style, but he didn't know what else to do. Michael was *here*. The last time Tristan had seen him, Tristan had been sneaking out of a hotel room.

'Hi,' Tristan said, running a nervous hand through his hair, recently cut short to keep himself cool.

'Hey,' said Michael.

True to the song, they couldn't take their eyes off of each other.

The mariachi band finished, and the leader asked if they'd like another. Michael said no and handed him a wad of dollar bills. *'Muchas gracias.'*

'Learning Spanish?' said Tristan, the corner of his mouth turning up.

'I had to. The man I love is hiding out in Mexico, and I thought I better learn some of the lingo if I was going to come and rescue him.'

Tristan's heart clattered in his chest. Did Michael just say he loved him? He swallowed hard. 'Does he need saving then?'

'Yes. From himself. Because he can be an idiot sometimes. *No offence.'*

A laugh exploded from Tristan's mouth. He remembered the kid in the phone repair shop implying that Michael should stick with being a courier because he didn't have what it took to be a model. Seemed so long ago now.

'I'm sorry,' Tristan said. 'I thought I was doing the right thing.'

Michael poked Tristan on his sweaty, bare chest. 'At first, I was really angry at you for leaving like that. I wish you'd had more faith in me... in us. But after I calmed down, I sort of understood. I'd hurt you before. And you didn't want to cause me any problems. But here's the thing: you will never be a problem to me. You are the solution. To everything. And I love you.'

'I love you, too,' Tristan said, meaning those words more than anything else he'd said in his entire life.

Michael's lips parted. Tristan cupped his face and leaned down. Unlike their heated kisses in Las Vegas, this kiss was slow and deliberate.

They had all the time in the world.

The only breeze came from Michael's neck fan, which whirred busily. After a minute, Michael pulled away, taking a step back so that Tristan's hands dropped.

'Sorry. It's just... I'm so *hot*.' Michael fanned himself, sweat dripping down his temple. Eyeing Tristan, he said, 'How is it that you look so sexy in this heat and I feel like a melting ice cream?'

'Practice,' joked Tristan. He didn't have the heart to tell Michael that this was the coolest part of the day. As Michael's hand flapped, Tristan caught sight of something black on his wrist. Reaching out, he grabbed Michael's arm and held it still. 'What's this?'

Michael looked sheepish. 'It's a phoenix. Just a small one. I... I got it because it made me feel closer to you. I couldn't come right away because of work, and I wanted a piece of you with me.'

With those words, Tristan's love grew a bit more. How was it even possible?

'It's fabulous, darling,' he said reverentially, lifting the phoenix to his mouth and kissing the ink. Then with a mischievous smirk, he said, 'Almost as fabulous as the one of David Hasselhoff I got to remind me of *you*.' He dropped Michael's hand and began to undo his shorts.

Under his sunburn, Michael paled. 'You didn't!'

Tristan stopped pretending. 'Of course I didn't.'

They kissed again—no hands this time so Michael didn't overheat.

In the distance, Tristan heard the musical cry of the tamale man coming their way: *'Ya lle-gar-on sus ric-os-ta-ma-les Oaxa-queños!'*

He remembered walking in Red Rocks Canyon and thinking Michael didn't deserve any delicious tamales. But now, Tristan wanted to share everything with Michael: feed him all the *garnachas* he could eat, take him to see the Aztec ruins, to the Frida Kahlo museum, to the floating gardens...

And after that, they'd figure it out. For the first time in ages, Tristan knew exactly what he wanted and who he wanted to do it with.

But first: 'Are you hungry?' Tristan asked. 'Fancy a tamale?'

'Is that code for something?' said Michael with a naughty gleam in his eye. He took off his Fedora and fanned himself with it.

Tristan laughed. 'Well, it *wasn't*, but...'

'Frankly, my dear, I'd sell a kidney for a cold shower and some water right now.'

'And then the tamale?' Tristan asked.

'And then the tamale,' Michael agreed.

And they weren't talking about food.

MEANWHILE IN LA...

Stella

'THERE'S A SWIMMING POOL!' SCREAMED GRACE AS SHE ZIPPED PAST Stella into the backyard of the house. 'And a swing!'

'Ahem,' said Stella. 'How about a hug for your mother?'

Grace stopped short and turned, running towards Stella and jumping into her arms. 'I missed you, mummy!' She wrapped her little legs around Stella's middle, and they clung to each other.

'Me, too, baby girl,' said Stella into her daughter's tangled red hair. Had Connor been brushing it at all?

Stella had flown to Los Angeles two weeks before Connor and Grace so she could ready their new house rental and start filming content for Knight School, while back in London, Connor dealt with the final details of their move.

'Hi,' said Connor, dropping their luggage on the kitchen floor. Without missing a beat, he joined the hug, kissing Stella on the lips when she offered them up to him.

'How was the flight?' she asked.

'Long. I will forever be amazed by a young child's ability to watch cartoons about Australian dogs for eleven hours straight.'

Done being the filling in the parent sandwich, Grace wiggled her way to the floor. She ran straight for the swing hanging from a sturdy old tree blooming with red flowers.

'Daddy, push me!' she demanded.

'Daddy needs a moment,' he said, taking Stella in his arms again and resting his forehead against hers. 'I missed you.'

'Me, too.'

'How's it all been going?'

'Really great. The studio is just south of here. Only half an hour in the car, mostly along the coast.' It was the perfect space: lots of storage for costumes, high ceilings, a beautiful frontage.

'Excellent.' He regarded the modern house they'd rented, so different from their 19th-century home in London. The idea was to live in this area for a while and, if they liked it, buy somewhere as an investment. Better than throwing their money away on rental fees.

So far, Stella loved it. After only two weeks, she didn't know how she could live anywhere except LA. Its amazing light was a photographer's dream. And she also loved that they had a pool. She might try some underwater shoots at some point because... why not?

The Knight School launch wasn't for two months yet, but they were busy creating content every day. Blake was handling the work visas, so at least that was one thing they didn't have to worry about.

'How was the final handover?' she asked with a wince, feeling guilty about everything she'd left in Connor's lap. Knowing his ADHD might cause him problems with all the organisational tasks, she'd created a detailed spreadsheet with manageable, daily to-dos to help him out. He'd dropped a few balls, but that was okay. When he dropped a ball, she did her best to pick it up for him and vice versa.

'It's done and we're alive, so I suppose it was a success,' he said with a tired rub of his eyes.

A noise coming from the laundry room made Connor turn his head. 'Is that my dad or the other thing?'

'The other thing. Your dad is at the yacht club. Again. It's Hawaii night.'

Armstrong was staying with them until he could find his own place, but he seemed to be making himself very comfortable in their guest bedroom. She didn't know how much house-hunting he was actually doing. Stella would leave it to Connor to handle that conversation.

Instead, Armstrong had quickly scouted out the local yacht club and spent most of his days there. He'd already signed up for sailing lessons, a cocktail-making course, life-model painting, and merengue dance classes. He was taking full advantage of retirement and only mentioned Liliwen once a day, sometimes twice.

'Should we show her now... or has she already had too much excitement?' asked Stella, watching Grace pump her little legs back and forth with determination while only moving the swing a few inches forwards or backwards.

'I still can't believe you gave in.' Connor smiled and kissed her on the nose.

She sighed. 'A promise is a promise. Besides she's kind of cute.'

'Okay, let's do it then. Shall I bring Grace over to the fire pit?' That was another thing Stella loved about this house: the sunken fire pit in the garden surrounded by sofas. She imagined evenings there, drinking a glass of California red with Connor and talking about their day, making love under the stars (another reason for Armstrong to move out).

'Sounds like a plan.'

'Gigi!' called Connor as he walked towards the swing. 'Mummy and daddy have a surprise for you.'

Stella went into the laundry to collect 'the surprise'. Carrying the medium-sized box to the fire pit, she placed it on a low table.

'What is it?' said Grace as the box hopped two inches to the left.

'Open it and see,' said Stella.

The box moved again, and Grace slowly reached out to remove the lid, as though afraid there might be a monster inside. As soon as the lid was off, two fluffy, cloud-like paws appeared, and a frizzy little head popped out.

'A puppy!' screamed Grace.

The dog yapped, and Connor rescued her from the box, holding her in his lap so Grace could pet her soft fur. The puppy licked her face.

Stella inhaled and exhaled steadily. She could do this. The dog that had bit her all those years ago was also small, also white. But logically, her brain knew that *this* was a nice dog: a Havanese, which had a reputation for being a great family pet *and* was hypo-allergenic.

The puppy was already twelve weeks old and had been fully vaccinated when Stella picked her up. Thankfully, Armstrong helped with dog care, taking her for walks and bringing her to the yacht club to socialise with other canines. He commented that having a dog was a great way to meet women (before wondering out loud what kind of dog Liliwen would want).

Watching Connor and Grace with the puppy, Stella knew she'd made the right choice. Both of them were besotted. 'What do you want to call her?' asked Stella, taking a risk. Princess Poopy Paws was still fresh in her head.

'Hmmm,' Grace screwed up her face, but she came to a decision surprisingly quickly. 'I think... Dildo!'

Connor coughed and laughed at the same time. 'I think you mean *Bilbo*, Gigi.' To Stella, he said, 'We've been reading *The Hobbit* at bedtime.'

Stella screwed up her face, imagining yelling 'Bilbo!' at the dog park. Well, it would be a conversation starter. 'I suppose I can live with Bilbo.'

Later, after putting Grace to bed, Connor and Stella snuggled together on the fire pit sofa, Bilbo curled up on her lap. They both leaned back against the cushions to look up at the stars.

Connor yawned.

'You must be exhausted,' Stella said.

'I am. It's very possible I'll fall asleep right here.'

'At your age...' she teased.

'Cheeky.'

As soon as they had returned from Las Vegas, they'd started seeing Magda, unequivocally the best marriage counsellor in existence. Stella would keep the woman in her pocket if she could. Magda gave the Dalai Lama a run for his money when it came to wisdom. They'd learned so much from her already.

Like the fact that most couples didn't know how to argue properly, just like Chris Seals said. The first thing she taught them was how to listen to each other and do conflict *well*.

Like the fact that, due to their upbringings, Stella saw love as attention while Connor saw it as independence. They needed to learn how to speak each other's love language.

Like the fact that Stella had to create her own self-esteem and self-worth. Nobody else could do that for her.

And there was no such thing as the wrong way. Only different ways.

The change in their relationship happened fast. After each session, Magda encouraged them to go out to dinner to discuss what they'd learned. Within weeks, Stella spoke better Connor, and Connor spoke better Stella.

They'd continue their sessions with Magda over Zoom on a monthly basis for now, to check in. But Stella's confidence in their relationship had grown so much. She now believed *every* couple should see a relationship counsellor to learn how to communicate better.

'Was Claudia helpful this week?' Stella asked. In her absence, Claudia had promised to keep Connor accountable to his to-do list and pick up Grace from school.

Connor groaned. 'She was a drill sergeant. When did you say Claudia and Magnus are coming out with the kids? I need to make sure my agent schedules some work for me that week,' he mumbled.

'Connor!' Stella reprimanded, smiling as she poked him in the ribs with her elbow. Thankfully, Connor's agent was thrilled to hear he was moving to LA. Plenty of work for him here with no need to travel so much. She had already booked him a few shoots locally—but only a few. Stella and Connor agreed that he'd slow down for a while, help settle Grace, do some more teaching instead.

He laughed at her faux outrage, and Bilbo barked.

'Sorry, Bilbo,' said Stella, scratching behind the dog's soft ears. 'In answer to your very impertinent question, they're coming in the school holidays. Late July.'

Stella couldn't wait. She planned to do a shoot of Claudia for Knight School and was already gathering outfits and making sketches.

Magnus, however, was still on her shit list after what Claudia revealed at her surprise going away party for the Knights.

Pulling Stella aside, Claudia had said, 'By the way, I know who dobbed you in to Blake Romero about the separation. It was my fucking husband. He's the absolute worst at keeping secrets.'

Apparently Magnus and Blake were old friends, and when Blake called to do his due diligence on Stella because he knew she was best friends with Claudia, Magnus sang like a canary. His heart was in the right place, thinking he was helping land Stella a huge opportunity.

He'd apologised profusely. In reality, she'd already forgiven him. But it was fun to let him think she was still irate. She planned to put him on permanent cocktail-making and dog-walking duty when they came to visit.

Besides, everything had worked out for the best in the end.

Next to her, Connor's body relaxed, and the sound of his gentle snores reached her ears. She leaned over and pressed a kiss to his stubbled jaw.

Laying her head on his shoulder, she looked up at the stars and smiled.

This was the life.

JULIA BOGGIO

. . .

THE END

**If you want one more glimpse of everyone's happily ever afters,
then go to
juliaboggio.com/exp-epi
to download an exclusive bonus epilogue about Michael and
Tristan's wedding!**

Thank you for reading!

ACKNOWLEDGMENTS

Finishing this book feels like the end of an era. I penned the first line of the Photographers Trilogy in 2019 and now, five years later, I've concluded Connor and Stella's story. I'll miss this crowd. They were so much fun to write.

Every book is a team effort and I have plenty of people to thank for their input in making *Exposure!* the story it is. First, to my amazing beta readers in the J Coven: Jayne Rice, Jessica Popplewell, Jo Lyons, Farrah Riaz, Juno Goldstone, and Amanda Scotland. You guys are the best. Thank you also to my best friend, Sarah Gillman, for her feedback and Amy Borg for being the editor with the mostest. Ugo Boggio (a.k.a. my dad), thank you for the illustration for the bookmarks and for checking the Italian and, Anne Hughes (a.k.a. my mother-in-law), thank you for the Welsh help.

Bailey McGinn, your covers have become the symbol of this series and I bless the day I found you.

While researching for this book, I met some amazing people who generously shared their stories and experiences with me. Nate Benson, thank you for your honesty. Tristan's character is stronger for it. Todd Rappaport, thanks for our chat over dinner. There's a bit of you in Michael. Poncho Cottier and Carlos Ascorve, thank you for your insight into Mexico City and gay culture in Mexico. Alice Wood, thank you for telling me about your travels in Mexico City and Oaxaca. I want to go now! To my sister Sarah, thanks for the nuggets about LA living.

Kelly Brown, thank you for chatting with me about your successful career as a photographer. You helped me realise just how full-on a conference like this is for the headline speakers (plus many more insights!).

Jason Marino, thank you for our chat about getting diagnosed with ADHD later in life. ADHD is a topic dear to my heart, so when I had the idea ages ago that it would be part of Connor's arc, I was excited to bring it to life for my readers. As with most other things, ADHD is different for every person who has it and affects us all in different ways. Some people see it as their superpower; some really, really don't. In Connor's case, he did. After talking with Jason about his experiences with meds, I made the decision not to put Connor on medication. However, ADHD medication is very helpful in many cases and I have absolutely nothing against it. People close to me are on it and it's a godsend.

A huge thank you to Juliette Smith, relationship coach and counsellor, for giving me her time to discuss the fictional marriage problems of Stella and Connor. She really helped to crystallise their issues, the journey they needed to take, and the outcome of that journey. Stella and Connor may be works of fiction, but their problems were very real and I highly recommend seeking help if your relationship is in crisis. Juliette had so much amazing insight. (juliettesmith.co.uk)

Jess Major and Connor McLaren, thanks for letting me earwig on your banter at F45 South Wimbledon. Never a dull moment.

Congratulations to Chris Seals and Therese Asplund, who were the joint winners of the photography competition I held for *Camera Shy*. Their prize was to have characters named after them in this book. I hope you enjoyed your fictional incarnations.

While writing this book, I was saddened by the death of the beautiful man who was Steve Scalone. Steve was part of the launch campaigns for both *Shooters* and *Chasing the Light*. He was the kindest of men, an amazing photographer, and a wonderful teacher. In *Exposure!*, I wanted to give him one last award: Photographer of the Year. Steve, you will be sorely missed.

Thank you as well to all the photographers who took part in the launch campaign for this book: Magda Sienicka, Maggie Robinson, Christina Lauder, Julia West, Fiona Elizabeth, Kelly Brown, Neil Shearer and Damian McGillicuddy.

To my family: James, G and H. I appreciate your putting up with my talking about my imaginary friends.

And finally, thank you to the readers who have travelled this journey with me. I am so grateful to each and every one of you for giving my words your time. If you want to see what I'm doing next, please sign up for my newsletter.

Goodbye, Connor and Stella (for now)! You've been a blast!

Julia x

If you enjoyed EXPOSURE! * * * * * * * *

please review it on Goodreads and Amazon! Reviews help new readers find my books!

♥ Julia

Thank you so much for READING!

All I Want for Christmas is Hugh

SPICING UP YOUR HOLIDAYS 2024

When American headshot photographer Henrietta Winkle moves to London, all she wants is to find her very own Hugh Grant.

Then she meets Graff Holden. He's ruggedly handsome, but he's also everything she doesn't want: grumpy, anti-social, and, worst of all, American. Trying to get a decent headshot of him is like trying to photograph a wild snow leopard.

But when he invites her to be his plus one at his publisher's Christmas party to make his ex-wife jealous, Henri can't help but notice how well he fills out a tux...

Find out what happens next to Henri and Graff in this uplifting, fake-dating festive love story.

PRE-ORDER NOW FROM AMAZON

Shooters

WINNER AT THE LONDON BOOK FAIR SELFIE AWARDS 2024

Stella Price thought she had her life all planned out, until it exploded in front of her. Desperate for a fresh start, she picks up her old camera and dives into the challenging world of wedding photography. But with fierce competition and a fast-approaching deadline, Stella is in danger of failing yet again.

That is, until she meets Connor Knight, the renowned 'king' of wedding photography. He's talented, arrogant, and undeniably attractive, but Stella can't stand him. However, when Connor becomes her mentor, she's forced to confront her preconceived opinions and work alongside him.

As they clash and push each other's buttons, a passionate spark ignites between them. But with Connor's cynical views on love and Stella's past mistakes, can they find a way to make it work? Or will their explosive chemistry fizzle out before they can capture their own happily ever after?

AVAILABLE ON AMAZON

Chasing the Light

SHORTLISTED FOR ROMCOM
OF THE YEAR IN THE RNA AWARDS 2024

On the outside, Francesca March is a confident
woman and an entrepreneur, but on the inside,
she's a quivering mess with a painful secret.

When she runs into ex-boyfriend Krish Kapadia,
old feelings bubble to the surface, but her instincts
tell her to push him away again.

He's still sexy. He still has a bad habit of rescuing
her. But she's still broken. Plus he's got a nice new
girlfriend who could easily win a beauty contest. His
life is working out just how he's always wanted.

But when Krish finally discovers her secret, will that
change his plans? Or will he stay the course with the
life he always said he wanted? And even if he did
choose her, will Francesca let him?

AVAILABLE ON AMAZON

Camera Shy

'Similar to Emily in Paris, but better.'
- Goodreads Review

Heartbroken after her almost-engagement was called off,
Jess goes on a mini-break to Paris seeking closure and
meets a hot French stranger called Gabriel. As sparks fly,
Jess, fearing she was dumped because she was boring,
vows to be more spontaneous, and she and Gabriel
have mind-blowing, earth-shattering sex.

With his troubled past and soulful eyes, Jess quickly
realises there's more to Gabriel than a great shag and,
when he whisks her away to his fixer-upper chateau in
the country, Jess thinks she might be falling for him—even
though they've only known each other a few days.

But is this what she wants? She was all for taking risks,
but risking her heart so soon after a break-up was not in
the cards, especially when Gabriel's troubled past arrives
in the present. Can they both heal their emotional wounds
and let love back into their lives before it's too late?

AVAILABLE ON AMAZON

ABOUT THE AUTHOR

Photo by Magdalena Sienicka

Originally from New Jersey, Julia moved to London in her early twenties. She worked as an advertising copywriter until discovering her love of photography on a 6-month trip around South America. She started a wedding photography business which received some great PR when her own *Dirty Dancing*-themed wedding dance went viral on YouTube. She appeared on *Richard & Judy* and *The Oprah Winfrey Show*, where she danced with Patrick Swayze. In 2009 she opened a luxury portrait studio and has photographed everyone from the Queen to Queen, the band. After 15 years as a photographer, she returned to her first love: writing. Her debut novel, *Shooters*, won the Selfie Awards 2024 at London Book Fair. Julia lives in Wimbledon with her Welsh husband, two children, and an extremely large cat with jealousy issues.

facebook.com/juliaboggio

instagram.com/juliaboggio

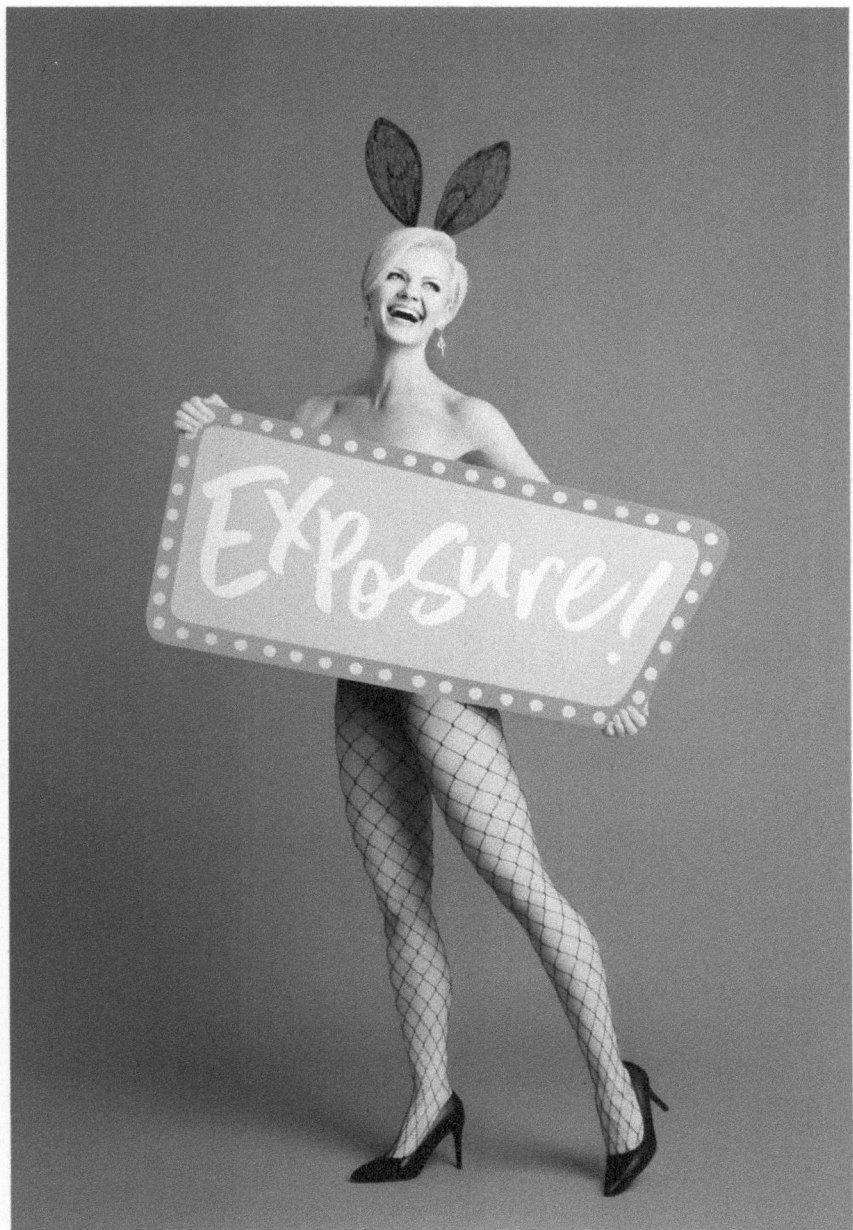

Australian photographer, Kelly Brown
Taken by Julia Boggio

British photographer, Christina Lauder and her dog, Blue
Taken by Magdalena Sienicka

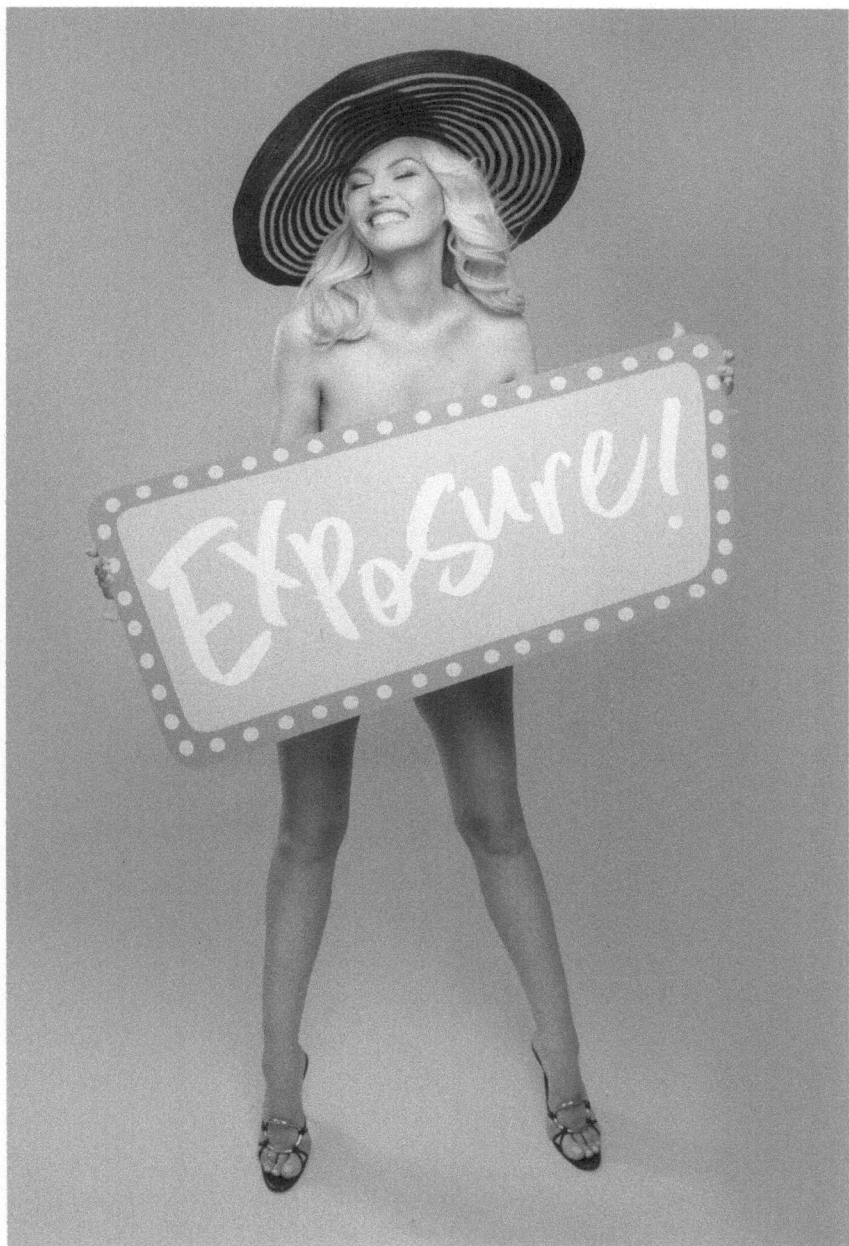

Polish photographer, Maggie Robinson
Taken by Magdalena Sienicka